PANVERSE

Panverse Publishing LLC
office.panpubs@gmail.com
707 718-6845

CHANNEL ZILCH
by Doug Sharp

Our entry for the 2013 Campbell Award,
with sincere thanks for your time and consideration

Dario Ciriello
Executive Editor
Panverse Publishing LLC

CHANNEL ZILCH

CHANNEL ZILCH

doug sharp

PANVERSE

CHANNEL ZILCH copyright © 2013 by Doug Sharp
Artwork by Aurelia Shaw

Published by Panverse Publishing LLC
2207 Holbrook Dr., Concord, CA 94519
www.panversepublishing.com

Printed in the U.S.A.

ISBN 978-1-940581-90-3

To
My First Reader

"Someday an awful lot of people are going to look back and kick themselves and say, 'What on Earth was I doing? Why was I sitting around watching television while the fate of all humankind hung in the balance and almost no one was doing anything?'"

—Eliezer Yudkowsky, *Research Fellow, The Singularity Institute for Artificial Intelligence*

CHAPTER ONE: THE FLYING COW

MY JOURNEY TO SPACE and godhood starts in a puddle of shit.

I'm flat on my back under my cantankerous, hard-working old DC-3, *The Flying Cow*, unclogging a manure spray nozzle. The nozzle drips liquefied cow poop on the hot cement a foot from my head—a swarm of eager flies.

It's a sticky Minnesota afternoon. The summer of 2007 is turning into another sweltering record-breaker. The stink of agriculture saturates the hangar. My bank account bleeds five dollars every minute the *Cow* spends grounded, so I'm intent on my task and don't hear their footsteps.

"Mick here's a real live asternaut." Nils' squeaky old rasp.

The hangar resonates with a tuba of a voice, "I am acutely aware of the young man's accomplishments. Might you persuade Mr. Oolfson to speak with me?"

Bent down next to Nils is a small, somewhat Asian fellow clad in a white suit. He shines me a smile that's a mite too genuine: salesman.

I turn back to the clogged nozzle. "Can't talk. Busy."

"Mr. Oolfson!" The guy's massive voice outweighs him a ton. I keep at my shitty task while he emotes as if addressing a multitude, "I salute your commendable labors. Aerial manure fertilization is an admirable vocation—nourishing the noble soybean from on high!—but I have a business proposition which I am confident shall intrigue you. I should like to offer you a position in your old profession."

I snort my disgust. "I'm out of the transport pilot racket. And I'm not a mercenary." Haul guns or cocaine—risk my ass for bloodstained cash? Not a chance in hell.

Then he emotes a miracle, "Your subsequent profession, Mr. Oolfson—the profession that so unjustly expelled you. My commercial enterprise has an employment opportunity for an experienced spacefarer. We are seeking a Chief Astronaut."

I whack my head on a crusty nozzle as I scramble from under the *Cow*. I smear manure on his hand shaking it but he just chuckles—the guy's all right.

This is THE CALL!

A bevy of geek moguls are building boosters. Mr. Musk's SpaceX has schlepped supplies and astrofolk to the ISS for years, but Elon never asked me to drive one of his Falcons. When Orbital Sciences got into the space business my hopes glimmered, but no joy. But I always knew someday a rich rocket freak would be desperate to find an experienced space jockey, look me up, and give me THE CALL.

Spraying manure just lost its allure.

Why did Manuel Chin hunt down Mick Oolfson to drive his rocketship?

My résumé:

- Intergalactic explorer: In my imagination (birth-present)
- Treasurer, Rocket Club, Cannon Valley High (Go Bombers!)
- Air Force Academy stud, Degree: Space Operations
- Hotshit air transport jock and instructor: C-130 Hercs
- Accepted into astronaut corps. WHEEE!
- Astronaut training. WHEEEEEE!
- Pilot of two shuttle missions. WHEEEEEEEEE!!!!!
- Shitcanned by NASA for *mumble, mumble*. I'll dredge up that little shitstorm later.
- Baron of the Aerial Manure Application Industry based at an itty-bitty grass-strip airport in Stanton, MN.

"I don't usually do job interviews when I'm dipped in manure, but if you're looking for an astronaut, I'm your man." I gesture toward my old grey metal desk in the corner of the hangar. "Step into my office, Mr. Chin."

I give Nils a smile and wink and hold a shush-finger to my lips. "Mum's the word."

Nils looks serious, nods intently, and heads for the door. By tomorrow everyone in Stanton will know about my job offer.

Manuel beams me a thousand-candlepower smile and says, "I am not going to pretend to interview you. I knew the instant I shook your hand that it was crucial Mick Oolfson become our Director of Space Operations and Chief Astronaut."

Hallelujah, Mommy—your little boy's gonna get to fly in space again! My voice comes out an octave high: "Well, all right! I've got a shitload of questions for you. Sit down and let's talk. Tell me about your launch tech."

Manuel beams brighter still. "I have a...technical associate who will brief you on our mission. Will you join us...?"

"We talking new or existing booster?"

Manuel holds up a hand. "Patience. If you would join my associate and me for dinner tonight all your questions will be answered."

"Dinner?"

"Please join us for a working dinner tonight at Chin Limited's expense."

My stomach throbs at the mention of money. Unclog the *Cow* and I can still squeeze in a half day of spraying beans. "Can we make it a late dinner, like ten? I gotta work until sundown. There's a storm system moving in that'll ground me for the next couple days and I need to make some dough in case your astronauting gig doesn't pan out."

Chin looks at me as if he's proud of my cleverness. "Admirable caution and enterprise, Mr. Oolfson. Ten o'clock. A late working dinner it shall be."

We exchange cards. Chin Ltd. has an address in St. Paul. I give him directions to the CrossRoads Bar, the local pilot/farmer hangout.

As I watch Manuel Chin's tiny, white-suited figure disappear out the hangar door, doubt bites hard. Don't waste a single ounce of hope thinking about this, Oolfson. People don't just drop by and offer astronaut jobs.

o   o   o

After a filthy hour under *The Flying Cow*[1] wrestling crusty nozzles and pipes, I admit defeat. The whole shebang has to be steam-cleaned: $175 plus tax and loss of prime spraying hours. My gut stress-knot seethes in the caustic coffee I've swilled.

I call the ag service and plead for an emergency steam-cleaning appointment but they're booked until three. No choice, so I take it. I can still spray maybe four hours before dusk.

I taxi the *Cow* out to the maintenance lot. Half a day pissed away with a major storm front looming. Ten hours until I find out whether Manuel Chin was a methane hallucination. I meander slowly back to the hangar, trying hard to enjoy the warm sun and sweet summer air, forbidding myself to think about Chin's implausible job offer.

My brain starts fretting about the *Cow*'s marginal propeller governor—a $3k repair I've been putting off. I hate the thought of crawling into Cannon Valley Bank on my knees to beg for another credit line extension.

I'm bad at worrying so I don't. I'm good at distracting myself, so I do that instead. Nothing takes Mick Oolfson's mind off the world and its mundane woes like playing tag with clouds. I need a fix of therapeutic flight, but can I squeeze in a glider ride before the *Cow* is finished with her steam enema?

I close my eyes and dream myself into the sailplane cockpit, banked tight in the heart of a booming thermal, hawk off my wingtip, reading the air's secrets with my gut and stick, carving a steep, climbing spiral up and up toward the churning base of a baby thunderhead, checkered green countryside hazily rotating under my wing, head empty of any thought but milking every inch of lift out of this bubble of warm rising air, doing what I was meant to.

I open my eyes and I'm still dead broke. I wish I was addicted to something cheap like heroin. Flying eats hundred-dollar bills like popcorn. No joyride.

---

1   After the immortal playground doggerel:
Birdy, birdy in the sky,
Why'd you do that in my eye?
Aren't you glad that cows don't fly?

When I get back to my desk and check the computer, weather.com tells me that the storm front will shut down flying by six today. There goes my half day of work. My half day of pay. I call Chin's cell number and he's delighted to move dinner forward to seven.

My default pastime is bank-balance friendly. When life is shit, grab a book. I keep a drawer full of classics in my desk for times when I'm losing money and all I can do is sit. I tune out the world and its mundane woes and dive into the world of Sterling's *Schismatrix*. My ass can't blast into space today so I launch my brain.

CHAPTER TWO: ROCKET JOCK FOR HIRE

I'M EARLY. I'M ANTSY.

The CrossRoads parking lot is half full, good crowd. Nothing but pickups and beaters, so tycoon Chin hasn't arrived. The looming storm front flickers and booms to the west.

I'm a Minnesota boy so I've got no use for optimism. Manuel Chin will disappoint me tonight. No use getting my hopes up. I rationed myself to thinking the words "Chief Astronaut" only a couple hundred times in the last few hours.

As I trot across the gravel lot, a gust of warm wind pelts me with the first licks of rain. I swing open the bar door, thinking, *I'll ask Rhonda to give us that corner table in the back room.*

"MISTER OOLFSON!" booms a distinctive voice. All eyes are on Manuel Chin, pristine in his white suit, happily beckoning me to join him in his booth.

He stands, hand outstretched. "What a pleasure to see you on this momentous evening, Mr. Oolfson."

"It's Mick," I say as he pumps my hand enthusiastically.

Chin beams and booms, "You must call me Manuel. Sit down, Mick."

"Hell of a set of vocal cords ya got there."

Chin turns on the high beams, "When I emote at maximum volume, my friends call it THE VOICE OF GOD!"

The bar is stunned to silence and all eyes are on us. Chin raises his glass, turns to the room and toasts pleasantly, "Pardon, all. Cheers." He turns back to me and dials his voice down to a conversational level, "My voice adds two feet to my height on the telephone—a bankable asset."

Chin says earnestly, "My technical associate will be here shortly. Until then, order a drink and let us get to know one another."

I like most folks but I'm not going to become Manuel's buddy before I know what his game is. I wave to Rhonda behind the bar and mime sipping a beer. When I look back at Manuel, his attention is fixed on me as if I'm a rare species of beetle. I'm blunt: "I'm sure you're a fascinating fellow, Manuel, but before we get all palsy I need to learn a LOT more about your space business."

"Surely we can wait until my associate…"

"The gist of the business. I'll dive into the tech with your associate."

Manuel takes a deep breath, focuses fully on me, and his small green eyes catch fire. "We call our enterprise Channel Zilch."

I smile at the name and Chin looks pleased.

He continues, "Channel Zilch will be a media sensation—a video station in outer space streaming sensational live content to an enthralled audience. I have projected revenues—"

I hold up my hand to restrain him. "Video space station. Got it. You're not here to hire an MBA or a media expert. I'm sure you can give me an overview of your rocket tech without your associate's help. How does Channel Zilch launch?"

Chin hesitates but relents. "I have some literature that may satisfy your appetite for nuts and bolts." From a briefcase he extracts a binder and opens it to a glossy photo of a familiar fat delta-winged white and black silhouette.

The Space Shuttle—impressive. This Channel Zilch business is legit. "Whoa, as a shuttle jock I approve. How'd you score a slot, and which shuttle?"

Chin shakes his head and with a smile slides the binder across the table to me. As I resolve the details in the photo, my hopes lurch.

I groan. "That's Buran, the dead Russian shuttle. You bought a launch on a discontinued rocketship. You got scammed and I'm wasting my time."

Chin. "Not the Buran—which is, of course, history. I trust you'll recognize the name of this prominent astronautical corporation."

In bold letters: "S. P. Korolev Rocket and Space Corporation Energia". I nod. "Ok, you're dealing with pros. Those guys have rock-solid booster tech."

This is getting realer, so I ask the 64k-buck question, "What's the budget?"

Chin brushes me off. "Ever the model worker. Let's leave discussions of finances until my associate has briefed you."

Not a good sign. I set my jaw and ask again. "I need a budget to make this thing real for me. Round it off to the nearest hundred million: a ballpark figure."

Chin gives me a look I can't decipher. I know he's trying to keep his fingers on my buttons. His brow wrinkles into fatherly concern. "I am quite prepared to commence negotiating your compensation this evening, but I would advise you to wait until you have talked to my associate."

It's my turn to give him a look: sour. "You buy me a tent and give me five bucks a day for burgers and I'm okay on the salary front."

He takes this in with evident satisfaction—I'm not what you'd call a savvy negotiator where subjects dear to my heart are concerned, and space is my one true love—and gives me a reassuring wink. "I think we can pay you a bit more than five dollars per day."

I put on my bulldog face. "My point being that I don't give a hill of beans about my salary, but I care a lot about having a real budget to work with. Space ain't cheap."

He nods and pumps bullshit again, "Much can be done with intelligence leverage."

7

As predicted, my space dream is crumbling. "Nobody I know has levered into orbit. Heard of space capsules? Life support systems? Ground control? Little things dear to the hearts of us astronauts. Little things you don't find at garage sales." I look into Chin's eyes and narrow mine. I won't get played. "The budget or I walk."

Chin clears his throat, looks down, and mumbles something with the word million in it.

"Didn't quite get that. How many million?"

"A healthy seven figure budget."

Peanut crumbs. I stand. "So long, Mr. Chin. Can't say I get the joke."

"My investment totals three million six hundred thousand dollars."

I think that through and sit. "That didn't hurt, did it? No reason to be embarrassed—you're CEO, right? You've got the clout but you're a minor investor. Give me the total."

Chin looks insulted. "I am sole investor."

And I am a jelly-brained sot.

Manuel turns on his charm, "I commend your skepticism about our lean budget. Channel Zilch would indeed be a feeble jest but for this fact: I have arranged for a free launch."

"Everyone knows there ain't no such thing as a—"

Chin holds up an imperious hand to stop me, leans toward me, and whispers, "I have bartered with a corrupt Russian space official for launch on an Energia."

My hopes are in freefall but I give him one more chance to sell me. "You bartered? For an Energia booster?"

Chin smiles. "A splendid deal! A shipping container full of classical rock and roll record albums."

"Classical rock and roll albums."

Chin says cheerfully, as if he's quite sane, "Monkees. Herman's Hermits."

I stand—"Good-bye, Mr. Chin."—and head for the door. I expected this. I am not disappointed.

But damn.

CHAPTER THREE: LUTEFISK SUSHI

AS I WALK through the dark bar toward the door, the storm lets loose a flashing-crashing-splashing hullabaloo. Nothing beats a full-bore Minnesota thunderstorm for special effects.

Manuel calls after me, "Please stay. My associate is minutes away and will convince you…"

I turn and snort derisively. "As much as I'd love to hear how you conned the poor bastard, I've wasted enough time listening to your claptrap. Good night, Mr. Chin."

Chin smiles, trying charm on me again. "I hesitate to embarrass you, but the poor bastardess is my quite legitimate daughter, Heloise Chin. She is the brain behind the Channel Zilch mission."

The bar door swings open behind me and the CrossRoads crowd goes dead silent as it slams. I turn.

In strides a stunning apparition clad in a dripping wet matte black jumpsuit. A grid of orange lights twinkles on her belly. The lights strobe and form

pointing upward at her face, framed in short black hair. Her eyes shine through pink-rimmed amber sunglasses glittering with rhinestones. The lenses flicker: a heads-up display. None of the commercial brands of spex. Definitely a hacker custom job.

She's wired and I'm riveted.

I was expecting a middle-aged standard-issue male Birkenstocked alpha geek and instead—WHOA!—a thirty-something alpha-geek's wet dream.

As she reaches to flip up the glasses I glimpse hairline strips of silver on the back of her fingers.

She is vivid and wiry. Her skin is satin honey. Ethnic background? Mongrel American: a stunning example of hybrid vigor.

And then her eyes. Light green eyes that glow like LED's. Barbed pupils that snag my gaze. Green, green eyes.

I was born to love women and Heloise Chin is female, female, female. Whip-thin, medium height, low-slung hips that mean business, small, high breasts like twin howitzer shells, ripe lower lip, straight black hair shorn severely, and did I mention the green, green eyes?

The button that says, "COBOL IS SEXAAY!" geek style with a twisted edge like it's a private joke and if you don't grok it that's jake with her. The silver Mylar bow in her hair.

She commands every iota of my attention. As she strides toward me, hormones slosh through my hydraulic system in a towering wave, drowning my IQ.

Heloise Chin stops in front of me and looks hard into my eyes.

"Uh, Heloise?" I splutter, "pleased, uh, real pleased to meet you. What is it you do?" Innocent question, I swear.

She shoots me a narrow-eyed, nostril-flared gaze that curls my toes, with a tight little smirk like I'd asked her the color of her panties. I see her fingers twitch and the light grid on her belly comes to life—flipping between

and

Pop Chin emits a guffaw. "Do not let my daughter pull your chain. Heloise has an unfortunate propensity to toy with men's psyches. What do you call this charming avocation, my dear?"

Heloise looks at me mock-sweetly and bats her lashes

TESTOSTERONE SURFING

Cue Beach Boys' "Surfing Safari".

"It would be cataclysmically rude of you to depart from us when my daughter has driven through a deadly storm to meet you," says Chin.

Mick Oolfson is never rude. I return to the booth and sit.

Heloise slides into the booth beside me, quite close. She smells of cinnamon and firecrackers. Her breath is a delicious breeze.

Chin smiles at his daughter. "Heloise has many engineering talents—hardware, software, social. My singular offspring is the brains behind the technology of Channel Zilch. I merely enumerate the legumes."

I ask, my eyes not leaving her, "Can she talk?"

That scores a genuine smile. "One."

YES/TRUE

Her voice is a flute in a cave. "I yack fine, astroboy."

DO YOU FLY?

I turn and watch the message scroll across the black matte fabric hugging her tight little belly.

I manage a limp, "Like a fish. But I don't do stupid things just to impress women."

She scintillates her eyes at me. "Points for that."

9.1

"Fill me in," I say, trying to act sentient. "Besides whipping up costumes for the centerfold of Wired magazine, what geek magic does Heloise Chin do?"

She reels off in a monotone, "Evolutionary robotics. Cortical multitasking. Loving AGI embodiment. Kickstarting an Open Source Singularity."

XKCDFXORTMAX

crawls sideways across her belly lights.

"Whoa! Impressive buzzword dump. I don't see how any of it helps an orbiting video station."

"I hack vid, computer, and comm tech with one hemisphere idle. I want space bad."

STARS IN HER EYES...

She's got that look I've seen in a thousand faces. People who've begged me to reveal the secret key to getting into space.

"Say not another word, Ms. Chin. I am with you there." I look into her green eyes and think: Heloise Chin wants something from Mick Oolfson. My Y chromosome does a happy dance. Even though I am old and dull and ugly, I've got a shot at this singular woman. Whatever happens tonight, I vow on my honor as a testicle-bearing citizen to ask Heloise Chin out on a date.

The bar's bachelor farmers in their John Deere caps give Heloise full attention from the corners of their eyes. Don't get many women costumed like a cross between a Hell's Angel and a Christmas tree in The CrossRoads. Her orange belly lights throb a soothing pattern of

###

to keep the Lutherans skittish.

I've got a hole in my soul that youthful Christianity used to fill. I want to believe in this mission.

Rhonda bustles up to our table full of curiosity. "How are you folks tonight?"

Chin answers grandly, "Most grateful for your hospitable tavern's shelter from nature's fury."

I feed Rhonda one of my stale yucks, "Bring me the usual—warm sake and lutefisk sushi."

Rhonda rolls her eyes. "Leinenkugel and fried cheese curds it is."

While Rhonda takes their order I eye the manipulative pair. They are most definitely sincere: they genuinely think they are assembling a space mission. I'm in no hurry to end our little soiree. Let's see how far these two have hoodwinked themselves. As Rhonda departs, curiosity unsated, I open the discussion. "I'm listening."

"Mick has questions about our Energia booster," Says Manuel.

I snort. "The free launch."

"Pop got the deal of the century on that Energia launch."

PEACHY CHEAP

"He got took. It's a scam."

Heloise puts her hand on mine to short out my logic circuits. Her small, cool, silver-backed fingers.... She runs her hand up my arm and rests it on my shoulder. "The Energia launch is on. Will Oolfson drive the rocket?"

"Um..." I articulate articulately. Heloise is boogie-boarding my man juice, but I can't get her out of my eyes. I gently take her wrist and feel it pulse once as I set her hand on the table. "You're a heck of a woman and I'm a big fan of womankind, but let this old rocket jock think straight for a sec."

Heloise and her dad exchange carnivorous grins without a trace of guilt.

Heloise produces a laptop and props it in front of me: a picture of a bizarre rocket stack—an Energia with a featureless white tapered cylinder attached to one side. I lean closer to the screen (and Heloise) but the thing remains a featureless white tapered cylinder. I shake my head sadly. Chin and his daughter are high off each other's adrenaline fumes. Orbit a homebrew capsule with the beefiest Russian booster ever launched?

Heloise points to angled orange struts on the white tube. "Here's where we attach the capsule to the Energia using existing Buran mountpoints."

I hold up my hand. "Whoa, whoa. Say again. Capsule? Buran mountpoints? Start with the mountpoints."

She says, "You know the USSR cancelled its Buran shuttle program after one unmanned mission."

I give her a pained look. Space history 101. I'm a shuttle pilot and Buran was the only competing shuttle. I know Buran and I know its history. I break the news to them, "The Buran hangar collapsed years ago. The last Energia/Buran combo was crushed. Tragic waste of a rocketship. You got took."

Heloise's eyes flash sparks of glee. "Zero, Mr. O!"

"Zero?"

T0/FALSE

Chin chimes in, "My daughter's word for negation. She is a font of verbal innovation."

I eke out a spark of cleverness, "Hell one! That Energia was squashed quite flat."

My use of "one" scores a point in Heloise's eyes but she states flatly, "Zero. Buran got gronked but the Energia is good to go for launch. Our corrupt bureaucrat in Kazakhstan stashed it in the building's rubble. He knew an ultraspiffy deal like Channel Zilch would make him rich."

I look from Heloise to Chin. "Rich on Monkees albums."

Chin smiles, supremely pleased with himself. "Herman's Hermits albums as well. And a splendid motorcycle. I don't pretend to understand Russian economics, but be assured that our entrepreneurial Russian friend is well satisfied."

Looked at with half-closed eyes and gullibility knob cranked to 11, this Channel Zilch scheme is inching into the neighborhood of the not-laughably-absurd. If an Energia survived the Buran hangar collapse, it stands to reason that Manuel Chin would sniff out a deal. Buran's Energia was rigged to carry a heavy weight on its side so it makes solid sense to bolt on a white cylinder and call it a capsule. It all makes perfectly logically reasonable everyday common sense.

Moon cheese and fairy farts! At least this evening will be a memorable one.

Time to gently let the laughing gas out of their Zeppelin. "Are you guys aware that astronauts like to travel inside something airtight? Is that albino cigar shape a placeholder graphic until you pick up a refurbished Soyuz capsule on eBay?"

Chin rubs his hands with eager pride. "Tell Mick what your clever friends have cooked up, dear."

Heloise's eyes do this cute little flicker as she clicks to the next picture. Heloise Chin loves her tech. I bend close to see what makes her smile: cross-section of a sleek metal-skinned core embedded in a white featureless cigar. Four astronauts strapped into a tiny space.

Heloise puts her finger on the core. "We bought the fuselage of a prototype supersonic business jet at a bankruptcy auction."

I nod. "Plausible. Other commercial space projects are using that approach—cladding an existing plane. But what the heck is that white thing?"

"The crew's capsule is embedded in solid foam heat shielding." She's serious. That absurdity makes me look at her hard. She's a woman to die for but is she all there? "So we float around in space locked in a foam cigar."

She taps my hand excitedly. "The foam is ablative. As we pass through the atmosphere it melts away. In orbit our capsule will be squeaky clean."

Madness. "You're talking boost-ablative, not re-entry ablative?"

"One. Foam sheath has a low melting point gradient." More marginally plausible kookoo talk.

I point to the tiny space crammed with its four astronauts. "That little thing is Channel Zilch's video space station?"

She beams. "Zero. Once in orbit we deploy a big balloon and rigidify it with foam. We'll broadcast our reality show from inside the balloon."

I pick one absurdity at random. "Reality show?"

Heloise leans close and tries to fog my mind with her sweet breath. "That's how we make dough. Channel Zilch is an orbiting reality show!"

I give her a look, searching for crazy in her eyes.

"You want Mick Oolfson as test pilot to bust the cherry on a homebrew capsule that will melt on its way into space? Then I'm going to climb into a balloon, star in an orbital freak show, and then...? What? Beg for a ride back to Earth?"

Chin looks concerned at my tone but nods emphatically.

"Channel Zilch will make Pop a squillionaire. We'll buy a return ticket from SpaceX or Orbital Sci. I bet Pop ten bucks that a commercial space biz will pay Channel Zilch to haul us back home for the PR boost."

"Of course." I nod, adding a sour smile. "Makes as much sense as the rest of it. Any other singular features of the mission you'd care to share?"

Heloise pauses and thinks. She smiles and tells me another one, "Zilch needs to broadcast from geosynchronous orbit, so we'll salvage a broken research satellite and boost orbit with its ion thruster."

Laughing, I throw back my head and crow, "Next stop THE MOON! Whee doggies, it must be fun to think like that. I'm a big sci-fi fan and I would pay full price to see a movie built around your crazy scheme. I give you guys full points for gumption, but Channel Zilch is not going to fly."

Don't want to dump all over their dream: I've vowed to ask Heloise out for a date. I give them the benefit of my wisdom to keep the evening rolling. "Have you talked to any of the new commercial space companies? Pay one to launch an unmanned Channel Zilch payload cheap on a test shot. Get your toes wet in the space business, make some money and work up to your orbiting reality show."

Chin looks at Heloise who sneers. His voice rises in volume and deepens in pitch. "Channel Zilch requires a crew from the start. Publicity is paramount. We are resourceful people. I have no doubt we can augment our admittedly modest capital with our cleverness, our desire, and our backbone."

Sure thing, Pops. Dad and daughter are sealed in their self-delusionary little bubble.

A wet gust rattles windows. Grounded for the next three days. Glad Chin is paying for dinner.

Chin's briefcase is full of space reference books. I grab a familiar Space Almanac and page morosely through it. I find my name in the list of shuttle astronauts.

I shake my head as I leaf through the book. "I don't know jack shit about Russki tech. Their stuff is controlled from the ground." As I page through the chapter on the space shuttle I wallow in self-pity, something I've got pretty good at in the past couple years. I sigh when I read the lament for the first space shuttle built, the prototype shuttle that never made it into space: "...Enterprise sits among weeds in the outback of Washington's Dulles International Airport, paint peeling, out of sight, out of mind.[2]"

---

2   p. 197, Space Almanac, Second Edition, Anthony R. Curtis, Editor.

I sigh, "Here's what you guys need, a real spaceship, a shuttle." I hold the book up to Heloise's green eyes and her belly lights up:

Heloise Chin flashes me a look hard as emerald and states flatly, "Enterprise is ours."

CHAPTER FOUR: A HALF-VAST PLAN

SNUG FROM THE meteorological extravaganza, inside our cozy bar, I'm thinking, *"Enterprise is ours." What the heck does that mean?*

Heloise asks briskly, "Can you leave tomorrow?"

"Leave? What? No. Uh, zero. I have to spray."

She points to the rain-smeared window. "Tomorrow?"

"Well, not tomorrow. I'm socked in the next three days."

She states as if it's decided, "So you *can* leave tomorrow."

"Wait. Where? Go where?"

Heloise shines her eyes' fully-rated candlepower right at me. "To Dulles to inspect Enterprise. We'll pay expenses and one k a day; call it three thousand."

Three thousand will fix the *Cow's* flakey prop governor!

Heloise sees me waver. "Unless you'd rather spend those three days losing money."

Pay for a needed repair, a chance to see shuttle Enterprise, maybe a chance to spend a little quality time with...

I ask, trying not to sound pathetically hopeful, "Will you...?"

Heloise looks sympathetic. "Wish I could come along. I have a Channel Zilch personnel interview to run on Monday."

Chin says, "The videographer? But I will be with Mick at Dulles. Reschedule the interview—"

I butt in, "Wai-wai-wai-wai-wait! Give me a chance to think this through." My money-spending lobe has already spent the three thousand dollars on my crotchety plane. Crapping on the Earth from a WWII-vintage airplane is a costly fetish. I clarify the task. "Inspect Enterprise? NASA security at Dulles isn't going to let me crawl around inside Enterprise with a screwdriver and blueprint."

Manuel answers, as if this was long-planned, "A cursory external inspection will inform us whether to pursue our acquisition of Enterprise as a key Channel Zilch asset."

I taste the word, "Acquisition."

Heloise rushes me past that little issue. "That isn't your concern. We will pay you three thousand dollars for a report on Enterprise's condition."

I want the money. Want to see Enterprise—the prototype of the shuttles I love. Want to see Heloise again. But I don't want to be played for a fool.

Time to see how much they want me. "Fifteen hundred a day is my rate for contract work."

Heloise looks at her father who smiles and shakes his head. "Hearken back to our earlier salary negotiation. How did you phrase it: five bucks a day for burgers?"

Savvy negotiator is me. "That was when I thought you had a real plan for blasting my ass into space. Fifteen hundred."

Chin says flatly, "My daughter's offer is generous." He waits. I shrug and nod. I can't bluff against these two. The Chins make it up as they go along like a well-tuned pair of grifters. Good thing I'm too broke to worry about them stealing my dough.

But I *can* make sure they don't steal my self-respect. If I inspect Enterprise I'm going to inspect it right. I collect people smarter than me. I get their help when I get in over my head, which happens. I say resolutely, "I want Gritch Neubart along on the scouting party."

Heloise, "Fewer better. Why?"

"Gritch is the world's best shuttle doctor. He retired last year and I bet he'd jump at the chance to inspect Enterprise. If Gritch gives Enterprise a thumbs up you'll know it's worth acq… whatever."

Chin says decisively, "I think not. Since we travel tomorrow to take advantage of the leisure afforded you by this inclement weather, best keep this initial reconnaissance simple. If you give

Enterprise a provisional bill of health, I will pay Mr. Neubart to conduct an in-depth inspection before we consider it for acquisition."

I'm not going to poke at that word "acquisition". My conscience may not be clear on this, but it's at least translucent.

Chin says, "Come to my office at ten tomorrow morning. I will secure passage to Dulles for tomorrow evening." He turns to Heloise. "You will move Monday's interview to tomorrow morning."

Heloise waves him off. "'t's OK, Pops. I can handle—"

"TOMORROW!" His megavoice shocks the restaurant to silence. Chin raises his glass to the stunned patrons and smiles ruefully. "Pardon."

Heloise leans close to me and whispers, "The other Mexican orphans called Pop 'Sirena'."

Chin says quietly, "Short for 'Sirena de Niebla': foghorn. My prodigious larynx was an asset for a tiny child in the rough and tumble of an understaffed orphanage. I sometimes use it reflexively and inappropriately."

Heloise needles him, "Pop shoots off his big mouth to get his way."

METATRON

"Metawho?"

"Voice of God."

Hard to imagine Chin's voice coming from something as dinky as a burning bush.

Chin says, "Returning to the subject at hand, and speaking with my *interior* voice: If it would please my darling daughter to indulge her imperious Pater, I ask humbly that the interview be moved to a later date so that I can participate."

Heloise looks sullen, but nods slowly. Looks like these two have some family issues.

I break the silence. "Who ya interviewing?"

Heloise lights up with excitement. "Channel Zilch's camera operator. I like her résumé."

Interviewing applicants for the Channel Zilch orbital reality show. There are so many layers of improbability wrapped around that concept that I don't even bother boggling at it.

My long day is catching up to me. I glance overtly at my watch.

Chin wraps things up, "It is late and tomorrow will be eventful," reaching into his jacket and pulling out his wallet. "Why don't you two kids enjoy a breath of air?"

I am suddenly very aware of Heloise Chin and my vow to ask her out.

Heloise stands and her belly lights scroll

CHANNEL ZILCH ❤ ENTERPRISE

Chin and I read the text and smile at Heloise and one another. We shake hands and I verify tomorrow's appointment details. Heloise heads to the parking lot and I follow.

I'm suave like a boulder's cuddly. Asking a woman for a date is a gut-check thing for me every time. As I follow Heloise, I painstakingly craft the perfect sentence, choosing words to say both 'How about a date?' and 'Mick Oolfson is awesomeness incarnate.'

We pause at the exit and look out its window into the heavy rain. As good a time as any to try out my devastating line: "Um... Heloise. Would you like to maybe go and see a movie sometime?"

Heloise looks at me like I've told her I have three buttocks. "Movie? Me? A date?"

I state it baldly, "One. A date. Maybe sometime next..."

She cocks her head. "I don't date people I work with."

Shit.

Then her belly gives me hope:

BUT SOMETIMES I FUCK 'EM

CHAPTER FIVE: NASA'S ZERO-TOLERANCE POLICY ON CANNIBALISM

As soon as I get home I google up some info on the Chins. I find a one-page Chin Ltd. website with an address in the industrial outskirts of St. Paul: "Chin, Ltd. Imports Exports Throughout the World, Bulk Maritime Byproducts a Specialty." Not a word about their Channel Zilch space show, which doesn't surprise me. Not a word about Heloise Chin, which disappoints me.

Late that night my doubts are winning—maybe I should keep my distance, bail out on the Dulles trip—when Chin phones me with flight details. Manuel convinces me to make the trip by actually offering to part with more money. "To further ensure mission security I offer you a bonus of five hundred dollars to take aggressive steps to ensure that Chin Ltd. leaves no traces of its interest in Enterprise."

Not a good sign. I say, "We're just taking pictures. Why the secrecy?"

Chin replies in a patient voice. "Competition between commercial entities demands tactical control of strategic information. Surely you've heard of industrial espionage."

Right. Mustn't let the other Maritime Byproduct Moguls steal your killer business plan to branch out into media by launching a space shuttle. I ask, "What sort of aggressive security steps are you talking about? Just because I'm an astronaut doesn't mean I'm part ninja. Nunchuks are hilarious in microgravity."

Chin, "Oh, nothing so heroic as that. Take prudent steps to minimize our exposure to surveillance cameras and Dulles personnel."

"Five hundred extra bucks if I plan a quick, smart inspection? I'll hit the Internet and route us in and out of Dulles like invisible men."

Manuel says, "I shall sleep soundly tonight because of your diligent efforts."

"Wish I could say the same. See ya at check-in, Manuel."

I spend a few hours googling maps of Dulles International Airport and laying out the safest route to and from Enterprise's hangar as the storm rattles my bedroom windows. As I drift off to sleep, visions of Heloise dance in my head.

A rumble of thunder shakes me awake.

Grounded. My brain kicks into the old familiar money fret but...Green eyes. Heloise. It replays. The whole crazy night. Her fragrance of cinnamon and sparklers. Belly lights taunting me then giving me hope. I'm hooked bad. When I think of her green, green eyes my heart kicks in like an afterburner.

Then I remember Channel Zilch. Shuttle Enterprise! My quest for Lady Heloise. A quest? Just a business trip. I smile and shake my head and picture Heloise, singular and vibrant and aimed straight at her target.

I'm not ready for a leap of faith but I'll take a short, paid hop to Dulles. A trip to see Enterprise, a minuscule chance for a space trip, and a shot at Heloise Chin are worth sticking my scrawny neck out as far as I can stretch it. Keep reminding myself that Channel Zilch is a harebrained scheme that's doomed to fail.

I recall the implacable look in Heloise's eyes and my doubt wavers.

Pilots make lousy passengers. I put in a couple of my best Air Force years at Little Rock AFB teaching boneheaded rookies how not to crash C-130 Hercs. I'm generally an easy-going guy but I do have strong and well-founded opinions about the proper way to fly a large airplane.

The surest way to stop a plane crash is to hook[3] a lousy student pilot. The pilot of our Dulles-bound Boeing 737 isn't a washout candidate; he's not dangerous, just marginal—a bottom-ten-percenter. His piloting sets my teeth on edge from the moment we taxi away from the Minneapolis/St. Paul terminal—sloppy in his turns and late and heavy on his brakes. I do *not* like riding in a plane mishandled by a lousy pilot. The guy's take-off is passable

3   Aviationese for flunk.

but the minute we're in the air he starts fiddling with the throttles.

As our plane climbs and points toward D.C. Manuel is eager to get to work. I put him off. "Let's talk when we reach altitude."

I pretend to scan the in-flight consumer-porn catalog but really I'm hoping the shiny pictures take my mind off the tragically marginal flying of Captain Twitchthrottle, who evidently has some original theories about the aerodynamics of the rudder. He fumbles with this sweet old Baby Boeing like he's wrestling a drunk pig.

I study a shiny picture of The Matrix CyberToiletSeat™, which I don't want anywhere near my nethers so I'll pass on that price reduction from $1,199 to $949. Wasting time, I turn pages, distracting myself by trying to figure out who buys this shit.

At long last we hit cruise altitude and Captain Swinegrappler engages the blessed autopilot. I can forget about ignoring his buffoonery, relax, and talk to Chin. First I take advantage of one of the few perks of being a passenger: I order a brace of Jim Beam miniatures.

I pour my tiny Jims into the plastic cup and raise it in an obvious toast, "To our Enterprise." Chin clinks me with his plastic cup of ginger ale, nods happily, and sips. I take a sweet sip of gold Kentucky fire and begin the briefing, "We'll make two trips to Enterprise—first a scouting trip late tonight to recon the area for access and security."

Chin nods eagerly. The guy's got a taste for adventure. That could be a problem.

I lean close again and share my biggest concern, "There is a NASA Security post on the Dulles Airport grounds about half a mile from our objective. We are going to give it a wide, wide berth." It's a small office used infrequently to host meetings on classified space missions. I sat in on a few briefings there before my second shuttle flight. It's not a major risk, but I'm a pilot: I attend to detail.

Chin leans even closer and whispers, "NASA Security? Do they guard Enterprise?"

I whisper back, "Scuttlebutt is that Enterprise is in a kind of jurisdictional limbo. It's parked in a Smithsonian storage lot, but NASA still has research rights to it. I'm counting on the fact that no sane person would swipe a shuttle. They just have to keep teenagers from spray-painting it so I'm figuring sporadic patrols by rent-a-cops. If we see a big NASA Security presence around Enterprise we'll have to throw in the towel. I don't want another run-in with Ishwald."

Chin tilts his head and waits.

I sigh and shake my head slowly. "Lieutenant Commander Tobias Ishwald, an officer in NASA Security. A dear, dear friend of mine."

Chin sits up straight. "A friend? So you have ties with an insider who can make our job very easy indeed."

I wince. "Ishwald would pay good money to feed me dick-first into a pencil sharpener. We've got a history that goes way back."

"You've led a fascinating life, Mr. Oolfson. Do go on." Chin settles himself with an expectant smile.

I take a hefty slurp of Mr. Beam's elixir and find it good. "Let me tell you a story about the first time I met Tobias Ishwald. Toby applied for the same astronaut class I did. I met him for the first time at a lunch interview. Four of us scared little candidates sweating and twitching and trying our darnedest to impress a real live NASA astronaut, whose name I won't drag into this. It was supposed to be an informal meet and greet, but I was so tense you couldn't drive a hatpin up my ass with a sledgehammer."

Chin listens, rapt, and we've got another hour in the air so I spin the tale. Pilots tell stories. "Tobias and I wound up sitting side-by-side during lunch and didn't exchange a word. Too busy straining to be gung-ho and brilliant for the real live astronaut. After dessert, the astronaut asked a question and had us each answer in turn: 'What can you do better than anyone at this table?'"

Chin says, "A standard but often enlightening query in a cutthroat group interview."

I say with feeling, "I hate questions like that, but Ishwald jumped right in. He picked up his butter knife and said, 'I can kill a human with this butter knife in more ways than any of you.'

Chin looks thrilled. "A visceral answer!"

I grimace at the memory. "It got visceraller. He turned to me and started stabbing and slashing in quick, precise strokes just short of my eye and temple and ear and throat, showing us all the fatal wounds he could make, and when Ishwald started stabbing and slicing his way down my chest our astronaut laughed and said, 'Got it. You're the SEAL, right?'"

Chin's eyes get very large. "A Navy SEAL?"

I nod and keep spinning, "Ishwald grinned real sweet and pretended to wipe my blood off his knife with his napkin. That boy knows how to make an impression."

Chin looks troubled. "And yet after that disturbing display of psychopathology, NASA invited this person to become an astronaut?"

"Lots of astronauts are into that macho shit. His Mick-killing demo set Toby apart from the pack of applicants."

Chin inquires, "What did Mick Oolfson answer to the astronaut's query? What expertise did you claim?"

"I forget." It was lame. After Tobias performed his grisly piece, all I could come up with was that I probably (not "for sure", being a good Minnesota boy) grew the tastiest potatoes.

Chin says, "So you met Tobias Ishwald at the point of a knife."

I smile with more than a dash of rue. "That set the tone for our relationship."

Chin looks puzzled. "Ishwald tried to join NASA as an astronaut, so how did he come to work in security? Isn't that a rather circuitous career path?"

"Toby was selected for the same crop of rookie astronauts I got into. To boil a saga down to a haiku: I made astronaut; he scrubbed out."

Chin pries, "Can you share the reason Mr. Ishwald did not pass muster into the elite astronautical corps?"

"Claustrophobia. A bad case. He went barking, biting psychotic when we did the basketball escape drill."

"The basketball?"

Whenever I talk about the basketball I tend to sympathize with Toby. "Nickname for the rescue sphere used in a shuttle emergency. It's a flexible hollow ball about a meter across. It holds enough air so you can be ferried from a stranded shuttle by an astronaut in a space suit."

"A meter-wide sphere. A bit snug." Chin shivers dramatically.

I nod emphatically, remembering the fetal helplessness inside it. "We were paired for the exercise. I went first and didn't like it one bit. When Tobias crawled into the basketball, he started screaming—sounded like a pig eating a monkey. When I reached into the basketball to pull him out, he bit me." I hold up my left forearm and roll down the sleeve: two arcs of white scars. "I punched him upside the head."

Chin examines my scar. "Which did nothing to cement an enduring emotional bond with Commander Ishwald."

"Lieutenant Commander. We've got an emotional bond all right. Not a blood brother thing—more like Cain and Abel or Sylvester and Tweety Pie. Hang on for the surprise ending."

"I await further revelations."

"I figured he'd be embarrassed by the whole thing, so I tried to make a joke about it the next day when I saw him—showed him my bandaged arm and asked him if he was aware of NASA's zero-tolerance policy on cannibalism."

"I take it that Tobias did not respond with a hearty guffaw."

"Ishwald spat piss and farted fire, then hightailed it straight to the personnel office and withdrew from astronaut training."

"Wouldn't claustrophobia have disqualified him from space flight in any case?"

"Sure, they canned every candidate who went weird in the basketball. But Ishwald got it all twisted in his mind like I was persecuting him for a medical condition, that it was my fault."

"Isn't he a rather odd choice to be head of NASA security?"

"Freaky odd, but ya gotta hand it to Tobias. Instead of slinking back into civilian life with his tail between his legs he got his foot in the door at NASA security and clawed his way to the top. His SEAL background intimidated rivals." I take a long sip of bourbon. Still far from Dulles. "I could go on about Ishwald and Oolfson—we've got history—but I don't want to hog the floor. So.... Tell me about Heloise."

Chin laughs. "Manuel's story doesn't interest you? My childhood spent at the Hogar de Niños del Ejército de Salvación Orphanage in Pijijiapan?"

It startles me when Chin switches accent from angular Midwest English to sinuous native Spanish.

Chin scolds me, "My adoption by Esther and Ted Gillibrand, a wonderful elderly Lutheran couple, and my adolescence in Coon Rapids, is too tedious to hold your ear?"

"Love to hear all about your life later, Manuel, but your daughter fascinates me."

Chin shrugs and smiles. "My extraordinary daughter is too long a topic for such a short flight. I am content to learn more of your history with the Lieutenant Commander. We approach his lair, after all."

I beg, "One story about Heloise."

"Perhaps on the return flight. As your employer I demand that you brief me fully on our opponent."

I throw Chin a sloppy salute. "At your command, sir. Let me tell you a little story about the last time I met Tobias Ishwald."

Chin settles back, looking deeply content with the evening's entertainment. I take a lingering sip, a deep breath, and start the woeful tale, "Once upon a time there was a rather stupid young astronaut who got himself into a shitload of trouble doing a dumb but perfectly safe maneuver with a space shuttle."

Chin inquires, "Was this young astronaut named Mick Oolfson?"

"You know my history. You're spoiling the flow of my narrative."

"I go silent."

"So anyhoo, the powerful wizards at NASA were mucho pissed and decided to decide this stupid lad's fate by convening a tribunal of the three wisest, most powerful ogres in the bureaucracy. And among the three chosen was the terrible Tobias of Ishwald."

Chin sighs on cue, "Ah."

I take another taste of Mr. Beam's finest. "Yes. And the tribunal did hear the evidence, which was indisputable, and did hear the young starfarer grovel and beg for clemency and kiss ass and promise to be a good little astronaut. And in their infinite mercy the three wise ogres did decide by a vote of two votes unto one that the naughty rocketboy should be shafted, banished from the starry vacuum he loved and made to crawl on the ground upon his belly like the lowly groundlings for the rest of his miserable days."

"Need I ask how Tobias of Ishwald voted?"

I seethe, "You should have seen the smug, self-righteous simper plastered on Ishwald's face. I nearly jumped across the table and chewed his larynx out."

Chin says earnestly, "Then by all means we shall do our utmost to avoid your friend Ishwald and his security building."

"Here's to that." I raise my glass and drain the last precious sip.

The landing changes my opinion of our pilot—despite a stiff crosswind he greases it.

As we exit, I compliment the guy, "Bit of crosswind."

The pilot jerks his thumb into the cockpit, "I leave the hairy landings to the young bucks. My co-pilot nailed it, though, didn't he? Take a bow, kid."

I'm thinking, *Find a job you're good at, old man. Maybe you'll actually enjoy it.* I'm only happy doing what I excel at. What do I excel at? Flying rocketships.

I avoid the pilot's eyes and turn to follow Chin down the tunnel to the terminal. Time to inspect a rocketship.

CHAPTER SIX: A FEW REVEALING PHOTOS

CHIN IS A SPEEDY little cuss. The emergency-orange suitcase he trundles behind him doesn't slow him a tick. I hustle to tail him through the echoey, shuttered Concourse A.

As we progress toward Passenger Pickup my eye is snagged by an enormous poster covering a twenty-foot span of the wall: Enterprise! "Return to Dulles International Airport this Winter to

Visit Space Shuttle Enterprise in the New National Air and Space Museum's Steven F. Udvar-Hazy Center". Enterprise looks cozy in its future shrine, a grand hangar thronged with tiny people and legendary planes.

I feel a twinge of pity for the captive bird. Enterprise was not built to squat motionless in a shelter—she's a rocketship!

Don't get me wrong, whenever I have free time in D.C. I spend it wandering the Air & Space Museum, but every visit I have the same fantasy: jailbreak! One by one the venerable birds' engines sputter to life as the crowd oohs and aahs. Long-shut doors swing open and visitors climb aboard laughing. Museum walls go poof! and one by one historic flying machines taxi out onto the Mall. The crowd cheers lustily as the Wright Brothers' Flyer lumbers down the Mall and slowly lifts into the air towing a Lilienthal glider. I'm strapped into Yeager's Bell X-1 hanging from the wing of Lindbergh's *Spirit of St. Louis*...

A piercing whistle snaps me back. Chin beckons from the exit door. I point to the huge poster of Enterprise and cock my head at him. He beams me a high-powered grin and jerks a big thumbs up.

I look up at the poster and laugh at my own sorry ass. I should be ashamed to take the Chins' money—the Smithsonian is building an expensive retirement home for Enterprise—but Chin's a big boy, and I like being paid.

Chin takes a detour to the luggage area to pick up some damn thing so I loiter in the lobby until he re-emerges.

As we exit Dulles Terminal to the pickup area, the chill air is smoky with exhaust. Few cars are waiting this late at night so it's easy to spot the culprit, an ancient, dust-grey Dodge Dart coughing noxious haze from its rattling exhaust.

Chin scans the cars and makes a beeline toward the doddering Dart. A tall Sikh gentleman (flowing black beard, distinctive white head wrap) opens the trunk and deposits Chin's suitcase. As I arrive at the smoking car the guy gives me a polite nod and walks quickly away.

I regard the Dart—a dull grey primer-splotched beater spewing blue-brown haze into the cold evening air—and don't say a word, just turn to Chin and raise an eyebrow.

He laughs. "Every dime is a child to me. We needn't drive a costly rental car, so I bartered with an ally who does business at Dulles."

I shrug. "I'm not bellyaching. I've got a thing for Dodge Darts." I learned to drive in Mom's baby blue 1972 Dart, so I'm content with our chariot, shabby though it be. "Best if I drive."

I climb in and smile at the Dart's familiar, faux-wood-trimmed instrument panel. A favorite old machine is comfort food to my spirit. I've spent my life trusting my ass to machines from doddering Dodge Darts to humongous Hercs to spectacular Space Shuttles. Machines have meaning to me.

Chin belts himself into shotgun. I spread out my maps and start the mission briefing. "Tonight we're doing a simple drive-by recon of Enterprise's hangar—" I tap on the red marker circling it "—to check security. That's a straight shot of a little over a mile up Autopilot Drive and then a short left on Wind Shear Road to Enterprise, which is stored in Hanger C-17."

I tap the big red X on Ishwald's outpost. "That NASA Security office is on Ariane Way, which parallels Autopilot a block east. After we scope out Enterprise, we come straight back down Autopilot to get to our motel—we never pass Ishwald's outpost."

Chin says emphatically, "We shall evade your nemesis Ishwald at all costs."

I try to calm him down a notch, "Like I said, Ishwald doesn't live in that building—NASA uses it for briefings about classified shuttle missions. The next mission is pure science and the next spook mission is five months off so I doubt if anyone's pulling an all-nighter there."

Chin's eyes sparkle. "But the prospect of tangling with your Ishwald will keep us coiled for action." Manuel is half-hoping for adventure. This whole Channel Zilch lark must be the thrill of a lifetime for a guy jaded with the maritime byproduct business.

I say, "Drive-by tonight, and if it looks like a reasonable risk we go in tomorrow and take pictures for Gritch."

Manuel nods earnestly. "You are well on your way to earning your five-hundred-dollar security bonus."

I'll splurge on a new axle for the *Cow's* tailwheel!

I ease out from the curb and the engine complains. Our Dart needs a tune-up, bad. As I navigate empty airport streets, we lay a nasty cloud in our wake.

I glance at Chin. He's got a tight grin on his mug—raring to go.

He gives a little gasp. Flashing lights ahead! My stomach cha-chas. Stay cool, Oolfson. Nothing illegal about driving a rattletrap around an airport. As we approach, the blinking lights resolve into safety flashers—workers setting up a backhoe for a night of road work. Barriers block part of the intersection, but the left turn lane is clear. I inch past the orange cones and breathe easier when I see the flashers dwindle in the mirror.

A sign points right to "Hangars C-16 to C-23".

I say, "This is it. Enterprise is stored inside hangar C-17—the second hangar in."

Chin says, "This is thrilling. All my senses are sharp with fear and anticipation."

I look over to see if he's shitting me, but the guy looks bright-eyed and eager.

As we cruise past the sign, huge hangars loom into view. Enterprise! Parked in the open! I can't help it—I stomp the brakes, which squeal like a gaggle of Japanese fangirls.

Enterprise! I haven't set my eyes on a real, live space shuttle in forty-three long months. Enterprise's beefy curves shine in bright light, stark white and black. I grin a goofy grin—what a beaut! Space shuttles are gorgeous, voluptuous, Rubenesque, every curve muscular, a real armful of rocketship. A tough, sweet bird to fly through vacuum, fire, and air. I'm one of the few who knows how to fly that thing. I'd give my left nut to fly Enterprise.

Not a person in sight for as far as I can see down the row of hangars. Looks like we can dial down the paranoia; this is a storage lot. I have *got* to lay my hands on that bird right now.

I lean toward Chin and goad him, "What say you, Manuel? Enterprise is out in the open with no one around. Who knows, they may wheel it back into the hangar tomorrow. Let's get our pictures tonight."

The whole point of this Dulles mission is to take pictures of Enterprise so my shuttle-fixing buddy Gritch Neubart can evaluate the bird. From here Enterprise looks to be in great shape, which makes me smile even wider and goofier.

Chin nods eagerly. "Let us seize this opportunity."

I swing the Dart slowly into the hangar lot, survey our options, and park behind a fuel truck near Enterprise's right wingtip.

I know we'll be on surveillance camera, so I devised a simple security plan: move fast and wear stupid shit.

Our costumes don't have to make sense, since we are only going to wear them if no one is around Enterprise. My getup is a purple plastic poncho, big blue mirrored sunglasses, and a long blond wig. Stylin!

Chin and I wriggle into our fancy duds side-by-side in the cramped front seat. He struggles into a long, purple terry cloth bathrobe, a Santa beard dyed canary yellow, and a straw boater. I stifle laughter when Chin looks at me with regal dignity and says, "For my crowning touch," as he dons a pair of familiar pink rhinestoned glasses. "Do they complement my look?" He looks like a deranged Cuban band leader.

"Sinister, Manuel. Let's do this thing. Remember, once we leave the car we've got three minutes to take pictures. Three minutes, then scram."

Chin says cheerfully through his golden beard, "Three minutes then scram it is! Let's to it!"

I put on my gloves and stomp the gas pedal hard, which the Dart protests.

As we approach Enterprise, I turn to look at Chin. He's lowered the pink glasses, and his eyes are huge; his head tilts back to take in Enterprise as it looms.

Manuel says quietly, "Space shuttles are quite sizable."

I've seen plenty of people look up at a shuttle with their chins dragging ground. Space shuttles are enormous: 56 feet high, 120 feet long, 78 feet wide from wingtip to wingtip, 106 tons (if the ashtrays are empty) of the best tech the seventies had to offer. Shuttles look dinkier strapped onto their huge launch boosters. It's an illusion—the suckers are BIG.

I pull the Dart close to the fuel tanker with a squeal of brakes and shout, "Start your timer. Go!"

We're out the door, clad like loonies and full of purpose. I've got the task of photographing Enterprise's undercarriage, wheel wells, bottom tiles. Chin hurries off to record the sides and nose and vertical stabilizer.

I look up at Enterprise's tiled black hide high above me—a wave of shuttle love pings from my aviator lobe. This is the prototype space shuttle. The only shuttle never to fly to space. She looks like her beautiful sisters, and I love every one of them.

Can't stand here imprinting on Enterprise like a baby duckling.

Chin bought a couple of decent digital cameras, so I disable the flash and take continuous shots, panning and zooming as I walk slowly along the trailing edge of the rear wing. I zoom tight into the seams of the elevons to catch juicy detail for Gritch.

I methodically work my way from the tail toward the nose, photographing the tiles of the rear wings' undersurface, which looms overhead like a high dark ceiling. Space shuttles sit ass high on the ground, so as I work my way forward, the tiles slope closer. When I reach the left main landing gear, I zoom into the wheel well from all angles.

I've got to lay my hands on this historic rocketship. I reach to touch a tire and feel its cold solidity—Enterprise comes to life for me. Maybe I'm projecting just a tad, but this shuttle wants to fly.

Beep. One minute down—first main gear—right on schedule. I give Enterprise's wheel a pat and resume clicking. I walk a zigzag pattern up the belly of Enterprise, snapping the tiles. Looks like the Smithsonian is taking decent care of her.

Beep. Shit. One minute left. Running a little long to get total coverage of the leading edge of the wing.

I hear the car coming before I see it—adrenaline gooses my heart. I signal Chin, "PSST!", and point to the nose gear. He double-times after me. I get there first and crouch behind the tiny wheels, less than three feet high.

The car enters the hangar lot slowly. I turn to urge Chin on just in time to see him trip and sprawl, still twenty feet from the gear's cover. His straw boater rolls toward me on its edge and I grab it as it wobbles by.

"Damn this robe!" Chin hisses and then lets out a harsh, "Oooh. That ankle does not feel right. I dare not walk. I shall crawl."

I whisper loudly, "Hunker down until the car drives past."

I peek over the wheel. The car—a red Civic—drives slowly past at a distance, oblivious to us and our useless fear. It dwindles slowly down the row of giant hangars until it turns behind one.

I sprint to Chin's side and bend to help him up. "We've got the pictures. We're out of here. I've got ya." As he rises slowly, I loop his arm over my shoulder and take his weight. He winces audibly. We start a three-legged shuffle toward the Dart, a sorry sight in our outlandish duds.

The Civic's headlights stab out from the road flanking Enterprise's empty hangar as its engine rumbles between the huge metal walls.

We freeze, clutching one another. I say, "Nose gear." We pivot and skip/walk/limp to the gear. The nose wheels are way too small for both of us to hide behind, but I lower Chin to the tarmac, and we try to squeeze our bodies into the tire's cover.

My damned plastic poncho crinkles like aluminum foil.

The Civic pulls to a stop a shuttle-length away under the wingtip opposite the one we parked by. The gas tanker blocks our Dart from their sight.

A thin white guy in a blue rent-a-cop uniform gets out followed by a small black guard. The two jabber a mile a minute, but they're a hundred feet away and I can't make out a syllable. They don't glance our way but turn and walk toward Enterprise's empty hangar, shining flashlight beams into the immense empty space.

Those guards will be back, and our Dart is a long way for Chin to hobble. Best piggyback him to the car and wait for the guards to split.

I stand and lean to help Chin up. "Hop on my back."

He rises gingerly, plops the straw boater back on his head, and grins a genuine grin. Manuel Chin is getting the adventure he itched for tonight. I smile a crooked smile, turn, bend, and Chin hops on my back, as heavy as a damp cat.

The wheel well doors hang down on both sides of us, hiding us and blocking our view. I walk us forward, and peer around the front edge of the hanging doors to check for the guards.

A flashlight shines dead in my eyes. Busted!

I duck back behind the door, let out a lungful of adrenaline fumes, and take two steps backwards. I point up into the wheel well, just above our heads.

I whisper urgently, "Grab the forward edge and pull yourself up. I'll boost."

A beam plays across the landing gear. I freeze. We are shrouded by the hanging doors so only the bottom of my purple poncho is visible from the guard's side. The light sweeps away but the guards' voices grow louder—headed straight toward us.

I hiss, "Now!" and stretch as tall as I can stretch.

Chin grabs and gives a mighty heave upwards and as I bend he swings a leg up but fouls it in the crinkly plastic of my poncho. Chin keeps his grip and—slow and quiet this time—swings his leg up and over my shoulder.

The guards' voices get louder. Chin hoiks his other leg up onto my shoulder. "Go!" I urge, and Chin boosts himself as the guards round the nose.

These two Shuttle Guard of the Year candidates would have walked by oblivious if not for Chin's straw boater, which tumbles from his head. I lunge for it and knock it toward them rolling on its edge across their path. They go quiet as their flashlight beams converge and follow the rolling hat for a full second before swinging back along its path to bathe us in incriminating photons.

Chin swings his robe shut in front of my eyes and hisses, "Run at 'em screaming."

The guards are speechless—their beams frozen on us.

Something in Chin's voice convinces me: COMMIT!

I lurch forward and summon a hoarse howl from deep in my gut. Chin bows to clear the wheel well and as we emerge from under Enterprise's nose he sits tall and foghorns in his Voice of God, "FE! FI! FO! FUM!"

"GIANT!" shrieks one of the guards. I hear him throw his flashlight and flee.

I lumber blindly forward, howling my guts out.

POP, POP, POP and the lights go out.

The other guard throws his flashlight and runs, screaming, "GIANT WITH A FUCKING GUN!"

CHAPTER SEVEN: I'LL GRIND HIS BONES TO MAKE MY BREAD

CHIN SPREADS HIS ROBE so I can watch the guards flee into the dark distance. "Run for the hills, Mick," he urges happily,

My shock at Chin's gunplay flares to anger as I piggyback Chin toward the Dart. I spit out the words, "A gun!"

Chin sounds supremely satisfied with himself, "A FUCKING GUN, Mick! Which I hold securely in my hand, safety engaged."

Guns are entropy pumps and pilots hate entropy. I prefer zero probability of perforation by fast bits of metal. "Throw it," I demand.

"It is secure."

"THROW IT!" I stop dead.

"I think not. My trusty PT111 is registered to Manuel Chin." Damn.

"The guards have disappeared into the alley between hangars," he says. "Let us flee before they return."

Gun anger later. Defer noncritical issues to noncritical times—time to get the hell out of Dodge. I resume piggybacking carwards.

I suck air hard as I carry Chin the last few yards to the Dart. I lean back against the passenger-side window and dump him on the roof. I mutter, "Get that f...that gun away from me." I stand and sear Chin with my harshest disapproving glare, which bounces off his serenely smug smile. I sprint to the driver's side and shuck the poncho before getting in.

I look out to see Chin's short legs dangling outside the passenger window—a long drop for a runt. Good! I can be a petty bastard. I remember Chin's bum ankle and feel like a shit as he gingerly slides off the roof and lands hard on his good foot.

Chin rips off his robe as he gets into the car. I start the Dart, and he retrieves a black plastic garbage bag from his briefcase. I stomp the gas, and the Dart takes its leisurely time accelerating.

"Come on, come on," I command the car. Yeah, I talk to machines. I keep the gas pedal floored, which the Dart finds amusing, engine wheezing its mirth as it slowly gathers speed.

Chin grabs the discarded robe from my lap and starts stuffing our stupid duds into the trash bag. As we turn onto the road, Chin's voice is tight with excitement. "No sign of the guards, Mick. A clean getaway!"

I relax a hair then remember I need to be pissed at Chin. I turn and shoot him a paint-scorching glower. "The gun…"

"GIANT WITH A FUCKING GUN!" roars Chin, and starts to giggle like a little girl with bronchitis.

My temperature kicks up a notch. "Not funny. So not, so unfunny…" I sputter, as I steer toward the exit. Manuel escalates his infernal giggling into piercing soprano guffaws.

Then it hits me: we did it! Despite the snafu we got our pictures and we got away. I verify, "My five hundred bucks?"

"Yours. Well earned. Now attend to the road. That construction has blocked our way."

The intersection is a floodlit hive of flashing lights and orange machinery. The backhoe works a trench that cuts Autopilot Drive—our route to the hotel. My pilot's mind shuts off emotion. I go icy calm.

"Get the maps. Stuff that bag in the back," I tell Chin, who obeys. I steer between the lines of orange cones which snake through the intersection. Once we're well clear I pull to the side of the road.

As I spread out the maps, I state, "We are *not* driving past the NASA security office." I trace our new route with my finger. "We turn left on Ariane instead of right, and head north away from…"

Chin, "Away from Ishwald and his incisors."

I ease the Dart back onto the road. "I'm sure old Toby is sleeping soundly somewhere."

I assume that Chin is unaware that his darling daughter's pink rhinestone sunglasses still adorn his face. I'm not telling.

I stomp the gas and the Dart surprises me by accelerating smartly. I enjoy the surging power and let our speed get a bit illegal. In the rear view mirror we're trailing serious smoke.

The traffic light ahead on Ariane is green. I'm going way too fast when it turns yellow. I stomp the brake hard. My foot sinks to the floor! "SHIT!"

The harsh reek of brake fluid fills the car. I grab the t-handle of the parking brake and yank hard—it comes free in my hand. "SHIT!"

I pull the wheel hard left, hoping to slow by drifting through the turn. Trees loom fast.

A red Mercedes Sportster barrels into the intersection from the right just as the light turns red. I jerk the wheel to cut behind him but the Sportster hits his brakes and...

SCREECHUNK! We scrape the back of the Sportster, and barrel into the tree line. Seatbelt slams my chest as we hit a tree and crunch to a halt. Smoke pours from under the hood. Adrenaline pumps, and things are sharp and slow.

I'm alive, so I ask, "You ok?"

Chin pats his chest and winces. "You will be pleased to know that I have a fucking gun-shaped bruise on my chest. Otherwise in fierce fettle."

The driver of the Mercedes screams, "You fucking idiot!" Sounds like he's in fierce fettle, too.

Chin says resolutely, "Let me deal with this."

I sigh. "It's all yours."

I groan and beat my forehead slowly against the steering wheel. The berserk guy gets out of his car. Another car door opens and slams—passenger, great.

He raves as he stomps toward our dead Dart, "You scum-sucking moron! You pinheaded little shit!"

The distinctive tenor voice freezes my adrenalized bloodstream: Ishwald!

I hiss, "RUN! It's Ishwald!"

Chin flashes me a determined smile—I remember his bum ankle—and kicks his door open. As I fumble with my own door I hear Manuel flee into the darkness, clutching his briefcase.

Stuck! Bent doorframe. I launch myself through the passenger door, but as my feet hit the ground, Lieutenant Commander Tobias Ishwald stands before me.

I stand straight and look Ishwald in the eye. His jaw is wide open and his eyes bulge. I haven't seen Tobias in a few years—since the tribunal that canned me from NASA. His crewcut is a bit greyer but he still looms over me, uniform taut over the bulk of his brawn. The scene is tinged the radioactive sepia of sodium streetlight.

Ishwald stares down silently at me for a beat, artery pulsing in his forehead. His bulldog chin swings wide, "OOLFSON! It's you, you desiccated little prick! This is a revenge thing, right? Blake, back me up here, we got a terrorist situation."

His passenger looms behind Ishwald aiming a wicked black pistol at my forehead, which starts to itch. "Gotcha covered, skipper."

Ishwald snaps, "Hands high, Oolfson. Tell the tall guy to throw his gun out of the car."

I raise my hands and ask, "Do you see a 'tall guy' in the vehicle?"

Ishwald sneers, "Don't feed me bullshit! The guards at Enterprise called us about a...a tall guy with a pistol. Blake?"

Blake bends and peers into the rear seat. "The giant ran. Shall I pursue?"

Ishwald says, "He's armed. I'll call a team to sweep the area."

I talk to give Chin time to get away, "This is all a misfired prank."

Ishwald says coldly, "Prank? Revenge! Couldn't forget the tribunal, huh, Oolfson? Had to try to kill me."

I've got to end this.

"Like you tried to kill me in astronaut training?" I start to roll up my right sleeve.

Ishwald growls menacingly. His sidekick looks interested and steps closer. He starts to ask but then thinks better of it.

I ask innocently, "Shall I tell your bodyguard about my funny little scar, Toby?" I'm gambling that Ishwald can't afford to let the story of his washout leak to his troops. It makes me feel like the desiccated little prick he just called me, but I need to slam the curtain on this scene any way handy.

Ishwald barks in my face, "Shut up. Blake, I know this punk, so I'll walk him back to the security building. It's only a mile. You take my car to Enterprise, and debrief the guards on the incident."

Blake, well-trained, sprints to Ishwald's dinged Mercedes.

Game over. Kiss my five hundred bye-bye. Kiss my silly little dream of space bye-bye. Wish I could kiss Heloise Chin bye-bye.

Since Chin got away, I resolve to play dumb until they link Chin to the rental car.

Ishwald tries to get my goat, "Start walking, washout."

I reply, "Lawyer." I've got nothing to say to Ishwald. He won. He gives up and we walk in silence.

As my adrenaline drains away, I review my situation. When all is said and done, the foulest crimes I've committed tonight are piggybacking a guy who shot out a couple hundred dollars worth of lights and driving a wee bit fast right before the brakes failed. Hardly hanging offenses, but it's back to pooping on beans from on high for Mick Oolfson. At least I gave it a shot.

Maybe Heloise will date me now that we're not business part-ners! I know that prospect is a loser even as my neurons form the thought.

At least I got to touch Enterprise.

As we walk silently, I keep my eyes on the ground so the twinkly-ass stars in the bitter black sky don't set me to sniffling.

CHAPTER EIGHT: RESET

I SPEND THE NIGHT in a 1½-star Fairfax County jail—my first night ever behind bars.

Lieutenant Commander Ishwald tries to make a Federal case out of the incident, but I play it as a dumb prank gone wrong. I stoutly embellish the mythos of the GIANT WITH TFG, claim I didn't know my tall companion was armed, but can't incriminate a friend.

Ishwald never links the incident to Chin because records of the Dart show it had been recycled years ago. Chin has clever friends. Wish they took better care of their cars.

I piss away a couple weeks of good summer flying days dealing with lawyers and judges and commuting between Stanton and Dulles. The last time I see Tobias Ishwald is at my sentencing. I swear he bares his teeth at me when the judge hands down a lenient sentence—three month suspended jail, a hundred hours of community service, and a $2,200 fine. Embarrassing.

Chin is a champ about it all. He shows genuine gratitude at getting away cleanly by slipping me a welcome bundle of cash. He pays for a shrewd lawyer, covers my fine, and gives me $10K for my trouble on top of my $3k fee. Manuel even takes the blame for our lousy Dart and pays my five hundred "security fee".

We agree that I best lose touch with Channel Zilch. I thank him for the adventure and tell him I'll keep an eye out for news of white cigars launching from Baikonur. He doesn't laugh.

Heloise Chin doesn't bother to call.

The Sands of Time pour relentlessly through the Great Cosmic Hourglass, and as the years drift by I embrace my dwindling future. Now that I've got a criminal record, I stop wasting hope on fantasies of commanding a rich geek's homebrew rocket.

I invest my windfall in *The Flying Cow* and clock a couple of good years and one wretched patch—weather, engine replacement—that nearly sinks Oolfson Aerial Fertilizing Service. I fight my way back to solvency and restructure *Flying Cow's* loan.

I nearly marry a sweet, pretty woman, but our hearts aren't in it, so I wind up with a Facebook friend.

I turn forty. I lose a good friend when Columbia dies.

I follow Enterprise's career. When she moves into her shiny new Smithsonian home, I think about visiting her, but know that seeing Enterprise would only stoke my sense of failure.

When NASA retires the shuttle fleet and Enterprise flies to her home in New York's Intrepid Sea, Air, & Space Museum, I take a weeklong trip into the Boundary Waters Canoe Area, so I don't have to watch the news.

I don't look up at the night sky much.

o o o

A few years later, innocently checking email late at night, I damn near spit hot decaf on my keyboard.

From: hel@channelzilch.com
To: beanpooper@yahoo.com
Date: 3 Jan, 2015 23:47

Subject: CZ

Spaceman,
Google "space shuttle enterprise dulles".
Channel Zilch is GO!

Hel

That name jolts me. I haven't thought of Heloise Chin in many moons. A whiff of cloves and a spark somewhat south of my heart.

I google "space shuttle enterprise dulles" and lose myself reading news reports about today's big NASA announcement: "Space Shuttle Reunion at Kennedy Space Center...three working shuttles and prototype Enterprise...Shuttle Carrier Aircraft and Enterprise stop at Dulles for weeklong display..."

Weeklong display at Dulles Airport. My mind replays our abortive inspection and Ishwald's triumph.

I click up more articles and a detail catches my eye: "Newly-appointed NASA Security Director Captain Tobias Ishwald's first big challenge is to oversee transportation of all four shuttles on their flights to Kennedy Space Center."

Captain(!) Ishwald head of NASA Security? I close my eyes and see the smug, self-satisfied simper plastered on his face at my NASA tribunal.

Dusty neurons sputter to life as I recall the Chin's demented plan to steal Enterprise. The crazy Channel Zilch reality show. Stolen Energia boosters. Green, green eyes. My Dream of Space. Am I demented enough to buy into that craziness again?

It would be sooo sweet to steal Enterprise from under Ishwald's nose.

Not a chance. Security will be airtight—not like it was when Enterprise rusted in a storage lot.

I don winter gear and take a long, cold, dark, thinky-feely walk around Stanton Air Field. Boredom, curiosity, and my life-long Dream of Space battle prudence and doubt. When I think of touching Enterprise, my eyes mist. When I think of Heloise Chin's green, green eyes, I feel an unaccustomed hunger. I am famished for dreams.

I picture Heloise beside me in the CrossRoads Bar clad in her outrageous geek suit. Her flute voice stating, "Enterprise is ours."

I level with myself: these people want to steal a space shuttle. If I so much as talk to them, I'm part of it. Can I live with that?

Let that question ride.

It's a bitter, clear, sharply moonlit Minnesota winter night. Snow-swaddled fields glow silver. It's been many years since I looked up wholeheartedly at the night. I lift my eyes to a sky full of stars studding the sweet black nothingness that used to be mine. The moon hangs just out of reach.

A star moves and I focus on it. The bright point glides slow and steady—a satellite in Low Earth Orbit. A shuttle? No—the fleet retired. No shuttle will orbit again.

Unless.

I picture Enterprise strapped to an Energia. What a launch that would be! I'm in the cockpit, Heloise in the Commander's seat, looking up through Enterprise's windshield at the Baikonur sky. My Russian isn't good enough to count down from ten.

And then Ishwald works his way into my little reverie, standing at the base of the Energia, kicking it and swearing. Energia's thrusters roar to life and Ishwald just has time to scream, "OOOLFSON!" before he's roasted by the flames.

Whoa! That scene got out of hand. But stealing Enterprise from Ishwald would be an epic burn.

When I open the door to my hangar, I look up at my old *Flying Cow* and all I see is Enterprise.

It's winter, and I've got time on my hands. I'll think myself a lesser man if I don't sink a month into pushing this Channel Zilch thing as far as I can.

I telephone Manuel Chin. Channel Zilch is most definitely a go and desperately needs Mick Oolfson. Manuel offers to buy *The Flying Cow* if I sign up.

I nix that idea. I'll give Channel Zilch a month but I'm not committing.

CHAPTER NINE: DON'T BE A DICK

MY VINTAGE ORANGE MGB GT loves to drive hard in a full-blooded thunderstorm. I crank up a classic rock station and make an ass of myself singing with Janice and Jimi and Joni on the forty-five-minute drive from Stanton to Chin HQ. Weekend traffic is light. I push the speed more than I should in the rain—sort of the point of a sports car.

I think about a certain green-eyed, twinkle-bellied geekstress. Can't remember the precise shape of her lower lip.

Chin Ltd. headquarters is in the St. Paul warehouse district south of the Mississippi. The old grey stone warehouse sports a modest sign echoing the text of their website: "Chin, Ltd. Imports Exports Throughout the World, Bulk Maritime Byproducts a Specialty."

I pull to a stop in the Chin HQ parking lot, but my mind is still in gear. Between my bouts of awful karaoke, I spent most of the drive up from Stanton in a state of mental frenzy, mostly throttling outbreaks of hope. I've got one toe sunk deep in the dream of Channel Zilch, and today will tell whether I'm diving in.

A quick pre-Heloise check in the rear view mirror—nothing dangling from my nose or wedged in my teeth. Fly zipped. Ready to engage.

I stride across the parking lot toward Channel Zilch and

Heloise, doing my best not to be hopeful. I stop dead to take in this flyer taped to the HQ door:

JOIN CHANNEL ZILCH!

We are searching for the next Video Hyperstar. Are you:
A Broadcast-Quality Journalist with a Camera-Ready Face?
More interested in Exposure, Adventure than Cash?

Channel Zilch
is being readied for launch.
Call Mr. Chin at 651-555-4799.

Searching for the next Video Hyperstar! I take a breath and think about the one angle of Channel Zilch that I've completely repressed: the reality show. I chew through the list one more time—all the reasons Chin and Heloise guaranteed would make Channel Zilch a cash gusher:

- The usual reality show vicarious emotional roller coaster: betrayal, benevolence, stupidity, alliance, tears, love. Who slips insult A into reputation B? Who slips tab M into slot H?
- The Geek demographic: Sci-fi fans are a natural audience and they love to spend money on stupid shit.
- Ingredient D: Danger. Snag the NASCAR and hockey and ledge-jumper fans.
- Infotainment: Awful word. Key ingredient to grabbing

snobby viewers who wouldn't stoop to watch *Survivor* or *Danger Dungeon* or *Supermodel Slumber Party*.

In our phone call, Manuel assured me he'd built spreadsheets demonstrating that Zilch'll suck in hundreds of millions a year from advertising, syndication, merchandizing, movie spin-offs, computer games, even religions, for all I know. Plenty of moolah to buy our return trip to Earth before our bones turn to mush. Sounds iffy, but what does Mick Oolfson know about media or money? I drive rockets, not cameras or spreadsheets.

I do a preflight zip check as I near Chin's office door, which is wide open, so I walk right in.

Heloise watches a TV screen. Beautiful and focused. Her hair is a bit longer but still cut severely. She doesn't notice me.

Oh yeah, Manuel is watching, too, as is a plump middle-aged woman with a startling penumbra of red curly hair.

I'm a tad deflated at my reception. All three are glued to the screen. Some sort of news show—a talking head jabbering on and on about some damn thing. I can't quite hear the guy, and they are engrossed, so I finally blurt, "Whatcha watching?"

They turn, and I swear that Heloise smiles for a fraction of a second.

Manuel, gesturing toward a chair: "Welcome, Mick. Take a seat and watch."

Heloise flicks her tongue at me in what I choose to interpret as a friendly fashion and turns back to the screen. Ms. Chin is dressed down in grey sweats today. I wonder if she still owns that geeky lightsuit. The red-haired woman smiles a smile so wholesome and warm, I swear I smell baking bread. I open my mouth to introduce myself, but she shakes her head and points at the screen.

This was not how I'd visualized the Channel Zilch reunion. My fantasies were pathetically Mick-centric.

I whisper, "What are we watching?" I decide to lean nonchalantly against the wall near Heloise so I start to make my way, but Manuel grabs my arm and sits me in an empty chair beside him. I ask again, "What...?"

Heloise shushes me emphatically and hisses, "Watch."

From the newsreader's tone of voice and expression, the news is rather sad, but then I hear his words, "...in the top part of your double boiler, first cooking for one or two minutes over direct heat..." His voice drops, and he looks out of the screen fathoms deep into my eyes and reveals to me in an aching voice, "...before placing over hot water. Continue cooking at least five minutes..."

His voice quavers, and sorrow seeps into my marrow, "...or longer, as desired..." His voice cracks, and his eyes become aching wounds, "...for more delicious flavor." I'm overwhelmed by manufactured grief. I reach up to wipe away a—can you believe it?—a freaking tear!

I blurt, "WHAT THE...!?"

Heloise looks peeved, but Manuel says, "Mick should see the complete presentation. Ms. Vader, queue it from the top." The red-haired woman flicks a handheld control, and when I look back at the screen the guy is looking straight into the camera with a Gigawatt smile.

The talking head is handsome but not distracting movie star handsome. Thin and fit, with top-of-the-line teeth, an expensive haircut, and a suit I couldn't afford. He holds up a cylindrical package to the camera and says simply, "Quaker Rolled White Oats."

I persist, "What...?!"

Manuel leans close and whispers, "Audition. Richard Head. Channel Zilch's spokesperson."

Ah, an audition tape. Looks suspiciously like the CZ gang has already mentally hired this guy.

Richard Head winks at us and starts to read the back of the box. This time he is elated to share the greatest news on Earth. His eyes twinkle, and his voice trumpets joy unbounded, "Quick Quaker Oats. Boil two and one half minutes." I have to grin at his contagious enthusiasm.

He leans into the camera to share a great joke, eyes sparkling, "Delicious economy meat loaf costs only a few cents per serving." I wait for the punch line, and he delivers, "Eight generous inch-thick slices." The way he says it bulls-eyes my funny bone, and I laugh with the others. Heloise giggles an endearing piccolo trill.

Mr. Head keeps going, his demeanor and voice for all the world as if the Twins won the World Series again, "One and a half pounds ground beef chuck." His voice tightens and his eyes narrow. Something awful has happened in the world and Mr. Head must share it dutifully and reluctantly, "One quarter pound pork loin ends. One quarter cup onion..."

He pauses, takes a breath and I'm on the edge of my seat waiting for him to deliver the awful news. In a low voice and with downcast eyes, "...cut fine."

I get it, but I don't like it. The guy is a virtuoso newsreader showing off that he can make an oatmeal recipe sound like the most sensational scoop since Madonna bore Cheney's love child. Impressive like a musical genius playing Bach on a whoopee cushion or an aerobatics champ entering a competition in a stock Erco Ercoupe.

Head sure is one handsome son of a buck with a riveting video presence. The guy knows how to play to a camera. His eyes are his money-makers: engaged eyes, empathetic eyes, deeply caring eyes.

I say, "Those eyes..."

Chin interrupts eagerly, "Richard's extraordinarily compelling oculars are money in the bank for Channel Zilch."

The red-haired woman fairly croons, "Eyes, voice, face—the whole package is terrific. I've pointed cameras at talking heads all my life, and Richard blows the rest away."

So Ms. Vader is a camera person. Got it. And I get that humongous numbers of humans glued to Channel Zilch mean shoals of shekels swimming Zilchwards. But this guy scares me.

I ask, "Did Mr. Head submit a resumé?"

They aren't listening. Head has launched into a hard-driving cadence modulated by herky-jerky dynamics that keeps you hanging on because he's always just on the verge of saying something astounding, "...this famous food is often introduced by child specialists into the diet..."

I force my eyes to leave the screen—Head's that good. I wave my hand slowly up and down in front of Manuel's face. "Yooohooo. Resumé?"

Manuel's eyes stay velcroed to the screen as his hands search his desk. Wouldn't want to miss a word of, "... whole-grain Quaker Oats provide the..."

Chin finds the sheet and passes it to me, saying, "The young man's *vita* is spotty, but Ms. Vader assures me that a media star's worth lies entirely on the screen."

I glance at the screen and Richard is in a dudgeon, spitting out words with a nasty sneer that makes me want to hate, "... riboflavin, four percent..." This guy has his fingers welded to my deepest buttons. That's not right.

Head's resumé is a one pager. I skip the intro B.S. and skim down the list of schools and jobs. Theology major? No degree, hmmm, dropout. Small town radio: Klamath Falls, Ponca City. Breakthrough into television: a few months as a weatherman in Portland and currently at a station in Minneapolis. But I'd remember him for sure. Oh, KPXM—Channel 41, one of the skip-over cable channels running infomercials that look like talk shows, except the coked-up host is interviewing some big-haired guy about an astounding low-calorie car wax or a sure-fire system for making a gajillion bucks by subleasing diseased poultry.

Meanwhile, Richard issues dire warnings to the world, "Cream shortening and sugar thoroughly. Beat in eggs..."

There are years between some of Richard's gigs. I've seen enough. Of Richard Head's face, audition tape, and resumé.

I say firmly, "I've seen enough. Turn it off, and let's talk this thing over."

Manuel and Heloise ignore me. Ms. Vader shushes me with a smile, "He's nearly done. Watch."

I watch. Richard is building toward a climactic summation. His voice rises in triumph, and a dumb little voice inside me wants to cheer as Head declares exultantly, "We guarantee you, too, will agree that Quaker Oats are the finest in quality of any oatmeal you have ever tasted, or we will gladly remit you the cost of the package."

The three addled loons applaud and cheer, and—dammit—I have to stop myself from clapping.

Heloise gives me the full force of her eyes. "How about our Richard?"

I don't know where to begin, so I blurt, "You're planning to haul a fast-talking failed priest who peddles car wax on a trip into space that may take... how long?"

"Nine months minimum to earn our passage back. Richard's magic eyes could make the bucks flow in faster—maybe six."

I soldier on against the tide of local opinion, "You're going to be living in a space the volume of an average living room—that's how much room a space shuttle's flightdeck and middeck add up to. You think you can live with that guy? He's a cold-blooded manipulator."

Heloise cows me with a disdainful sneer. "I'm not afraid of Richard's voodoo eyes."

"So this is a done deal? You guys have already decided to hire him."

Manuel points: Head's face at rest—blank and bland—still commands the screen, "We must harness that face to Channel Zilch."

"And I don't get a say?"

"You are saying your say. I am listening. Of course, I listen more closely on this matter to Ms. Vader and my daughter, who are conversant with the art and business of media. If there are issues pertaining to astronautics that disqualify Richard, please disclose them."

Cute. Ok, then, let's see if this little astronaut can march Hyperstar Head to the chopping block. "Here's the astronautical issue: crew cohesion."

Chin waves his hand disdainfully, "You are all professionals."

I flail. "Professionals? If he's such a professional TV god why is he doing infomercials on a backwater cable channel?"

Ms. Vader explains slowly, "I spotted Richard on Channel 41 months ago and have been watching him. I turned Helgirl onto Richard, and she's a fan. I invited Richard to interview for our announcer slot. He's the one Channel Zilch needs."

Heloise nods slow and big, as if to a child. "Darthy knows faces."

I tilt my head, and Heloise says, "Darthy Vader is the best newsroom videographer I know. That's why she's Channel Zilch's camera operator."

That takes the wind out of my sails, but I give it one last shot. "People can go gaga on long space flights. Some of those half-year ISS and Mir guys went off the deep end, and some of them never found their way back to their old minds—cults and visions and fits of epic doggerel and such. You want a crewmate who at least starts near normal."

Heloise snorts. "Normal is average."

"Did you even look at his resumé? Big gaps between jobs—year and a half here, two years there. How do we know he wasn't shooting smack or stuck in some cult craziness?"

Heloise starts to smirk. I keep pushing. "Did you look into the guy's eyes? You want to live cheek by jowl with that? What if Mr. Head flips out and comes after you while you're sleeping?"

Manuel sits up straight and looks attentive. I'm finally getting through. I go for the kill. "I look into that guy's eyes and I see light-years of crazy. He made me cry at an oatmeal box, and that magnitude of sickness just won't cut it on..."

Manuel clears his throat and points behind me. Heloise covers her mouth and stifles an ugly snort of laughter.

I turn, and there, as large as life, is Richard Head. I sag with embarrassment. My Minnesota Nice kicks me hard for the awful things he just heard me say about him. To make it ten times worse, Richard Head is smiling hugely at me and sticking his hand out to shake mine. I'm wrong about him—the guy can take heat without being a jerk.

My MNice takes control and overcompensates to make up for things. I grab his hand and pump it enthusiastically. "Richard!"

He reaches to his neck and pulls off a pair of earbuds. "Sorry. I was listening to Ms. Vader's cues."

The instant relief makes me even friendlier, so I try desperately to break more ice, get on a nickname basis. "Can I call you Dick Hea..."

My mouth knows it's done wrong as I bite off the word.

Richard "Richard" Head jerks his hand back and his eyes go small and hard. My Minnesota Nice writhes on the ground whimpering for forgiveness, for oblivion.

I say the only thing I can say, "Richard.... Richard Head. That was an awesome audition, just excellent. You lit up the screen."

Richard thaws instantly—starts to smile. I turn and look from Manuel to Heloise. Their eyes tell me what to do.

I turn back to Richard and my Minnesota Nice thoroughly enjoys asking him, "How'd you like to be Channel Zilch's Hyperstar?

CHAPTER TEN: SPACE 'N' VADER

HEAD DOESN'T TAPDANCE with glee at my job offer. He waves his hand dismissively and looks at his watch. "You've seen my work. You have my *vita*. Email me your proposed contract and my agent will consider it. I must be off to prepare for my afternoon's broadcast."

As Head turns to leave I decide it best to leave the goodbyes to the others, who flank Head as he heads for the exit, Manuel's huge voice extolling the opportunity Channel Zilch offers.

I look around Chin's empty office, disappointingly generic, seeing not a shred of evidence that these people are actually planning a space mission. I'm still a bit drained from the emotional workout Head put me through.

Rising voices interrupt my reverie. Manuel strides back into the room with his hand outstretched and his face lit with a toothy smile. "Well played, Oolfson. I thought you'd cost us a spacecaster, but you recovered splendidly."

I open my mouth to expound on my ambivalence toward Head and leave it hanging as Heloise runs straight at me, green eyes blazing. I extend my hand, but she ignores it, wraps her arms around me, and hugs me tight. I look down at the top of her head and gingerly embrace her. Wisps of her black hair and spiced-lightning scent tickle my nose. I feel the warmth of her and the shape of her and am speechless. Heloise's tight little tummy breathes against me as she says, "Welcome aboard, spaceman."

I've had a recent dry spell in my so-called "sex life," so I have to break the clinch before an involuntary biohydraulic response kicks in.

Heloise looks so happy that it's hard for me to say, "Let's get this straight: I am *not* aboard Channel Zilch. I drove up today to give you a shot at convincing me to help you with your Channel Zilch scheme, and instead I wind up offering a job to a..."

Smiling, she says, "To our new Channel Zilch announcer. Optimal, Mick."

I say, "Unless you satisfy my doubts on a few key points about Zilch, I won't ever see the guy again... Unless I'm channel-flipping in the wee hours. Did you tell him the little detail that your hyperstar gig is conditional on a risky trip to space?"

Manuel looks troubled for a fraction of a second but then turns on his confident, toothy smile. "Richard's hasty exit precluded full disclosure, but we have arranged to meet for full and frank discussions later this week."

I say, with feeling, "Don't forget that I'm not onboard yet. I don't like that guy, and I like most people."

Heloise's hug and the memory of Richard Head rattle me. I realize I'm being rude to Ms. Vader who stands politely waiting to meet me. Her frizzy red hair billows around her head like a fiery afro lion's mane. I turn and shake her hand—firm and sure, as is the steady look she gives me. She's an impressive woman, not so much short as concentrated.

I start to introduce myself, but Chin butts in: "Forgive my rudeness, Ms. Vader. Let me introduce a man who needs no introduction, Channel Zilch's Chief Astronaut, Mick Oolfson."

"Nice to meet you, Ms. Vader. I'm not part of Channel Zilch. More of a contractor."

She gives me a fresh-baked smile. "I *am* part of Channel Zilch—the camera operator. Call me Darthy."

"Dorothy?"

"Darthy. D-A-R."

"Darthy?" Odd. Then it hits me. I say gingerly, "Darthy Vader[4]?"

She grins and says, "That's me. I used to be D-O-R-O-thy Vader but got it legally changed."

---

4   Later she tells me she gets a lot of mileage out of playing Darthy Vader at sci-fi conventions. Wears a costume and plays a hardcore shrew who makes hubby Darth iron his own cape.

I have to ask. "You know all about this crazy Channel Zilch plan, and yet you want in. You seem like a smart person. Why the heck would you get mixed up in such a load of malarkey?"

Darthy holds up her clenched fist and counts. "Three reasons. One: I need to get into space before I die. Non-negotiable."

I nod. Lot of that going around.

Darthy continues counting, "Two: Heloise Chin. Three: Heloise Chin."

I nod. Can't argue with that. I turn to Heloise, "Why Darthy Vader?"

Heloise says simply, "I know vid, and Darthy's the best. She may have orbited the sun too many times for Pop—" Chin snorts "—but I need her in orbit for CZ because she's a brilliant videographer, and she's got all sorts of skills we need."

Heloise sees my puzzled look and explains. "Dad has an orbit-count fixation. Darthy suffers from excess birthdays. Pop didn't want to hire her because she's not Barbie enough for our reality show."

Ok. I get it, but I don't like it. Darthy is fiftyish and like I said: not thin. Observers trained to Western standards of feminine beauty may see Darthy as plain and dumpy. This boils my piss. Mick's heartfelt sermon follows: That's a person you're talking about, friend. If you see a person as ugly, you're a spiritual vandal. I pity you your bleak and pinch-hearted world.

Manuel turns to me. "Heloise would have you think me ageist. As if reality television is not notoriously the province of the young and beautiful. Contrary to my daughter's suggestion, I find Ms. Vader extremely attractive. I like a substantial woman, and her unruly red hair is sensational. Were she not a Channel Zilch employee, I would be so forward as to ask Ms. Vader to dinner and a movie."

Darthy swats Manuel's shoulder, and he grins. She says, "I may be a fat-assed old cow, but I gave Manuel two hundred thousand good reasons to hire me. I'm paying for my ride on Enterprise with my ass-freezing fund."

I tilt my head and wait.

Darthy says matter-of-factly, "I saved that money to freeze my body when I die. Cryonics, you've heard of it?"

I nod. Wow! Darthy is an immortalist hypergeek. Our Ms. Vader wants to die on a gurney in a cryonics lab. When her brainwave goes flat, med techs will flush her blood with anti-freeze and dip her corpse in liquid nitrogen. After a restful spell spent floating among the corpsicles in a giant thermos, Doctor-Bots will thaw Darthy and pump her full of FutureBlood and wake her to a FutureLife of RocketChairs and SmartShoes and weekend picnics in the Oort Cloud. A wickedly weird retirement plan. Cryonic embalming would frighten and confuse our ances-tors—that's Progress! Balls-to-the-wall weirdness is mother's milk to Darthy V. so no wonder she's hip deep in this Channel Zilch madness.

Heloise says, "Once Pop found out all Darthy's space geek skills, he had to hire her. Her cryobucks clinched it."

I say, "I'm listening."

Darthy says proudly, "I speak Russian fluently; I minored in college. I've been studying spacecraft life support systems for years—since Helgirl clued me in."

Helgirl, cute. Hel, even.

"I can service all current microgravity air-scrubbing and water filtration systems. I have studied all current Russian and American spacesuits and am familiar with..."

As Darthy keeps ticking off pertinent skills, I find myself re-laxing. She's a treasure.

Darthy continues, "I've got advanced EMT training and three years of volunteer ambulance experience. I can handle most common medical emergencies—broken bones, sutures, minor surgery. I have read every unclassified paper on zero-g medicine, nutrition, and exercise."

I turn to Chin and say, trying not to be over-sincere, "Gotta admit, Manuel, the fact that Darthy Vader buys into Channel Zilch makes me more open-minded about your plan." In a crazy way, I mean it. Darthy's got the stink of competence on her—as-tronauts develop a nose for that. With Darthy behind Channel Zilch the whole nutty scheme just got more likely. Fudging all the factors rigorously, I estimate that Channel Zilch's probability of reaching orbit just rocketed from 2.9% to 3.2%.

Hel and Darthy and Manuel are listening, so I hold the floor. "I'm impressed with Ms. Vader, but I told Manuel on the phone exactly what I need to see today. We're talking felonies with this Enterprise caper, so I want solid proof that this launch is not a scam."

"You're ours, then," says Darthy. "Show him the goods, Helgrrrl."

"Allow me," says Manuel, "to describe how I bargained for our launch while my daughter prepares her presentation on Channel Zilch's technological particulars."

Hel puts her hand on my shoulder and leans close to me, playing with my circuits. "You are going to drool over my Energia pix." She runs out the door, glancing back to wink and leave me blushing.

Manuel orates, "Let me allay your fears about the business side of Channel Zilch's launch."

I put on my listening face, sure my red cheeks make me look a fool. Manuel's voice fills the office.

"You are no doubt well aware that Russia is traveling a long, bumpy road from the Dark Age of communist thought-slavery to the Golden Age of capitalist wage-slavery. Greasing palms is still an integral part of business. Years ago, before our aborted scouting trip to Dulles, my formidable daughter was determined to find a way to get her beloved Channel Zilch into space. She asked me to attend something called the Russian Space Industry Exposition in Moscow, certain that I could sniff out a deal.

"At that point I was a skeptic about Heloise's Channel Zilch, but I love my daughter, and I love to travel, and quite candidly I was bored to tears with scheduling shipments of emulsified fish entrails. At the expo I struck pay dirt when I approached Vasili Kropotkin, Assistant Director of Operations for Baikonur Cosmodrome[5].

---

5   Baikonur is Russia's Kennedy Space Center even though it's in Kazakhstan. It's not really at Baikonur either, but near Tyuratam. They named it after the little town of Baikonur 150 miles away in a slick security move that buffaloed U.S. intelligence for five nanoseconds.

"When I let Kropotkin know that I was willing to pay well for a discreetly-conducted manned launch, he told me his dreams of retirement: a little dacha nestled in a birch forest by a lake, a kickass sound system with refrigerator-sized speakers, blissful days listening to his collection of classic Western rock and roll recordings: The Monkees, Herman's Hermits, The Turtles played at such a copious volume as to quake the birch leaves. When he talked about the particulars of his retirement plan, I knew that I had found my daughter her coveted launch."

Darthy pipes up, "Vasili is a great guy. I've talked to him a few times about tech issues. You'll love him."

"If Vasili gets me back into space, I'll get down on my knees and propose to the corrupt S.O.B."

Manuel, "Prepare your wedding vows, because I assure you that Vasili Kropotkin has in his possession a rocket booster capable of launching Enterprise."

"As much as I need to get back into space, I wouldn't ride for free on one of their Zenit boosters."

Chin humphs, "I am aware of that. We are talking about another booster entirely—the Energia."

An Energia? My jaw drops. We're back in cloud-cuckooland.

I'm not going to even think about that absurdity, so I ask, "But does he have a secret launch site? I assume the guards at Baikonur would notice if we pull up at the gate towing an American space shuttle."

Manuel radiates assurance with a restrained smile. "That issue was still unresolved when you and I staged our daring photoreconnaissance mission, but Vasili's career at Baikonur has flourished. His mixed Russian-Kazakh ancestry serves him well. He was recently promoted to Director of Operations of Baikonur Cosmodrome. Russia is building its own Cosmodrome on Russian soil."

I say, "Russia's been talking about opening a Cosmodrome at Vostochny for years, especially now that Kazakhstan has started getting picky about where they can drop their spent boosters."

Manuel acknowledges my knowledge with a nod. "Vasili has scheduled a week-long mass retraining exercise at the new

Vostochny Cosmodrome, conveniently scheduled for one month after Enterprise's scheduled reunion with the retired shuttle fleet. All Russian personnel will attend, leaving behind a core of Kazakh techs loyal to Vasili. Baikonur will be a ghost facility when Enterprise arrives."

Time to drop a big, ugly fact. "This all hinges on Vasili getting his hands on a booster. You say he owns the Energia inside the Buran building that caved in. I googled up pictures on the net and that Energia is crushed beyond repair, a total write-off. No way can it be salvaged."

Manuel says, "There were three Energias stored in that building and indeed all but one were crushed by the fallen roof. When they determined that an Energia was still fully operational, Vasili and his entrepreneurial Kazakh compatriots sealed off the building with a story of a lethal chemical spill. But why am I telling you this? Heloise will allay all your doubts with incontrovertible and—to a spaceman—no doubt alluring photographic evidence."

Manuel leads us out the door to a neighboring office. Darthy walks beside me, looking smug. She's sure Heloise has the astronautical goods to convince me.

Hel's office is small and severely under-decorated—a beat-up desk with a large flatscreen monitor, a couple chairs, nothing on the wall but a poster of Enterprise in its New York retirement home. Hel turns from the screen and points to a chair right beside her, so I sit dutifully.

"Nice office," I lie.

"Your office," Hel says, and mouses up a fullscreen picture that grabs my entire attention: an Energia rocket booster lying on its side taken from an angle that shows in the background a swath of blue sky through a gaping hole in the roof. Rubble is piled high around the enormous rocket, and as I bend forward to take in details I see three techs standing on top of the booster, hard at work on some task.

I've lost track of where I am, so Hel's voice startles me, "Two Energias were squashed quite flat by Site 112's collapse, but in clearing the fallen roof, Vasili and his Kazakhs found this one still intact, spared by fortuitously-angled fallen girders. They've walled the booster off with rubble and—"

"I can see that. What are those workers doing?"

Hel says eagerly, "Vasili took this pic last week. His Kazakh techs are modifying Energia's Buran mountpoints so Enterprise will snap right on."

I've had no trouble keeping my Dream of Space chained and starving in my mental basement because Channel Zilch has always been unlikelihood piled on impossibility teetering on it-just-won't-happen. Seeing the legendary Energia—obviously real, hidden, and being modified for Channel Zilch's crazy mission—is a banquet for my hopes. I am so focused on the Energia picture that Heloise might as well be a sack full of rutabagas. I demand, "More. Other angles. I want to see the thrusters."

She flips past pictures of details—close-ups of mountpoints, hydraulic couplings, plumbing—until the screen fills with an array of twenty gorgeous massive bell shapes: four big thrusters in the center surrounded by four clusters of four smaller ones. No visible damage. Twenty of Russia's best rocket engines waiting to boost my ass back into space.

"I want a close-up of that work...the mountpoints they were working on in the first photo."

Hel clicks through pictures. "Vasili decided to get a head start by modifying the Energia/Buran mountpoints to match Enterprise's standard mounting strut configuration." Each picture Hel flips through makes the Energia more real for me. She stops on a close-up. The metalwork is fresh and shiny, and I recognize a very standard fixture for a mounting strut.

I know I'm getting ahead of myself, but I blurt, "Gotta show these to Gritch. May I look through them?"

Hel nods and I grab the mouse. "I want to see..." I stop and think. I want nothing more than to lose a couple of hours rocket-science-geeking-out with this cache of Energia photos. The Chins have grabbed me by my dreams. All it takes is a few pretty pictures of Energia, and Mr. Skeptical is ready to become Reverend Zilch. Not so fast, Oolfson.

I tear my eyes from the screen, certain that the Chins and Darthy know my defenses are disintegrating. I say, "Very impressive pictures. But Channel Zilch is still so full of holes I'd be a fool to get my hopes up. For one thing, what about the free launch nonsense?"

Manuel corrects me, "Barter."

I swivel my chair to put the Energia picture out of sight. "Barter. For rock and roll, correct? You said you're trading CD's for the launch. That's just nuts."

Manuel corrects me again, "Not compact disks, but rare vinyl record albums."

Doubt revives big-time. "I don't believe a word of that."

Darthy says, "Show him."

Manuel smiles and beckons me to follow him. I stand and hustle after him down a long hallway, Hel and Darthy following. He opens a battered swinging door and we enter a large dark warehouse. When the lights go on, Manuel is pointing proudly upward to a wall of grey metal warehouse shelving stacked full of small cardboard boxes.

I give my patented Oolfson dumb look and Darthy steps to the shelving and opens a box. She pulls out an LP and holds it up to me to read: "Monkees Anniversary Tour 1986." I look up at the shelves full of boxes and shake my head. I admit, "It doesn't make sense...but it makes it real."

Manuel's voice echoes through the warehouse. "I bargained for a wonderful deal on a shipment of remaindered albums from three of Kropotkin's favorite artists. If you care to inspect further you'll find classic Turtles and Herman's Hermits albums in mint condition. One hundred and twenty-three thousand albums."

I scrunch my mouth. "And that's gonna buy us a launch?"

Manuel shakes his head. "I had to sweeten the deal. When Vasili balked at my initial bid, I offered him a piece of history." He walks to a shrouded pile and whips off the blue tarp. Gleaming under the stark warehouse lights sits one righteous chromed Harley-Davidson Hydra-Glide chopper with a Stars-and-Stripes-painted gas tank, low-slung profile, raked front wheel, and high-rise backrest and even higher apehanger handlebars—a gorgeous machine.

Manuel continues, "This is Captain America's chopper—Peter

Fonda's iconic motorcycle from the film *Easy Rider*."

"Ah." Knew I'd seen the cycle somewhere.

"It was stolen after the film was completed and given to me eleven years ago in payment for a substantial debt. I stored it in anticipation of just such a deal-clinching eventuality."

Chin radiates a wicked reality distortion field. The air fairly shimmers and warps around his head when he's cranking it out—reality has to give way to the improbable vision emanating from the tough little guy's brainium.

I'm in ChinWorld. I stare at the gaudy cycle and then up at the shelves stacked with boxed albums. In ChinWorld it's completely reasonable to buy a rocket launch with Monkees albums and a cinematic chopper.

I flash back to Heloise's pictures of the Energia: the twenty gorgeous rocket bells, the mountpoint work. Vasili Kropotkin is a citizen of ChinWorld, too.

It doesn't have to make sense. It just has to be real.

CHAPTER ELEVEN: OUR NOBLE ENTERPRISE

MANUEL AND HEL have their hook sunk deep in my Dream of Space. I give one last try at spitting it out: "Let's talk Enterprise. From your email, I take it that you plan to steal Enterprise from Dulles when it's on its way to the shuttle reunion."

Heloise says, "I've got a friend who works at Dulles who can get us into the Shuttle Carrier Aircraft[6] the night before it flies. You can fly the SCA, right?"

"Sure, I wheeled my way into copiloting an SCA for a leg of a return flight from Edwards. It's a handful, but it flies."

Darthy says, as if all is settled, "Well, there you go."

6   The Shuttle Carrier Aircraft (SCA) are Boeing 747 Jumbos modified to piggyback space shuttles. Their interiors are stripped to save weight, and they've got two additional vertical stabilizers to deal with the turbulence of the shuttle.

I hold up a hand. "Wait. I can fly the SCA, but Dulles is twenty miles from Washington, D.C. That's the most heavily defended airspace in the world. I'm a hell of a pilot, but no way I'm going to win a dogfight with an F-35 when I'm driving a jumbo piggybacking a shuttle."

Hel says, "I'm going to hack the SCA's transponders to tell the Air Traffic Control System that we're a top-secret spook flight. We won't show up on the ATC system."

"Oh, right. Heloise Chin downloaded schematics of the SCA's transponder from the web and magicked up a hack that will make us invisible. If it was that easy drug runners would have found the hack years ago."

"A friend wrote part of the ATC tracking system. He gave me the hack."

"If your friend found a security hole in the ATC system, he'd better report it!"

Hel soothes me: "He'll report it the day after we exploit it."

"Who the hell *are* these friends of yours?"

Darthy chimes in, "Hel is in a secret club of AI enthusiasts."

I nod blankly. Dar and Hel and their damned geekery.

I search for further objections, not quite ready to take the plunge. With the vision of flying the SCA lodged deep in my pilot lobe, I know I'm not thinking straight. "We'll still show up on radar even if your transponder hack works."

Hel pulls my pilot chain, "Fly low, flyboy—nap of the earth. Too hard for you?"

"Terrain hugging in a loaded SCA?" But I'm thinking, damn, that will be fun!

Here's the break point: "I need Gritch Neubart on our team now. The Smithsonian restored Enterprise and the Intrepid Museum fixed its Hurricane Sandy damage, but we'll need a head start on designing extended life-support systems and new maneuvering thrusters."

Manuel nods. "Please contact Mr. Neubart using utmost discretion. If he agrees to operational secrecy, I welcome him to the Channel Zilch team."

I mull for another few seconds. Stealing from a museum sucks any way you spell it.

I've never been allergic to breaking rules for a good cause. I say what they want me to say, but I put a time limit on it—a fig leaf of pride, "You cover my finances and I'll commit a month to this Channel Zilch craziness. One month, and then I reassess."

I might as well have held up a sign saying, "I NEED A GROUP HUG."

After we disengage from our team-building scrum it hits me: I've got a shitload of hard work to do to make this thing real.

I shut down Oolfson's Aerial Spraying for a month, lease *The Flying Cow* to Cannon Valley Aero-Ag, and give them my spraying contracts. CVAA owner Matt Otterness has always admired *The Flying Cow* and I trust him as a pilot. I pull up stakes from Stanton and move into my bare little office at Chin Ltd. HQ.

I know the guts of all the flying shuttles, but Enterprise is a prototype, with thousands of subtle and blatant differences. Hel's geek friends come through once more with a motherlode of Enterprise data: the documentation and 3D computer models the Smithsonian used to restore her. I immerse myself in thousands of pages, highlighting and digesting reams of mechanical drawings and dry, precise prose. It's the type of brain-numbing work that an astronaut has to do sometimes. I wear out my eyes winkling out variations in hatch locations, electrical system layout, and all the other doodads they upgraded between building Enterprise and Columbia.

The Channel Zilch team knows how to get work done.

Chin spends slabs of time on the phone to Russia with Darthy translating. Darthy spends the rest of her time with Richard Head, practicing their star and cameraperson routine. Heloise spends her time poring over schematics of the shuttle's computer and electrical system and buying techy stuff.

I was going to say that Heloise behaves towards me like a particularly snooty cat, but I'm reluctant to libel felines. She behaves more like an iguana or boa sizing me up as a snack. Many days I can't even get a "Hi" out of her. Then she switches gears and launches a testosterone wave, and my glands spew their mind-altering juices...and later on I realize she'd got me to help her with some really tedious shuttle system analysis which I would have helped with if she just asked me straight out.

Hel keeps dangling herself in front of me like a prize to be won. It's blatant and insulting and exciting. I know I'm alive when I'm around her. I'm not a complicated guy, just middling screwed up like most of us. Ms. Chin learns where my buttons are.

In the years since our dinner at The CrossRoads Bar, Hel upgraded her suit's orange bellylights to arrays of tiny video screens. Heloise wears the lightsuit sometimes and other times dresses like a normal geek-type female in jeans, tee shirts, sweats. When dealing with outsiders she dresses for success—simple, classy stuff. She uses her image as a tool to get what she wants. Whatever she wears, her clothes come to life on her body. She could wear a burqa, clown shoes, and a life vest and still top my best-dressed list.

But always, even when she dresses for the public, the backs of her fingers sport thin silver traces. Even when she wears no bellylights her fingers fidget in midair, typing something, sending messages somewhere, connecting to someone.

One early evening I'm working alone at Chin HQ while Dar and the Chins are off meeting Richard for their big recruiting dinner. They're going to break the little detail that the Channel Zilch hyperstar job requires space travel—which I fervently hope makes Richard bolt for the door. I'm in Manuel's office to drop off a schematic when the phone rings. I'm not a snoop but the caller ID says "HEAD, R." so I do the polite thing and pick it up.

"Chin Limited. Richard?"

"This is Richard Head. To whom am I speaking?"

"Mick Oolfson. How'd your dinner go?"

Richard says blandly, "I am calling to withdraw my name from consideration for your Channel Zilch position."

I try to keep my glee out of my voice, "That so? Really sorry to hear that, Richard. Space travel is dangerous and I'm sure no one will blame you for—"

"Space travel?"

I commiserate. "You're doing the right thing, Richard. You

don't seem like the kind of guy who would thrive orbiting the earth for months cooped up with three geeks. Smarter to let some newsreading newbie risk his ass as Channel Zilch's spacecaster."

Richard's voice comes alive, "Channel Zilch will broadcast from *space?*"

Shit! "Didn't Manuel Chin let you in on that little secret at dinner?"

Richard says, "Since I decided to withdraw my candidacy for the post, I decided not to attend tonight's recruiting dinner. But you have rekindled my interest in Channel Zilch. I sense opportunity for fame. I shall call Manuel's cellphone to let him know I will arrive late for dinner."

I try to pull my foot out. "Wait—I'm the guy you should talk to about the Channel Zilch space program. I'm an astronaut, and I wouldn't recommend…"

Richard's voice is eager, "An astronaut. So this plan is real. I'm so glad I reached you… Mike, is it?"

I let a little venom into my voice, "It's Mick. Mick Oolfson. Thank you for withdrawing, Dick."

Silence. Then Richard says, "Resentment. You don't want me to be part of Channel Zilch. You know I shall outshine you, is that it? You see talent and can't bear to have it near you."

I flounder. "I just don't think you're the type who will…*thrive* in space. Space travel is a team game, and…"

Richard says coldly, "I am used to being opposed by lesser men in my career. I will attend this dinner, and I will…" He hangs up.

When the Channel Zilch team returns late to HQ, they are quite pleased with themselves for hiring Richard Head as Spacecaster for Channel Zilch.

This is why I boss machines instead of humans.

After a week of wrestling my stack of Enterprise documentation, I know it's time to call Gritch. If Gritch Neubart feels that there's a good chance the mission will kill us, I bail on Channel Zilch. I'm not talking about the 98%+ safety margin that NASA somehow achieves. I figure anything over seventy-five confidence for the mission makes it a go, given the high motivation of the crew.

I have a straight talk with each of them to lay out my safety criteria. They all agree. Heloise listens up good for once during that little chat.

Time to call Gritch Neubart.

CHAPTER TWELVE: GRITCH

ASTRONAUTS, TOO, DREAM of dandling grandwhelps. The Dream of Space is stronger. Astronauts don't dwell on danger or we wouldn't be astronauts. Somewhere along the line we beat our survival instinct into submission.

But we're not stupid. That's why I need Gritch.

Gritch Neubart was a legend at NASA. He'd risen from mechanic's gofer to head the Rapid Response Repair Squad for the whole shuttle program. He knows space shuttles nose to thrusters, and if his team couldn't fix a problem, they knew who could.

Every astronaut knew Gritch, and the smart ones let him know how much they respected him. Not by praising him— Gritch can't abide a compliment—but by the way they shook his hand and looked him in the eye. You can't fake respect.

Gritch didn't care if you loved him or hated him; the shuttle was his baby. He always gave his best, and his best was stellar.

A year before our ill-fated Dulles reconnaissance, Gritch did something NASA couldn't forgive: the silly bastard turned 65, and NASA gave him the golden boot. Gritch suddenly had lots of time on his hands. When I heard the news I called Gritch to see if he'd like to join me in the booming aerial manure broadcasting industry. He thought maybe he'd try sitting on his ass in a boat and drowning worms instead.

Time to call him again. I take a deep breath and punch in his number, greet him raucously, and then lay out the crazy plan as straight as I can: Channel Zilch, Enterprise, Energia, Baikonur, Hel's friend at Dulles—the lot.

He listens. Doesn't interrupt with hysterical laughter.

So I make my pitch, "We need your help, Gritch. If anyone can pull this crazy mission off, it's Gritch Neubart."

Gritch asks his first question, "No reentry?"

"That's right. Enterprise just needs to get us into orbit. We'll buy a trip down from SpaceX or Orbital Science."

"Ha. More'n likely beg your way down, if you ever get up in the first place."

I nod silently into my phone.

Gritch's tone of voice says he's actually thinking this thing over, "So Enterprise has gotta get ya up there and keep ya breathing."

I assure him, "That's all, Gritch."

He snorts. "That's all, he says. Astronaut thinks his rocket's got an easy job."

"Sorry, Gritch. I mean, yes, Enterprise does have to accomplish the awesome task of getting us simple astronauts into space alive."

"At's better, ya ungrateful pup. Remind me again—whatsa launch weight of a Buran?"

He's biting. "Just over a hundred tons, Gritch."

"Buran and shuttles are twins. What I thought. Energia can carry a Buran it'll carry a shuttle."

I can hear him smile over the phone as he thinks this through. "Slick. Always wanted to monkey with an Energia."

Then he asks another good question, "Say you get Enterprise up in orbit—what's to keep the Pentagon from shooting you down? You know we've got the tech."

I know three ways the US government can bring down a satellite in Low Earth Orbit, but the issue never worried me. "Think about it, Gritch. Shooting down an unarmed, manned video station? PR fallout would be abysmal."

"I'll buy that. Just so ya thought it through."

Gritch's voice goes eager: "Now tell me—can we kick the tires before we steal Enterprise?"

I yell into the phone, "You said WE! YOU'RE IN!"

Gritch sniffs, "Ain't saying I'd bet a nickel on this Channel Zilch foolishness, but getting outwitted by fish day after day wears on a fella's ego. Always wanted to lay my hands on old Enterprise. Here's hoping the Intrepid Museum did a bangup job repairing the damage Hurricane Sandy did to at old girl. I'll play along till the joke gets old."

I wind up telling him the whole story of my Dulles run-in with the new head of NASA security.

Which sets Gritch off big-time. "WhooWEEE! So old Toby was nailin up wanted posters for a GIANT WITH A FUCKING GUN! I want me a seed cap with that one on it." His voice goes low and cold, "Never did see eye to eye with ol Captain Itchwad. The peckersniff pulled my bank records back in oh-two when some dumbshit on my crew misplaced a maintenance van. Toby thought I was ripping off NASA—ME! I'd pay good money to see the look on his ugly face if this crazy scheme flies."

I give an internal cheer. Gritch is famous for holding grudges; or rather, he's famous for getting even if you cross him. One of my fellow astronauts, who shall remain nameless, got on Gritch's ugly side by questioning whether a key shuttle maintenance procedure was done properly. When he got into orbit, turns out his personal luggage had been edited. Instead of the usual stylish pumpkin NASA jumpsuit, he found a lime-green polyester leisure suit.

Gritch isn't one for long conversations. His voice goes flat and calm. "You know what I need to do this thing?"

"Tell me, Gritch. Whatever—name it—it's yours."

"I gotta know that if I give thumbs down, you'll drop it. If I'm part of the Channel Zilch launch team, I gotta have go/no-go say."

"Done, Gritch. Done." I'm grinning from nape to nape. Channel Zilch's probability of launching just went through the roof.

CHAPTER THIRTEEN: ONE-WORD MOTTO

Mick Oolfson's motto: Commit.

There's a lot packed in that word: a Goal to commit to, the Decision to commit, the Will to stay committed to the Goal.

Back in the days when NASA launched Mick Oolfson, three hundred Shuttle Launch Team console jocks helped the Launch Director decide whether to commit to blast my ass into space. Shuttle Launch Commit Criteria demands a GO! from every one. Once the Director lights the shuttle's solid boosters, they stay lit. There is no UNLAUNCH button on the Launch Director's console.

Good thing I no longer have three hundred nitpicky hypernerds monitoring every parameter of my life. Talk about constraints and open issues! But with Gritch on board Channel Zilch, I can no longer pretend that I'm just putting my toe in the water. I'm in.

Commitment says I know the future will fight like hell to drag itself off on some random tangent, but I'll fight harder to wrestle it back on track to my goal.

Astronauts are experts at committing to outrageous goals and slaving and fighting and conniving and clawing to make them real. What are the odds of a space-crazy kid becoming an astronaut? Millions to one! Fifth-grade Mick Oolfson committed to becoming an astronaut and worked hard and smart to drive that childish dream from model rockets to an Astronaut pin. I'm good at this commitment thing.

Promises are nukes, and some people treat them like cap guns. That may be the shoddiest metaphor ever to sully paper, but you know what I mean.

I promise carefully. Being Mick Oolfson means I make promises I can keep.

o   o   o

I knock on Manuel's office door, and he booms, "Enter. Ah, and how went your momentous discussion with Mr. Neubart?"

I say, "Gritch just signed on to prep Enterprise, so forget my one month time limit. I promise to do my damnedest to get Channel Zilch into orbit."

Manuel rises from his chair and shakes my hand across his desk. His voice fills the room, "Excellent! Welcome aboard Channel Zilch, Commander Oolfson! Let us make history together."

I'm going to do my damnedest to make this Channel Zilch happen, and I am going to do my damnedest to bring every one of my passengers home. Alive.

I'm careful what I promise. I promised Manuel Chin I'd do my damnedest, and Mick Oolfson's damnedest is damn good.

As Tobias Ishwald will soon be reminded.

As Heloise Chin will soon discover.

My best quality: I don't give up.

My worst quality: I don't give up.

Chin's word is good. He moves quickly to buy me out, and when I arrive back at Chin HQ, all I have to do is sign a few papers, and *The Flying Cow* is his. For a fair dollar amount, too, which I appreciate, as I am rotten at pricing family members. Chin sees how I feel about selling my cranky old metal bird and promises he'll find a good home for it.

When I return to the hangar at Stanton, *The Cow* is gone. I appreciate that, Manuel.

I wind up my Minnesota life, telling acquaintances I've got a long term contract, and that they'll hear from me, not telling them they'll likely hear *about* me, for good or ill, on the evening news.

I call Mom and tell her I've got a fat contract that will take me out of the country for a while. Being an astronaut's mom, she's used to my travels. We arrange for a farewell dinner at her favorite restaurant.

I was marking time in Stanton. I've got a mission again.

CHAPTER FOURTEEN: BUGS! BUGS! BUGS! BUGS!

It's my job to pilot our aerial getaway car, the Shuttle Carrier Aircraft. I spend hours in my office flying a simulator to refresh my skill at wrestling that two-hundred-and-fifty-ton, aerodynamically dirty contraption around the sky.

After a particularly good sim landing I stand and stretch. It's late, and I haven't laid my eyes on Heloise for a few hours. With all the unfinished tasks, it's easy to come up with a topic. In my head I rehearse a scintillating conversational gambit: Heloise, I need to go over a few details of that thruster-control software you're writing. Perfect.

I step into the dark hallway and in my peripheral catch a small shape scurrying away from me with a metallic scuttle, like it's wearing taps. Heavy footsteps behind me turn out to be Heloise, breathing hard. She demands, "Where?"

I point after the thing, and she takes off full tilt after it. I tag along at a trot. The thing skitters metallically in front of her, too small and fast for me to ID it.

The thing scrabbles a hard left into an empty room. Heloise's boots squeal as she zigs after it. When I catch up she's cornered the tiny escapee. Hel lunges downward and snares the varmint.

Heloise walks toward me with her hands cupped tight together like she's packing a snowball. "A bug with a bug."

I try to play along. "The tarantula is sick? That thing scuttled pretty sprightly for a diseased spider."

"Look." She moves her hands toward me, flinches, and sucks in her breath. She opens her hand—a red slice about two inches long angles across her palm.

She dashes the insect hard against the floor. It crunches tinnily, twitches, sparks—a little plume of greyblue smoke. Hel sucks her palm while she stomps the remains with her matte black boot.

"You okay? Is it poisonous?"

"Bot sliced me. I don't build venom into my bugs."

"You built it?" I look down at the still form—a delicate construct of dull grey metal and black plastic, smashed quite flat.

"I built the parts. It built itself. Built itself nasty. Evolved to sharpen a leg and cut a hole in the door. The simulator didn't catch that case." We watch the scarlet line of blood well to a gleaming pool in her hand. She says quietly, "Never figured one would learn how to sharpen a leg. Can't wait to dump its build code."

Heloise Chin isn't omniscient? Stop the presses! "Wait, wait, slow down. You're hitting my limit here. You need to get stitched up. Fill me in while I drive you to a doctor."

"Zero. Vader can show off her Girl Scout skills. Got a rag?"

"Uh, sure." I pull out my pocketknife and cut a long rent in my left sleeve, give it a yank, ripping a long strip free.

She grimaces and shakes her head. "Remind me to hit you up if I get caught short of sanitary pads." Pure Hel, shoving me off-kilter even when I'm trying to be a hero. She takes the strip and wraps it a couple times around her palm.

Darthy is rock-steady as she sews shut the wound. "I'm designated medic on the flight. Can't let a chance to stitch a little flesh wound slip by. Were you juggling machetes again, dear?" Only Darthy Vader can get away with *dear*-ing Heloise Chin.

"A rogue bug busted out and nipped me."

I expect Darthy to be stymied by this statement, but she just tut-tuts, "I told you to watch those little beasties, Heloise. Darwin-power is way smarter than one brainy girl."

Once more I unveil my depths of ignorance. "You know about the electric spiders?"

Darthy pats my arm. "Heloise has many fascinating hobbies."

I say, "Run this by me again. We're working our asses off to launch, and Heloise is breeding slasher robot crabs?"

Heloise grimaces as Vader wraps the bandage tight around her palm. "That's right, astroboy; I'm sitting on my ass playing with toys while you carry the project."

Wrong. Heloise Chin is cranking hard and accomplishing great slabs of work, clocking time deep into the night and making stunning progress. I've watched her detailed plans evolve. I've checked out the progress of her flight control computers as best as I can. Whatever she is playing at isn't hurting her productivity.

"I didn't say you're slacking. I'm sure there's a great reason for you to build metal bugs that get loose and cut up your hand. I'm just a simple astronaut, so my IQ deficit leaves me bewildered. Explain."

Darthy finishes snipping loose bandage ends, and Heloise rises and heads for the door. She turns and waves me to follow. "I'll do better than explain. I'll show. You coming, Dar?"

"Got work to do. Give your buggies a big hug for me and don't scare the boy more than you have to." She gives her Darthy Vader patented throaty chuckle and sits back down to a glowing spreadsheet.

Heloise's black combat boots echo down the empty hallway as she tromps in front of me. She makes a commotion for such a compact woman. Despite the splendid view of her achingly beautiful...nape, I hustle to pull level with her.

"Any hints about what I'm going to see?"

She turns, narrows her eyes at me, and purses her lips. Trying to make a joke about something deeply rooted. "Darwin in hyperdrive."

I whisper theatrically, "At last I find out your little secret."

Her voice goes tight and blunt, "I don't do secrets. Secrecy is death. Secrecy is lies. Intelligence will rout the secrets damning us to die like beasts in pain and ignorance."

She turns and stomps off, leaving me stunned and silent. I've collided with something very near the deep heart of Heloise Chin. She doesn't do secrets. What the hell does that mean?

When I catch up to her, she's entering a workroom I've never seen. I follow her past tables heaped with humming PC's, through the oily light sprayed from monitors. I follow her to a door in the back. She points to a window set in the door. I peek through it and she snaps a light switch.

Dim purple light glows from the ceiling of the storeroom. A mound about the size of a prone horse lies in the center of the room. The mound ripples and twitches. I squint and slowly resolve hundreds of tiny angular shapes in spastic motion. It looks like a mob of ants on a baby bird. The damn mound is made of Heloise's frigging bugs.

"Gross! What are those things eating? Is that a dead horse?"

"Glitchbrain, botbugs don't eat flesh."

I point to the cut on her hand. "They sucking a horse dry of blood?"

"Yeah, and you're next. Close your eyes."

"I'm not sure about this."

"Shut 'em."

Trust. Stupid. I scrunch my eyes tight.

She flips a switch and a red light jolts through my clenched lids.

"Open em." She flips another switch, and stark florescent light winks on inside the room. "The light knocks them out."

"I'm going to see something yucky, aren't I? Something your bugs killed." I hate gruesome sights. Never seen *Alien* all the way through. I can just about stomach *Bambi*.

"Look." She grabs my shoulder and shoves me to the window.

There lies a beautiful model of a space shuttle about the size of a prone horse, constructed out of Lego bricks, gleaming black and white with clear cockpit windows promising compulsively accurate details inside. Strewn around the model on the floor, lying inert in heaps—hundreds of robot bugs.

She looks into the room over my shoulder. "My bots built that shuttle model." She sounds like a proud mom at her daughter's first recital.

I have to ask, "Why, Heloise? Why the bugs?"

Hel laughs a high, pealing note, looks at me, says, "Always wanted a big family."

o o o

It's hard for me to write about Richard Head because I generally like people. On his infrequent visits to Chin HQ we always manage to rub up against one another—minor interpersonal friction that doesn't bode well for crew cohesion.

Head doesn't like me. I return the favor.

Richard is firmly wedged in the Channel Zilch plan. Not a chance of ditching him.

We work round the clock, which is the only way to prepare for a trip into space. Time rips by.

Way too soon, the Channel Zilch team moves to a cheap motel near Dulles Airport. Gritch joins us.

NASA sticks to their shuttle reunion schedule, which plays into our hands: they bolt Enterprise to the top of the Shuttle Carrier Aircraft and fly it to Dulles for a weeklong exhibit. They park it next to a glass observation tower so that crowds can look into the SCA and the shuttle and oooh and aaaah at all the buttons.

Heloise and Gritch and I are the team who will "acquire" Enterprise. Hel's moles inform us that the SCA will fuel up for its trip on the last day of the exhibit. We have one night to steal the shuttle.

As the last days count down, I watch a late winter storm develop with much satisfaction. Poor visibility the night of the heist will help our cause.

On the final day, the last pieces of the plan fall into place. The boat that will carry Enterprise across the Atlantic is stationed off the coast, ready to meet us at an abandoned Wallops Island loading dock. Hel's friends report that they've got the booster-hefting dockside crane running.

The morning of the op, Gritch and I huddle in our motel room going over the plan. Hel enters, wearing a pair of sleek, black-rimmed, clear glasses, with an odd bump on one side.

"Spex? Are those the latest Google Glasses or the new Apple iGlasses?"

"Custom. ArduOS-based, almost all 3D-printed except for the lenses and CPU."

I shake my head. "Doesn't matter if they're custom. Airports have jammed cellular and wireless for over a year now since cell bombs took out Singapore Changi Airport. You know that."

Hel rolls her eyes. "These are designed to penetrate the jam. Signal path is wire and photons." She hands us each a pair. As she turns her head, the lenses flicker with shards of video.

"You ever used Spex, spaceman?"

"Never owned a pair. Tried Google Glasses 1.3 and got a headache."

"Latency and resolution issues. These are top."

Gritch growls, "Ain't never had no use for them things. But I learn quick."

Heloise pulls the bump from her glasses. A fine wire spools from the thing as she holds it out towards us—a tiny black suction cup. Hel strides toward the curtain, draws it back, and sticks her sucker to the glass. "Yoohoo. Gents."

Gritch gives a goofy grin. "Shee-it, why the hell not?" he says and slips on his spex.

I don mine as I follow Gritch to the window.

Hel points to her sucker stuck to the glass. "Do it."

We stick our suckers.

Hel explains, "These suckers are laser transmitter/receivers. Stick em on a window and they'll find a way to bounce their light signal to all other Spex suckers nearby."

"So radio spectrum jamming doesn't jam these."

Hel rewards me with a smile. "One, fanboy. I'll clue you how to share video and audio. Pay attention, boys. These Spex are running a suite of prototype special ops apps." She taps the side of her spex with a finger. "I'll teach you tap and voice commands for sharing vid and chatter."

The lesson and the cool new toy take my mind off the fact that tonight we steal Enterprise.

From Dulles Airport. From Captain Tobias Ishwald.

CHAPTER FIFTEEN: AMSCRAY UTTLESHAY

I'm wedged in a small dark space, bored out of my cranium and beginning to have glute spasms. I cheer silently when my cell phone tickles my hip: 9:20 P.M. I flip the latch, unfold myself from my hiding place, and suck a lungful of cool, sweet air.

The interior of the Shuttle Carrier Aircraft is dimly lit—a huge, empty, bare-ribbed, floored cylinder stripped of seats except for a few at the front. Not a sound.

I reach for the ceiling and bend sideways to get the kinks out. Listen—still nothing—and walk forward to the rows of seats. As promised, the last onboard guard left at seven when the exhibit closed.

I whisper loudly, "Hel? We're alone."

Hel's voice echoes through the place, "Olly olly oxen free!"

A rattling from the rear of the fuselage, and Heloise Chin emerges from her hiding place clad all in matte black and wearing her spex.

How'd we break into the Shuttle Carrier? A variant of the old Trojan horse wheeze: think food trolley, and when I say "food trolley," I mean trash cart, by which I mean MYOB. People crash airplanes into buildings to make theological points these days, so I am *not* going to give detailed instructions on how to steal a 747 from Dulles. Not going to happen.

Besides—getting inside the SCA was boring, the way a great plan ought to be. Sure boosted my opinion of Hel's buddies. The fine folk who helped us pull off the Enterprise heist stand to land in a swimming pool of diarrhea for their good deeds, so for the record: NO NASA PERSONNEL ASSISTED IN THE STEALING OF SPACE SHUTTLE ENTERPRISE. What matters is that Hel and I are inside the Shuttle Carrier Aircraft, and Enterprise is securely bolted on top, ready to steal.

Gritch's hidey-hole is outside in a truck. Hel trots toward a window and does the spex-sucker-to-glass routine. She's already chatting with Gritch when I stick mine to the glass.

Gritch's spex-filtered voice shrills, "...ain't seed no one in the viewing decks. Get your sorry ass on up to the cockpit, Oolfson. Prep that monster to fly."

"Roger that, Gritch. I'll link with you from the cockpit."

Hel stretches, but there's no time to appreciate the sight. I hustle up the spiral staircase to the cockpit.

The instrument panel is familiar; no changes since I last flew the SCA. As I sink into the sheepskin of the pilot seat, I glance out my side window. A glassed-in observation room looms a few feet away. Dark and empty after hours. Wonder how many thousand school kids fidgeted in line to peek into this cockpit and boggle at all the instruments?

I stick my spex-sucker to the glass and whisper, "Gritch?"

"Sheee-ut up n get to work."

It's great to work with Gritch again.

The wall of glass just feet away gives me the willies. According to Hel's Dulles insider, the whole observation deck gets shut down securely at eight, but I can't help picturing a janitor wandering in and busting us. I rummage through the cockpit until I find the stiff sun shades and wedge them into the two deck-side windshields. Without the potential audience, I relax a hair.

Now the hard part: to sit here for three to six hours listening to Dulles Tower chatter. Sometime between one and four A.M., I will decide that our time has come to take Enterprise.

First run the preflight checklist up to engine start. My pilot brain gives a satisfied sigh as it dives into the familiar routine of methodically waking up a big plane.

Hel startles me: "You're cute when you play pilot."

I sit up straight, turn—Hel stands in the cockpit doorway. "Cuter when I fly a space shuttle."

Hel says pityingly, "Still hope I'll turn astrogroupie? Not into NASCAR." Right. I'm just Channel Zilch's driver. I try a winning smile but she snorts.

I soothe my chastened ego by diving back into piloting--back to my checklist. Hel settles into the co-pilot seat and lays open a toolkit on her lap. She's got a transponder to hack. Let's call it parallel play, side-by-side focused on our tasks.

Dulles Tower announces a twenty-minute suspension of landings to clear snow from the runways. Damn, I don't want traffic stacked up after midnight. I tick off my last pre-engine-start task and slump back against the sheepskin. Hours to go before one A.M.

Hel is deep in her hardware hacking, focused on the gizmo on her lap, tip of her tongue peeking between her lips. She picks up the transponder and gives it a close squint. "Done. This will make the Air Traffic Control system classify us as a top-secret flight and ignore us." She slides it back into the panel.

Hel claims that her hacker friends are a bunch of freaking geniuses. A Sidewinder up the tailpipe would be a brutal way to learn that Hel overestimates her geek pals' expertise.

Light dazzles me—a bank of lights on the observation structure glares through the windshield. Hel and I exchange wide-eyed stares. My seat is shaded by the sun shields, but Hel is lit by the full glare. I motion her to get behind me. She nods hard and snaps shut her toolkit.

I whisper, "Gritch! What's with the lights?"

Gritch's hiding place is on the tarmac in a vehicle with a view of the observation deck. His voice over spex, "Looks like we got us a damn inconvenient VIP family tour. Zoomin."

Gritch's vid pops up in a window on my spex—a tight shot of the nose of our 747 backlit by the observation window. The shadows of two adults and two children. The silhouette of the tallest adult is huge and odd, with a grotesquely large head.

"The hell is that?" says Gritch.

The misshapen shadow is obviously lecturing. It points up at a detail on Enterprise and its contours come into focus. I suck in a breath. "A helmet."

"Big guy's wearin some sort of bulletproof vest."

Hel says from behind me, "A security guard giving a VIP family tour."

I whisper, reassuring myself, "They can't see us, so hang tight, gang."

Gritch keeps his spex focused on the window and we watch in shadow puppetry the armored guide pointing and lecturing, obviously well-versed in the lore of the SCA/Enterprise hybrid. The taller kid asks questions, and the smaller adult, obviously Mom, listens attentively—a heartwarming little scene if it wasn't playing out in an adrenaline buzz in the middle of my first shuttle heist.

Hel whispers, "I'm heading downstairs. I have work to do."

"Wait. Don't touch the door. Looks like the tour is over."

The smaller kid is now sitting on the floor, a tired pup. The armored hulk looks talked out. He stoops and picks up the tyke—must be the guard's family—and walks away from the window, shadows shrinking.

I say, "They're leaving."

"I'm out." Hel swings open the cockpit door.

I let out a lungful of pure relief, close my eyes and relax back into the sheepskin, just as Heloise slams the door, creating a puff of breeze scented with her electric spice—a puff just strong enough to dislodge one of the sun shields. I hear a rustle and open my eyes to see a bloom of light as the thing falls into my lap.

I look down at the fallen sun shield, gasp a heartfelt, "Shit!" and look back through the unblocked windshield straight into the eyes of a towheaded boy about eight years old. I force my shocked gape into a smile but the kid isn't buying it. I try a little wave to put him at ease, but the kid frowns. I wink and raise a finger to my lips, but he mouths the word, "Dad."

The big guy turns and beckons the kid to follow. I scooch lower in my seat. The kid mouths, "Look," and points right between my eyes.

The guard tips back the visor of his helmet, and Captain Tobias Ishwald looks at me with a puzzled head tilt, eyes going wide and his mouth opening wider, bellowing silently, "OOLFSON!"

A jolt of adrenaline right up my spine! I bolt upright and shout, "ISHWALD! GO! *Now, Gritch!*"

Gritch's voice through the spex, "Ats Itchwad? Sheeit! I'm on it."

Ishwald motions his wife and kids to get back from the window and unholsters a black, angular pistol. He aims his gun right between my eyes and I stare back, motionless, body clenched, forehead itching.

Hel swings open the door and walks into the cockpit. Ishwald swivels his gun toward her. Hel says quietly, "That's got to be bulletproof glass."

Ishwald focuses his eyes and gun on me again.

I feel in my gut that I can beat Ishwald tonight so I commit to making it happen. I have an impulse to give him the finger but remember his kids so… Mess with Cap'n I. I wink theatrically and blow Tobias a kiss. Hel laughs. Ishwald's jaw drops and his eyes bug, but he slowly lowers his gun. I turn to the controls and flip the switch to fire up the APU. Far back in the 747, the turbine coughs into life and settles down to a hum.

I look back into the observation room—Ishwald is gone! His family still looks at the exit he used. His wife carries the little one, and the blonde son hops in agitation.

I yell at Hel, "Lock the jetway cabin door! Ishwald's heading down."

Hel says, "Let's burn Ishwald!"

I don't turn to watch her leave. I pop out the other sun shield which gives me a view of the empty, bright-lit, glass-walled jetway. Ishwald has to get down at least one flight of stairs and—I hope—through a few locked doors.

Hel reports, "Cabin door locked," just as Ishwald appears, running hard, at the far end of the jetway.

I say, "He's in the jetway. Gritch, where the hell…?"

"Got the chocks out, now I'm gettin in the tractor."

"Ishwald's going to be banging on the door any moment. Pushback!"

"I'm on it."

I watch Ishwald barrel down the jetway. Airliner doors are designed to be easily opened from outside in case of emergency. If Gritch doesn't push us back from the jetway, Ishwald will pop the jetway door and nail us. My brain earns its keep and delivers a doozy of an inspiration. "Hel, see that lever at the top of the door?"

Hel points on video, "This?"

"Do it."

She laughs. "Did it!"

I've got no preflight tasks until Gritch pushes us back, so I take in the whole scene. Ishwald's family watches Poppa Tobias charging down the jetway to deal with us baddies.

"Gritch, buddy. You're killing us. Pushback!"

"Startin her NOW!" he barks.

The tractor engine rumbles to life right below the 747's nose. I stand and lean against the side windshield to keep Ishwald in sight as he sprints the final stretch of jetway.

I say, "Don't answer the doorbell."

"I see him," says Hel.

Ishwald reaches the door, reads the door-armed indicator, and stomps the ground in rage. He looks up at his family in the observation room and I follow his eyes. The blonde kid waves excitedly. Tobias stands straight and returns a single wave. He turns back toward the door, brain percolating.

"Pushback," I whisper. "C'mon."

Gritch says, "Gotta warm her up or she'll—"

Ishwald opens his flak jacket and pulls out a—

I shout, "He's got a hatchet! Just GO!"

I feel the welcome jerk of the tractor as Ishwald raises his arm and strikes, tomahawk sinking into the metal of the door.

The tug's engine coughs to a halt. "SheeIT! Toldja it needs warmin." The engine roars back to life.

Ishwald chops again and again, his tomahawk sinking deeper into the door.

"Not good, Mick." I open Hel's vid stream and hear ripping metal as the axe head slashes through the door, letting in a streak of light.

I shout, "Blow it!" and hold my breath as Heloise yanks the door release.

The door swings outward. Ishwald looms in the doorway, tomahawk raised. A billow of grey erupts from the floor with a steam-engine hiss: evacuation slide deployed! I get a great view of the slide unfurling into the glass jetway. As it pushes him back, Ishwald jumps on top of the grey mass and scrambles to swim his way into the plane. I lose sight of him as the jetway fills with doughy grey swelling lumps. As the slide engorges itself down the narrow chute, Ishwald reappears, squeezed flat against the glass and struggling madly.

I say, "Check my vid."

"Sweet!"

Ishwald wriggles against the glass, ripping at the slide with his tomahawk. The slide starts to sag around him and suddenly he's got room. Ishwald clears a space, draws his pistol, and aims at a spot right below me.

"Haul, Gritch!" I yell, "He's going for the front tires!"

The tug's engine surges, and with a jerk we start to move.

Ishwald's gun flashes. The jetway glass spiderwebs but holds. Through the cracks, I see his body stretched on a mound of slide.

"Shit! Stop! Ishwald shot himself!" Ricochet off the bombproof glass. This thing is over. I look at his family, pressed against the observation glass. I can't make out their faces. I feel like King Jerk.

Gritch says, "SheeIT!" and the SCA slows.

The blonde boy waves and hops excitedly. Behind the shattered glass Ishwald is up and determinedly hacking his way through the mass of deflating slide.

I shout, "Ishwald up. GO!"

The SCA gives a jerk and resumes pushback. As we reverse, the jetway roof obscures Ishwald; when he comes into view again, I see that we're pulling the slide from the jetway.

"Turn hard NOW, Gritch. We're unbottling Ishwald."

As our big jet turns, Hel says, "Rope ladder deployed."

"Let's do this!" Sit and grab the checklist. As I fire up engine four, Gritch swings us in a tight turn. At our new angle I can watch Ishwald slash furiously at the sagging slide still plugging the jetway exit.

I fire up engine one. "Get your scrawny old butt in here, Gritch. I'll watch Tobias." I alternate between watching the engines warm up and watching Ishwald slash at the shrinking mound blocking the exit. Ishwald breaks off his assault on the slide to watch Gritch climb up the rope ladder into our getaway jet.

As the engines spool up, I wave to Ishwald. He slashes at the glass with his axe, cracking it.

Whoa! "Close that cabin door and hang on!"

"Door's jammed by the damn slide. Git!"

I ease the throttles forward, and the mighty SCA/Enterprise trundles toward the taxiway. Let's get far, far away from mad Captain Ishwald.

Next task: clearance for takeoff. I hate to be a dick to Air Traffic Controllers, but tonight I am King Jerk. I select Dulles tower freq, clear my throat, and say blandly, "Shuttle Carrier Aircraft NASA 905 requests clearance for takeoff on Runway 19C."

Dulles Tower, shocked: "Say again! *NASA 905?*"

I've been over this moment in my mind more than a few times. No way to bluff, just brazen through, "NASA 905 requires emergency takeoff clearance."

"All runways are closed for snow removal. Return to your gate, NASA 905."

As the slide-plugged jetway slips from view, I turn to watch. The slide goes taut and uncorks the receding jetway with a flurry of flaccid grey. No sign of Ishwald. I turn back to the task at hand. "No can do. NASA 905 *will* take off on runway 19C. Instruct all snow removal vehicles to clear taxiways and runway."

That silences the tower, but sirens start to wail—which doesn't help me relax, frankly.

Hel whispers, "He's going for his gun!"

I groan. No way we can dodge bullets aimed at our landing gear. "He's fumbling for it."

Gritch shouts, "YEEHAA! Musta dropped his pistol in the jetway. Itchwad is hoppin mad!"

Watching a video while taxiing an aircraft is frowned upon, but when Hel shouts, "Look at this!" I spex her vid: Ishwald on the ground running full tilt toward the edge of the dragging slide, tomahawk held high. I goose the throttles, and he leaps onto the slide right where it droops to the ground. The slide is slick and I give a cheer as he starts to slip, go quiet as Ishwald chops his axe into the grey fabric and hangs on. Gotta shake him off.

But first I give full attention to turning onto the taxiway toward 19C. When I look back at Hel's vid, Ishwald is still riding the slide, gripping his tomahawk.

Gritch, "Itchwad's hangin on. Can't release the slide. You gonna hafta shake him off."

The tower adds its racket, "Negative, 905. No authorization. Return to—"

I cut in with my best stone-cold psycho voice, "905 *will* take off. It's your choice whether to keep ground crew safe. Signing off." I click off the useless chatter and turn my attention to shaking Ishwald.

Through the light snow, I see the long queue of snow-delayed jets on the taxiway to the left of the runway we're heading for. Our taxiway from the SCA/Enterprise Exhibit is empty, so I ease the throttles forward to build speed.

I glance at Hel's vid: Ishwald clings tight to his axe embedded in the dragging slide. I give the nose wheel a tap—the slide slews sideways, but Ishwald hangs on. I zag, and the slide starts to oscillate in the slipstream. The struts holding Enterprise groan with the sway.

Hel says, "Keep juking. He's... Wait, reaching in his jacket. A knife!" She zooms in on Ishwald. He hangs onto his embedded handaxe with one hand while the other brandishes a hefty blade. He yanks himself forward with the axe and stabs forward with the knife, burying it into the slide. The knife starts to slice the fabric; he twists it, and it holds.

I tap the nose wheel, and the slide whips sideways, but Ishwald is a limpet. "Almost at the runway. Takeoff speed will strip him."

"He's climbing with the knife and axe!" says Hel. "That's no butter knife."

Back in Hel's vid window, Ishwald is closer and bigger, hauling himself up the slope toward the cabin door. He stabs and chops his way forward, dragging himself upward, grim smile lighting his face, already tasting the familiar savor of Oolfson's whipped ass.

If Ishwald climbs into the cabin I'll have to abort. "Throw something at him! Almost at the runway!"

"Clear the door, sugar," says Gritch. I flip to his vid just in time to watch a food cart sail through the cabin door with a bit too much push—it sails over Ishwald's head. Ishwald gives a triumphant, silent roar and stabs forward up the shuddering slide toward the cabin door.

I clear my spex to concentrate on the turn. As I swing the nose wheel, the 747 sways, frame groaning like a chorus of sick robot walruses. Don't flip her, Oolfson! I widen the turn and ease out of it, pointing our nose down the runway. Dulles Tower has come through for the cause of ground crew safety—a half-dozen snowplows are parked well off the runway, yellow lights flashing in the falling snow.

I announce, "Cleared for takeoff, Channel Zilch 1. Hang on, gang. This will strip Ishwald." I shove the throttles forward—I love takeoffs!—and revel in the ass-kick of the roaring Pratt and Whitney engines.

As we surge down the runway a shimmy kicks in. The SCA/Enterprise combo is aerodynamically dirty and the dangling slide's asymmetric drag is killing our takeoff. I fight to keep our nose straight but my pilot's brain screams, "Abort!"

Hel's vid: Ishwald isn't climbing, but he's holding on, staring straight into Hel's spex, teeth bared in a voracious grin. He knows I won't take off with him hanging there. Ishwald beat me again and he knows it.

I sigh wretchedly, "Sorry, gang," and reach for the throttle, but a flash of light ahead stops me. Dead ahead, a snowplow pulls from the left verge into the runway, yellow lights flashing. Some hero trying to stop me?

I jink the nose right and as we miss the plow Gritch hoots, "Yeehaa! Slide snagged on sumpn." His vid: a dark, empty cabin door—slide and Ishwald stripped away by the snowplow.

Clean of the drag, the SCA tears down the runway straight and roaring to fly.

I shout, "Shut that door!"

As I lift the nose wheel, I feel and hear the rumble of a shuttle-laden SCA. I ease back on the yoke and say, "Beat ya, Toby!" and our wheels leave the ground.

Enterprise is ours!

CHAPTER SIXTEEN: WORLD'S SECOND LARGEST BIPLANE

AS WE MOUNT THE SKY, the SCA/Enterprise rumbles like a herd of clog-dancing hippos. At five hundred feet I bank right and feel the full 350-ton mass of a jumbo piggybacking a shuttle. I lean the plane harder and hear the struts groan and feel the shuttle's dirty airstream buffet the SCA's vertical stabilizers. I straighten out heading west, away from Washington D.C. and the greatest concentration of radar and interceptors on Earth, away from being labeled a terrorist threat, away from our destination.

I let out a huge breath, give myself a mental pat on the back, look at the GPS point dead ahead to our first waypoint at Bowmanton, and throttle up to cruise at 320. Time to see if Hel's transponder hack confuses aerial predators. Military interceptors patrol D.C. airspace 24/7 and a half-dozen military airstrips are minutes away.

Hel, sounding genuine, says, "Kudos, Mick." She called me Mick!

And Gritch: "Fuckin nuts, Oolfson, but ya did it! Keep her steady. Here I come!"

One minute to Bowmanton. I announce in my best airline pilot drawl, "Ladies and Gentlemen, welcome aboard Channel Zilch Flight 1. We will land at Wallops Island Airfield in approximately forty minutes. ETA 10:26. Please honor the seatbelt light."

I ease our ungainly flying contraption lower to the deck. The closer I fly to the nap of the earth the less chance we'll light up the radar of a prowling interceptor. Snowfall is a pixellated fog. Hazy lights of houses and farms zip by below at our 320 airspeed.

Gritch rattles through the cockpit door, saying, "Don't get up." and when I turn, the hatchet-faced skinny runt is already strapping himself into the co-pilot's seat.

"Just told Pops that we'll be arriving at Wallops hours early," says Hel. "He's scrambling the troops to get the boat docked and the runway lit."

"How's the weather at Wallops?" I ask.

Hel says cheerfully, as if it's great news, "Fog and snow. Great for security. I get all gooey around studly pilots who can land in zero visibility."

"Unless you can find me a hundred-yard-long white cane we'll need those runway lights."

"Working on it."

"Bowmanton waypoint in thirty seconds," I announce.

We'll turn south in the radar shadow of the Bull Run Mountains. Early in my Air Force career I had a boring deskbound assignment at Andrews AFB, so to stay sane a buddy and I would head to that ancient mountain range to hang-glide. Hundreds of flights taught me every wrinkle of that tree-infested heap of hills.

I'm startled by a touch on my shoulder and swivel to give Gritch some grief but see a small silver-filigreed hand. Hel's green eyes look right into mine, and when she smiles my toes curl. She leans toward me and whispers, "We did it, Mick."

I grin and shake my head in disbelief. "You called it: Enterprise is ours."

Hel's smile turns hard. "Snitching Enterprise in front of Ishwald's family—harsh, Oolfish."

I grimace, feeling a twinge of King Jerkhood for making Captain Toby fail so epically in front of his kids and wife. I retreat to pilot mode, "Seatbelts, Ms. Chin. We are at our first waypoint."

Bowmanton is on the north shoulder of the Bull Run range, and as I ease into my left turn we emerge from the safety of our cloud cover into a clear moonlit winter night.

"Shit," I opine with much feeling.

The radio delivers a jolt, "Visual contact with fugitive SCA. Got him on radar. Closing."

Twin points of light ahead swell into two fighters that streak by to our right. The next thirty seconds is one of those everything-happens-at-once slices of airborne near-mayhem that pilots dread and live for.

Lead fighter radios, "SCA. SCA. Do you read me? Ascend to 5,000 feet and we will escort you back to Dulles. Acknowledge."

My brain hangs fire as I watch the radar; the fighters make an impossibly tight turn, continuing to bark orders at us, "Start your ascent NOW, SCA! We have authorization to bring you down. Acknowledge."

Out of the night the fighters' flashing lights ease up to our right: a pair of spanking-new F-35A's. I glance to my left and see the safety of snow clouds looming out of reach over the solid wall of the Bull Run Mountains. A shard of moonlight glints from the ground. I've landed by that farm pond a dozen times. I visualize it and commit.

"Hold on!" I wrench us hard into a steep left bank and dive into the tight valley of Jackson Hollow.

I swear both Gritch and Hel let out soprano "*EEP!*"s.

G-tortured airframes shriek in the turn. As we enter the mountain notch, the roar of our engines echoes thunderously. No time to think—I shrug my right wing to clear a snowy knoll, juke right, left—flashes of snowy treed ridges—and we're through the tight little valley, under clouds again, flat land ahead.

Those F-35's are miles away on the other side of the mountains. I ease down to 200 feet to evade radar and to scare the shit out of some cows. The only sound in the cockpit is the rumble and roar of the SCA. I replay the last few seconds in my mind and look over my shoulder to Heloise with a smug grin. She opens her mouth but nothing comes out. I turn back to fly, full to the brim with myself.

Gritch finally says, "Thought you was gonna wreck my shuttle with your damn aerobatics there. Take it you flown that mountain."

I fake a yawn and drawl, "Jes feelin lucky. Wanna do it again?"

"I hope some fool was campin on top of that mountain and looked down to see a space shuttle fly by."

"I'm skipping our Airlie waypoint," I announce.

Hel says quietly, "So I notice."

I punch in the edit to the nav computer. "Wallops ETA is now 10:22."

While Hel mumbles into her spex, I examine the new leg of our route. No town between here and our Cookstown waypoint. Weather shows solid cloud cover and light snow all the way.

Hel says, "Boat's going to dock soon, but they can't find our runway light guy. Working on it."

Our destination, NASA's Wallops Island facility, is not real famous with the general public. It's a piece of NASA turf dangling off the snout of Maryland into the Atlantic, great place to fling big burning tubes of metal over water. With NASA tightening its belt,

Wallops is pretty much a ghost facility, perfect for slipping Enterprise out the door on the QT. Just for tonight we're reactivating a mothballed runway and decommissioned rocket-shipping dock.

I say, "If there are no runway lights we'd better hope that the coast is literally clear. I am not going to land a shuttle-laden SCA blind."

Gritch suggests, "Maybe circle over the ocean to burn some time?"

"Unadvisable. We lucked out with that F-35 patrol. I expect every operational fighter on the East Coast is scrambling to find us right now. We've got enough fuel for about two hours more flight. I'm leaving plenty of fuel to fly back to Dulles if we get shut out of landing at Wallops."

"Let's throw ourselves on Ishwald's tender mercies," says Hel, in a small, helpless voice. Gritch snorts appreciatively. A freshly-goaded Ishwald wasn't part of our exit strategy.

Time slows down as I concentrate on flying low. Hel gives a depressing update on Wallops: the runway lights are dead and the fog is pea soup.

I tune in weather info for the coast. "That damned fog is not going anywhere. It's gonna get thicker so we've only got a couple shots at landing."

We hit the Rappahannock River at Payne's Island. There are no power lines for thirty miles of the river so I get seriously low—even waggle my wings at a lit-up yacht.

Hel reports, "Can't find our runway lights guy. Pop says that the runway reflectors are in good shape, so if we get down low…"

"Not landing in fog without runway lights."

"How bout they park some cars at the end o' the runway," says Gritch, "turn on their high beams." Hel relays the suggestion.

I pull up to five hundred feet as we near the end of the Rappahannock to cross the wide mouth of Chesapeake Bay. The coastal fog bank merges with the clouds and we go blind as we cross the lowland of Virginia's shore.

Hel reports, "Pop's got two cars parked at the south end of the runway."

We emerge from clouds into a pocket of clear air over the Atlantic. When I turn north to parallel the coast, I take a good long gander at the fogbank. A few dim lights glimmer at its edge. Our runway runs south/north parallel to that line of solid fog.

"I'll get us down to 100 feet and make a pass over the runway. I'm going to be riding the GPS so you two keep a lookout for the headlights."

"Pop says high beams are on."

I ease down to 200 feet and turn left into the fogbank. As murk envelops us, I bank right and align with the GPS image of the runway. As I slow down and lower the gear, Gritch stands, and Hel leans over me to get a good field of view.

I narrate our progress toward the runway, "Closing, closing, look NOW." I tear my eyes from the GPS and strain to make out a glimmer in the dark.

Gritch pleads, "C'mon headlights. Give us some damn photons."

Hel, "Is that...? No."

Solid dark. Not a flicker.

As I cycle the gear and bank the SCA right for another pass, the full weight of tonight's caper hits me hard. I feel a dreadful certainty that Tobias Ishwald is going to get a bang-up finale to his so far rather disappointing evening.

I say to no one, "We tried." I crane my neck to study the moonlit fogbank. It's crept out over the beach, and I can't see any of the dim lights that gave me some hope on the first pass. "Fog is getting thicker, folks. One more approach and I call it a night. Not going to kill us all and trash Enterprise for a reality show. If we miss this landing, I'll pop up to 10,000 feet and call for a fighter escort back to Dulles. Park this baby right back up against the observation deck and look contrite while Ishwald cuffs me."

Gritch says, "Scalps ya more'n likely."

No one says another word as I circle back to head into the fogbank. As we dive into the grey wall of fog, I say, "Last shot. Going in low and slow."

I bank right and align once again with the GPS map's runway. Gritch and Hel are up out of their seats, eyes front and wide.

Hel says, "Cool, Pop," into her spex; and to us, "Look for fire. Dead center south end of runway."

I fine tune our course as I narrate our approach, "Closing. Closing."

Gritch mutters, "Nothin. Nothin."

Hel says, "There. No. THERE!"

A yellow flicker. "Got it!"

A bonfire lights a small pocket of fog. I nudge left to fly over the pyre. As I flip on our landing lights the fog glows, but the runway reflectors glare through it like beacons.

I grease the landing; don't want to rattle the shuttle. Taxi off the runway onto a service road leading to the docks.

As we taxi Hel exults, "Enterprise is ours!"

Gritch is sour. "We done the easy part—snitchin old Enterprise. Now we got us some real work to do—preppin a shuttle for launch on an Energia."

As we taxi on in silence, I reflect on the evening. I want space bad—bad enough to paper over some gaping ethical holes in the Zilch plan—but up until our battle with Toby and our wild flight I still felt queasy about stealing Enterprise. I shake that guilt tonight. We broke every law in reach, but we worked hard and risked our asses to free Enterprise. Channel Zilch earned itself a space shuttle tonight. Too bad we gave Ishwald excellent cause to be very, very peeved at us.

As we rumble toward the dock, the promised boat emerges from the fog—a grim-looking freighter. Closer doesn't make it prettier. It's a workhorse, not a yacht. Another Chin bargain.

I nose the jumbo out onto the massive dock to get the shuttle within reach of the monster dockside crane. I look down at the waiting boat and see three crewmembers standing at the rail gawking up at us. Two of them wear turbans. The other is massive and bald with a long white beard tucked into his grey trousers. White-beard harangues one of the turbaned ones, pointing up at the shuttle and shaking his pink-domed head.

Set the brakes and cut the engines. One more step back to outer space.

As my adrenaline drains, I sniff the air. The tang of ancient sardine.

CHAPTER SEVENTEEN: THE POTENT BULL

"No DIRER THAN inserting one's nose into the rectum of a deceased walrus, wouldn't you agree, sir?" The huge, white-bearded guy guffaws way too loudly.

I smile weakly, swallow a dry retch, and hold out my hand. "Mick Oolfson."

His great paw engulfs my hand in a warm, emphatic shake. "Lafcadio Hearn. Welcome aboard the *Potent Bull*—foulest-smelling ship to sail the high seas."

"The *Potent Bull*?"

"Powerful image to the Turks, a manly race."

Above us on the dock, a swarm of ship's crew labor to attach Enterprise to the rocket-loading crane. A light snow makes the intense scene cozy—snow globish.

"How long until we…?"

Hearn tuts. "We will depart the moment your shuttle is secure. I have received firm estimates of just over a single hour."

Can't place Hearns' accent. Irish?

I sniff the air and make a face. "What the…are you carrying on this ship?"

"We're loaded to the beams with space shuttles. *Potent Bull* is ranked among the more discreet space-shuttle-smuggling freighters registered out of Turkey."

I stare at him.

He sighs. "I see you're a tired man. Pray you aren't always thick as two short planks. I was after having a bit of fun with you."

I smile weakly. "I see—humor. I'll take your word for it. Long night. Coffee. This smell…"

The ramp heaves slowly as we talk. The rancid stench is a terrible cruelty.

Hearn shakes his head and tsks sagely. "Takes it right out of a lad, up all night stealing a space shuttle. But I haven't answered your query. I take it the freight with the brutal aroma is the object of your enquiry."

"Oh? Yes, right, that." My stomach burbles from rocking and reek.

Hearn leans close, so that his long white beard brushes my chest, and his smoky, sweet breath warms my face. "Don't dare crack a smile while I tell you this. Turks are powerful tetchy when it comes to their cultural singularities. We are carrying eight hundred barrels of the prized Turkish delicacy I alluded to."

"You didn't." I rack what's left of my brain and gulp down an acidic belch. "You made what you claimed was a joke about being a discreet space shuttle freighter."

He leans closer and whispers into my ear, "Eight hundred leaky wooden barrels of pickled walrus anuses."

"Uhhhh..." Bile squirms in my gut.

"Only slagging you, lad. What do you Yanks call it, a gag?" He beams and claps me on my back, not what I need right this moment.

"Scuse..."

I stumble to the railing and spew coffee-flavored puke down into the dark sea. My vomit spreads and sinks amid the shimmer of oil slicks and plops of melting snow. Some damn fish rises to nibble at it. Which sight triggers another heroic retch.

Hearn manhandles me below to my cabin where I eject the rest of my gut's throat-searing offal into a toilet. Flop onto the mattress and spiral away from consciousness.

I startle awake to a tap on my shoulder. Manuel Chin bends over me, concerned. Bass thrumming throbs through my cabin. The breath would gag a tobacco-chewing dung beetle.

This isn't like me. I should be up on deck helping. I apologize for my weakness. "Chin. Sorry—dozing. Any word of Ishwald? Did we get away clean?"

Chin smiles grimly. "No sign of pursuit as yet. The shuttle is loaded and secured. The *Potent Bull* will put to sea within the half hour, well before one A.M. You shall be well at sea by dawn."

I crack my jaw yawning. "How long did I sleep?"

"Just under an hour. You may resume your slumbers after I

impart a few words."

I offer weakly, "I should help tie down Enterprise. Is Gritch on board?"

Chin nods respectfully. "He is, fine man, hard at work inspecting what must be inspected, securing what must be secured. Ms. Vader and Richard Head have retired to their cabins. We were all most impressed—entertained is perhaps the better word—with your escape from the tomahawk-wielding Ishwald at Dulles, your valiant flight and escape through the mountain pass, and your superb landing in the fog."

I'm not much for ego but when I do good I'm not going to pretend I didn't. "Thanks. A night to remember. Couldn't have made that landing without your signal fire. How'd you pull a bonfire out of your ass?"

Manuel looks pleased. "When I realized that fog and snow obscured our headlights from your view I drew my trusty PT111 and emptied eleven bullets into the gas tank. As the tank drained I used the last bullet to ignite the conflagration. Oh, how we cheered when you emerged from that fog."

During the nap my smell receptors must have deadened to the fish-stench. I hope. Then I take a deeper breath and nausea comes on strong—my gut rumbles in outrage.

"What is that god-awful stink? Hearn told me it was an obscene Turkish delicacy."

Chin laughs. "Hearn is rather a card, I fear. The *Potent Bull* recently offloaded a cargo of herring oil in New Jersey. It is highly prized by the fertilizer industry. I seem to remember that you were once a baron of that industry. Our first meeting was remarkable for a similarly unsavory fragrance."

I shake my head. Never thought I'd miss the old, familiar perfume of honest cow manure. "Spraying shit from the air, those were the days! Cow shit you get used to, but this stuff—don't think so. They just unloaded? So the reek will fade after a couple days?"

A sigh of sympathy. "Almost certainly not. Hearn informed me that The *Potent Bull* has transported herring oil for over twenty years. The aroma is indelible. The best you can hope for is desensitization."

I joke feebly, "I'll have Heloise rewire my odor circuits. I'm sure she'd be happy to pop open my skull and root around with wire snippers and a soldering iron."

Chin smiles pityingly. "You know my daughter well. In the few minutes left to us before I disembark I would like to enhance that knowledge."

"Enhance away." He's got my attention.

"I have observed that Heloise has engaged your affections."

My shoulders droop. "You could put it that way. Fat lot of good it does me—she treats me like a lab rat."

Chin says, "She has behaved toward all her suitors in a similar fashion, although one forlorn chap told me that the rodent he identified with was a feeder mouse in a reptile cage."

I nod but try to hedge, "I wouldn't call myself a suitor, exactly."

"Permit me the usages of my antiquated lexicon, Mick. I am well aware that my daughter is beautiful, intelligent, and quite thoroughly cold-blooded: a formidable mélange, but not quite human. You, on the other hand, are a rather simple romantic, and I mean that in a most positive sense."

I nod him on.

"Do not underestimate the lengths to which Heloise Chin will go to amuse herself with your psyche. Warned is armed."

I give him my best I'm-on-tenterhooks nod and eyebrow-lift.

"You must promise never to betray this secret."

I raise my right hand and intone solemnly, "I, Mick Oolfson, promise never to tell your attractive but cold-hearted daughter, Heloise Chin, whatever the hell you are about to tell me." And I'm thinking: *secrets, secrets, she doesn't have secrets, secrets are death, secrets are lies*.

Chin says, quite seriously, "I take you at your word. Let me first state that were you not about to travel in virtual isolation with Heloise, I would never commit this indiscretion."

"Check, got it."

"Furthermore, I've grown quite fond of you myself, and would like to afford you a sporting chance against my indomitable off-spring."

"I really and truly appreciate it, Manuel." I give an encouraging nod to prod him to spit it out.

"To understand what I am about to disclose, I must first tell you about Heloise's mother—her name was Maureen Makuku—a stunning but infinitely confused black Irishwoman."

"Heloise has never mentioned her." I'm stunned to think Hel *has* a Mom.

"She doesn't, nor do I."

"You're telling me that Heloise is part Mexican, part Chinese, part African-American, and..."

Chin holds up his hand for silence. "Her mother and I adopted Heloise during a brief period of marital accord. The orphanage had no record of her parents, so any speculations as to Hel's ethnic heritage are speculations. Her mother was convinced that Heloise was a rare blend of Semite and Hillbilly."

Hmmm. Could be.

I ask a delicate question, but I am dying to know. "What's Hel's Mom like?"

Chin's eyes go grim. "I harbor undying hatred for that damnable... I am sure Heloise's emotions are more complex. Maureen was a fanatical peace activist, an anti-nuclear bomb firebrand. The day—June 2nd, 1987. Our marriage was long over by then. Maureen had custody of the children."

That shocks me. "Children?"

Chin pauses, breathes, and then continues softly, "Heloise has a twin brother, Harold. We adopted both of them, and though our marriage soured, Harold and Heloise were and are a source of great pride and joy. Until that day, Heloise and Harold were inseparable, a binary star system, both piercingly bright and full of audacious cerebral energy. Until that day. They were eight years old."

Chin stops breathing and looks away.

He turns back and speaks angrily. "It was to be a glorious blow against nuclear weapon testing. The first protest to shut down a nuclear bomb test. Maureen sent telegrams telling various agencies of the government exactly what she intended to do and when. And then she did what she promised to do. She surreptitiously entered the Nevada Test Site with Harold and Heloise, hiked miles across the desert. It must have seemed a magnificent crusade to the children, stopping an atomic bomb blast, saving Humankind! What power! What a lark! But of course the authorities very reasonably chose to regard her letters as the ravings of a crank." Chin sighs and looks at the ceiling.

I shake my head slowly. "No."

"Yes. The bomb was detonated as scheduled."

"I may be way out of bounds asking, but are you shitting me? Heloise lived through an atomic bomb explosion?"

Chin corrects me. "Hydrogen bomb. It was an underground test. When the bomb detonated the earth heaved, a human-engendered earthquake. My family was within a mile." He turns half away from me. "Ejected debris injured Maureen mortally and severely wounded Harold. Only Heloise escaped."

He continues in a dead monotone, "My daughter spent an hour trying desperately to save her family before an armored vehicle full of scientists arrived to gather samples and were appalled to find them. In that hour, Heloise listened to her mother die. She watched the light leave her brother's eyes and his whimpering turn to screams and then to silence. She tried valiantly to help them. An eight year-old-child fashioning tourniquets, hands wet with the blood of her wounded mother, brother. Heloise suffered, though her injuries were to her personhood, her Self." His voice is a shuddering whisper. He aches to his roots for his little girl.

I try to imagine the pain Heloise carries. "So Heloise couldn't save them. A child would... might blame herself for their deaths."

Chin turns to me and speaks with his usual energy. "Two errors there, Mick. Both happy ones, in a sense. Heloise never blamed herself. She was smart enough to understand their injuries were beyond her childish power to treat. And I do so hope she nailed the blame to her mother's carcass where it belongs. Your second error is—"

A ship's whistle shrills. And again.

Chin glances worriedly at his watch. "Five minute debarcation warning. The *Potent Bull* departs earlier than planned. Perhaps there is word of Ishwald in pursuit."

I can't let him drop it now. "Go on, Manuel. My second error?"

Chin looks puzzled. "I don't follow you. Oh, where was I? Not important. I must compress my analysis of the effects of this incident on my daughter. Good Captain Bogfyuk will undock his ship shortly." He hurries on, "Heloise was ravaged by sadness, loss, anger, relief, fear. Did she take the normal, the human, course and let time erode the searing pain? As you are aware, my daughter is in no sense normal. She analyzed her torment and identified her tormentor: emotion. She vowed to defeat emotion, to tame emotion, to control emotion.

"I believe she has succeeded. Her will cracks the whip and her feelings obey. Her intellect commands. She deploys emotion or perhaps simulates it only to optimize her effectiveness in human interaction. She manipulates the emotions of others as a kind of ongoing experiment or even a peculiar art form or hobby—who can say? I find it best not to anthropomorphize my own daughter. Heloise is what she is, and what she is, is remarkable.

"I tell you this so you have some small appreciation for what you face in Heloise. The feelings you seek to ignite in her are not yours to summon. What emerged from that bomb blast is not fully human and will likely never be so. Though I love her dearly, I expect no equivalent sentiment in return."

I sit at a loss, nauseous, overawed with the enormity of this data, unable to get a grip on it. Secrets are death. "I do appreciate the confidence, but what should I do with it? Should I try to engage your daughter in a purely intellectual relationship?"

Chin snorts. "Don't delude yourself, my young friend. If it becomes a duel of intellects between Mick Oolfson and Heloise Chin, you are flinging sharpened sticks at a cruise missile."

I grimace ruefully. "Ouch. Point taken. She's the brain—I'm a glorified bus driver, as she loves to remind me. What should I do with this? Where does it leave me?"

"You've heard of the renowned Shit Creek? You are well up it but I have just handed you a paddle. Paddle away from Heloise quickly to a safe, professional distance."

Chin purses his lips. "Will you heed my advice? I think not. She will make you suffer. But my warning will give you some perspective on your pain and assuage any guilt I might feel for not warning you. Now I must run to make my way ashore before *Potent Bull* sets sail. I wish you a successful voyage, Mick Oolfson. And congratulations once again on your exemplary actions in acquiring—"

"Stealing," I correct him.

"Stealing Space Shuttle Enterprise." Manuel extends his hand.

"Thank you." I stand and shake it.

Chin asks, "Will you accompany me to the deck?"

I start to say, "Sure," but my stomach does a flip. I make a sick face and point to the bathroom.

Manuel nods sadly, gives me a complicated look, and leaves me to my gastric misery.

CHAPTER EIGHTEEN: NEWS FLASH

CHIN DEPARTS. *Potent Bull* sets sail. I crash hard. Not sure in what order. When I wake we are far at sea under low, grey skies.

I wobble through a twisty maze of corridors until I find my way outside to look at my baby. The Enterprise is lashed down to the deck, swaddled in huge black sheets of plastic that do nothing to hide her gorgeous, fat-assed contours. Even under wraps she looms beautiful and proud.

I see Hel and duck her. What can I say to her? How bright do your bones glow? Care to achieve critical mass with me? I promised Chin I would keep the secret secret, but my tongue has a mind of its own. Do I dare ever talk to Heloise again?

Haven't set eyes on Head or Darthy. I hear they've turned Darthy's room into a video studio and are practicing. Practicing pointing a camera and talking I guess.

Right now Gritch is inside Enterprise inspecting his picky little heart out. Nothing I can do about that. In a few hours, Gritch is going to give his hands-on assessment of whether we can prep our stolen bird for extended space habitation in the time we have. Gritch'll either stick his thumb way up or we turn around, park Enterprise ashore, say bye-bye to *Potent Bull,* and face the music.

Gritch sends a crewman to my sickroom with a succinct note: "Get your ass up here." The Gritchlike tone of the note gives me hope. If he was going to call a no-go he'd be polite.

I find Gritch standing under the black-shrouded wing of the shuttle where it's almost warm in the blustery deck gale. The black plastic flaps like dry thunder. My empty gut is clenched. I'm jumpy as a clown in a pie factory. Can't read Gritch's face. He's poker-faced on purpose—another good sign. The best shuttle doc in the world just spent hours going over Enterprise from nose to tail. As far as I'm concerned, one word from Gritch and I kiss my space bug good-bye for all time.

I take a breath and dive in. "Spill it, Gritch. Is it possible to do this crazy thing or are we screwed? Should I tell the captain to turn this tub around and write the whole thing off as a bad joke?"

Gritch's cheek bulges with a big chaw of gum and his jaw muscles work while I ramble. "You finished?" Chew, chew. "Good. I'll put it like this—I went through a box of hankies crying my nuts off inspecting ol Enterprise."

"Shit, Gritch. I mean… shit." I thought I was ready for this moment, but now I have to face it. Back to face a victorious Ishwald, a few years in jail, and a bright future in the aerial diarrhea racket.

Worth it? Yep.

Gritch looks at his clipboard and breaks the news, "What was the Smithsonian thinking not restoring the computer bay to working order? And those leaky escape hatches for the test pilots to punch out—you guys gonna learn to breath vacuum?"

With each word of Gritch's speech my heart sinks further until it scrapes along the bottom of the sea floor. I smile weakly. "Shit, Gritch."

Gritch nods blankly. "Yeah, I know. Boy's got a space-monkey on his back, that monkey needs to chow down regular. Listen up; what's a redneck's last words?"

I shrug.

"Hey, ya'll, watch this!" Chew, chew. "Get it?"

I shrug harder. Can't look him in the eye.

"Redneck's doing some crazy-ass stunt, pleased as shit with hisself, wants everyone lookin at him. He yells, 'Hey, watch this!', and BOOM, the dumbshit's dead."

I don't get it and I'm not sure I want it. "Everyone tries humor on me when I'm like this. Sorry, Gritch."

Gritch gives me a pitying look. "You the sorry one. Don't you get it? You gonna be the redneck riding that thing. 'Hey, watch this!' I can't guarantee the punch line. There's a slim chance you'll live through it."

I protest, "But the problems—the computer bay and the escape hatch."

Gritch looks pleased with himself. "Just jerkin yer dipstick. I'm a bastard like at. We save time on the computer bay because the little freaky geek lady told me she needs those old computers ripped out. Sealing the escape hatches add maybe twelve hours.

"Gotta admit the Intrepid Museum folk did a topnotch job fixin the Hurricane Sandy damage. With what I know right now I'm figuring if I tack on one week to my prep schedule I give you pissants about a one in five or six chance of BOOM! That all right with you?"

I get that one loud and clear! "All right? Let me kiss you, you ugly runt. I got the crew to agree to a seventy-five percent best-guess survival odds."

Gritch shakes his head, smiling broadly. "About what I figured. We both know those safety-margin numbers are bogus, but I respect you as one of Jehovah's own crazy astrofolk so I'm cutting a few miles of slack here. I woulda shot someone if they let this crate fly when I ran the duct tape squad at NASA."

My heart shoots from the depths up into the sky. "YEEEE HAAAA! Gritch, buddy, you made my life."

"If you was planning to land this crate, I'd give you a big no go." Columbia.

"This ain't no money-back guarantee, but I'll work my balls off to get this bird fit to fly."

Happy, happy, joy, joy! "You just do your best. I don't have to tell you that, Gritch. Every one of the crew is dying to blast off into space and do the Channel Zilch thing."

Gritch shakes his head, bemused. "Ain't that the story of flight, though? Y'all are carrying on the grand tradition of flying fools." He puts on his business face. "That bullshit's out of the way. You done your victry dance. Let's get down to serious bidness."

Gritch leans close to me and confides, "Tell me bout the spooky lady. WhooEEE, that broad is a firecracker."

I snort—an atomic firecracker. "Heloise? Chin's daughter. I could tell you stories about her." Gritch would get a big bang out of anyone who rode an H-bomb blast. Watch your tongue, Oolfson.

"You porkin her?"

I explain carefully, "She and I are colleagues."

Gritch looks surprised. "Serious?"

I look him in the eye and nod, too embarrassed to spill my awkward teenage yearning.

Gritch pumps his fist. "YEEEHA! That leaves a clear deck for old Gritch. I got about eight days to make this a Love Boat cruise. You watch Gritch in action, brother, learn you a thing or two about romancin."

I wince. "I could use some pointers." I don't admit to him that it's been over half a year since I "porked" a woman.

"Let's hit the chow line. You missed lunch."

Food? No. "I plan to fast for the rest of this voyage. This god-awful smell and the boat…"

Gritch fairly drools the words, "Wait'll you get a whiff of old Hearn's cooking. Set the wolf to howlin in your gut."

"Hearn *cooks?*" Appalling. The memory of his disgusting walro-anal confection sets my back teeth quivering.

Gritch pats his tiny gut. "Ship's cook. Man's a genius. Stuffed myself on lunch till I was fit to puke."

I wave him away. "I puke fine without eating Hearn's cooking. Go pig out. I want to take a peek inside the bird."

The distant look in Gritch's eyes tells me he's thinking about Hearn's food. "Whatever. Catch you."

I turn toward the access ladder as Heloise runs up yelling, "Mick, Gritch, come dig this prime newscast—your psycho NASA buddy wants to drink our blood. Channel Zilch is legend."

We trot after Heloise. I savor the sight of her slender calves pumping briskly. She leads us through bathroom-green corridors lit by caged bulbs and slams open a door marked RECREATION. Inside the room an old couch faces a TV showing a soccer game. Two turbaned crewmen turn to watch us enter and smile when they see Heloise.

Darthy waves from a ratty chair. "How's Mick?"

I roll my eyes and grimace. Then I remember! "Gritch says old Enterprise is in good shape and that he thinks he can make the mods in the time we have. Channel Zilch is GO!"

Darthy stands up and gives me a tight, warm hug. She looks up at me with radiant eyes. "I'm going to ride a rocketship, Mick."

I can't help saying, "And maybe even make it all the way to space."

Hel emits a trill of laughter. "BOOM! What a way to go, huh?"

I know that thought. "Beats dying on a sickbed."

Darthy gives me a squeeze and says, "Hel and I are working on that one."

Hel flutes a burst of mirth. "Naughty Darthy."

These two have their inside jokes.

Darthy says, "Come sit beside me. I hear this is good."

A crewman comes through the door followed by Gritch and (TA-DA!) Richard "Richard" Head. I give him a polite wave and he nods at me without expression.

Gritch stands straight when he sees Hel and gives her a wink and an embarrassing leer. "Hey, little lady. Watcha got cooking?"

Heloise blows him a sarcastic kiss which Gritch accepts at face value. Foolish old horndog dogpaddling eagerly toward the maelstrom.

Hel makes an interrogatory gesture toward the TV. The crewmen nod and make affirmative sounds. She slots a tape into the ancient VCR, hits PLAY. "Didn't get the first few words, but I got the juicy part."

Onscreen is an old shot of Enterprise. A voice-over, "...the strange disappearance of the space shuttle Enterprise. CNN's

Myra Condran talks to recently-appointed NASA security chief Captain Tobias Ishwald."

Ms. Condran's face projects a mix of concern and incredulity. I don't feel it—she's not Richard Head. "Could you tell us how Enterprise was stolen, Captain?"

Cut to none other than my old pal Ishwald, who looks like he just gargled paint thinner after an all-night bender. "I'm afraid I can't discuss the details of the incident at this point in time. We will release all pertinent information during the trial of the perpetrators."

Condran smirks. "Could you comment on this video, Captain Ishwald?"

Cut to a shaky handheld shot of a throng of partiers dancing on the deck of a brightly-lit-up yacht. The camera shakily pans over the water and a smudge of light grows into our Enterprise/SCA biplane flying low. We dip a wing—I remember waggling that waggle!—and fly out of frame. Condran narrates, "This footage of the stolen Enterprise was taken by startled partiers attending a corporate function in a hired yacht on the Rappahannock River. These next sequences of incredible video clips show a dramatic moment in Enterprise's daring getaway—an aerobatic flight through a narrow notch in the Bull Run Mountains. We will show this sequence at one eighth speed."

Onscreen, the video cuts to a black and white shot of a snowy hillside. The SCA/Enterprise enters the frame banked nearly vertically, shuttle starkly white and totally alien against the background of snow-clad pine. As we exit the frame turbulence shakes the trees—a flurry of scattered snow.

Gritch hoots, "They got yer damn showoffy mountain pass stunt!"

"These incredible shots—" Condran's voice-over "—of the stolen Enterprise and carrier were taken by wildlife biologists conducting an automated video census of nocturnal bird migration through the Bull Run Mountain Range."

The next shot shows a bare rocky ridge in the foreground. The SCA/Enterprise enters the frame nearly edge-on and flicks its wing up to miss the ridge, raising a puff of snow.

Damn! Didn't know I was that close.

Gritch whistles. "Nearly shortened our wing there, hotshot"

Condran, "Earlier this month biologists from George Mason University placed over fifty night-vision owl-census cameras on the Bull Run Mountain range and seventeen of them captured images of the fugitive shuttle." More glimpses of our bulky biplane dancing with the tight, rocky walls of the twisty notch at Jackson Hollow.

Darthy teases, "You'll want to favorite that clip on YouTube, Mickster."

Back to Ishwald, his lips compressed in fury and his eyes glowing slits. He twitches as Condran asks, "Any reaction to that footage, Captain?"

Head intones disdainfully, "Amateur!"

"We know exactly how the shuttle was stolen," Ishwald sputters. "I can reveal that it was taken to an abandoned dock at NASA's Wallop Island facility. We recovered the Shuttle Carrier there just over an hour ago."

Condran asks, "Any sign of Enterprise?"

Ishwald hesitates, then says quietly, "I cannot comment or speculate verbally on that matter at this point in time. But I can tell you that I know the identity of the deranged punk who ripped off Enterprise."

Condran probes, "NASA employee? Al Qaeda terrorist?"

Darthy sucks in her breath.

Ishwald glares out of the screen directly at me, eyes cold with rage. "He's an ex-astronaut, a NASA washout, a flake, a disgruntled loser."

Gritch turns to me and winks, stifling a chuckle.

Veins bulge on Ishwald's glistening forehead. "I can't divulge his name at this point in time, but I've got a message for the pathetic little [BLEEP]. Listen, mister, and listen good. I'm going to personally skin your [BLEEP] and nail it to my wall, got that?"

Condran needles, "Why the rage, Captain? Is it because the theft undermines faith in your competence as newly-appointed Director of NASA Security?"

Ishwald flinches and starts to say something, but shuts his mouth in a lopsided grimace and shakes his head, not looking into the camera.

Condran pushes, "Is there any truth to the rumor that Enterprise was stolen while you were guarding it personally?"

Ishwald sits up straight and says very slowly, "I was off duty."

"Do you deny that you were at Dulles and witnessed the theft?"

Ishwald forces himself to talk. "I've been preparing for the space shuttles' move since I was appointed Director. I've spent no time with my family for weeks. So last night I decided to give my family a personal tour of the SCA/Shuttle. The theft did occur at that point in time."

Cut to Condran, whose eyes have doubled in size. "Stolen from under your nose in front of your family? How does that feel, Captain Ishwald?"

Ishwald's face goes dead. He smiles a dead smile and says, "My family is proud of the risks I took trying to stop the theft," while his eyes stare down at his hands.

The camera stays on Ishwald as Condran states, "You must hate the NASA employee you suspect of perpetrating the theft."

Ishwald stares deep into the camera and his eyes burn. His mouth opens and shuts and opens, "It's not just one individual. I am after every single one of the perpetrators."

Darthy says, with feeling, "Swim out and get us, Captain."

Ishwald takes a breath and composes his face into stern resolve. "Catching these crooks is personal, because my duties are my life. No one steals our nation's astronautical heritage while Captain Tobias Ishwald stands guard."

Condran needles, "The facts say otherwise, Captain."

Ishwald stares 50-caliber slugs into the camera, then sits straight and juts his chin. "I vow to the American public that I will recover Enterprise. Every American surveillance satellite, ship, and aircraft will hunt these [BLEEP] down like the [BLEEP] they are. I vow that Enterprise will attend the shuttle reunion on schedule. I urge all your viewers to visit the Cape to see all the shuttles together for the first time."

Condran: "You ducked my question, Captain. What is your relationship with the allegedly disgruntled former NASA employee?"

Ishwald hits the table with his fist. "The man is a menace, a psychopath evidently fixated on Enterprise. He tried to kill me years ago by ramming my car."

Cut to Condran, looking concerned and gleeful. "You expect this fugitive to kill you with the stolen space shuttle? Could you describe how he might accomplish this?"

Ishwald's sweaty face fills the screen, tight close-up, chipmunk-in-the-headlights stare on his face. "I never said..."

Cut to Condran, who is not bothering to suppress a smirk. "Thank you, Captain Ishwald. America can sleep soundly tonight knowing you are in charge of NASA security." She wraps it: "That was Captain Tobias Ishwald, Chief of NASA Security, commenting on the theft of space shuttle Enterprise. The Enterprise was stolen late last night from Dulles International Airport. Captain Ishwald has just confirmed that he was personally guarding Enterprise when it was stolen and that his family witnessed his fruitless efforts to stop the theft. Enterprise's current whereabouts is unknown. Captain Ishwald's credibility is weakened by his bizarre claim that the thieves stole the shuttle in order to attack him."

Cut to Ishwald, ashen, shaky. "I never said..."

Cut to a concerned Condran. "Stay tuned for further developments."

Cut to Ishwald, face buried in his hands, unaware his misery is being broadcast to the world.

Condran shifts into anchor mode. "To recap: early this morning, the space shuttle Enterprise was stolen from Dulles International Airport where it was exhibited prior to flying to the cape for the scheduled space shuttle reunion. The thieves are still at large."

The crew of Channel Zilch, even Richard, applaud loudly. The turbaned crewmen smile and applaud right along. I grin, clap, and laugh like an idiot with the rest of them. Richard requisitions the Ishwald tape and hands it to Darthy for the "Channel Zilch archive."

As the laughter glow fades my gut clenches from more than the stink and the sea's incessant rocking. Ishwald doesn't like me one little bit and he's throwing the full resources of the U.S. military into hunting me down: cloud-penetrating radar, air searches, blockades for all I know. We're toast; just a matter of time. Might as well enjoy the rest of the ride.

CHAPTER NINETEEN: A JOLLY ROGERING

I'M ONE OF THOSE lucky astronauts who don't puke in microgravity. Luck of the genes—some hotshot veterans are wretchedly ill for their first dozen orbits every mission. But I never sailed in anything bigger than a canoe, so up until the voyage of *Potent Bull* I didn't know that Lord Neptune hates me personally and has a direct line to my stomach's purge pump.

On the second day of our voyage I'm still no use to Gritch or myself but I go whole hours without worshipping at the porcelain throne. My stomach is so empty I fantasize puking myself inside out. Hell of a way to go: ralphing up chunks of my own pelvis.

After two solid hours lying in bed without hurling, I decide to get on my feet and make an appearance. I'm weak and still feel like shit, but I'm not much for lying in bed while others are doing my work. As a species, astronauts are doers rather than shirkers.

I'm in no shape for another deck excursion—don't want to see the sea. Time to chomp the slug and pay my respects to Head. Richy and I are slated to be roommates on Enterprise's flight-deck, so diplomacy is called for.

The hallways of The *Potent Bull* are a twisty little maze of passages, all alike. I flag down the first crewman I stumble upon and mime a video camera. Which confuses the poor sailor, who is eager to help, until I cock my nose in the air and the light goes on: Head the Arrogant.

He leads me to the Channel Zilch video studio. A red light burns above the door so I do the polite thing and don't barge in—I knock hard to get Darthy's attention.

Which is evidently a horrific mistake. Incoherent bellows erupt from behind the green door in Head's unmistakably resonant baritone. Darthy pops open the door and I hear Head clearly. "... atrocious studio discipline. HOW can I—"

Dar steps into the hallway and slams the door behind her. "No noise when the red light is on, Mick," she whispers. "I should have warned you. We're recording. Richard is having a bad day. Little things set him off."

The one and only Richard "Richard" Head bangs open the door and glares at me. "Oolfson! I should have known. Trying to throw off my game. I will *not* be rattled. Apologize, and off with you."

I despise drama even on a happy stomach; my MNnice wants to say sorry, but as pilot of this mission I shouldn't beg forgiveness. If I grovel now, our crew dynamic will start out way off kilter. I look Head straight in the eye and say firmly, "Get a grip, Richard. Show some professionalism."

Head's brow bunches and his mouth goes ugly with rage. "Professionalism? I'm not the one ignoring the recording light, banging on a studio door like a feckless dreg."

"'Feckless dreg,'" I needle. "That would be a swell inscription on my tombstone. Thanks, Richard."

Which stops him cold except for ragged breaths that get louder and faster with each lungful. Darthy looks alarmed, grabs Head's arm, yanks him back into the studio. Head gets off a parting shot, holding open the door as Darthy struggles to shut it.

"I know your type, Oolfson. Jealous of talent. Undermining. Corrosive. I've got my eye on you."

Darthy yanks his arm and slams the door without letting me goad him.

I don't know what gets into me when Richard is around. I can't think of another person who brings out the worst in me. He's my roomie on Enterprise so somehow I've got to file off the rough spots on our animosity. I'll settle for a coldly civil working relationship; Dick and I are never going to be pals.

I take a minute to think through my next move. Am I really sharp enough to brave an audience with Heloise Chin? I try to think of something Helworthy and fail. Can't produce a decent sentence even for the noble cause of impressing Hel.

Impressing Hel? That's rich. Best I can hope for is not to make a drooling ass out of myself. That hopeless thought drives home that maybe I better call getting yelled at by Head a good day's work and retire to my vomitorium.

As I mentioned, the corridors of the *Potent Bull* are a maze of twisty little passages, all alike. I try to remember which one the nice crewman led me down, and fail. What's the trick to getting out of a maze? Keep a hand on the wall and walk as long as it takes. Seems to me there's a gotcha in that, but it's the best I can recall.

I touch the cold green wall with my left fingertips and start walking, left at the first corner, and there she is: the very woman I need to avoid in my feeble state: Heloise Chin, decked out in full cybersuit regalia, belly lights atwinkle.

She smiles a smile that looks genuine. She shifts gears and her smile goes crooked and hard. "Time to earn your chow. Follow."

LAZARUS WALKS

She clomps past and turns the corner back to the studio. I follow and nearly bump into her as I round the corner.

"Whoa!" I say loudly.

"SHHH! Dar and Rick are recording. I'll bug Dar later. Boop beep, spacer." She turns and clomps off.

"Wait, wait." I call after her. "Can you help me find my room?"

She stops, turns, snickers. "Spiffy pickup line, M."

TOO MUCH?

"Give me a break, Heloise. I'm lost." Maybe I put a little too much whine in that.

"It's not going to happen." Her eyes are hard and pitiless.

"Wha...?"

"You and me."

LIP BLOCKADE

So you say, Heloise Chin. "I just want to find my way back to my room so I can die in peace."

She turns. "Follow." And clomps down the hall.

I hurry to walk beside her. Think, Oolfson. What's a subject dear to whatever Hel uses for a heart? Computers!

I take a breath and go for it. "Fill me in on the computers you're installing in Enterprise."

She turns, face already sneering. "Are you claiming to have a clue about computers?" She turns and stops so I can read her scrolling ego-stomp.

DELUSIONS OF NONSUCKAGE

"Cut me some slack. I'm just trying to understand as much as I can of every part of Enterprise."

Hel looks at me like I'm an uppity insect. "Listen up, astronaut hero man, best not aspire out of your skill set. You're operating at the ragged edges of your competence."

∷∷∷∷∷∷∷∷∷∷∷∷

Nothing in the belly lights. At least she had to use her whole brain to think up that insult.

When in doubt, play dumb. "Sorry, went right over my head. Was that a compliment? Us flyboys aren't used to ginormous words."

Hel sneers. "Hard to sustain a technical discourse employing monosyllables."

SEE WATT RUN

"Let's give it a try," I soldier on. Hel still faces me in the hallway. She wants me to read her tummy talk.

Hel gives a shrug. "Listen hard. I'm installing a cluster of 1,023 Sinclair ZX-81's arranged in a 4.3-dimensional hypercubic network topology connected over quantum entangled heliograph links talking in the Gopher protocol with apps coded in interpreted Ada and UI coded in embedded FORTH on top of Multix. Got that?"

YANGTUT

I watch the crypticism scroll across her bellylights. I shrug and give her the Oolfson dumb look.

"You Are Not Expected To Understand This," she de-acronymizes for me.

I defend myself, "Write that computer stuff down and turn me loose on Google—I'll figure it out. I did get some of it, but you threw it at me way too fast."

"Enlighten me, Mickster. Prove your geekhood. Tell me what you got." She thinks I didn't catch a thing.

YOU TECHNOSTUD YOU

I can't keep myself from trying. "You're installing some model of Sinclair computer, right?"

Hel nods and mimes shock.

FOOD PELLET

"Now I'll try for extra points. The Sinclairs run on a network. Some kind of quantum thing going on. I want to hear more about that later. And I did catch the lame joke about talking to gophers. I knew you'd throw in some garbage to trick me."

Hel slumps against the wall theatrically playing awed stupefaction. "Awesome mental horsepower. Remind me to eat your brain."

BRAINSTEM MCNUGGETS

I watch that one scroll by on her belly. "How do you carry on a conversation with your voice and your belly lights at the same time?"

"Scope my twitching digits."

MY FINGERS DO THE TALKING

Her fingers wiggle like they always do.

"I figured that. The silver strips let you play air typewriter." I wiggle my fingers in the air.

Hel looks disgusted. "You figured it but you're asking. Like to feel your larynx vibrate?"

STARSTARBRAIN

I keep trying. "My question is how do you generate two streams of language at once?"

Hel rolls her eyes. "Such a deep, probing question. You trying to get me all hot and bothered by showing off your man-sized appetite for knowledge?"

BULGING FRONTAL LOBES

"Give me a break. I'm curious."

"I'll spill my girlish little secret. Parallel cortical processing. I can partition my brain into an arbitrary number of autonomous consciousnesses."

JEALOUS, SINGLE MINDED ONE?

"Sounds like a lot of work to me."

"It's my life's work—re-engineering my mind on the inefficient substrate of my brain. Tame your brain. Thought, emotion, personality—own them or they own you."

I SELF HACK THEREFORE I AM SQUARED

I shake my head. "Whew, either you are doing something real scary to yourself or you have a rich fantasy life."

"That's not really an *OR*, so I choose Option A *AND* Option B. Pray continue lecturing on the frontiers of computer science. I'm learning loads."

WHAT'S WATT, TEACH?

"So I get to parade my ignorance while you stomp all over my ego, is that the game today?"

"And every day. Builds character." She stomps the floor with her black shiny rock star boots.

EGO-STOMPIN MOMMA

"I'll play. First, I know that a computer needs bits to operate."
"Needs bits, that's a revelation. Remind me what a bit is."

ITTY-BITTY

I grope for the right words. "It's like an atom of information."
"Where'd you read that, boy? I'm totally devastated by your insight. Allow me to bear you many strong sons." She flutters her eyelids and whispers the last word while her bellylights twinkle:

SEMINAL IDEAS

I'll show her I can keep my libido muzzled. "Let's keep focused. I was parading my ignorance."
"Stomping on your ego."
A door opens. I welcome the interruption. Darthy emerges from the Channel Zilch studio. The red light is off.
Dar gives us one of her fresh-baked-bread smiles. "Hope I'm not disturbing anything. I was going to hunt you down, Helgirl. I need a custom cable."
"Help you in a pico. But first listen to Mr. Albert Edison here explain his latest invention: the computer."

MIND OVER BLATHER

Darthy looks at me with a lift of her brow. "You taking over Heloise's job, Mick?"
I probably look woeful. "She's just applying her hobnails to my tender male ego."
Darthy tuts, "The nerve of that gal."
I try to shoo her away. "You might want to leave. I'll soon be lying on the floor writhing in embarrassment."
"Can I stay, Mick? I'd really like to hear what you've figured out."
Heloise smirks.

MCKMIND MONSTERS MON

Darthy swats her on the arm. "Heloise, you're terrible. Let the boy talk."

Hel, "Tell us more about bits."

BOY

I've wandered this far into a blank spot in my brain—Forward! "Usually the bits are stuck to the hard drive, but sometimes they get scooped up off the drive and fed into the RAM so the intel can get at them."

Darthy explodes with a whinnying shriek of laughter and Heloise stands straight, salutes me, and pretends to faint into my arms, which is fun in a cruel sort of way.

Her belly reads:

MAXIMALLY SUBOPTIMAL

So you see, I am a singularly clueless individual where the cybernetic arts are concerned. Next I'm going to explain the video camera to Darthy. I'm pretty sure that works by capturing souls.

As Darthy leads me back to my cabin, wounded pride throbbing, a loudspeaker blares, "BLACKOUT! All hands. BLACKOUT!" The message repeats in diverse languages. Door slams echo down the hall.

Darthy and I give each other looks. What...?

A crewman hustles toward us. Darthy stops him. "What's up?"

He knows English. "Hearn says Captain B saw a plane he didn't like. Thinks a search is on for Enterprise."

Ishwald!

CHAPTER TWENTY: CHANNEL HEL

ADVENTURES ON THE HIGH SEAS: the thrill of hunting for a non-metric torque wrench, the heart-stopping drama of disassembling a storage cabinet, the primordial battle of human versus task schedule. Complain all you want, but I'm going to skip all that grindage for the juicy scenes.

In a fit of camaraderie after watching the Ishwald video, I accompany Heloise and Gritch to dinner. I even manage to force down a biscuit.

Dar and Head sit at their own table. Darthy gives me a little wave. Richard looks right through me.

The extravagantly-bearded Lafcadio struts out of the kitchen to check on how his food is playing with the crowd. He guffaws when he spots me. I manage a wry smile—at least I'm trying for wry.

Gritch sits between Heloise and me, doing his 66-year-old best to hustle her. I expect Hel to bite his head off down to the ankles, but she bathes him in the emerald power of her eyes. Gritch thinks Heloise plays normal boy/girl games. Poor guy thinks he has a chance. I lean back in my chair and smile tiredly at nobody while keeping an eye on them.

As Heloise downs the last bite of her cherry pie, Gritch goes, "So if you need Gritch to tuck you in, honey, just give a holler. I don't get many complaints from the ladies."

Hel bends close to Gritch and whispers loud so the whole room can hear, "I have a peachy idea, Gritch-boy. You come to my cabin and I'll do you until you beg for mercy."

Gritch sits bolt upright. His head snaps back. "*Do* me?"

I wait for the punch line.

Heloise leans closer to Gritch. "If you're a virgin I'll start gentle. Your safe word is 'potato'."

I excuse myself and head back to my room. She's hanging ten in Gritch's glandular secretions. He's a big boy and I'm dead beat.

I get lost in the rolling, pale-green, bare-bulb-bright corridors. I realize I've circled back to the mess when I turn a corner and encounter Hearn.

He beams and opens his arms. "Foraging? Nothing like sea air to sharpen a man's appetite."

"Cut the crap, Hearn."

Hearn does a shocked take. "Lacerate the feces? I'm afraid you've mistaken me for an incompetent proctologist."

I groan and Hearn bows and says apologetically, "Not my best, but consider the hour."

"Can you tell me how to get back to my cabin? I'm beat."

Hearn tut-tuts and waggles his massive white beard. "Turning in so soon? On your first healthy night aboard? Can't have that. Come meet the crew. You've been so engrossed in your regurgitations that your manners have withered. Your reputation as a *bon vivant* has suffered. You must demonstrate to your fellow man that you adhere to the social compact."

"I'm way past beat. Just point me home, and I'll try hard to be genial in the morning."

Hearns wraps his huge arm around me and leads me like a tired child. "The recreation suite abuts the passage to your stateroom. I will introduce you to my crewmates, after which I will personally piggyback you to your kip and tuck you in and sing Turkish lullabies until your wee little eyes drift shut."

I walk with him. The warm bulk of his arm around my shoulders overlays my fatigue to lull me into a childishly dependent state—rather pleasant.

"Did Ms. Chin apprise you of the promising developments *vis-á-vis* your chum Ishwald?"

"We haven't chatted about Toby in a while."

"Scuttlebutt among Hel's NASA sources is that Tobias severely damaged his credibility: first, by allowing Enterprise's theft from under his nose; second, by his disastrous television meltdown."

"Which helps us how?"

"Captain Toby's position as Director of NASA Security hangs by a thread. Almost every branch of the U.S. military has refused to provide Tobias with the surveillance resources he requires to hunt the *Potent Bull.*"

"*Almost* every branch?"

"Ishwald has a single high-ranking friend in the Navy who has assigned a small task force to pursue our gallant ship."

"How about the NRO?"

"Acronyms are not my strong suit."

"National Reconnaissance Office. They run Uncle Sam's spy sats. Those guys can spot a flea from orbit through a hurricane. If the NRO gives Ishwald the cold shoulder we can party hearty."

"I shall enquire when next I talk with the estimable Heloise. I welcome opportunities to converse with her." He monologues as we progress, "You must tell me about Ms. Chin. Fascinating article. Truly a girl made of piss and vinegar and a wee dram of angel jez as my poor besainted Ma never said. I saw Ms. Chin lead a visibly agitated Mr. Gritch Neubart to her private suite with salacious intent. Is she a fancier of unsightly old gents?"

Poor Gritch. I'm sure he had high hopes on that little walk. "She likes to play with men's heads."

Hearn sighs feelingly. "She'd be most welcome to dandle my cranium upon her lap. And, speak of the devil's playthings, here is where our stouthearted crew bring their idle hands: the *Potent Bull's* recreation complex."

He opens the door and announces grandly, "All rise for the Duke of Deep Space, Mr. Mick Oolfson."

His big hand propels me into a room I recognize. This is where Heloise played the tape of Ishwald's vow to flay my naughty bits. The three turbaned crewmen on the sofa turn from the television to watch my entrance.

Hearn enters and addresses them, "I applaud your relentless study of the anatomical sciences, gentlemen, but allow me to mute the sound until civilities are attended to."

Porn plays on the TV. The back of a woman dressed in black, riding upright on the loins of a recumbent skinny gent whose face is off-camera. A whiteboard beside the bed is covered with equations—kinky detail. Video-blurred flesh undulates while a muffled female voice recites equations until Hearn douses the volume.

"Allow me to introduce, from the left, Ahmet, Mehmet, and most particularly Yeter, my stalwart steward who has an ambitious relationship with the English tongue."

Yeter smiles, nods, and gestures to an empty chair beside the television. "Please relieve yourself."

Though I'll deny it, I've got a peer-pressure button about a yard square. I sit.

Hearn sits down in an empty leather chair that is obviously his accustomed throne and produces a bottle. "Let's drink to our glorious Enterprise."

The three crewmen extend their coffee mugs and Hearn pours each a long glistening ribbon of bright orange liquor. He watches me examine the stream. "Glorious shade of crimson gold, eh, lad? Tuvak is a rare Turkish brandy distilled from frost-damaged kumquats. The pulp is trod by the bare feet of a monastical convent of hermaphrodites, adherents of a resurgent cult of Bacchus. A sip won't mangle you."

I'm comfy. Hearn will do all the talking. Might as well bond with the crew. A rocketship is just a type of ship. A crew is a crew. Does that mean anything or am I just really, really tired?

I accept a generous mug of the brew. I take a peek at the screen—I'm a guy. Still just the black-clothed back of a woman taking a ride on an anonymous gent next to an equation-covered whiteboard. The usual.

Hearn raises his mug. "To starship Enterprise."

The crewmen raise their mugs and I join the toast. The liquor bites and cloys. I recognize the taste instantly. "Turkish brandy? Bullshit! This is NASA Punch—Tang and whatever rotgut you have lying around."

"Then I'll have to throttle the wretched vendor who charged me forty dollars for the bottle," Hearn pronounces complacently.

We sip in silence.

Hearn chuckles. "I should go fetch the good Captain B. to round out our little tea party."

Yeter holds up both hands, palms forward, and says earnestly, "Captain is driving *Potent Bull*."

Hearn shakes his head and grimaces sincerely. "The *Potent Bull* is a happy ship, by and large, but even I fear our Captain, Mick."

What did Manuel call the captain? "I haven't met Captain... what is his name?"

Hearn shudders and downs a gulp. "Pray you never do. Captain Boogfyook, Hnazdrysz Boogfiuk. A singular moniker even by Turkish standards. A singular man."

"What did Yeter mean about the Captain driving the ship?"

Hearn says quietly, almost reverently, "Our Captain mans the bridge alone every night from eleven until five-thirty in the morning."

"Odd for a captain to take night shift."

Hearn shrugs. "None are privy to the captain's thoughts or motives. I postulate that he needs night and privacy to further his quest."

I wait. Hearn will tell his tale with no prompting from me.

"Yes, his quest. It is my theory that our captain searches all the Oceans of the World for the Great White Herring."

He waits a beat and sighs at my silence. "Not a literary man, I take it."

I give him the satisfaction of his jest. "Whale oil—herring oil. Great White Whale—Great White Herring. Captain Ahab—Captain Boogwhatever. Which means your middle name is Ishmael. I took freshman English."

Hearn is delighted with my grasp of literary canon. "A man of culture after all. I salute NASA for their discerning judgment in selecting you."

I shrug. "Yeah, I'm the original renaissance faire man. What's up with the captain?"

Hearn pouts, "You doubt my Moby Sprat theory? Very well. The truth is that no one knows what makes Captain B be Captain B. Other than those dark hours piloting the ship, our captain stays snug in his cabin, communicates through written commands, and is never to be summoned unless the *Potent Bull* is in desperate need of a Captain's judgment.

"I leave dinner on a tray outside his door at ten-forty and my first task upon waking is to cook a simple breakfast which Yeter delivers to his cabin door at six."

The familiar flavor of Tang-laced booze puts me in a mood to sit and listen. Booze doesn't make me giddy or sleepy; it just puts me in a zone of I-don't-care, bleary whateverness. "Tell me a tale about our big bad Captain Bahoosiewhatsit. I'll take a bedtime story instead of that lullaby you threatened me with."

Hearn smiles and rubs his hands thoughtfully. "Once upon a time our good Captain found Mehmet sleeping on his lookout watch as we sailed into the crowded Chesapeake Bay."

Yeter frowns and murmurs quickly to Mehmet. Mehmet bangs down his mug and spits out an untranscribable burst of forceful syllables.

Hearn nods pleasantly. "Mehmet modestly declines the honor of being enshrined in verbal lore. I will instead tell you the tale of the time I brought our good Captain poached eggs for breakfast." He shudders. "This tale will drain my reservoirs of language. I shall consult a thesaurus and exhaust its synonyms for terror, anger, and cowardice."

I shrug. "It'd be wasted on me, Hearn. Use any old words. Shorter the better."

The crew returns their attention to the soundless porn behind me while I sip the potent brew in my mug.

Hearn hesitates to begin his tale, the first time I've seen him at a loss for words, so I lend a hand. "Try 'Once upon a time'."

He nods, mock-earnest. "Once upon a time, the good ship *Potent Bull* went voyaging from her home port in Turkey, holds bulging with glass beads, to the coast of wild Amerikay to trade with the primitive natives for those odoriferous delicacies so prized in Istanbul." Hearn winks at me, and I shudder at the sick twang in my gut.

Hearn continues, "On board was a new member of the crew, a cook of rare culinary talent and impressive physical stature, Lafcadio Hearn by name. On his first evening, to show his new Captain what a cook of a cook he was, Lafcadio planned to poach a pair of perfect poultry embryos, though the Captain had expressed in forceful written orders that his late dinner be four cold salt herring on burnt rye toast every evening of the trip.

"Hearn had never set eyes on his Captain, and being of a narrative bent, wished and fully expected to win praise, camaraderie, and ultimately friendship in gratitude for his culinary skill. So he poached those eggs to ovine perfection, made up a handsome tray, and handed it to his steward to set down outside the Captain's door. The steward was terrified. He wouldn't touch the tray though Hearn shouted dire threats and waved his cleaver in best mad cookish tradition.

"The eggs threatened to grow cold, so Hearn took up the tray, sneered at the cowardly steward, and marched off to present the Captain with his poached masterpiece." Hearn frowns, interrupting himself. "Yeter, kindly tell your crewmates to pipe down."

The crew's been getting louder, talking and gesturing at the screen. Yeter laughs. "Old man needs helping."

Hearn barks sternly at him, "I am speaking, Yeter. And when Hearn speaks, what do you do?"

Yeter looks down at his lap, chastened, "Hearing." He looks up and can't keep his eyes from the screen. He bursts into a shrieking giggle and points to the screen. Mehmet and Ahmet likewise convulse.

Hearn turns his contemptuous gaze toward the television. He opens his mouth to make a withering remark but stops cold. "Lights on her belly? Could it be...?"

I hop out of my chair to get a peek. It's Heloise, dressed in the top half of her lightsuit, standing before the equation-covered whiteboard. She's heatedly chastising someone off camera. I turn and yell at the crew, "Turn it off!" I stride to the console. The ancient videotape player is off. "Hearn, is there a tape machine broadcasting this to the whole boat?"

Hearn shakes his head. "No such thing. I suppose it would be too much to ask you to increase the volume. Please don't think me a cad, but I would dearly like to hear what the vixen is saying to Mr. Neubart."

"Gritch? What the hell..." I squint at the screen where, sure enough, Heloise has Gritch by the arm. She gestures toward the bed while he shakes his head emphatically.

I yell at Yeter, "Where did you get this tape?"

Yeter shrugs and shakes his head, "No tape. Camera."

Outrage! "You bastards rigged a video camera in her room?" Fuck Channel Zilch, I'm going to sink this boat and all aboard her and row Heloise to safety in a lifeboat.

The crew bursts into laughter. I peek at the screen.

Gritch is gone. Heloise kicks one leg of the whiteboard, her mouth going a mile a minute, obviously swearing a blue streak.

Hearn wheedles, "I know this is unforgivably, reprehensibly ungentlemanly, but would you be so kind as to turn up the sound?"

I'm done. "You want a sound? Here's a sound!" I grab my mug. As I hurl it I see an image of Heloise looking right at me, shrugging comically for a sliver of a second before the mug shatters the picture tube and lights flicker and sparks spray and smoke pukes from the smashed TV.

Silence. I stand with my hand pointing along the mug's trajectory trying to decipher that last glimpse of Heloise. She was looking, most definitely looking, right into the camera.

Pungent smoke of fried plastic and hot metal.

The door flings open and everyone turns. Gritch rushes into the room, a towel clutched around his middle, breathing hard, a haggard old man. He takes us in and his head jerks back when he sees the wrecked TV. His voice is steady when it comes, "Mick. Got me a code yellow, buddy. Step out here and let's us talk private."

I turn to glower at the others. They look concerned; the hysteria is over. I'll return to butcher them lingeringly.

Outside in the green of the hall I wait for Gritch to begin. He's scrawnier than ever with his bony legs bare and his old man's crepe skin draped loose on his bones. He's thinking hard.

I do my usual, go for the joke, "Don't tell me, Gritch, you went skinny-dipping in the Atlantic and someone swiped your clothes?"

Gritch grimaces. "How long dyall peep on us?"

She knew and she told him. "I smashed the TV the instant I saw who it was."

Gritch smiles with half his mouth and shakes his head. "That's one dead TV set. The way you were standin there it musta just happened."

I reach out and pat his slumped shoulder. "What gives? Did she discover the camera and freak out?"

Gritch looks up at me with something just short of horror in his eyes. "You got the freak part right. That little lady is one freaky scary piece of bidness. That lightshow on her belly and her damn sex algebra. She didn't discover that camera—she put it there. She told me about it right when I was fixing to pop my rocks."

How can I stay pissed at the crew? Heloise set up the sordid episode, can't blame them for playing along with the crazy American exhibitionist.

I'm going to cut short this squalid vignette because the sensational parts are pretty much over. There's a good moment later that night when I pound on Heloise's door for an explanation and she sticks her head out, sticks her tongue out at me, slams and locks it.

Gritch gets settled down and put to bed, vowing to keep his dipstick locked up for the rest of the voyage.

Just what the hell is that woman built from? Guess she wants the world to know that she isn't made of human stuff.

And what did Gritch mean by "her damn sex algebra"? I can't get that phrase out of my mind.

CHAPTER TWENTY-ONE: THIS OLD SHUTTLE

I WRIGGLE IN through the familiar circular hatch and stand up inside Enterprise's middeck—the first shuttle I've been inside for way too many years. Gritch's head sticks out from an open panel in the wall. "Look who shows up right when we bout to take a break," he gripes cheerfully.

Work is well underway. Storage locker doors are off and stacked against the wall. Missing wall panels expose the veins and guts of Enterprise.

I take a deep breath, trying to smell space shuttle but mostly smelling dust. Gritch scooches out of his hole and says, with a big grin, "WooEEE! Craziest job I ever signed onto."

"Looks like you've got a good start on it."

I hear a muffled voice from flightdeck. "Who ya got working with you?"

Gritch looks over his shoulder. "Got two of the *Bull* crew—Mehmet and Cal. Guys know how to work once I show em what I want."

"Can I...?"

"I know what you want. Sit your ass in the pilot's seat and jerk the joystick n make rocket noises."

I climb the ladder and nod at Mehmet and Cal as my head clears the hatch. Flightdeck is starkly lit by two worklights. As soon as my foot hits the floor, I'm focused on the flight controls and pilot stations.

The general layout of flightdeck is the same as all the shuttles, but the details are all wrong on Enterprise. Enterprise got bare-bones instrumentation because she never flew in space. Cue flashback to Enterprise's traumatic childhood—soundtrack: a mournful violin and the sloshing of a bucketful of tears.

Enterprise was NASA's first-born shuttle, but she was Cinderella from the start—worked hard, dressed in rags, treated like shit, and kept home from the big party all her sisters were invited to. I guess that makes me her fairy godmother.

When NASA built her, they didn't give her orbital maneuvering rockets or main engines, just mockups that weighed the same. She didn't get the deluxe dashboard package—no Heads-Up Displays, no navigation or guidance instrumentation. Her crew compartment has no galley, lockers, bunks, or showers. Her skin is cheap polyurethane, rather than the pricey ceramic foam tiles worn by her sisters.

But when they rolled her out on September 17, 1976, she sported one very cool adornment—about a gallon of heat-resistant black paint that spelled out "Enterprise". The first shuttle was slated to be named "Constitution" until Star Trek fans deluged the White House with mail demanding she be christened after their favorite fictional space ship. Darthy Vader wrote one of those letters.

Enterprise was a hard worker from the start. She went through nine months of approach and landing tests, first to see how she taxied and flew when mounted on the Shuttle Carrier Aircraft, and then a taste, but only a taste, of the real thing. Enterprise flew five free flights, flights in which she was strapped to the jumbo, flown five miles high and cut loose to glide to Earth under her own control. Enterprise flew free—a quarter century ago, but she flew—in air, never in vacuum.

After that taste of glory, Enterprise was battered with a vengeance. They called it the Mated Vertical Ground Vibration Test series. Engineers pummeled her with carefully positioned "exciters". Sounds kinky until you hear that the fifty-six exciters they had strapped to her could each deliver half a ton of instantaneous pressure. Sadistic test techs rocked my bird hard to make sure her sister shuttles wouldn't crack under the stress of launch.

After this pounding, Enterprise was slated to go back to the manufacturers and get retrofitted into a spaceworthy shuttle—main engines and guidance thrusters and instruments and space toilets and real ceramic tiles. But NASA shafted Enterprise right up the nozzle. They'd learned so much from building and testing her that they changed their shuttle designs in a hundred thousand big and little ways. It would cost more to bring Enterprise up to revised specs than to build a new one from scratch.

Well done, and screw you, Enterprise.

They kept her around for a few years for more tests and PR events. Meanwhile her sisters went to the Big Cosmic Ball.

In '81, Columbia made the first shuttle space flight.

In '83, Challenger made her maiden flight. That year, Enterprise got a jumbo-back flight to Europe to star in air shows.

By '84, NASA had ten shuttle missions under its belt. Enterprise starred in the World's Fair in New Orleans. Discovery launched.

In '85, they flew Enterprise to Dulles to rot in storage.

In '04, they spruced her up (and did a fine job) and moved her into the Smithsonian's new Steven F. Udvar-Hazy Center retirement home.

In '12, she became the centerpiece of New York's Intrepid Sea, Air, and Space Museum until we nabbed her on her way to a family reunion.

Now it's up to us to beef up Enterprise's life-support, computers, and thrusters, and take her to the Big Cosmic Ball.

I vow to put my shoulder to the wheel to make up for my downtime. Gritch looks skeptical but my stomach feels invulnerable inside the shuttle. I feel a pang of hunger and decide I'd better fill up on Hearn's cooking before I swing a hammer. I excuse myself and promise to be right back.

I throw open the shuttle hatch and take one look at the sea, one whiff of herring. I scramble down the ladder and barely make it to the railing.

CHAPTER TWENTY-TWO: DAMN SPACE HIPPIE

THUNDER WAKES ME—someone pounding on my door. *"What...?"*

Hearns' voice booms, "Arise and greet our astronautical co-conspirators who have made a perilous mid-sea rendezvous with *Potent Bull.*"

The *Potent Bull's* engines are silent. My cabin rocks slowly but my stomach is too empty to care.

"Gritch and Ms. Chin and I await you on deck."

I fumble in the dark for the light switch. Dress fast.. I'm not going to miss this, even with an iffy gut.

On deck, wet air bites cold. Fog greys meager dawn light. Gritch waits, standing a ways away from Heloise, who looks down over the railing. I join him. Ignore the video harlot. Dar vowed to interview Hel about her televised sex show. I'll likely learn more than I care to about Helsex from watching that.

We don't talk. Gritch points down to the fogged lights of a smaller boat tied to the *Potent Bull*. Captain Bougfyuk has delivered: a meeting in mid-sea, well beyond U.S. territorial limits.

We take on board two wooden crates, each about the size of a dumpster, and a dozen smaller crates. We welcome aboard four technicians—specialists in installing rocket engines.

Weeks before we "acquired" Enterprise, Gritch specified and located these engines. He called buddies in the emerging commercial space industry and swore them to secrecy before easing slowly into the details of the deal: he was in the market for rocket engines, in the market cheap and secret. He needed a couple of medium thrusters to move a vehicle into new orbits—what we call the Orbital Maneuvering System (OMS). He needed a bunch of smaller rockets to rotate a ship and to make bitty changes in its speed—the Reaction Control System (RCS). And, oh yeah, he needed all those rocket engines installed in an unnamed space vehicle.

He gave them weight and dimensions of our unidentified rocketship and let them do the obvious math: shuttle. At this point they usually shook their heads and his hand, promised to keep his secret, and wished him luck. And keep out of trouble, ya hear? Wink, wink.

One company didn't spook: AmeRocket Inc. Once Gritch and his pals at AmeRocket reached an understanding, Heloise took a look under the hood and approved of their control hardware and software. As soon as Manuel closed the deal, she started integrating AmeRocket's software into her Enterprise Systems Control software suite.

A key part of our deal with AmeRocket was that they wouldn't deliver the goods to us inside American territory. Some sort of legal BS: exporting military-grade tech, tax evasion, liability and warranty stuff—jaywalking, for all I know.

As the crew hauls the precious containers of rocket tech up on deck Darthy, shows up with her video camera. She gives me a wave and starts to film.

I rush towards her shouting, "Whoa! CUT! Stop!"

She gives me a quizzical look.

I can tell Gritch is pissed at the security breach. I don't want him anywhere near Darthy so when I reach her I'm quick and firm. "Shut that thing off, Darthy. Now. Please."

"But Richard wants…"

"No pictures of the rocket engines. None. Or the techs."

"But…"

I grow a little heated. "What the hell has Head done to you? Show some common sense, Dar. AmeRocket is going way out on a limb for Channel Zilch."

Darthy looks abashed. "Sorry, Mick. Richard—"

"Screw Richard!" The intense emotion upsets more than my tranquility. I've eaten nothing since yesterday's tea, but it wants out now. I sprint to feed the fish.

Everyone but Darthy clears away from me to give me room to hurl. When I'm done, I'm woozy-dizzy. Darthy lets me lean on her as she walks me back to my room.

When she has me cleaned up and tucked in bed, I ask her to stay. I know I'm not going to sleep—just had eighteen hours of shuteye—and I'm not up for another bout of lying in bed feeling sorry for myself. I'm also dying of curiosity.

"How'd the interview with Hel go?"

Darthy lets out a true Darthy laugh—from the gut. "That girl is something else. She wouldn't talk about the Gritch incident at all. She turned the whole interview into an infomercial for her book. Richard was not pleased."

Curiouser. "She's writing a book? About Channel Zilch?"

Darthy rolls her eyes. "Hel's book is something else, believe me. It's filled with erotic equations. Richard is the one who is planning to write the definitive book about Channel Zilch. "

"Ouch. Maybe I better suck up to him."

Darthy finds this amusing. "He's a fine reporter, Mick. Richard's personal likes and dislikes won't enter into it."

I find *that* amusing but don't show it. "So what's Hel writing? Love poems to her computer?"

Darthy almost chokes. "Close, Mick. Scary close. She calls it the ErotoMathematicon."

"Her sex algebra! So Gritch heard right."

Darthy scrunches up her mouth at that, not quite smiling. "She was mean to Gritch. That wasn't right."

"You're telling me. So she screwed Gritch for this book, huh?"

She looks puzzled. "I have no idea why she did that to Gritch. I've known Hel for years and she still stumps me."

I pry, "How'd you two meet?"

"In the Choir." She pronounces Choir with a capital C.

I make a ?-face.

She brushes me off. "We'll talk about that later."

I pry hard, "Now would be a great time to tell Mick a story

about this Choir. I take it you're not talking Third-Lutheran-Church-A-Mighty-Fortress-is-our-Lord-type Choir."

Darthy starts to say something but thinks better of it. "Later, Mick."

"Indulge an invalid." I clutch my throat and fake a cough.

Darthy looks at her watch. "Richard…"

I whine dramatically, "C'mon, Darthy. Tell Mick a little story."

"Words aren't my thing, Mick. How about I go fetch a laptop and my demo reel DVD—show off my video chops."

"If you won't spill the beans on Hel, tell me a story about Darthy Vader. How'd a nice girl like you get sucked into this Channel Zilch foolishness?"

Darthy settles back in her chair. "I always loved rock and roll and rocket ships."

"Damn space hippie." I growl.

Which pleases Darthy. "Space hippie! Guilty as charged."

I put my arms behind my head on the pillow and look at her expectantly. "Go on."

Darthy takes a breath and tells her story, "I was nine years old when Gagarin orbited, fifteen when Sgt. Pepper's Lonely Hearts Club Band lit up my mind, and seventeen when Armstrong moonwalked. I loved Hendrix and the Atlas Booster and The Grateful Dead and Gene Kranz[7] and incense from the poster shop. I owned two lava lamps and a telescope."

I urge her on. "Makes sense to me."

She smiles the best Darthy smile I've seen in days. "It all fit together—space and bongs and rock and roll. I knew that I'd visit the moon someday. I dreamed about retiring to a commune on a space station. I knew that some of my grandkids would grow up without touching the ground."

I chime in, "I can see how you'd get that impression. It only took twelve years from Sputnik to the moon. Did you ever apply for the astronaut corps?"

She scoffs, "Didn't waste my time. In the sixties it was a fundamental law of physics that Americans needed a penis to reach

---

7   The Michael Jordan of NASA Flight Directors. He was a big reason the Apollo 13 crew survived.

escape velocity. I decided to save bucks for my ticket to the moon by shaking the flowers out of my hair and learning a high-paying trade as a videographer. Then Uncle Sam got cold feet and NASA went from space race to snail's pace. Sorry, Mick, but space flight got bogged down in the shuttle era."

I grimace and nod. "As much as I love shuttles I know they are a long, expensive detour from exploring space."

Darthy is rolling now. "When I hit forty I realized that tickets to the moon might not go on sale until after I was dead. I couldn't let that happen. I couldn't let myself die Earthbound."

I butt in, "Your ass-saving fund deal."

"That's right. If the future wouldn't come to me, I would go to the future. Cryonics is the only mode of time-travel presently booking seats. I saved $200,000 to have myself cryonically preserved. A future that can thaw a humansicle should have coach seating to Mars."

I laugh, "Makes perfect sense, if you're a damn space hippie."

Darthy beams. "It does, Mick. Once I had my cryonic nest egg banked I got real, real safety conscious. No way would I risk smashing my precious brain in an accident. I stopped driving a car and wouldn't fly. I spent a lot of time at home listening to Procol Harum and Jefferson Airplane and watching Star Trek and smoking ganja and meditating. And then Heloise Chin comes along with her crazy Channel Zilch scam." Darthy smiles a blinding smile. "I'm going to do it, Mick. I'm going to ride a rocket and orbit the Earth."

I shake my head and say, mock old-man-grouchy, "We're going to have to..." I laugh. "...to find a tie-dyed spacesuit for you."

She squeals with delight. "Please! Now I have to go practice with Richard."

I shake my finger at her. "No shots of AmeRocket tech or personnel."

She nods contritely.

"And watch out with Richard, Dar. I know he's way under your skin, but that doesn't excuse your lapses in judgment. I'm counting on you to rein him in when he pushes things too far."

Darthy nods, not looking at me.

I give her a shot of love to send her on her way. "Now scram. Let an astronaut die in peace, ya damn space hippie."

On our third day at sea, I finally keep my tea down and put in some real work.

While the AmeRocket techs mount their engines, Gritch and I concentrate on making Enterprise airtight.

We're not insane—just determinedly delusional. We know Enterprise could never survive the heat, buffeting, and pressure of reentry. Columbia was clad in real heat tiles and the violence of reentry still killed her. We'll leave the teeny problem of surviving our trip down to the engineers at whatever commercial space entity we hire to haul our sorry asses back to planet Earth.

Blastoff is nowhere near as torturous as reentry, but it can still kill you fast if your spaceship falls apart.

Heat's not a huge threat during the boost phase—by the time we hit escape velocity of 17,000 M.P.H. the air's thinned to nothing. The force of atmospheric drag hits a peak about 20 miles up—Max Q[8]—when the speed is high and the air is thin. That's what we have to fix her up to survive.

We weld aluminum panels to secure the cockpit ceiling where Enterprise sported two flimsy ejection panels in case Crippen and Young, the free-flight test pilots, had to punch out to save their asses. We caulk like crazy with space-rated sealant and run leakage tests. We'd prefer air to stay inside the ship where our lungs can get at it.

To hell with Heloise Chin—I throw myself into getting Enterprise spaceworthy. We all put in long, hard hours.

I dig the intensity of the preparation. It feels like a funky version of the old NASA preflight push. I hang with Gritch and thruster contractors and ship's crew late at night when we're all too bushed to see straight. We guzzle Tang and vodka cocktails, laugh ourselves silly, and turn in for four to six hours of heavy snoring.

---

8   "Max Q is a Houston-based rock band whose members are all NASA Astronauts." –Wikipedia.org
        "Max Q kicks ass. Check 'em on YouTube." –Mick Oolfson, fan.

My nose goes numb to *Potent Bull*'s aroma and I regain a pound or two. Hearn boils up pots of chewy Turkish coffee in the morning to kickstart our brains. He keeps a steady stream of snacks and meals and coffee and more coffee coming our way throughout the day. The man is never happier than watching a famished worker wolf down his grub.

Heloise works as hard as or harder than the rest of us mortals, but she retires to her cabin when she's off-duty. Somewhere inside her psyche, hidden under some rock, she has to be ashamed of her filthy trick on Gritch. She acts brazen about it, tried to embarrass him the first time our paths crossed. She's in her own moral orbit and we don't intersect. We talk business when we do talk, though not all my thoughts are businesslike. Hel deals mostly with the AmeRocket techs because she's got to control the thrusters with her magic cyberboxes.

She starts by installing a rack of servers in the empty computer bay. She spouts cryptic hacker sarcasm about the old shuttle computers. Evidently there has been some progress made in cybernetics in the nearly half-century since Enterprise's systems were built. She mates her precious brainboxes with the AmeRocket thruster. She is supremely happy when she communes with her damned hopped-up adding machines.

Captain Bogfyuk keeps to his solitary habits. I see him once through the wheelhouse window during a late night shuttle-caulking session. I can't make out his features. The light is low and he's a ghostly smudge. I wave, but he doesn't acknowledge me.

Potent Bull sails East with its crew of holy fools.

Somewhere, Captain Tobias Ishwald spends every waking hour hunting my ass.

CHAPTER TWENTY-TWO: DÉJÀ CHEW

ON THE FIFTH WORKDAY of the cruise, I'm taking an involuntary break in the rec room. Heloise ordered Gritch and me to stay below because she wants the deck clear for Enterprise's first live thruster test. It's not fair—Darthy gets to stay on deck to record the test from Hel's safety bunker.

Captain B used the cover of last night to sail us to the edge of a new storm system, safe from the eyes of the satellites and recon planes Ishwald doubtless set on our tail. We're especially vulnerable during the thruster test because we've stripped the black plastic from the shuttle to reduce risk of fire. Enterprise is highly visible on deck in all her buck naked, lily-white glory.

The knuckle-bleaching aspect of this extended rocket test is that we have no blast bunker for it. Best we can do is surround Enterprise's tail with thick steel plates angled up at the sky. If Enterprise explodes, most of the blast goes up instead of sideways. Theoretically. The AmeRocket techs tested all our thrusters back in Arizona, so odds are palatable that none of them will blow.

The beefiest baffle faces the OMS thrusters to deflect the rocket flame skyward. Pumps flood seawater down the deflector to keep it from melting.

Hel cares deeply about our safety, the little darling. Problem is, I never get tired of watching rocket engines fire. Gritch is of the same mind. No way we're gonna miss this show. We've decided to piss Hel off by strolling out on deck when we hear the rockets howl.

We make fake marshmallows out of Styrofoam and stick 'em on straightened coat hangers. Best joke we could come up with in our dog-tired state.

Weather's harsh out there today. Sweat trickles down my chest, steamed by my rain gear. *Potent Bull* keeps skirting the nasty storm—so nasty that Captain B himself is manning the wheel during daylight, sailing us northeast, staying under cover of the bad stuff. Is he chewing on burnt toast and herring?

The AmeRocket techs scrammed by helicopter late last night after they finished a startup test of each thruster, so the rec room is pretty empty. Gritch and I kick back, high on caffeine and sleep deprivation, glugging thick coffee and pigging on fresh-baked peach pie. Eyes drift shut now and then.

Wham, bam! Heloise crashes into the room. She's breathing hard and takes a moment to catch her breath. I take the opportunity to admire her black t-shirt which advertises in large white letters what is evidently a musical ensemble called The Turbogrind Terrorizers—no doubt a bunch of sweet, talented boys on the verge of becoming the next Beatles. What kind of dreck does Hel put in her ears?

Hel takes one last deep breath and all of a sudden she's cranked to full volume. "Butts on deck, white boys!"

Gritch's head snaps back and he goes tight-faced. Heloise does that to him.

I pipe up, peeved, "That test was awful quiet."

"Big trouble. Ishwald trouble. Upstairs NOW!" She snaps back out the door.

We drop our fake marshmallow sticks and hightail after her. She slams open the hatch and we scramble out on deck. The stiff gale almost bowls us over. The deep whine of a strange engine drowns the *Potent Bull's* familiar din. Heloise points straight up.

I look. "Damn."

Gritch, "Shitfire!"

A big blue Navy copter—a Super Seasprite—hovers fifty feet up. A commando with a gun slung on his back dangles from its winch-line. The copter lowers him slowly toward one wing of the Enterprise.

Potent Bull is heeled over, making a sharp turn at speed. The chopper tracks us like it's nailed to the sky. Damn fine flying. Darthy has her videocam trained on the copter, getting some great footage for Ishwald to use at our trial.

A rumble cuts through the chopper noise. An F/A-18A shrieks by at deck level, ruffling the sea. Gorgeous vicious, grimgrey bird. Never thought I'd fear one. I fear it.

I tell Hel. "Game over. Ishwald nailed us."

Hel gives me a scowl and mumbles into a walkie-talkie. She puts her face right into mine and yells. "Boogfyok says we gotta buy him fifteen minutes."

I shake my head emphatically. "Byogfuk talked to you? So what? We're history. Did you see the ordnance hung on that plane? Those bomb-shaped things? The missiles? The NRO must be tracking us with spy sats. Shut down the ship and let the waterboys board us."

Hel grabs the front of my slicker. "You quit? Get your ASS off deck. OUT of my FACE, loser!"

I knock her hand away. "It's over. That's the U.S. Navy up there, not rent-a-cops."

Heloise sneers. "Watch me. You go whimper in the corner."

I'll watch her all right—watch her so she doesn't do something stupid. Gritch sidles up beside me, a what-the-hell-it-was-fun-while-it-lasted grin pasted crooked on his gum-chewing mug.

Boogfyuch's tactic is plain. Steer into the storm, a storm that means nothing to the cloud-piercing eyes of spy sats. Ahead, sea and sky swirl together in awful greys. The chopper swerves and wobbles in a roaring gust and the dangling commando swings in a wide arc.

Heloise crouches and pops an antenna out of her cyber backpack. She slips the pink rhinestone display glasses out of her pocket and over her eyes. Nope, not gonna let her kill the chopper crew. I crouch down beside her and order, "Put that thing away. You're not going to hack the chopper. No one dies to save a damn reality show."

She scorches me with a dismissive glare. "Navy doesn't expose vehicle-control software for remote hacking. This isn't a shit-for-brains magic hacker movie. Just gonna give our friends a little warning."

The Hornet screams by. Its sweet monstrous roar rattles my bowels. That's a Navy plane. The Falcons kicked Navy's ass in football last year so if they know I'm an Air Force Academy grad, we're sunk.

Heloise looks into me. Pushes her screwy pink glasses up her forehead. Her green eyes radiate sincerity. "I gotta try to save Zilch. But no one gets dinged here, okay? I'm still vaguely human. Watch me closely."

Still vaguely human? *Trust* her? I will watch her closely. I look into Heloise's eyes and feel a spark. We connect. Commit. I tell her, "Go for it."

She grins. "One, Mickdude. This be spiffy fun." She flips her glasses down, and her eyes sparkle through the amber lenses. Her graceful fingers spasm messages into the air. It's a game to her. Her voice goes girlish. "Tell me when soldier-on-a-rope swings to one side, even a few meters."

I look up. The chopper hovers precisely overhead. GI Joe dangles twenty feet above the shuttle's wing. A gust sweeps in from the side and swings him wide. "NOW!"

Hel's fingers twitch.

Pumped seawater pours over the baffle. A loud pop, and BOOMROOOAR: the thrilling sound of rocket power in Sensurround. Enterprise surges forward against its cables. *Potent Bull* seems to settle a few yards into the sea. The baffles divert the rocket's torch skyward and the chopper veers sharply away from the geyser of flame and steam, trailing the twirling commando. Heloise looks at me and laughs. Her OMS/RCS test is on and the Navy has been warned.

I run to the railing to look down the length of the shuttle. Beautiful flame roars from the thrusters. The deflector is holding. Steam explodes from flame-broiled brine. Brown-stained blue flame roars raggedly into the grey sky in a billow of white. Darthy focuses her camera on the flames. Gritch grins wickedly and jerks two middle fingers up at the copter.

I hang onto the railing and give thumbs up to Hel. She air-types a command, and the thunder dies.

The chopper hesitates a beat and starts to track back to us. I point into the sky and nod hard to Heloise. She types, and the OMS howls back to life. Chopper skids to a halt and the commando swings toward the torch. I slash a finger across my throat and Hel cuts the thruster. Navy dude swings through air still rippling with heat—but the flame is out. I sag with relief.

Rain starts to pelt the deck. The F-18 screams by, farther off this time. He's not going to sink us. They want Enterprise for their museum, not double-parked next to the Titanic.

The chopper surges toward the front of the ship. Its pilot aims to drop the SEAL on the foredeck in front of the shuttle's nose. I point forward and Heloise looks up to track it.

The chopper slows to fly dead above the bow. I can read what's going through the pilot's mind. Not enough clearance—if he lowers the commando over the front deck his rear rotor will get pummeled by the thruster turbulence.

Potent Bull plunges forward into the angry seas and driving wind; the chopper stays nailed right over the bow.

The pilot rotates his craft so he's flying ass backward. He flies that way for about half a minute, getting a feel for flying in reverse in heavy wind. When the pilot has the touch he sidles his chopper toward the *Potent Bull* well clear of the OMS flame zone.

Flying a chopper backwards in a storm! I'll buy that pilot a pitcher of Jim Beam any day. But right now we have to screw him royally.

Heloise air-types, and a small torch of flame shoots up from one of the RCS thrusters mounted on the nose of Enterprise. Chopper stops, thinks, and inches away. Score another point for Heloise.

A cold lash of rain veils the chopper. When it reappears, it's winching Mr. Commando into its belly, kicking and shaking his fist up at the whirlybird, insanely pissed at not getting to play pirate. I wave at him, and Heloise stands and joins me. Don't see Gritch. SEAL looks down, sees us waving bye-bye, goes rigid. The chopper winches him the last few feet then peels off and ghosts into the grey gale.

A wave hits the side of the ship and slops ice water over us. I yell and Heloise slips and bumps me. I grab her with both arms to balance and she comes in under my radar—green, green eyes blazing up into my face, eyes filled with triumph. She opens her mouth and licks her tongue crudely around her lips in a slow circle. It's an ugly gesture that reaches deep into my circuits. I go hard and dumb.

Her hands flutter below, but not on me. I look down; she's typing into the air again. She opens her coat and her belly lights scroll:

I'M WET. NOW HEAT ME UP.

Hel laughs when I grimace. I let go of her and turn away—hard rain blinds me. She grabs my ear, twists, and hauls my face painfully down to hers, mashes her lips against my numb mouth. I tense with shock, then ease against her to feel it. Her mouth twitches. She's laughing!

I jerk away, mindfucked. I stumble toward the railing to escape her clutch. Branded deep into my heart: Heloise Chin is not human. I turn back to look at her, but can't meet her eyes. I read her t-shirt—Turbogrind Terrorizers—read it again and look away.

So many shades of whitish black.

A dark manshape looms through the rain and swings back into the greys. I grab Hel and point to where he vanished. I shout, "Rambo's back!"

A rift in the rain shows the chopper flying formation with *Potent Bull*. A hundred feet high and twenty feet off our side. The gutsy guy swings on his rope like Tarzan. Ballsy stupid stunt—gotta be a SEAL. He gets on board, it's all over. One SEAL could take down this whole crew without breaking a sweat. And our SEAL is pissed. I bet SEAL-Alumnus Ishwald picked this one out special for his sweet temper.

The copter jukes toward us to give the guy's swing some extra oomph. Where'd that chopper pilot come from? Planet X?

The SEAL swings at us, arms outstretched. Hel and I hustle toward the spot he's swinging for. Hands on the railing—the deck is wicked slick. He snags the top rail with one hand and pulls himself in. We converge on his handhold. Heloise kicks high and smashes his fingers. His hand slips and he swings away.

This whole screwy scene feels like a lame computer game running inside our heads. To make it more unreal, I see Darthy with her camera catching all the action. Did she film the fucked up kiss?

Hel waves me away. That girl's brain is always in gear. Spread out to cover more of the railing. He slows at the far end of his arc. The chopper jukes a couple feet to swing him harder. His return swing aims at the same spot between us.

We meet there and thrust our arms out over the railing to block him. He swoops in fast and big.

A gust slews him to our right. Before we react, he slams into the railing and wraps both arms around it. He swings his leg up and hooks it over the top rail before I get to him. Grab his boot and twist and push.

A frigid wave slams hard and sweeps my legs from under me. I lose my grip, fall sideways against the railing; his arm clamps around my neck. He jerks against my throat and wraps his other arm around, squeezing my neck against the rail. I yell, but it chokes in my throat.

I'm throttled helpless backwards against the rail. Hel runs slow and slower. Things twinkle. Black smears inward from the sides like a high-G blackout. Training kicks in and I clench every muscle to force blood to my brain.

If this is a game, I'm losing bad.

Hel arrives. I admire her slo-mo leg as her boot swings up and taps his ankle. Her boot keeps going and the SEAL's leg flips free, but he's got both arms around my neck and his full weight hangs on my throat. Naptime.

A wave slams hard—wet cold shocks me back to here-and-now and falling. The SEAL's weight hangs from my neck, drags me over the railing. My back is gonna snap. Feet rise off the deck. Railing digs hard into my spine as I slide over the rail. Going over.

Always figured I'd die fast in a bad launch. Don't know how to drown.

Hel tackles my legs and stops my backflip. The weight of the three of us wedges the railing hard between two vertebrae. Looking up at the fierce grey cloud, gritting my teeth and waiting to hear my spine shatter.

The commando's got a stranglehold grip, his head mashed into my shoulder. I jerk my head round to find his face so I can aim a punch.

My eyes lock on his. "Ishwald!"

Tobias howls, "In front of my kids!"

I smash my bare forearm into Ishwald's mouth and rock his face back. He bites and the pain pumps me to frenzy. I punch with my free hand, punch hard into his nose and rear back to....

His arms go slack and slip off my neck, but his teeth stay clenched deep in my forearm. Tension builds, and my ass slips over the railing. I fall back as Ishwald's teeth drag me overboard. Heloise hangs on, arms wrapped around my ankles.

The pain in my arm sears away thought. I shake my arm to stop the bite. Pain goes white and I blank.

A wave sloshes me to consciousness. Cold brine rasps my wounded arm.

I dangle head down to the sea, hanging from knees, kinked painful over the railing. Heloise lies prone on the deck gripping my ankles, keeping me on board with her negligible weight and concentrated strength.

Upside down the chopper is small, Ishwald a livid dangling dot. They smudge in a lash of rain and dissolve into the mad grey.

Gritch leans way over the rail and grabs my belt. Heloise hauls on my ankles, and Gritch pulls me up and over. I'm numb with wet and cold. All I can feel is Ishwald's searing bite. Don't feel a thing as they drag me over the railing.

Darthy's got her camera pointed straight at us.

Boogfyuc sails the *Potent Bull* onward into the dark heart of the storm.

I'm the proud owner of a hole in my arm where Ishwald bit my skin away, twin to his chomp mark on my right.

Heloise Chin chewed another chunk of my heart. And spit it out.

Pure frigging poetry.

CHAPTER TWENTY-THREE: DIRE STRAIT

IF FORCED TO CHOOSE between getting chewed by a dog or a human, go with the mutt. Human mouths are jam-packed with nasty little creatures who love to party in a wound. I hope that before he did his Tarzan act Ishwald brushed his teeth and got current on all his shots.

The *Potent Bull's* infirmary is small but spotless. The PB's medic (and electrician) is a quiet man named Turgay who gets a kick out of working with Darthy on patching the hole in my arm. They agree that the sea water that scorched my arm did me a favor by scouring the wound, and that it would be foolish to stitch up the bite until the risk of infection passes. They numb my arm and clean and bandage it while I look in the other direction and try not to think about Heloise. Or Ishwald. Or Heloise.

A familiar face, Hearn's pal Yeter, leans in from the hallway. "Hearn has for you," he says, and hands a note to Darthy.

Darthy reads in her best faux-Irish Hearn voice, "Please assemble for a Council of War in the dining room at your earliest convenience. Sweets and coffee will be served."

War with Ishwald it is. The Great Shuttle Reunion at The Cape opened today, and despite Ishwald's vow, Enterprise is conspicuously missing from her family get-together.

Sorry, Toby. I'm taking Cinderella Enterprise to her own cosmic party.

Sweets and coffee? My stomach rumbles in a good way. Beating Commando Ishwald burnt some calories.

I've finally come around to appreciating the culinary genius of Lafcadio Hearn. The smell of coffee and pastry that wafts from the dining room propels me through the door. Hearn is at the serving table, doling out plates full of warm apple crisp. Gritch and a few of the crew are already seated and hard at work snarfing their snacks.

"A lavish portion for our near-martyr!" Hearn dishes me a heaping bowl and tops it with custard. My dormant appetite kicks in hard. He shakes his head at my bandaged arm. "I hear the mad snapper made another impromptu meal of a bit of your dermis."

I take my tray with my good arm. "The Captain Tobias Ishwald weight loss plan. He got a good ounce of me this time."

Darthy holds out her tray. "Quite some Council of War you're hosting here."

Hearn says primly, "War is best waged on a full stomach. They also serve who serve dessert. Now who are we missing?"

As I turn to carry my tray of goodies to a table, Heloise enters. My brain tries to feel seventeen emotions at once and goes bonk. "Hi," I say flatly.

Heloise winks at me. "We did it, spaceman. Beat Toby and danced on his grave."

I nod vacantly and carry my tray to Gritch's table. He looks up from scraping his bowl. "Your workin' arm out of commission?"

I say, "They saved the arm. Thanks for your concern, Gritch. Means a lot to me."

He burps loudly. "Can ya swing a hammer?"

I am working on a reply when the door swings open and Richard strides into the room looking like the canary that ate the cat. "Ms. Vader, you outdid yourself, my girl. I reviewed your tapes of Captain Ishwald's abortive raid—breathtaking video of riveting action. Channel Zilch's first broadcast is in the can. Well done, dear."

Darthy stands silent, slowly going pink, not saying a word. She smiles at me and follows Heloise to a table across the room. I'd be nervous, but on the way to the infirmary Darthy swore to me she never saw, much less videotaped, Hel's hellish osculation.

When all are seated, Hearn pulls a sheet of paper from his pocket and clears his throat.

"Captain Bougfiuk congratulates the crew of Channel Zilch for their heroic performance in repelling the would-be pirates."

Gritch butts in, "Ol' Boogys got quite the way with words. Funny how he writes like you talk. He write that?"

Hearn, with all his considerable dignity, "I translate from Turkish with no loss of meaning. I am not an automaton."

Gritch, cranky and exhausted, "Spit it out."

Hearn continues, "Captain B goes on to say that unfortunately Captain Ishwald now knows our boat, our position, our direction, and our speed..."

Where's Heisenberg when you need him?

"...and that by drawing a line from Wallops Island through the point at which he intercepted us, just east of the Azores, Ishwald will discern with certainty that tomorrow night *Potent Bull* intends to smuggle Enterprise through the Straits of Gibraltar."

Gritch is on his feet. "How big's at Strait?"

"Less than eight nautical miles in breadth."

"Captain Itchwad got a day n a half to set up a blockade. Plenty of US Navy ships in Europe to lend a hand. The Captain planning to take a shortcut round Africa?"

Hearn assures us, "Our wise and devious Captain plans no detour. He is a man who relishes a challenge, and your Ishwald has piqued his ire. I assure you in His Name that The *Potent Bull* will sail through the Straits on schedule."

Foolhardy. I raise my hand. The anesthetic is starting to wear off and I feel a throb of pain from Ishwald's bite. I grit my teeth and ask, "I love Tobias dearly, but do we have to gift-wrap ourselves for him? Ishwald knows this ship, knows we've got Enterprise on deck, knows we're headed through the Strait. He's also got spy sats painting a bullseye on us for the Navy."

Hel butts in. "Newsflash, Spaceboy. I just got word that Ishwald's commando fiasco gave the NRO an excuse to pull their spy sats from the hunt."

That puts a big smile on my face. Gritch does his best to remove it. "Ya still ain't told us how we gonna get through the Strait. Itchwad don't need no spy sat to set his Navy ships cross that bottleneck to nab us."

Hearn waves away Gritch's concern. "We shall ride the brunt of our cloaking storm in the black of a moonless night. The *Potent Bull*'s hull type is as common as Honda Civics in the Med. Over two hundred ships a day steam through the Strait and your Navy must now rely on luck to intercept us. Most importantly, our Captain and your Mr. Chin have many powerful friends in this part of the world. May I refresh your coffees before I detail the plan?"

I stare at my empty cup. The room heels hard as a big wave breaks outside. Hope Enterprise is tied down tight. This insane day is catching up with me fast, but I've got to hear what Hearn has to say.

o   o   o

I crash hard after the Council of War and wake the next morning to a raging headache and a throbbing arm. Evidently Ishwald neglected to floss his teeth before he chomped me. Over the next few hours my forearm swells into a giant purple sea cucumber and throbs like hell when I retch. Hearn plays nursemaid. He changes the bandage on my déjà chew, keeps me drugged, tries to force soup into me. No more gross jibes about walrus heinies—I nearly took a lethal dive for smelly old *Potent Bull*. A real hero, me: nearly die being clumsy, and get saved by a girl.

Gritch stops by once during the day to update me on shuttle-fixing progress. It doesn't help that the team makes good progress without me. Bastards. I console myself that in my sorry state I'm doing the mission a favor not to touch a damn thing.

As I lay wasted on Dramamine, antibiotics, morphine, and fever, my mind often wobbles back to Heloise. Belly lights teasing, grinding on top of Gritch, seizing that crude thing that was not a kiss, clinging to my legs as I dangled over the sea. She fucked my mind and then she saved my ass.

Ms. Chin doesn't bother to drop by.

Hearn insists I follow him to the deck, that the rare sight to be seen is well worth the pain, anguish, and travail it will undoubtedly cost me. He swaddles me in warm clothes and a yellow slicker and rubber boots and practically carries me up the last few steps to the deck. The wind is nippy but blowing merely brisk, not a deadly howl. A rip in the clouds exposes a slash of purple sky. Hearn points at a distinctive shape on the horizon.

"Gibraltar?"

Hearn replies, "The Queen's own Rock."

Gritch joins us at the rail. "Oooeee, at's one hell of a pebble."

The setting sun finds a crack in the clouds and paints a gold highlight on the wet flank of Gibraltar. We stand silent for one oscillation of the ship.

Gritch complains, "Hey, where's our storm at? We go through the strait in good weather, darkness ain't gonna cut it as camo."

Hearn reassures, "Our guardian tempest is slated to assail the Straits with renewed vigor within hours. We shall sail through

Hercules' Pillars to the safety of the Middle Sea in the heart of a meteorological tumult."

I'm in no shape to appreciate the view. I register the rock's awesomeness, but it doesn't stir anything in me. Gotta be polite, though. "Beautiful, Lafcadio. Thanks a bunch. You're going to have to carry me..."

Hearn looks at his watch, "Patience, my friend. You yearn to resume your regurgitations, but I can *not* in good conscience allow you to miss this next spectacle."

At that instant the big rock is blotted out and the sky goes black. A mountain has risen from the sea. Hearn points upwards and I see an edge and follow it with my eyes. A rope is thrown down from the sky, and crewmen rush to grab it. *Potent Bull* is dwarfed by a humongous oil tanker with not a light alight.

I ask in genuine awe, "Powerful friends?"

"Indeed," says Hearn, with supreme satisfaction.

As much as I want to see what happens next, I'm just not up to it. Hearn helps me below and I crash hard for a few hours.

The *Potent Bull*'s growling engines shake me from a dream I won't bore you with. I'm tired of being useless. The scrap of sleep sets me up enough to venture on deck to see how the "plan" is coming. I finally discover the arcane secret to finding my way up to the deck (follow the EXIT signs, duh.)

I grab a yellow rain slicker but can't find rubber boots. Once I take a step onto the deck, I realize the slicker is three sizes too small. My pants and shoes soak through in seconds.

The cold wet gale clears my head. The mountainous tanker looms not twenty yards off the *Potent Bull*'s starboard, surging forward through the waves, every light lit, blazing like a refinery. The pelting rain is a luminous cloud round the tanker.

Potent Bull is blacked out, hiding in the visual and radar shadow of our powerful friend. The tanker plows through the rolling waves while *Potent Bull* rides each one. The tanker's glow makes it easy to see on PB's deck, but from any distance through the rain, the *Potent Bull* would be a blemish on the hull of our gargantuan escort.

When I look away from the tanker for a moment, my eyes adjust and I see a handful of tiny, dimly lit ships through the cold rain. Which ones are US Navy?

The gale makes the night unfit for flying, although I wouldn't put it past that hotshot Navy chopper pilot.

I make my way forward to see Enterprise. I see the unbelievable pile of orange and stop to take it in.

Enterprise lies buried under huge coils of plastic colored a particularly urgent wavelength of emergency orange by the tanker's sodium lights. The plastic is a soft tube about large enough to crawl through, partially inflated so that the shape of Enterprise is obscured under the wobbling mass.

Gritch splashes up to me, wearing a yellow raincoat with a shit-eating grin on his face. "Got us some camouflage and a travelling buddy."

I goggle at the orange mass. "Camouflage isn't the word you want here, Gritch, unless we're planning on hunkering down in the entrails of a blue whale with jaundice."

"Whatever, Webster. Point is, once we're in the Med no fly-over recon photo gonna show Enterprise."

I say, "No, just a *Potent Bull*-sized ship with an Enterprise-sized emergency orange mound on her deck. That should baffle 'em."

Gritch sniffs pityingly. "Ain't you the gloomy Gus? Ever figure our foreign friends here maybe have more'n half a brain? Mericans ain't cornered the market on smarts, ya know. Hearn tells me that tomorrow half the ships our size sailing the Med gonna have orange piles a boom on their deck. Ol Chin and Capn Boogers got some dedicated buddies."

I ask, "How's Enterprise taking all this?"

Gritch lights up. "Shoulda seen the slick operation to cover her up. The crew on the tanker lowers this plastic orange boom over the side and our crew start coiling it over the shuttle. I lend a hand to make sure we leave room to get at the shuttle hatch."

I smile. "And to make sure they don't scratch your precious shuttle."

"Bet your candy ass. They was gonna climb right on up the shuttle bay door till I cussed em out. So we get the shuttle all wrapped up in about half mile of that boom. The last of it drops down on deck and they lower a work crew with some paint tech I never seen before. Repainted our hull and superstructure down to the water-line the same ugly orange color as our big buddy's hull. Ship don't look a thing like the *Potent Bull* ol Itchwad got a gander at."

I feel a tap on my shoulder, and I turn to stare into the lens of Darthy's video cam. She says, "Smile, Mick. I'm going to shoot lots of good footage tonight."

"Where's Head?"

Dar looks away and back. "I had to give him a sleeping pill. He had a hard day." And, brightly, to change the subject, "Look who's here!"

Lafcadio Hearn looms out of the rain. "Our hero walks! Splendid, I can't wait to put some meat on your bones. Ms. Vader, I hope you'll forgive my lack of television makeup. You caught me unprepared for my cameo."

Darthy films him quietly.

I point out to sea at the dim ship lights. "How many of those are Navy boats looking for us?"

Hearn replies dismissively, "The chance of interception on a night like this is scant. While riding in the shadow of our copious friend we are as safe as at Ma's pap."

On cue, a blinding shaft of light stabs out of the storm, lighting *Potent Bull* starkly. A hellaciously-amplified voice blasts through the waves and rain. "HAUL UP AND PREPARE TO BE BOARDED."

Gritch yells, "Suck a duck! Ats a Mark V Special Ops Craft! Ishwald done sicced em SEALs on us again."

I look up at Hearn. He looks troubled for a breath, then smiles a broad smile. "A challenge our Captain shall relish. Watch the master work his magic."

Gritch says disgustedly, "Them V's got 50 calibers can cut *Potent Bull* in half."

Hearns reassures us, "They will most certainly not fire when a tanker full of oil looms behind us."

Darthy pans from the craft to our little group, weaving her video magic. Makes me a tad self-conscious, but I guess I better get used to the fact that the most stressful moments of my life are now media fodder for the masses.

I play my part of Nordic pessimist. "But they nailed our tanker buddy's ID. Navy's gonna come down hard on that ship."

Hearns smiles a broad smile that ripples down his wet beard and points up at our companion's bow. "An old seafaring tradition—masquerade."

And painted in large white letters on the tanker's orange bow: "YOUR MOMMA."

Hearns continues, "Identifying features of the superstructure have been altered, transponder falsified. Unless the Navy boards her she will retain her anonymity."

The tanker surges forward into the storm, and *Potent Bull's* engines roar louder to match her burst of speed. The gale kicks up a notch and I lean forward into the shelter of Hearns' towering bulk. My legs and feet can't get any wetter.

The bright light of the Navy boat falls behind and dims in the rain. Can't be that easy.

Gritch splutters through dripping lips, "They just give up? No way. Let's go keep an eye on that boat."

Hearns, Gritch, and I, trailed by Darthy plying her camera, walk to the stern in single file. I keep a firm grip on the slick railing and pause a beat at the spot where I nearly took a dive in Ishwald's arms. My arm throbs in memory.

Darthy asks, "Watcha thinking? Care to tell the viewers."

I shake my head and move on. My head is clear and I don't wobble as I follow Hearns and Gritch through the pouring rain.

As we reach the back of the ship, the lights of the Navy craft show that it's swinging in behind us. Hearns laughs. "A stern chase. I can predict with certainty our Captain's answer to that maneuver."

Gritch and I look up at him, but Hearns shakes his head. "Watch and learn." He points across the stern deck to where a gang of crewmen emerge carrying something bulky and soft.

Gritch shouts into the wind, "Bet the Navy's gonna get close and fire their fifties at our screws leavin us dead meat in the water."

Hearns' face clenches with concern. "I must tell the crew to hurry. This tactic is most often used for stern chases when a lightly-armed pursuer is within shouting range." Hearns surprises me with his speed as he runs to confer with the waiting crewmen.

The Navy craft's lights are faint smudges through the bucketing rain. Outrun them?

Gritch stomps on that hope. "Hearns better hurry. Mark V's got fifteen knots speed on the *Bull* easy."

The pursuer's lights sharpen and shine perceptibly brighter. And brighter.

The SEALcraft's Voice of God booms, "CUT YOUR ENGINES AND PREPARE TO BE BOARDED." A New England accent—not Ishwald. The spotlight gets steadily brighter and the amplified voice louder, "THIS IS YOUR LAST WARNING. CUT YOUR ENGINES!"

A large door opens beside the crewmen and Hearns. Two crewman push a dolly bearing a crate the size of a fridge. Hearns makes a sweeping arm gesture to urge them on. One of them pops open the front of the crate, and a mass of ropes and shiny baubles, glass fishing floats, spills out.

A hissing sound from the scrum of crewmen, and a red weather balloon is inflated to the height of a child. A crewman ties off the balloon and ties it to the mass of rope. Two crewmen grab the rope and begin feeding it over the railing. They inflate another balloon and attach it further down the rope as it is fed over the side, dragging the balloon from view. The *Potent Bull* turns sharply away from the tanker as the crew keep up their laying of the trap.

A burst of blazing tracers zip overhead followed by the clamor of heavy gunfire. Oh shit, oh shit!

"STOP YOUR ENGINES!"

My knees go weak. As stated prev., I am allergic to fast bits of metal.

Darthy exults, "Got it on vid. Tracers in the rain should look sweet onscreen."

Gritch says gloomily, "A little closer and they shoot out our damn screws. You watch."

Captain B swerves the *Bull* back toward the tanker as the crewmen keep feeding rope and the occasional balloon over the side, leaving a scalloped curve of cable in the path of the pursuer.

The silhouette of the Navy craft emerges from the driving rain as it encounters the first balloon. Its voice squawks, "CLEAR THAT TRASH!" Quad 50 calibers spit fire down into the water. Tracers obliterate the balloon. The sea around its bow becomes a boiling cauldron lashed by bolts of flame.

The *Potent Bull* swerves steadily from side to side and the trap-laying crewmen don't miss a beat.

Out of the corner of my eye I see Hearn approaching. Gritch calls out to him, "Old Boogy done met his match. Them 50 cals gonna chop up his puny little tripline."

Hearns closes his eyes and smiles beatifically. "Highly doubtful. Even if a lucky bullet hit the cable, it is made of tough stuff which, once it wraps around our pursuer, will tangle his props. Let us enjoy the next few minutes." He leans on the stern railing and Gritch and I turn back to watch. Darthy keeps her camera trained on the deadly fireworks in the rain.

Gritch, "It better work quick or they'll be within shootin range of our prop."

The Mark V surges on, tracers lancing down from its nose in a sweeping pattern through the balloons and floating cable. Its spotlight kicks in and I blink my eyes against the glare.

The spotlight jerks to the side and a clattering racket overpowers the sound of the 50's. "CUT THE... *SHIT!*" The craft wobbles, and the racket shifts into a high-pitched snarl.

Hearns laughs.

SCREE-BOOM!—something in the craft's drive train fails. Silence, but for the storm and *Potent Bull*. The crew cheers, and Gritch lets out a whoop. The lights of the stalled pursuer dim, fade, disappear.

I shake my head and smile up at Hearn. "Gotta hand it to you guys."

Hearn looks quite smug. "Apology accepted. Now let us get you below. Warm sheets and a steaming rum toddy will hasten deep and dreamless sleep."

I assure him. "I'm over the worst. I could use a good sleep, but my arm is feeling vaguely human again. I'll take you up on the nightcap, though. And a hot basin of water to thaw out my toes."

Gritch scowls over the railing into the dark storm. "Fore you two party better looky here. Looks like our buddies done untangled their prop."

A dim light suddenly flares through the storm as the pursuing craft surges after us.

Hearn says with feeling, maxing his Irishness, "Divil hound all SEAL gobshites. Captain B will sort those gammy gits."

Gritch says, "Them SEALs is gonna do the sortin. Captain B planning to outrun em?"

Hearn answers, "Sailors capable of beating our Captain are rarer than rockinghorse turds. Watch and learn from the master."

We watch silently as the pursuing craft's lights draw nearer and the dim outline of the boat emerges once more from the dark rain. Our oil tanker companion keeps pace beside us, doing us no good because the pursuer's guns are behind us and can riddle PB without hitting its oil-filled hull.

Light flickers as tracers lance from the nose of the craft into the water behind us.

Gritch groans, "They gettin our range. Gonna take out our props."

The twin streams of tracers chew up the water behind us, walking toward our stern. The falling rain glows brighter as 50-caliber slugs roil the water closer and closer.

Lafcadio starts to laugh and I turn to see what's up. He's looking away from our pursuer with a face full of glee. I follow his eyes and see a huge, well-lit ship loom from the rain, leaving a gap for *Potent Bull* to squeeze between her hull and our tanker's.

Gritch takes in the sight and says, "Squeeze play, huh? Too bad our SEAL buddies' boat's smaller n the *Bull*. They just follow on right behind us."

The tracers stop as our pursuers take in the sight of the fast-approaching ship. Booms and nets hang high over the sides of the ship, some sort of factory fishing trawler.

Hearn repeats with relish, "Learn from the master."

"Our Navy buddies ain't slowin a hair," Gritch retorts.

I turn to watch our pursuer gain as we rush toward the trawler. As it closes the distance, we enter a steel canyon: tanker pacing us on our left, trawler passing us on our right. *Potent Bull* bucks in the turbulent waters— horrendous din of storm and waves and engine noise. Sagging nets pass over us as *Potent Bull* keeps its course.

I look up just in time to see a net shake and the first fish begin to fall. Gritch yells, "WHOEEE! It's rainin herring!"

The *Potent Bull* surges forward, and a sprinkle of glistening fish hit the water right behind us. The net sags, parts, and the sky behind us fills with falling fish. The 50-calibers lance skyward into the falling mass but go silent as tons of dead fish bury the pursuing SEALs. The small craft founders, piled high with fish, and then it's gone in the dark rain as *Potent Bull* plows onward.

No one speaks as we watch the trawler disappear behind us into the storm. Finally, Gritch pushes back from the railing, looks at me hard, and shakes his head. "That 50 cal just made it rain fish guts."

"It'll look great on video," Darthy enthuses. "Tracers lighting up a torrent of sparkly wet fish. I'm heading straight to the studio to look at this on a decent monitor."

Hearn smiles smugly and says to me, "Your hot toddy awaits."

Gritch busts in, "'Fore you two do your pat-yerseff-on-the-back polka think on this. That boat we just buried in sardines is onna radio right now giving ol Itchwad our GPS coords and make, model, and color of *Potent Bull* and our big buddy tanker. Ishwald gotta have more'n that one dinky Special Ops craft on our ass. Bet a bigger and nastier Navy vehicle is headin right at us."

Hearn listens quietly. "I assure you that our Captain is cognizant of that possibility and is taking steps."

The *Potent Bull* heels hard to port and the tanker slowly turns away from us.

Hearn breathes satisfaction. "As I foretold. Captain Byugfoc is taking steps."

The storm-roiled water between the tanker and the *Bull* stretches wider. As the tanker recedes into the rain, its lights go black. Within seconds its dim outline is erased by the storm. *Potent Bull* sails alone into the Med.

Hearn: "By morning our big friend will have a different name and look quite different abovedeck."

I wave a thanks.

Gritch, "Cut me in on that nightcap. Gonna need it. Bet ya pennies to pig nuts ol Itchwad ain't thoo with us yet."

CHAPTER TWENTY-FOUR: CALM SEAS AND A FOLLOWING BREEZE

HEARN'S HOT RUM TODDY goes down and stays down. I know you probably can't get enough details about my nausea, but my stomach finally gets its sea legs. My arm is sore but healing. I try to sleep, but my head is full of tracers and tankers and Tobias Ishwald. For once Heloise doesn't make the cut.

I manage a few hours of shuteye. My eyes pop open at some ship noise and I can't get back to sleep. After twenty minutes of tossing and turning I get out of bed, do a bunch of pushups to get the corpuscles humming, dress and head deckside. I grab a slicker and boots, but when I open the door the sea is calm and only a light drizzle falls. The clouds are barely lit by the dawn sun.

The deck is empty. I walk to the railing and look out onto the dimly-mottled sea. A few distant shiplights. Which ones are Ishwald's eyes looking for us?

I've gotta see Enterprise. When I round the corner, the orange mound towers over the deck. Details I didn't catch last night—cords tied over the bundle to keep the wind from unraveling the lightweight boom; a three-foot diameter plastic corrugated tube big enough to crawl through poking from bottom of the pile.

I knew that Gritch would leave some sort of access to Enterprise—there's work to be done. Way past time for me to lend a hand.

The long tube is dark and winding but fun to crawl through in a grade-school-haunted-house kind of way. A worklight at the end of the tunnel illuminates the ladder to Enterprise's access hatch.

I climb and find the hatch open to let electrical cords in. I bend low for the circular opening and feel a pang of shuttle-nostalgia as I crawl through the portal.

The middeck of Enterprise is dimly lit by a single weak bulb. Gritch wasn't shitting about the progress they made without me. The walls and ceiling of middeck are stripped to the metal. Evidently Gritch is keeping the stock off-white flooring. The shape of the middeck space is familiar from days spent in orbit and years spent in sims.

Flightdeck is what I want to see. I climb up the temporary ladder, smiling already. It's dark at the top. I know Gritch—he's thorough—so I feel around and find the switch within easy reach. I flip it and a bank of lights flare like high noon.

"AlIIeeeSHHHEEEEIT!" Gritch lurches upright in the CDR's chair.

"Sorry, Gritch. Didn't know you were..."

"Ain't no sorry about it. Ya caught me sleepin in. Shoulda been up hours ago." Gritch hops out of the chair and stretches. "Gotta get going on the wiring. The crazy lady got me to gree to put in a new data port on middeck. Says she's gotta talk to some damn computers in the bay."

I bet Gritch got all of three hours sleep last night. You get used to that at NASA.

I ask about details and Gritch responds. Before you know it we're deep in the intense familiar feel of mission prep.

If you want to be a happy astronaut you better like mission prep, because most of an astronaut's career hours are clocked in cramming and practicing for the next mission or supporting another crew's prep.

I only hear the klaxon because Gritch and I are quietly tracing through a wiring diagram. It's got to be a loud one to cut through the pile of boom and Enterprise's hull.

Gritch slams the binder shut and barks, "Ishwald! Hop it."

He's down the ladder and I'm right after him.

When we emerge from the crawltube the deck is hopping with Zilchonauts and PB crew. Most of them are lining the railing so we hustle to take a look. I squeeze in beside Darthy who's attached to Head.

Darthy points, "We've got company."

A small sailboat sailing at right angles to our path.

"*Potent Bull* can't outrun a sailboat?"

Darthy points more emphatically. "Just beyond that to the left. Hearn says the Captain picked up a big, fast ship on radar. It's heading our way."

I see a tiny grey fleck nearly at the horizon. I watch long enough to see it grow. Doesn't take long—that sucker has some serious velocity on it, and it's headed straight at us.

Gritch has binoculars trained on our pursuer. "Atsa US Navy destroyer. This year's model—Burke Class. Crammed full of missiles n long guns n Gatling cannons n paid killers."

Richard Head gasps. Darthy turns to him. "I'll fetch the cam."

Head replies in a devastated voice, "Don't waste my time. A destroyer hunts us. Your camera will be destroyed. We will be destroyed. It's over. Excuse me." He heaves a wrenching sigh, turns, and walks away.

Darthy gives me an anxious look. "I'm going to fetch the cam."

I add, "And check on Richard."

She nods and hurries away.

Hearn, further down the railing, is talking to a scrum of crew. Gritch grabs my arm and we join them.

Hearn switches from Turkish to address us, "Don't be unduly alarmed, gents. Captain Boogf..."

Gritch interrupts, "Booger's gonna try the tripline on a destroyer. Somepin tells me that little gag ain't gonna..."

Hearn, "Our Captain is a man of many gags. We are entering the Sea of Alboran, notorious for eating ships with its savage shoals and submerged rocks and ravenous sea monsters. Our Captain came of age in these waters."

Gritch spits over the railing. "So we skulk in there while the whole US Navy throws a cordon around the area. We gonna blow up all them weather balloons and float The *Bull* to Russia?"

Hearn laughs, "I'm surprised you don't offer to fire up your Enterprise's rockets and lift *Potent Bull* to safety."

Gritch likes that image; a crooked smile wriggles out despite his best effort to stay pissed. He snorts wryly, "We runnin short on propellant after Mizz Chin done tried to fry Itchwad. Otherwise Mick'd fire up Enterprise and blast us all off to the mooOOn. Ain't at right?"

But I'm watching the distant grey ship get less distant by the second. Details emerge—a white V of foam peeling from its bow, little lethal bumps on the top. I imagine Ishwald standing on the bow leering at me through binoculars, already digesting his victory. Hope Captain Boogphyk's got a corker up his sleeve.

Our engine downshifts dramatically and the deck wind dies as *Potent Bull* slows.

Gritch, "Bout what I figgered. A US Navy destroyer on your ass even Capn Boogums gotta pull over."

Hearn gestures to a floating red barrel. "That buoy marks the boundary of a shallow shoal of jagged rocks called Dientes de la Muerte—Teeth of Death. Even our Captain must sail slowly to thread his way among the sunken hazards. The chase is over. A larger ship than *Potent Bull* cannot clear the rocks."

With *Potent Bull* slowed to quarter speed the destroyer surges closer with a vengeance. Gritch is able to read the name—"USS Hopper"—before it slows down violently with a great sploshing of propwash and lumbers to a halt about a quarter mile away.

Potent Bull putts slowly away from the immobile Hopper.

Gritch looks up at Hearn and grouses, "So Mr. Destroyer gonna shadow us, keep us on radar till we come out the other side a these rocks. Don't see what pissin off the US Navy is gonna buy us."

Hearn strokes his beard over and over. I've never seen Lafcadio nervous but that's how it reads. He doesn't say a thing, which says a lot. Not good.

Hearn brightens with purpose. "I shall make buckwheat pancakes for breakfast. Expect a steward within the half hour to announce the feast." He looks straight at me when he says, "I shall break out my private stock of maple syrup."

I can hear the promised wolf howling in my gut. I hungrily watch Hearn make his way toward the door to belowdeck.

I don't like being a passenger in the middle of a crisis. I'm fit and ready to act, but my only choice is to put my hands in my pockets and ride the ride. Better go wave bye-bye to that destroyer.

Hearn lets out a whoop. "You gave me a shock there, Richard!"

I turn back. Richard Head is standing in the doorway carrying a large suitcase. He doesn't acknowledge Hearn, steps out onto the deck and carries his luggage to the rail. Darthy follows. She's got her cam but it hangs dead from a shoulder strap. All her concern is focused on Richard.

Crew parts to let Richard make his way to the railing. He sets down his suitcase and sits on top of it and seems content to stare at the sea.

I look again at the destroyer and am delighted at how it's dwindled. It's sweet to have perspective on our side as we sail slowly away—the destroyer shrinks until it's hard to take seriously as a threat. Gritch keeps his binoculars zeroed on it. He's been a worry wart the past couple of days so it doesn't shake me to my core when he yells, "ZODIAC!"

I squint my eyes to try to see it. "What are you...?"

Gritch shouts to the crowd, "Suckers launched a Zodiac inflatable. It's scootin our way fast."

A crewman yells that he sees it and then another. I finally make out the tiny craft bouncing over the water. It closes with us at a mighty clip.

Richard bellows, "I SURRENDER! I GIVE UP! I WAS KIDNAPPED!" He's stripped to the waist waving his white shirt above his head.

The crew looks uneasily from the crazy man to the oncoming boat which is undoubtedly filled to the brim with pissed-off SEALs.

Darthy stands behind Head, whispering into his ear. She says the right thing because Richard sags, drops his white shirt, and sits heavily on his suitcase, bare-chested and defeated. Darthy leans towards him and shakes something from a bottle into his hand. He pops the pills into his mouth and chews.

Darthy grimaces and then sees me watching this transaction. She mouths silently at me, "MEDICATION." I nod and fake a smile. Head shivers, and Darthy whips off her jacket and drapes it over his shoulders. I look away, not happy I just saw that, back to the Zodiac.

I don't know where she came from, but suddenly Heloise is here. Gritch and Heloise and I huddle, embarrassments forgotten.

Gritch, "Whata we got can slow em down?"

Hel, "Enterprise's thrusters won't hold off a boat."

Me, "Too bad we used up all the balloons and floating line."

Gritch, "Anybody got a shower of fish handy? C'mon. Whata we got...?"

We think it together. Gritch says, "You thinkin...?" just as I jerk my thumb back toward Enterprise. Hel is already running full tilt to grab the orange boom.

Hel yells back over her shoulder, "Darthy Vader, get to work—show time, grrrlio!"

I yell to Gritch, "Line up the crew to feed the boom over the stern." I take off after Heloise. When I get to the mound of orange she's already sawing at one of the restraining cords.

She yells, "Pull the boom free. Get it started. I'll cut cords." She hacks the first cord apart and plastic boom slithers out over us. I grab a loop with both arms and haul it away from the mass. Hel cuts cords.

The boom resists. I put my legs and back into pulling on it but it's wrapped around something. My arm starts to throb hard. I yell to Gritch, "I need a couple more hands."

Hel cuts the last of the cord on this side of Enterprise as three crewmen arrive. One of them slices through the looped plastic tube so we can tug on one end. Together we yank the boom free—it unravels quickly from the great orange pile—and haul it down the deck to the waiting line of crew. Gritch has spaced them every few feet along the twenty yards to the stern. The first hands grab the boom and feed it hand over hand down the line.

I let go, winded and glad to let the *Potent Bull*'s crew do the work. Heloise sprints past on her way to the stern. Doesn't say a thing. Ok—I sprint after her. Gotta see this.

As I make it to the stern and join Heloise at the rail a megaphonic voice booms, "HALT TO BE BOARDED!" The voice of—who else?—Captain Tobias Ishwald! "I REPEAT. STOP YOUR ENGINES AND PREPARE TO BE BOARDED!"

Darthy arrives, camera blazing. She leans over the rail and draws a bead on the Zodiac, which zooms up fast.

The leading edge of the boom has reached the stern. Heloise runs over to confer with the crew at the railing. She gestures and they start to coil it on the deck.

The Zodiac zooms closer and Ishwald is visible, bullhorn hiding his face.

"IT'S OVER, OOLFSON! HAUL UP AND LET US BOARD!"

Two other SEALs in the Zodiac, which pulls into the shadow of the *Potent Bull* and throttles down to close the last dozen yards.

"OOBLICK!" yells Heloise—the crew pitches the coiled pile over the railing.

Ishwald drops his bullhorn and stares up in disbelief at the tangled orange boom plummeting from the sky. He raises his arms to shield himself from the mass as it envelops the Zodiac. Where the Zodiac was is a snarled heap of orange, wiggling in the middle where the three SEALs struggle.

"PULL! PULL!" yells Hel to spur the crew to keep feeding boom over the stern. The pilot of the Zodiac kills its engine and *Potent Bull* starts to pull away.

Darthy leans way out over the railing, immortalizing the whole fiasco for Ishwald's memory book.

Ishwald pops up from the plastic mess and starts heaving boom off the Zodiac. Hel and her work crew keep it spilling off the stern to coil on the open water.

"Richard!" Darthy's startled voice startles me.

Head's voice is strong, "Film this, my dear." He steps to the railing and waits for Darthy to frame and focus him. The boom crew grinds to a halt as even Hel gives Richard her full attention.

Head angles his face toward the sea and says in his bravest voice, "Captain Tobias Ishwald, it is I, Richard Head, who defeats you!" Richard looks toward the camera and brandishes a gun toward the sky!

I yell, "No!" and start to run at him. Gritch grabs my sleeve and says, "Flare gun. Let him be. Gonna see some fireworks."

Heloise yells at her crew to keep feeding boom. I've got to watch the Richard Head Show. Head barks a cryptic command at Darthy and she moves back from the railing to get both Head and dwindling Ishwald in the frame.

Richard turns toward the sea and roars, "Eat flaming death!" He waits a beat and then lowers the flare gun and sights it at the entangled Zodiac. Before I can shout, Head pulls the trigger—BLOOP!—and the flaming orange flare flies straight and true into the center of the orange mass.

Richard raises his gun and blows the smoke from its barrel. He turns toward Darthy, smiling broadly. "Captain Tobias Ishwald will not imperil Channel Zilch's mission. Richard Head took up arms..."

I let Richard rave to the camera. His flare didn't do a thing. A second SEAL emerges from under the heap of boom and starts working with Ishwald to untangle their craft.

Hel's gang keeps feeding boom overboard but if that Zodiac cuts free it can scoot around and over it. I try to remember tips from pirate movies on repelling boarders. Must complain to Hearn about the shortage of cutlasses and flintlock pistols.

The third SEAL struggles free, yelling something lost in the wind. He pushes a mass of boom over the side of the craft and jumps into the sea. A puff of black smoke wafts from the craft and thickens instantly into a spewing cloud. As boom slithers over the side of the craft, the bright red flame of the flare lights up the smoke. More yells and Ishwald and the other SEAL jump overboard.

The explosion is small but loud. Something fast and metal ricochets off the *Potent Bull*'s hull and we all hit the deck. All except Richard, who stands looking over the railing triumphantly.

Hel's work crew are all as prone as I am. Face down on the deck, I can't see the Zodiac. A second small BOOM! and smoke billows into the sky. I inch forward, not putting weight on my Ishwald-bit arm, and when I get to the edge, look down.

The center of the orange boom pile is blazing, sending greasy smoke boiling into the sky. Darthy crawls up beside me, and without saying a word aims her cam at the flaming craft. The heads of the three SEALs bob in open, choppy waters well away from the fire.

Gritch says from above. "Ya can stand up. Look at ol Ishwald swim! Hey, Oolfson—NURR NIH... NURR NIH..." The Jaws theme song, droll.

The SEALs are swimming flat out to grab the boom floating near the burning Zodiac. One by one they reach it and latch on. Darthy continues to point her cam at the receding wreckage. Richard stands beside her, looking rather proud. He's got to go.

I turn to get a glimpse of Heloise. She is leaning against the railing, watching Ishwald and co. dwindle in the distance. I learned again today that when you need her, Heloise is there.

I say to Hearn, "About those pancakes..."

Darthy and Richard are missing from the feast. I put that issue to one side and stuff myself to bursting with Lafcadio's amazing hotcakes.

"Don't tell my Aunt Margaret, but these are the best I've ever eaten."

Hearn looks immoderately pleased at my compliment. "Mum's the word. Good to see your stomach finally doing justice to my art."

He addresses the diners. "I urge you all to take a stroll on deck. I have been told that there is a sight well worth the seeing."

When we emerge on deck the sea is packed with ships—ships the size and shape of *Potent Bull* with dull orange hulls and mounds of orange boom coiled high on their deck. Somehow a freaking flotilla of decoy ships surround us as we sail away from the setting sun.

Gritch is high as a kite on the spectacle. "I count nine boats lookin just like ol *Potent Bull*. Talk about powerful friends!"

Two *Potent Bull* clones pull abreast on either side and the flotilla eases to a stop. Gangplanks sprout and a swarm of workers descend on *Potent Bull*. In under an hour The *Potent Bull*'s hull is painted a dull blue, the incriminating orange boom is whisked away, and one of the boats uses a loading boom to stack shipping containers around Enterprise, hiding it from view.

After the work crews go back to their ships, the flotilla sets sail. The PB clones slowly diverge from our path.

Heloise stands with Hearn, smiling wide at our dispersing flotilla of clones. Gritch and I join them at the railing and try to make sense of the scene.

"This costing somebody millions," says Gritch. "Can't see Capn Boogs payin for it."

Hearn admits, "This display is beyond the power of even our good Captain to conjure."

"Pocket change to Pops," jokes Hel.

I'm still baffled. "Your Dad isn't this rich. He's got less than four mill sunk in Channel Zilch."

Gritch snorts, "Saved him a bunch by rentin a fired astronaut."

I watch Heloise as I ask, "How does a merchant from Minnesota organize a *Potent Bull* impersonators convention in the middle of the Med?"

"Pops is tight with God."

"God?"

Hearn gestures grandly in a sweeping arc at the receding clone ships. "Behold the handiwork of Merzifon Karabuk, as close to a deity as you'll find in this unholy middle sea."

CHAPTER TWENTY-FIVE: ISTANBUL, CONSTANTINOPLE

GRITCH ASKS, "You fit to swing a hammer, Mick?"

I want to say yes, but I know my limits. "Give me one good night of shuteye and I'll turn in an honest day's work tomorrow."

"At'll be a first."

Hearn tut-tuts, "Lay off the boy, Mr. Neubart. He needs some few days more of dedicated gorging. Mick is a wisp of a boy. The merest breeze will waft him from the ship."

Gritch will have none of it. "He's young. He'll bounce back quick. I need him bad. Running behind schedule."

Nice to be needed. "What's next to on the task list?"

"Got the high-cap carbon air filters to plumb in. If the damn thing works you guys won't have to suffocate on your own farts and b.o."

"I'll see you in the morning, hammer in hand."

Gritch smiles and spits a loogee of chewing gum juice over the side.

Hearn shakes his head. "I do so loathe an emaciated man. An affront to my culinary genius."

I head to bed. Tomorrow I work.

I sleep soundly and wake to a light tap on my shoulder. Hearn leans over me bearing a tray. The smell of muffins and coffee. I reflexively push the tray away but feel an unfamiliar pang. "Give me a shovel, I'm starved."

We get solid work done during the two days we sail in the Med. We gain back twelve hours on Gritch's schedule.

We're in the Aegean, sailing by the island of Lesbos at dusk when Ishwald nails us again. Replay: a Navy F/A-18A buzzes us three times at sea level. This action movie stuff is getting tiresome. I used up this month's allotment of adrenaline about a month ago.

Hearn gathers Gritch, Heloise, Darthy, and me together to give us the lowdown from Captain Boogfyuik. Even Head shows up. It's the first time I've seen Heloise for days. I ration myself to a brief pang before tuning in to Hearn's voice.

"Our good Captain has done me the signal honor of appointing me to read a message pertaining to our course of action."

Gritch, tired, says, "Spit it out."

Hearn rolls his eyes theatrically. "The Captain has seen fit to share his plans with us. He could just as well have kept us in the dark."

"Spit it out."

Hearn gives Gritch a look. "Ahem. As it is evident that Ishwald has divined our destination—Istanbul and the Dardanelles passage—we shall divert to a covert port mere hours from our present position. Our revised destination is a shipyard on the Turkish coast. It occupies an artificial harbor near the delightful and historic port of Ayvalik." He looks around as if seeking approval.

"That's it?" says Hel. "That's the plan? We get arrested in Ayvalik instead of Istanbul? A higher class jail there?"

Gritch yawns. "We gonna shoot all the dockworkers to keep em quiet? Capn Bugfuck's quite the genius."

Hearn, patiently: "It is owing to your Manuel Chin that we can avail ourselves of this option. His good friend Merzifon Kara-buk is a mogul of the tanker refitting industry. His shipyard is comprised of not a few covered docks which are of so capacious a volume as to swallow the most gargantuan of oil tankers. Our valiant little vessel will be as a minnow among—"

Gritch, "We get it. *Potent Bull* gonna sail itsef into a big covered dock."

I pipe up, "What if we want to discuss this with Captain B.? Maybe make a few suggestions."

Hearn shudders.

Potent Bull extinguishes all lights and pours on the coal.

Somewhere south of four in the morning we pull into sight of the promised land. None of us got a wink of shut-eye, working hard hours. I'm halfway hallucinating from exhaustion.

Astronauts get used to BIG, but I can't grasp the size of what I'm looking at. The laws of perspective are rubbery. As *Potent Bull* rumbles into the harbor, the far covered docks look like single-car garages. As the *Bull* draws close, they loom larger than the Vehicle Assembly Building at the Cape.

There's something about bright lights and sleepiness that glazes things with fakeness. It all looks plastic. I am one tuckered shuttle thief.

We putter toward the maw of one of the bigger dock hangars, or whatever they're called. The oil tanker tied up inside gives it scale: monstrously humongously gigantiomous. We grumble slowly into the cavernous space and tie up beside the tanker. Feel like a hamster staring up at a cow.

The bass growl of the *Potent Bull*'s engines, our constant com-panion for what seems forever, sputters to silence.

We're all on deck taking in our change of fortune. Heloise, Gritch, Darthy, Head, me—glaze-eyed, pumped, wrung out by our hard work and escapes from Ishwald, blinking up at the big ship and the actinic arclights. Heloise wears her blue-black peacoat and black stocking cap. She's got her back to me and I take the opportunity to examine the way her jean-sheathed legs disappear up under her coat. I'm tired, not dead.

She turns around, catches me gawking, shakes her finger at me, and points up to a huge orange sign on the wall of the dock. "Chiokis Tanker Construction Corp." it reads.

"Curiouser and curiouser." She's talking at me. "Chiokis, Mick." She expects me to know this.

I shrug. "Nope."

Gritch chimes in "Chiokis? Whooee! Enterprise sure got its butt hauled to the right place."

I give my patented Oolfson dumb look.

Gritch shakes his head at me, "Chiokis. Anybody's built a spaceship knows that name. Built the original Enterprise for Captain Kirk. Chiokis Starship Construction Corp."

I groan, "It's a Star Trek thing."

Heloise claps. "Give Mick a food pellet. Isn't he Star Trek literate?"

Gritch shakes his head. "Mick's screwed up by a deprived childhood. No TV. No cigarettes. No comic books."

Heloise recoils in mock horror.

I shrug. Old story. I have survived all that.

Gritch wrinkles his brow. "I'm guessing that whoever owns this dockyard is one hell of a rich Trekkie."

For four in the morning the dock sure has a shitload of workers on hand. Every one of them converges on *Potent Bull*. Gritch slaps some palms and is immediately welcomed into conference with a couple of the bosses. I've seen it before with American and Russian astronauts—you got the skills, you got The Dream, you're one of us.

Gritch and his new buddies swing into action like they've been planning this operation for weeks. Cranes swing over *Potent Bull* and whisk away the shipping containers hiding Enterprise.

Looking good, Lady E. The new team takes a break to gawk. Enterprise might look dinky next to a tanker, but she is still one big, sweet bird. Gritch struts around her, pointing out features like a proud parent. I amble up to the small knot of crew. Gritch points out the locations of the load-bearing areas on Enterprises underbelly. He waves me off and I wander over to the railing to be useless.

My eyes slide down the railing to the spot where Ishwald nearly boarded. Where I nearly got dragged over to a long wet nap. Where I got bit. Where I got "kissed."

I feel a throb of pain on every pulse—pain in my infected arm, pain in my infected heart. Someday I'm going to learn to play guitar and sing, and then you're all in trouble.

The new team settles into a choreographed effort. The Chiokis crew knows how to get things done. A gargantuan crane swings out over the side of the tanker. Within half an hour they have Enterprise in a freight sling and haul it aboard, Gritch bustling like a mother hen. As she swings up aboard the gigantic ship my pretty bird dwindles. It's about the size of a paper airplane at arm's length as it slips from view over the deck of the supertanker.

Things move faster than possible. Hearn tells the Channel Zilch crew to pack—we're moving out. I amble down to my cabin and gather my duds. A lot happened in this cabin. A lot of puke got puked, physical and emotional.

When I emerge onto the deck Yeter trots over and grabs the biggest duffle from my hand. Fine fellow. I look around at the vast, brilliant space. The huge tanker. The walls of the ship hangar. Plasticky. Unreal, like everything else since I hooked up with the Zilch crazies. This is coming from an ex-astronaut who has pretty damn loose reality boundaries. Or whatever. Too tired to think.

Yeter leads me across the deck to the top of the gangway. *Potent Bull's* crew is gathered. I grasp the hand of each in turn and say a simple, "Thanks."

We're all smiling, stifling emotions we're too manly to hint at. We've shared danger, boredom, hard work, triumph—an adventure. Good people. Yeter carries my bag down the gangway.

Hearn, Gritch, and Heloise wait at the bottom, bags piled onto carts. I shake Yeter's hand. He turns the handshake into a muscular hug. "Best lucking."

"Thanks."

Hearn is full of purpose. Good thing he's on the ball—we're zombies. Even Heloise is dragging her tail feathers.

As we hustle toward the tanker, I nearly forget to give a glance back, and when I do it hits me that I'll never step on board that little ship's deck again. After I finally got used to the "assertive aroma." A rueful pang. I look up at the pilot house. Its window is dark, but the grey blotch must be him. I wave my arm in a slow sweep. A small white smudge travels slowly in a single arc. Goodbye and thanks, Cap'n B-whatever.

Hearn shepherds us along the dock to the bottom of the tanker's long walkway. "Up we go, my heavy-eyed friends. Leave your bundles with these exemplary gentlemen here. They will safely reach your cabins. Depend upon it."

As if I'm awake enough to worry. It takes us a good ten minutes to trundle our way up the gangway, switchback after switchback. My lungs burn when we reach the top.

Hearn claps his hands to get our attention. "Now trail behind me docilely into a proper stateroom, you Yank rabble. I'm about to introduce you to Manuel Chin's godlike friend, Merzifon Karabuk, the gentleman what's saving your neck and mine. I won't have you expectorating tobacco juice on his priceless carpets or excavating grotesque morsels from your hideous snouts. Labor to deceive the world into believing that you are civilized beings, all evidence to the contrary."

The tanker's corridors are a maze of twisting little passages but somehow Hearn knows the way. I trudge behind him, dumb. He leads us down a long, red-carpeted corridor up to a massive rosewood door. The door bears a large circular insignia: an atom with three circles at its center.

Darthy digs her elbow into Gritch's side.

He whispers, "Got it. Logo of a Starfleet Executive Science Officer."

I roll my eyes at the pathetic fanboys. Hearn knocks. The door swings deliberately, silently, majestically open. A small, graceful Turkish man darts out and beams a radiant smile at us. He raises his right hand in the Spock Vulcan salute—V'ed ringman and middle finger[9]—and says with an upper-crust English accent, "Live long and prosper."

[9]   Even I know that one. It's a fairly common mock salutation among drunk astronauts.

Heloise, Gritch, Darthy, and I return the salute. Hearn and Head stand speechless and baffled. First time for everything.

Our host nods his head politely. "I am Merzifon Karabuk, lifelong fan and student of the inspiring universe of Star Trek. I welcome your gloriously-named spaceship Enterprise aboard my humble vessel. I shall endeavor with all my heart, mentation, and considerable financial and technical resources to make your mission a success. My skilled colleagues shall also labor in your service. In Turkey, Enterprise and her crew have many competent friends."

Merzifon bows low and sweeps his arm toward the room beyond the open door. Hel and I exchange genuine grins as we walk into the room. Sweet to have powerful pals.

The room is decorated in Turko-Trekian style. The floor is layered with Turkish carpets that have Star Trek insignia woven into the patterns, as do the mosaics in the wall. At first I'm afraid I'll get the giggles, but something clicks and I realize I'm onboard a luxurious Islamic space station. The guy's got imagination, money, and taste.

Merzifon smiles hugely when he sees us gawking at his room.

Hel bursts out, "You're out there, guy!"

Merzifon giggles a surprisingly manly giggle. "Out there! Delightful, a condition I aspire to greatly." He gestures to heaps of gaudy pillows. "Sit down, one and all. We shall talk and dine as my ship, which you must treat as your ship now, the tanker Vulcan, transports us and valiant Enterprise to Istanbul and beyond."

I watch Karabuk nestle into a pillow, and sigh a grateful sigh as I shimmy my butt down into welcome comfort.

Hearn stays standing. "As much as I long to stay and partake in what will surely be a stimulating and diverting gabfest, duty dictates I return to *Potent Bull*. The crew would mutiny without my cooking."

Merzifon laughs. "Mutiny against the legendary Captain Bob Falk? No mortal would dare. But I respect the call of duty."

Hearn turns to Heloise. "Good-bye, lovely lady. I hope you find in space the thing you seek."

Heloise narrows her eyes and snaps a terse, ambiguous wave.

I rise to shake Hearn's hand. "Good-bye, Lafcadio. You know, when I first met you, I wanted to heave you right over the side."

Hearn looks down at his feet. "I blush to think how I tormented you in your weakness that day. I trust I atoned for my prankish gall by playing Florence Nightingale."

When I say, "Those pancakes made up for everything," Hearn beams and crushes me in an ursine embrace. He turns respectfully to Gritch. "I trust you to do your considerable best to ensure that these mentally unsound specimens survive their fiery ascent."

Gritch shrugs. "You set your ass on a rocket, you take your chances. Notice I don't ride em things."

Hearn takes Head's hand and leans close to him. He says something I can't hear. Head looks startled, then pleased. He pumps Hearn's hand.

At last he turns to Darthy. He takes her hand in both of his, bends, and kisses it tenderly. Her smile turns a little sad. Hearn starts to speak but stops short and bows slowly. His eyes linger on Darthy as he turns.

Merzifon sees Hearn to the door, and I feel a pang as I watch the white-bearded giant exit.

Merzifon returns to sit in his command pillow. He taps the communicator pin on his chest and says forcefully, "Engage." The mighty throb of distant engines signals the resumption of our journey. We'll work on Enterprise at a safer Chiokis dock.

I vaguely recall goblets of brandy. Merzifon's Islamic glass of Dr. Pepper. High spirits all around. I believe we toasted many toasts to the Enterprise, to boldly going etc., confusion to Tobias Ishwald.

Somehow during all that tired partying Gritch and Merzifon sketch out a ten day schedule for finishing Enterprise's refit.

By morning we are at a shipyard on the outskirts of Istanbul, berthed in another big, big covered ship-refitting dock.

For security, Merzifon's people stay in a barracks for the duration of our visit. Only the most trustworthy are given slots in the shuttle team. But even so, no leaving the dockyard, no cell phones. Everyone gets triple pay. The rest of the workers at Chiokis get a surprise vacation, so everybody's happy.

We are pampered like deities by Merzifon and his staff in our few resting hours, fed until we burst with pungent foods and jellied sweets, serenaded by musicians playing instruments I don't recognize. During the days we put in long, hard hours, and in four days we knock seven days off Gritch's estimated refitting schedule. We work together with a small army of Merzifon's technicians. Gritch and his Turkish boss-buddies deploy them masterfully—setting up round-the-clock shifts and charting parallel tasks so there is little wasted effort tripping over one another or waiting for another team to complete a prerequisite task.

Gritch acts as delegator, trainer, quality inspector. He works with the team leaders to schedule tasks. He shows the techs how to do a piece of work. When it's finished, he checks the workmanship and gives it thumbs up more often than not. Merzifon's troops are pro. They're not afraid to ask when they don't know something. They're not afraid to tell their boss if they hit a snag or fall behind schedule. A lot of laughter, a bit of cursing, young guys looking over old guys' shoulders. A healthy workplace.

The bosses and techs respect Gritch from day one. It's obvious that they idolize Merzifon. It's like good days at NASA, with everyone putting out their finest effort for the team and their own pride. I lend a hand where needed, mostly running tests from the pilot's seat.

Not quite everyone is putting shoulder to the wheel. Head is confined to quarters with the collywobbles. Darthy keeps avoiding a talk about Head, and I admit I put it off, too. She knows what I think. I want Manuel Chin by my side when we fire the guy. It's quite all right with me that I rarely see him.

Gritch corners me on flight deck with an update. He's got the distracted, annoyed look on his face that means he's having a good old time. Time, and working daily with Heloise, means that Gritch can talk about her without turning apple-cheeked. "Hel wants to run some more captive RCS tests."

Sounds like a good idea. "Can you fire the rockets in this dock?"

"Ats not the problem. When she tried to fricassee Itchwad's ass she burnt some serious prop. We low on tet."

Ouch. "That stuff's not easy to find. Any nitrogen tetroxide blend fueling stations between here and Baikonur?"

Gritch smiles, problem already solved, "Got me a old NASA buddy retired to Istanbul, a propellant specialist name of Dover Hedsel. I give Dover a call—don't fret, I cleared it with Merz—and let him know I was in the market. Spectin to hear back from him on a pickup time. Only need maybe hundred fifty liters. When the call comes in I want you ridin shotgun."

"Done, Gritch. Love to do some sightseeing."

The bunks, galley facility, and personal lockers are installed and Gritch-certified. Seems shuttle fittings are pretty much like top-quality boat doodads. Chiokis is sure not intimidated by big projects. Enterprise is a tub toy compared to the tankers they're used to.

In a lull between work shifts I spend a few minutes alone in the shuttle's middeck. Déjà vu up the wazoo. I've spent hundreds of hours in shuttle middecks on my three missions and thousands of hours in mockup training.

Gritch has followed the same general layout as the "real" shuttles, but everything is different. We use different materials, different fixtures, different colors on the Enterprise. I truly believe our new facilities will work, maybe in some ways better than the "real" shuttles.

I'm going to spend a long, long time in this old rocketship. No way can I live cheek-by-jowl in this small space with Richard Head.

We work hard, damned hard. By any reasonable yardstick we should collapse into twitching puddles of drool and fatigue. I'm an expert at running sleep-deprivation experiments on myself—a bad habit I started in the Air Force Academy.

Ishwald is worth six cups of coffee a day.

CHAPTER TWENTY-SIX: BULL SESSION

ON THE FOURTH NIGHT of Karabuk's post-workday hospitality, the Channel Zilch gang sprawls on piles of plump silk pillows. My fingers are honey-sticky from flaky pastries I've snatched from silver trays, and my tummy is well satisfied.

Heloise is dressed down in grey sweats. She graces a heap of shiny varicolored pillows piled in a crook of Karabuk's cabin wall.

Despite being a hermit during our long workdays, Richard is a regular at Merzifon's late-night soirées. He's surprisingly quiet and on his best behavior. Darthy always sits beside him, across the room from me. She knows I'm planning to talk to Manuel about firing Richard. It's put a little kink in our friendship.

Put a defrocked astronaut, a geek goddess, a space hippie, a rocketship mechanic, and a billionaire Trekkie in one room and conversation naturally turns to The Future.

We just watched an episode of classic Star Trek on a wall-sized video screen. It was about the usual: Enterprise pops a rivet; forehead aliens do something alien; unnamed redshirted crewman dies; Kirk punches and smooches; inter-species understanding dawns; Spock says something wise-sounding and ambiguous. THE END. Must be the superb acting that draws the fans.

Merzifon has the floor. "I do so love the fictional Enterprise and her crew. Though I am a fan of Star Trek, nay, a Trek scholar, I am not foolish enough to believe it predicts the future in any real sense."

"Good on you, Merz." Heloise lies gracefully sprawled in her grey sweats. "How'd you figure that one out?"

Merzifon stretches. He loves to talk. "I drink voraciously of science fiction in all its forms of literary and cinematic drama, but I also read philosophical journals and websites of futurist thought. The world of Star Trek projects an old-fashioned future without nanotechnology or Singularity."

Hel teases, "You buy that Singularity crap, huh, Merz?"

Karabuk's eyes stay wide with astonishment. "Heloise Chin a

cybernetic pessimist? Can you, of all people, deny that progress is ever swiftening? Does not Moore teach us that computers double in capacity every eighteen months?"

"Moore's Law is going to haul us all to Singufairyland, huh? You forget hardware's the easy part."

Gritch butts in, "What's this Singularity bidness you all yammering about? Care to break it down for us simple rocket science types."

Hel doesn't jump right in and I've read plenty of sci-fi, so I decide to stick my neck out. "The Singularity... That's Vernor Vinge, right? Computers jacking up their own brainpower until they have an IQ orgasm."

That stops conversation dead. I've stunned them into silence. Dar and Karabuk look at me with pained expressions. Gritch burps. Head ignores me.

Hel rewards me with a real laugh. "IQ orgasm—IQgasm—gonna use that, spacehead. Go ahead, Merz, fill Gritchman in on the Singularity. I see Kurzweil on your shelf; you're the expert on the Geek Rapture."

"Expert on the Singularity?" says Karabuk. "I make no such claim. I am an amateur enthusiast. I watch Singularity University videos and RSS Singularity Hub. But I can do no better than to paraphrase the prophets of the Singularity. Vernor Vinge defines the Singularity as the imminent rise of superhuman intelligences and the end of the human era. Raymond Kurzweil defines the Singularity as... Here I quote from memory, 'a future period during which the pace of technological change will get so rapid, its impact so deep, that human life will be irreversibly transformed.'"

Darthy adds urgently, "We want to... The Singularity people are trying to build a friendly god."

Richard speaks up at that, "You know people who are building a God? How is that possible?"

Hel teases, "Easy as kicking dead whales down a beach. Just build a human-smart computer and let it do the work. Its first priority will be to max its intelligence—optimize its code, optimize its hardware, optimize its world."

Gritch says, "Oh, that Singularity. Yeah, I seen the Terminator flicks. You think that shit's gonna happen off-screen?"

"No one's working on an evil overlord," says Darthy. "People are building a friendly god. The Google guys hired Kurzweil because they want to upgrade their search engine into a patented, money-making deity."

Hel growls, "Nobody should own the source code of god. That's why Dar and I work towards an open-source Singularity."

Sounds swell whatever the hell it means. Richard turns to Darthy. "A God in a computer. Is this possible?"

"Everyone will own a custom god," Darthy replies.

"Damn space hippie," says Gritch.

But Richard is riveted. He goes into reporter mode. "You talk as if you know these God builders. Tell me more about them."

Darthy shakes her head emphatically. "I follow their blogs. I'm a Singularity enthusiast like Merzifon."

Heloise flutes a derisive trill. "Darthy's being modest. She's incubating a godling in her laptop. Show Richard the latest build of Opencog."

Darthy wads up a napkin and throws it at Heloise, who bats it away. Gritch yawns a big fake one.

"Too rich for you, Gritch?" says Hel.

Gritch sniffs. "Bullshit's bullshit. I'm listenin. So you the Terminator's nooky? Splains a lot."

Hel throws back her head and laughs, "All Hail Skynet! I'm a huge cheerleader for the Singularity, but I'm only in it for the spiffy spin-offs—immortality, omniscience, omnipotence. You studied that stuff for your theology degree, didn't you Richard?"

Head turns to Heloise and starts to grill her. "You know these Godbuilding people. By cheerleader do you mean…"

"I'm a big fan of The Project. I like to talk it up."

"The Project?"

Darthy, "Building the Singularity is The Project because it's the big one."

"The Project is the only thing worth doing," says Hel.

"If," Head asks, "this Godmaking is so important to you, why embark upon Channel Zilch?"

Heloise says simply, as if it is obvious, "Channel Zilch is going to kickstart the Singularity."

Darthy chuckles. "Helgirl is getting a little tired. Time to—"

"I don't do secrets."

Secrets are death. Secrets are lies.

Hel is on a roll. "This is a bull session, one? Let's amp it. Raise your hand if you'd like to live ten thousand years."

All but Gritch raise their hand. That surprises me so I ask, "Gritch, you...?"

He raises his hand and mutters, "All right, all right, I'll play."

Heloise beams at us. "Interesting people like life."

"Want y'all to know I think this Singularity bidness is all fried farts and cracker crumbs," Gritch grouses. "Don't believe a word of it. But I like livin."

Hel goes lectury, "Mortality is the crux, The Problem with a capital P. Solve The Problem and everything follows. Engineer immortal bodies or the tech for downloading minds into computers."

Darthy dives in. "Mortality is an engineering problem. There's nothing magic in a sperm or ovum, no pixie dust sprinkled on the molecules of DNA. We are built of fundamental particles, atoms, molecules, biological systems that we can study and understand. What we understand we can hack and improve."

I goad them, "But what about our immortal souls?"

Heloise's head swivels slowly toward me. Her green eyes goggle in disbelief. Karabuk's mouth hangs open. Head actually looks at me.

I giggle. "Got ya."

Heloise cracks up and Karabuk smiles a toothy smile. He shakes his head. "Ah, the barbaric era we live in. Mick reminds us that even as we fashion ourselves into gods, among us live those haunted by ghosts of ancient memes."

"Screen yer memes," Hel aphorizes.

Karabuk nods. "Screen your memes. Amen to that judicious principle. Astringent skepticism is necessary cognitive hygiene."

"I fail to see the humor," says Head. He's heated. "Surely a working copy of Richard Head must contain a copy of Richard Head's soul."

Heloise nearly spits the words, "If the soul exists, it's a negligible parasite."

Gritch doesn't like that. "Cold."

Which stops conversation until our host restores the flow. "Let us not be diverted by Mick's japes from our compelling dialogue. Heloise Chin, you talk as if it is in your power to ignite the Singularity. Surely an ambitious agenda even for so remarkable a woman as yourself."

Even dog-tired, this debate is worth gawking at. It's nice to be on the sidelines, out of Hel's line of fire.

Heloise unfolds upwards and walks to stand dead in front of Karabuk, bending to glare at him. She strikes a strange, focused pose, arms stretched wide, palms turned upward. "I don't mouth an agenda—I'm going to ram my vision down the jaws of history. I'm going to force-feed humanity fifty years of progress in the next decade."

"You go, grrrl!" Darthy amens.

Karabuk smiles and shakes his head. "Heloise Chin cannot 'cook up' this future all alone, though she is a formidable human. Be mindful of the tens of thousands of scientists laboring to discover, engineers working to invent, technicians working to build. Your ego astounds me, Ms. Chin."

Helsnort. "I didn't say little old me is going to build the future. One person, one lifetime is diddley-squat in terms of cranking out the progress we need. Tens of thousands of lifetimes are squat if we want to kill death in the next fifty years—the only years I got. We need millions of brains online ASAP, thinking, hacking, jawing nonstop—focused on The Problem. We have seven billion minds on earth today and ninety-nine-point-too-many-nines percent of them are wasted. That waste is going to kill everyone in this room if we let it."

I hurl my tuppence, "Killing death is another of your spare-time projects?"

She turns and sneers all over me. "Zero, brain-free zone. Zilch is my only project. I am not pissing away my energy. I focus on the goal."

"Immortality and omniscience are pretty cool spin-offs. I've read the sci-fi, so I get it, and I really dig living and thinking. What I don't get is how's a pirate TV space station reality show going to kickstart the Singularity? And like Merzifon said, isn't progress speeding up enough already?"

Heloise steps toward me, green eyes slitted, lips curled in a snarl, mind racing to phrase an insult that will sprawl me mewling and spewing vital fluids on the floor. Karabuk, smiling, moves to placate her. "I see that we are all techno-optimists in this room. It seems we disagree about implementation."

Hel takes two deep breaths and speaks low and fast. "A good engineer overdesigns for multiple, simultaneous worst cases when lives are at stake. Lives are at stake. My life, your life. I want fault-tolerant backup tech in place NOW. Cause maybe, just maybe, the seers are wrong and it's gonna take eighty years to solve The Problem. I'm dead meat. We're carrion. I can't allow that."

Karabuk says, "But cryonic suspension—"

"You've got a brain freeze contract?"

He nods.

"Chancy. Very. So far they can't thaw a live hamster after a week frozen. Darthy gave up her corpsicle contract to fly with Channel Zilch."

Karabuk breaks into an appreciative series of chuckles. "I admire your hubris. Ignite the Singularity, and the name of Heloise Chin will echo down the ages."

Hel directs her sneer at him. "That's right Merz. I'm in this game to be the next Elvis. I want people to paint me on black velvet and name their cats after me. You got me pegged. Must be why you're this awesome business god."

"I apologize if my clumsy rhetorical gambit sailed astray. In heated debate an attack on an assertion too often seems to target the asserter."

Hel waves it off. "Sticks and stones can break my bones, but your clumsy rhetorical gambit can kiss my royal mongrel ass."

Merz processes that one while Heloise ambles back and lowers her regal derriere onto a pile of shiny rainbow pillows.

Darthy announces, as if it's a common parlor game, "I know. Let's play Singularity Claus. What will you ask the Singularity for, Mick? It can build anything you want."

"Anything?"

"Anything physically possible. When the Singularity comes, you can be as rich as you want. Things are just atoms and information and energy. Matter will be programmable. Just give the nanobots a recipe and raw ingredients and power, and they'll build anything you want, atom by atom."

I beg off. "You go first. What is Singularity Santa going to leave under your tree?"

Darthy smiles and looks sheepish. "I know what you all are going to call me, but I have to be honest. As long we feed our cows better than we feed every single human child, we are barbarians. I'd ask for food for all the starving kids, no more hunger."

"And how would St. Singularity work this miracle?"

Dar gives a wide-eyed search-me shrug. "Maybe it will invent a hat-sized nano-brewery that eats dead leaves and sunlight and excretes nourishing butterscotch pudding. Who knows, Mick? It's the fucking Singularity."

Which cracks us up.

Hel: "Great slogan, Dar: Work for the Fucking Singularity and ye shall sup eternally on butterscotch hat poop."

"I've just got one thing to say to you, Darthy Vader," I reply. "You are a tie-dyed, zero-g, space hippie."

She's amused. "Guilty as charged, your honor. After all the kids are fed, all I want out of life is to listen to In-A-Gadda-Da-Vida on earbuds while building an awesome snow fort in Saturn's rings. Is that too much to ask?"

"Sounds perfectly reasonable to me."

"Your turn, then, Mickster."

I know exactly what I want. "Easy. I want to be an Apollo Lunar Mission reenactor. I want a Saturn 5, a command module, a LEM, all stock... Authentic."

Gritch approves. "Hell of a hobby."

"I want that Saturn 5 stacked on the original launch pad at the Cape and topped up with LOX and liquid H. I want to train for the mission with two of my astronaut buddies. Then I want to reenact a whole Apollo moon mission—one of the longer, later ones with the Rover—all the way from training to blasting off to flying the mission to walking the moon to reentry to the ticker-tape parade."

Merzifon says, "Well played, Mick. An admirable goal. Who shall...?"

I hold up my hand. "Wait a minute, wait a minute, I'm not done. Since we're talking crazy talk, I do request one upgrade to the stock Apollo astronaut life. You know how they let us astronauts fly those sexy little T-38 Talon jets? I want an upgraded ride. I want my own personal SR-71 Blackbird painted candy-flake burgundy—and make it a convertible, because I like to feel the wind in my hair."

Gritch cackles, "That Mach 3 wind gonna light your hair like striking a match."

I amend, "Oh, and give me titanium hair."

Merzifon claps and everyone smiles, even Heloise!

I pass the baton while I'm ahead. "Your turn, Merz. What's a billionaire got on his wish list? What would make your eyes light up if you found it under your Singularity tree?"

Merzifon considers and decides. "I would wish for a bigger brain to think with as I make my wish. Any wish I make with my current brain will seem trivial to Karabuk-to-be. When I was a child I doted upon raspberry sherbet, and if you had asked me then what was my ultimate wish I might have answered, 'A mountain of raspberry sherbet.' A bigger brain before I make my wish."

Gritch, "Sure you don't want more cash? You only got—what?—four billion dollars I heard. How long's that gonna last ya?"

Karabuk considers this seriously. "Money I have enough of. There are too few worthwhile things to spend it on, alas. Post-Singularity money will be as glass beads. I agree with the lamented Scottish science fiction writer Iain Banks that 'Money is a sign of poverty.' I will be content only when every human is as rich as I."

Gritch growls genially, "Sound like a socialist, there, Merz. They gonna kick you out of the yacht club."

I chime in with a point unpopular with my conservative military brethren, "I worked in the most socialist organization in the

US—the military. Government medicine, housing, schooling, even clothing. Covering the basics let us get on with our work."

Merzifon expounds, "We are a social species, and socialism begins at the mother's breast; the natural state of a single human in nature is dead. But enough politics, let us return to our game. My current brain would ask the Singularity for one gift, a gift which you brave crew of Enterprise will soon receive—to travel into space for however brief a moment, to look down on our Earth while floating weightless."

Gritch approves. "Lot of that wish goin round. Won't catch me ridin a rocketship even if I got my immortality guarantee notarized by the Terminator hisself. I know how them rocketships work so you ain't gettin me to risk my ass ridin one."

I prod him. "So what would you ask Singularity Claus for, Gritch? A magic hook that catches a fish every time you cast it?"

"I'm off fishin for a couple decades. Lessee, I got all the time in the world, right? Everone here knows I think this is a bullshit game but I'm a sport. What I want? Easy. I want to build all five shuttles all on my ownsome. I want to make every part, every tile, circuit board, rocket nozzle—every part of all five shuttles, starting with our old Enterprise up to Endeavor. Then I want to put together them parts to make five working shuttles. That's it—just want to build all five space shuttles with my own hands."

What a bunch of space geeks. "I'll be your driver, Gritch. Wring those birds out for you."

Gritch shakes his head. "No way I'm letting one of you rocket jocks touch my babies. I don't want no one to fly em—they gone stay pristine forever, ya hear?"

I tease him. "Shame to let those ships just sit there collecting dust."

Gritch doesn't relent. "Shame the way you astronauts bring those shuttles back after a mission—tiles all dinged up and smellin like a locker room. My shuttles gonna stay pristine, I tell ya. Not that I believe a word of it."

Conversation stops as a steward enters, carrying a silver tray of plums and dates and figs. I pat my stomach and shake my head ruefully to show I'm stuffed—nice to enjoy my gastrointestinal system again.

Darthy turns to Richard and asks, "How about you, Richard? What would you like Singularity Claus to bring you?"

Richard clarifies, "This Singularity—it's a godlike mind in a computer, correct?"

Darthy nods.

Richard says, as if it's not insane, "Richard Head's goal is Fame. How can this Singularity serve Richard Head's end? It must embed Richard Head deep in every human mind. I want every human to know my face and name, love my work, know my favorite color and shoe size and zodiac sign. I don't just want to be the most famous person alive; I want to be the most famous person possible."

Heloise is impressed. "Whoa there, Headspace. Optimal fame—cool goal. Race ya."

Head looks concerned. "I asked first."

She laughs and tweaks him. "You're thinking small. How about this, Richman: The Singularity can build you an audience way bigger than a dinky seven billion humans."

Richard leans forward in his pile of pillows, listening raptly.

Heloise holds up a cushion. "Doesn't it kill you that this pillow doesn't know Richard Head's birthplace? How about that rug? No way does it know your favorite toothpaste. The Singularity could turn all that wasted matter into tiny robotic fan brains that love Richard Head round the clock."

Richard's eyes unfocus and he looks into the distance, tasting this new thought. He smiles.

Hel piles it on. "It could turn all the stuff of Earth into tiny robotic Richard fans and then reach out into the Universe at near lightspeed, converting planets and comets and suns into swarms of tiny minds that worship Richard Head. An expanding bubble of Richardmania will eventually turn every atom in the Universe into a Richard-worshipping mind."

Hel watches the effect of her words on Richard and is pleased at the havoc she's wrought on the frail reed of his psyche. "That optimal enough for ya, Richhead?"

Richard trumps her bull. "I must meet this Singularity and make her mine. Darthy, Heloise, you know this Goddess's makers. When will she be old enough to entertain suitors?"

Darthy starts to laugh but covers it in a cough. Hel flops back in her pillows and laughs a laugh you could dance to. It doesn't faze Head one bit. His mind spins with this new vision of truly Universal fame.

I've got to ask. "Turnabout time. What does the singular Ms. Chin want from the Singularity?"

Heloise sits up straight and smiles. "I want everything... ev... er... y... thing. I want to multiply myself so I can get to know every human being."

Richard says fervently, "Amen to fame!"

Hel rolls her eyes and says, "Every human can be famous if our memories are pooled."

"Everyone?" He looks troubled.

Hel nods. "I'm going to spearhead an Open Memory Standard so humans can store and share memories."

Richard asks. "My fans will be able to remember my memories?"

Hel says, "Those you share."

Darthy says, "No geeking out, Helgrrrl. What else will Singularity Claus grant you?"

Hel says, "I want to fuck every adult who'll have me."

I open my mouth but nothing comes to mind. She continues as if she hasn't poleaxed me, "I'm going to eradicate suffering. Not only kill death, but make humans unkillable. I'm going to end carnivorism in all species—lions and lambs will have slumber parties. I've got further optimizations planned but I don't want to hog the floor."

I wouldn't mind listening to Heloise all night. She continues, "I'm going to read every book, play every game, hear every song, taste every vegetable and fruit. I don't give a shit about fashion but I want to be on Project Runway's 345,000th season. I want to write a great book in every genre—even theomantic fanfic like the Bible. I'm going to write at least one play better than King Lear. Same with games, musical instruments..."

Darthy says, "I'll teach you accordion!"

Which gets a laugh out of Hel. "Almost every musical instrument...and every artform, including chainsaw sculpture. I'm even going to write a decent opera. I'll visit and get to know every planet and every star in every galaxy."

Gotta admire her desire. I say, "You want it all—the American Dream."

"I'm going to understand physics in my bones. I'll know what a star knows when it goes supernova. I'll unwind the universe back to the Big Bang by reading the information in the total Hawking Radiation of every black hole. "

"The Transhuman Dream," says Darthy.

"We wouldn't have to dream it," Hel snaps, "if the ultra-affluent backed Singularity research instead of building bigger tub toys."

Gritch objects, "Whoa, whoa, little lady! Merz's tub toys are savin Enterprise's ass. He don't deserve you bitchin at him."

Merzifon sighs, "It is likely that I deserve Ms. Chin's chastening. Do you hate all wealthy people, Ms. Chin?"

She barks an ugly laugh. "I hate a few, sure—greedheads who shit in gold toilets while kids eat rocks in Sudan. Hmmm, oh, yeah—has-been geek moguls who slow the Singularity by patent-trolling get box seats in the 7th Ring of Hel's special hell. But how can I hate on all you dumb fucks? In a hundred years people will laugh at the rich idiots of today 'til guts squirt out their noses. All these rich dudes hogging their cool toys in their cold coffins. If they'd invested in human minds they could have licked death and lived forever as gods, but they died clutching a bunch of pathetic, expensive, primitive baubles.

"Brains are the wealth. Squandered." Hel's eyes blaze emerald. "I don't mean wealth as in every mother's child is so, so precious. I mean wealth as in substance of ultimate value."

Karabuk looks peeved and thoughtful. "I am persuaded. I will invest in your Channel Zilch scheme. Your father did not confide that the Singularity was at issue."

Heloise laughs a short high chime. "Pop doesn't know. Channel Zilch doesn't need investors. How about investing in the movie?"

"You are planning a movie?"

Hel says, as if to a child, "Of course there's going to be a Chanel Zilch movie! We just stole a fucking space shuttle."

Darthy adds, "If we make it into orbit, it'll be a feature film instead of movie of the week."

"So who will play Heloise Chin?" I ask.

"I'm not a movie maker, so we'll leave that to the director," says Hel. "I may try out for the part of Heloise Chin."

Dar laughs. "They're gonna go for a star. Hel doesn't want to admit she looks like... Who is it? That singer. What's her name?"

Hel tries to hide a pleased smile. "I know who will play Mick Oolfson: Wil Wheaton."

I shrug ignorance. Around Heloise, my baffled-shrug muscles get a workout.

Karabuk says happily, "Wil Wheaton played the young Wesley Crusher in The New Generation."

I remember that guy. "But that guy was an egotistical little smartass. Don't Trekkies hate his guts?"

Darthy laughs, "The geek world has forgiven him."

"Wheaton is geek bait," says Hel, "and I'll give him points in the picture if he helps fundraise among the cyberbarons."

I've got to laugh at the idea of someone pretending to be me in a moving picture. "You know I'm not a Trekkie, but I can picture this Crusher guy—kind of a pugnosed cherub face, right? You really think he can play me?"

Karabuk says enthusiastically, "Wesley Crusher deserves to pilot Enterprise! It is a matter of cosmic justice. I am most eager to invest in this movie." On cue a cell phone plays the Star Trek theme. He laughs. "I would take that as an omen if I were a soft-headed man." He reaches into his jacket and says, "Security. Please excuse me."

Karabuk talks to his phone as we all look wide-eyed at one another. I haven't thought about Ishwald all evening.

Merzifon stands and walks toward Gritch with the phone outstretched, saying, "Your friend Dover Hedsel. He has the propellant required and insists most emphatically that we pick it up tonight."

CHAPTER TWENTY-SEVEN: REFOOL

THE STREET OUTSIDE Karabuk's compound is empty and still, a narrow paved alleyway lined with shuttered shops. The sea-damp night smells of wood smoke and licorice. A tinny radio in the distance keens a wobbly, passionate banjoish solo. This ain't Minnesota.

My get-up-and-go has got up and went. It's been a long, tough day but we've got a critical task to do. We need to pick up that fuel for thruster tests to track down control anomalies.

Karabuk insists on accompanying us. That guy always goes the extra mile. I still shake my head when I remember the flotilla of faux *Potent* Bulls he assembled in the middle of the Med. When I laughed at Chin for insisting we could leverage his few measly millions to get Channel Zilch off the ground I had no clue he had deity-calibre chums like Merzifon Karabuk.

Hel has attached herself to the expedition. She wears the thin, rigid, primer-grey backpack that houses her mobile data center.

None of us talk as we wait for transport. The bull session tapped us out and this impromptu work detail is going to shave hours off tonight's ration of shut-eye. Good thing I'm getting fond of gnawing on Turkish coffee.

A black, shiny Ford Explorer pulls into the narrow street and eases to a stop. Gritch pointedly gets into the passenger seat. Hel, Merz, and I take the back. I've seen the driver around Chiokis, a quiet, small, muscular man always hurrying or standing still, watching.

Heloise. Although Merzifon sits between us, I register her proximity, her electric spice scent. After all the shit she's put my head and heart through I can't switch off my adolescent yearning.

Merzifon introduces the driver. "Ercument Gorgul, head of Chiokis Security."

Ercument nods and we're off. A fast, smooth ride through deserted streets. I look away from Hel and space out watching the alien townscape drift by punctuated by minarets and domes that remind me I'm far from home and lightly passing through. I'll come back here someday and stay at the Holiday Inn.

Karabuk interrupts my reverie, "Ms. Chin, pardon me. I have just realized that there is no reason for you to accompany us on this tedious errand. Please allow us to return you to Chiokis so that you might sleep some well-earned sleep."

Hel is not well pleased by Karabuk's kindness. She gives him a flat, "Zero."

Merzifon rashly persists. "Weeks of hard work lie ahead of you, Ms. Chin. Sleep for your health's sake when possible. Do not be deceived by youthful ignorance of the body's limits."

I reassure him, "Don't sweat it, Merz, if Hel can ride an H-bomb she can survive an all-nighter."

Shit. My sleepy frigging mouth blabbed what? I'm toast. I look across Karabuk's head—Heloise's eyes gape, then clench to furious gouges spitting green sparks. Her mouth mouths silent syllables I don't care to interpret.

Karabuk continues, as if a billion watts of annihilating energy weren't crackling over his head, "That is a figure of speech I have not heard. To 'ride an H-bomb'—the English language continues to spawn expressive novelties."

Hel's words are too high-pitched and clearly enunciated to match the flat tone she speaks in, "Mick Oolfson, I have some business to talk over with you later tonight."

"Roger that." What do I want for my last meal? The usual: a bowl of Captain Crunch cereal and a pitcher of Jim Beam.

"Cancel that. Pause game." She takes a breath and closes her eyes. Her hand darts toward her pocket.

My hippocampus (or whatever they call the brain's cowardice center) slaps my glands awake to pump a high-octane cocktail into my bloodstream. My poor, pooped muscles are pointlessly primed to sprint. Big thanks to evolution for oxygen-starving my brain, shunting blood to my muscles just when I need to sit still and think.

Gritch turns around and looks back at me from the front seat. "Y'all havin fun back air with yer crazy talk?"

I give him a genuine pained look. Heloise pulls out her pair of pink rhinestone computer shades and slides them over her eyes. She slumps; her fingers quiver in the air.

Karabuk's eyes go large at Hel's behavior. He looks at me in silent interrogation and I hold a finger to my lips. I give a slow nod and reassuring wink to put the guy at ease. I spin my forefinger around my ear and glance at Hel to mime that she is slightly mental right now. He shudders and looks out the window. Guess my gesture didn't translate into Turkish.

Hel's head pops up and she turns toward me with an electric smile radiating elation from beneath the amber lenses. "Hello, World! Hel One here. Pardon my atrocious manners, boys. Sometimes a little change does a young lady a world of good." Her voice has a julepy, southern belle intimacy that pelts through my psyche like warm rain through a cotton T-shirt.

"Why, look at you, Mick, honey. You are all aquiver, how beguiling! Did you think lil ol Heloise would slap you silly over a silly lil slip of the tongue? Heloise doesn't hold with secrets. I told you that and a lady's word must be treated as gospel by well-bred, fine-looking gentlemen."

Gritch snorts hard but stares straight ahead. Hel tosses her head in the direction of Karabuk, who looks roundly nonplussed, and places her hand coquettishly on his chest. "Merzifon, dear, let me explain this awkwardness. You must surely find all this mystifying. Mick here feels just awful right now. Don't you, Mick, dear?"

I nod, but pathetically relish that 'dear'.

"He just touched rather clumsily upon a family tragedy to which I was not aware he was privy. Undoubtedly my darling father thought Mick would benefit from possessing this information. Being the caring father that he is, Papa urged Mick to keep silent on the subject, making him swear a solemn oath not to divulge his knowledge so as not to upset the sensitive blossom that is Heloise Chin. Isn't that right, Mick, honey?" She swings around to regard me with a flirtatious tilt of her head, eyes screened behind her flickering amber spex.

My expression tells her all and I hang my head. Her lovey-doviness unnerves me. She tousles my hair. "Mick Oolfson, you are the sweetest thing. I could just eat you alive."

Gulp. Um. Yay?

"Mick expected I was going to go into a tizzy at his little indiscretion and so the cute lil astronaut is as bewildered as you are." She focuses her belle persona on Karabuk. "Are you the sort of man who savors gossip concerning distressing details of a woman's past?"

Taking the hobnails to my psyche again. I earned it. Might as well savor each stomp.

Karabuk comes to life. "I don't recall Mick spilling indelicate tales of your youth."

There is hope. Heloise will let it pass since Karabuk didn't get it.

"The wicked scoundrel told you I rode an H-bomb."

Karabuk nods. Hel leans across him and commands, "Fill him in." Then she puts her hand on my thigh and leans close and whispers in my ear, "Hel One thinks you're cute."

?

I try translating from Heltalk: Hel Yes thinks you're cute.

?!

I look at her achingly lovely face and once again fail to fathom what's going on behind those glittering glasses inside that infernal engine she thinks with. No way can I fit *her* mind in *my* brain. I shake my head and stare out at the sleeping streets of Istanbul sliding by the window of the SUV.

Hel takes her hand off my thigh and sits back. "Mick is sulking like a naughty little boy. He's such a deliciously sensitive specimen. Shall I satisfy your curiosity about the H-bomb, Merzifon?"

Merzifon tries to quiet her. "I have no such need to know these things. Please, the late hour wears on us all."

Gritch turns around to face us. "Ok. Ya got me wondrin. Tell ol Gritch what the hell ridin a H-bomb means. Some kinda twisted sex kink, right?"

Ercument says something Turkish, and Merzifon, relieved, interrupts our discussion. "Let us resume this topic later. We are blocks away from your friend's fuel storage yard." He asks Heloise with real concern, "Before we arrive I must ascertain—are you well, my dear Heloise?"

She removes the damnable glasses from her eyes. "Default Hel Zero process." Blinks and shakes her head. "That went off track, but, yeah, fine now."

Something got away from Heloise Chin right there. Doesn't even begin to make sense. None of us says a thing. Hel is her own category.

The car slows. We're in an industrial district. About as exotic as Des Moines if you don't try to read the signs. Ercument points to a high weathered wood fence. The bulbous tops of a few immense rusted storage tanks loom above it in the enclosed yard.

Karabuk speaks, "Your friend gave this address. That gate would appear to be the entrance."

I ask, "Ready to get some prop, Gritch?" Gritch's friend has specified that he wants to meet only the two of us old NASA hands.

Ercument speaks and Merzifon translates. "We, of course will remain in the car. If we spot anything suspicious we will alert you."

I'm thinking, *suspicious?* but Gritch agrees, "Sure thing, you see one a Ishwald's destroyers just honk your horn and we'll come runnin."

I suggest something a bit more subtle, "Merz, can you whistle?"

Karabuk looks offended. "No Turk whistles. It is considered a grossly uncivil practice."

Heloise goes wide-eyed. "Whatever. Just do a wild animal call, then."

Merzifon nods, "Like this?", screws up his face and puffs his cheeks and makes a choking sound way back in his throat that starts low and warbles up into a hoarse screeching cough.

I stare hard. "The fuck was that?"

"You do not have them in America? About this big, amphibious, green smooth skin, with a horned throat ruff of scarlet tissue?" He holds his hands apart about three feet.

"Squirrels?" I ask helpfully.

Heloise looks at me and shakes her head. "The man said green."

Karabuk elaborates, "They gorge on the marrow of their living prey. Live singly in seaside grottoes. Migrate on floating driftwood. Magnificent beasts driven to the doorstop of extinction." Karabuk looks at us hopefully.

"Beagles?" I'm groping now.

Karabuk nods thoughtfully. "Perhaps."

Heloise makes a chopping motion with her hand. "I don't want to know what that was about. Get going, you two."

Gritch and I get out, and I follow him to the gate. He knocks and a low voice comes from inside, American, "State your name."

Gritch says sourly, "You always was a stickler, Dover. Who ya think come knockin this time a night?"

"State your name."

Gritch snarls, "Daisy Fuckin Duck. Now open this gate, Hedsel, or we'll take our bidness down the street."

The latch clunks; the gate opens. A tall, thin, ruddy man with a trim ginger beard leans out and waves us in.

I turn and wave back to Heloise.

Gritch sticks his hand out to his old buddy. "Thanks for..."

Hedsel is nervous, "Get inside."

We step into the storage yard and my eyes adjust to the dim, uneven light cast by a distant streetlight. The fenced lot is glutted with cylindrical metal tanks of all sizes. A few huge rusty tanks loom over heaps of propane tanks. Parked right in front of us are a few small trailers loaded with green jerry cans. Gritch points to one. "That ours, Dover?"

Dover answers quietly from behind us. "I'm sorry, Gritch. Can't let you get away with it."

From behind us, "Hands up, Oolfson!" The voice is uniquely that of my main man: Captain Tobias Ishwald.

As I reach for the sky, I stifle my shock and shout loud enough for Hel to hear, "If it isn't Captain Ishwald!"

"Shut up!" Ishwald's dulcet tones, right behind us. "Now turn around."

I turn and there he is in all his glory, big grin on his face, eyes wide with glee. The two soldiers who flank him level nasty angular black weapons at my navel, which starts to itch: my allergy to the prospect of rapid metal.

Ishwald says coldly but with satisfaction, "Gritch Neubart. I'm disappointed in you, old man."

Gritch, "Ats what you said when you tol NASA I stole that van. This time ya maybe got a point."

Ishwald looks at me, smiling wide, and speaks slowly to savor each syllable, "Oolfson, I told you I'd—"

Outside the gate a car door slams and Heloise shouts, "GO! GO! I'm staying with Zilch!" The Explorer's engine roars to life and accelerates into the distance.

Ishwald snaps, "All of you, follow me!" To his soldiers, "Keep them covered. Cut them down if they run." He walks out of the gate and one of the soldiers urges me to follow with a wave of his weapon.

I wonder aloud, "I wonder if this guy would really shoot if..."

The soldier dips his gun to point it at my knees. He stands straighter and smiles right at me.

I assure him, "Got it. I'm right behind the Captain."

As I walk out the gate I think—too bad it had to happen this way. Wonder how many years of jail time I'll draw? Plenty of time to finish my memoir. Too bad it'll end with a thud.

Heloise stands in front of Ishwald, her hands held high. The good Captain has a pistol aimed at her gut. I don't like that at all, but there are too many guns around for me to try anything stupid.

Ishwald barks, "Halt." We halt. He motions with his pistol for Hel to join us.

As the soldiers walk wide to stand by Ishwald they keep their guns trained on us. Hel walks straight toward me, looking right into my eyes. She flashes me an exaggerated wink and a wicked smile. I relax a notch—Hel's got something cooking.

As she nears Gritch and me, she whispers, "Close your eyes when I say 'persimmon'." She starts to pass between us.

Ishwald yells. "Halt. Good. Now turn around." I see Heloise out the corner of my eye. She turns and continues to rotate.

Ishwald's happy face turns sour. "What is she doing?"

Heloise says while turning in circles, "You told me to turn around. I obey big brave penisfolk with guns."

I help, "You didn't tell her to stop. She works with computers."

"Stop!" Ishwald is pissed that his moment of triumph is getting messy.

"You didn't say 'Simon says'." Heloise continues to spin slowly. Her fingers air-type above her head.

Ishwald yells, "Oolfson! Make that woman stop spinning."

I say, grinning, "I don't control her."

Heloise giggles. "Gonna bite me, Toby? Or you only chow on Mick?"

Ishwald steps forward to grab her shoulder, and Heloise says evenly, "VOICE COMMAND 509."

Ishwald jerks back and shouts, "What the?" A swarm of beetlish black shapes drips from Hel's backpack and spreads out from her. Ishwald squeals and starts stomping. The soldiers back away pointing their guns down at the swarming bugbots.

"COMMAND PERSIMMON STROKE 47." I close my eyes just as bright screaming heck erupts from the ground. Shrieking whistles accompany a light show that shines bright through my eyelids. Sparks pepper my hands as the squealing fireworks build to a crescendo. A small hand grips mine and tugs. Heloise jerks me out of the insane screeching light. I open my eyes to see the way, the glaring shrieks behind us. Gritch holds tight to her other hand.

Hel looks at me, her face lit with excitement. "Scamper!"

I laugh. "With you, crazy lady!"

"Go!" The three of us run hand in hand down the street to freedom.

"Where to?" I ask, just as the ungodly howl of Merzifon's Turkish Death Beagle curdles the night air and triggers my brakes. Heloise wobbles and pitches toward the ground, but Gritch and I catch her before she falls.

"There they are!" Ishwald shouts. I look back. The crazed inferno sputters behind him.

The big black friendly Explorer roars down the street and screes to a halt beside us. A door swings open and Merzifon urges from inside, "Quickly now. Quickly." I push Heloise into the car and then Gritch. A burst of shots—I fling myself across their laps as Ercument slams the accelerator. Gunshots rattle and echo as we accelerate hard.

My head is on Merzifon's lap, my feet on Gritch's. Luckily I'm facing up because Hel supports mid-Mick.

More shots and a pattering on the back window. Merzifon smiles down at me. "Quite bulletproof. Ercument has earned a substantial bonus tonight."

I sit up, scooting gingerly off Hel's lap toward Gritch, and look out the back window. An Ishwald-shaped shadow spasms in rage against the dying flickers of Heloise's robotic pyre.

Merzifon enquire of Heloise, "The fireworks?"

Heloise says proudly, "Bots with phosphorus copter-shrieker-blades. Drop from my pack, disperse and deploy blades from wetbaths, fly and shriek on voice command. Blades ignite when airborne."

Gritch says tartly, "Bet atsa hit in the bedroom."

We didn't get the tet. Ishwald gets half a point for that.

CHAPTER TWENTY-EIGHT: BAIKONUR BECKONS—BACK ROADS, BLUFFERY, BULLY-BOYS, AND BAKSHEESH

WE CATCH OUR BREATHS as the Explorer whisks us back to the docks of Chiokis. Heloise's hip touches mine firmly. In terms of automotive etiquette, I believe that with four of us squeezed in the back seat it's kosher for me not to scoot away—if I sit still and don't enjoy the feel of her hip against mine too much.

Gritch finally speaks, "Sorry bout ol Dover. Didn't remember what a stickler he was. Spose I wanted that fuel a mite too much."

Merzifon says, "It is but human nature to—"

"Yeah, I'm a sap. Upshot is ol Enterprise gotta hit the road. Spect Itchwad and his SEAL buddies gonna be combing every inch of waterfront startin bout five minutes ago."

"I won't hear of it. You may depend upon Chiokis Security. Enterprise's refitting is far from complete."

I weigh in, "You're a real pal to Enterprise, Merz, but we can't let Channel Zilch take you down. Ishwald knows we're in Istanbul. We gotta hit the trail."

"Chiokis gave our schedule a big boost," says Gritch. We the ones owe you big-time. We ain't gonna risk your ass for no space video. I hear Turkish prison ain't ezactly Mr. Roger's neighborhood."

Hel says, "You're a champ, Merz, but we'll scram."

Ercument says something to Merzifon who listens and nods slowly. "Ercument concurs with your assessment. As much as it grieves me to send you on your way with much work to do, I accept that it must be so."

"Tell ya what, Merz," says Gritch. You lend us ten a your top techs and we'll put em to good use on our joyride across the Black Sea."

"You shall have twenty. I can send them with you only as far as the Georgian coast. I do no business in the wreckage of the USSR. That region's lawlessness precludes an honest profit. Beyond the Black Sea the name of Merzifon Karabuk will be of no assistance to you."

Gritch says sincerely, "We owe ya big-time, buddy."

We leave Istanbul at dusk the next day on one of Karabuk's mini-tankers, Enterprise shrouded by a tent of waterproof, army-green fabric on the deck. Our parting from Karabuk is strained: though there is lots of gratitude on our side, a feeling of lost opportunity hangs over it all.

Heloise in her opaque mode grins and scowls at random intervals. She's not diddling anyone's brain at the moment. She's plotting the next fourteen moves in the game. Haven't seen a trace of her Southern Belle character since the H-bomb leak. Hasn't called me 'dear' since.

Darthy and Head make themselves scarce. They've got no refitting tasks, so I never see them. I'm not looking forward to kicking Head off the crew, but that's my first order of business with Manuel when we get off this damned boat. I know I'll have a fight on my hands.

It's a 40-hour trip across the Black Sea during which neither Heloise, Gritch, nor I get one REM of sleep, working like caffeine-fueled zombies to squeeze the last hours of skilled labor out of Karabuk's techs.

We don't have the fuel we need to run live thruster tests, so Hel decides to tear out and reinstall all the RCS wiring. She and two Chiokis techs wrestle with the cabling while I sit in pilot seat feeding them joystick input when they need to run a diagnostic.

Hel and Gritch have to work together and so they grow to tolerate one another. Neither of them refers back to their special night on the video screen.

Hel and I start out all business, then as the hours grind by we get too tired to care, and even share a few fatigue-drunk giggles that make my heart do its hopeful little flutter and my crotch twang. It's been over half a year since I've made love to a real, live female so it's a wonder that Heloise can't *hear* the twang.

Don't get me wrong. Heloise Chin is a human-shaped hunk of antimatter, an emotional vortex, a sexual vandal. She's also competent as hell, which attracts me. And her face and body are objectively stunning, which short-circuits my few remaining sensible neurons.

It's hopeless.

I'm playing the long game now. I'm not going to score with Hel on this journey, that's clear, and admitting that takes some pressure off me. Heloise is bound to fall for me once we get into space. Outer space is where I shine. Mick Oolfson is a patient man.

The last task Gritch wrings out of Karabuk's techs is to attach the beefy mounting struts to Enterprise that will mate with the Buran mountpoints on the Energia.

When we steam into harbor at Poti on the Black Sea coast of Georgia under a grey noon sky, I follow Gritch and Hel as they wander groggily to the ship's rail to take a first, bleary-eyed squint at Russia. Course it's not really Russia proper, but the Republic of Georgia was once locked up in the good old Evil Empire.

Last year's Russia-Georgia flareup didn't affect Poti; in fact, the port was thriving. Our tanker wends its way past the busy docks to a deserted stretch of coastline. Looks like an abandoned military base.

Down on the dock we spot the unmistakable figure of Manuel Chin. He doesn't even glance up at us as we tie up. He's deep in conversation with a group of three gents whom we are soon to know all too intimately.

Gritch and I follow Hel down the ramp to meet Manuel, who waits at the bottom. From a distance it's apparent that his white suit is wrinkled and dust-stained. He looks tuckered out. Didn't know Chin was mortal like that.

He hugs Hel, which seems to surprise them both. Manuel smiles and looks me in the eye when he shakes my hand. Good to see him. After greeting Gritch, he booms ceremoniously, "Let me introduce our new business associates, Struggli, Bom, and Clint."

Cool customers. We get a squint-eyed nod from the one in the shiny blue suit and a laconic mock salute out of the one in the black leather jacket and jeans. "They will be expediting our passage to our destination. These gentlemen are members of a well-respected professional fraternal organization." Translation: Russian Mafiya.

Chin turns to the third, dressed in mismatched military gear and wearing a crack-lipped grin revealing a shortage of incisors— by far the friendliest-looking of the three. Chin can't help smiling at the fellow. "This is Bom—a Russian Army combat engineer on a kind of extended entrepreneurial leave." Turns out he's AWOL from the latest flare-up of the Chechen quagmire.

The three wait expectantly, eyes glued to Heloise.

Chin points. "Gritch. He fixes rockets."

Clint—leather jacket—translates.

Chin points again. "Mick. He drives rockets."

Clint does the Russian and they all nod at me. Bom pumps me a big, beefy handshake. The guy works for a living—calluses.

And the one they've all been waiting for, Chin puts his arm around Hel's shoulders. "Heloise, my daughter. Technical expert."

Clint translates as he shakes her hand, then Struggli's turn, and after Bom gives her a two-handed shake, smiling a glorious gap-toothed smile, he reaches into the pocket of his duffel coat and pulls out a sausage and knife and slices a generous hunk, which Heloise graciously accepts and chews appreciatively. She can deploy the social graces when it's useful.

Chin announces grandly, "Clint and Struggli and Bom are to escort you to our launch site, attending to security and border niceties and any practical matters that should arise. Darthy and Richard and I shall fly ahead to Baikonur to expedite preparations for launch."

Richard expediting prep? Most likely Dar will lock him in a closet with some pills. I *will* talk to Chin about Richard. Alone.

Chin continues proudly, "To demonstrate what fine and capable fellows are these three gentlemen, I direct your attention to that sizable container of liquid."

A large grey-green fuel tank on wheels.

Gritch asks, "Bourbon?"

Chin booms, "Twelve hundred liters of the purest nitrogen tetroxide."

That puts a smile on all our faces. Live thruster tests are GO!

Chin lowers his voice. "On a less pleasant note, your good friend Captain Ishwald continues to hound us."

Damn! "Ishwald's in Georgia?"

Chin looks grim. "I have no knowledge of his whereabouts. His trouble comes in the form of a well-publicized reward: one million dollars for information leading to the recovery of Enterprise. Our shuttle's absence from the reunion at The Cape has become a major scandal."

Gritch grouses, "We gotta drag Enterprise all that way with a target painted on our ass? I hear this ain't exactly Iowa."

Chin says, "Clint has news that should reassure you of your safety."

Clint stands up straight and informs us, "Your Ishvalt say reward for Enterprise one million dollars. My boss say reward also. Is reward for person rats on Enterprise. Reward is one bullet." He mimes a pistol shot to the back of his neck. "All persons here know this."

I look at Chin hard. He's smiling at Clint as if this was some pre-game pep rally.

I've got to say this, "I just want to point out that we're talking about shooting people for a video station. That's a little rich for my blood."

Chin says firmly, "No one will be shot because no one will dare turn in Enterprise. The reward is a matter of deterrence."

Clint squints and smiles me an ugly smile. "My boss name Hwadco Delp is respeck. Is fear."

Chin adds, "Darthy and Richard will accompany me to meet Mr. Delp. His private plane awaits us."

I must get Manuel alone to talk over Head.

Chin turns to head up the ramp to the ship. "I will wait here only as long as it takes to offload Enterprise. Let us all go aboard to prepare our spaceship for hoisting."

Gritch snaps, "Not so fast. I gotta raise a big red flag right here. We behind schedule on refitting Enterprise. Your friend in Baikonur says we gotta launch in ten days. Your boys here got us some fuel, any way they can get us three more days at Baikonur?"

Chin turns to Clint, "Could Mr. Delp buy us three more days at Baikonur?"

Clint smiles and brushes aside the problem, "I tell him three days more. Delp name is respeck."

The dock is deserted—no ships tied up at what looks like a normally busy cargo offloading center. Our babysitters have arranged for a "holiday" for the workers.

Karabuk's twenty techs stay belowdeck on Merzifon's orders. He's serious about not getting entangled in the ex-USSR. Those folk turned in some good, hard hours for Zilch. Enterprise is going to be damn near ready to mount on that Energia when we hit Baikonur.

The tanker crew and our new Mafiya pals all pitch in to prep Enterprise for offloading. Even Richard finally makes an appearance, although he doesn't get his hands dirty. Darthy stays near Head and avoids me—fine with me.

No chance to corner Chin. Moving a shuttle is always a hairy undertaking and we're shorthanded, so all spare hands wrestle the massive cargo netting. Gritch sweats bullets watching his baby manhandled.

Bom climbs into the control booth of the massive crane and it grinds to life. We hold our breath as the netting tightens. The shuttle strains free of the deck—a metal screech rattles my fillings and the crane's yellow arm sags. Enterprise whomps hard back onto the deck.

Gritch screeches, "Cut the cable. Back off! That fuckin crane's gonna crush my shuttle!"

We get a taste of our babysitters' Mr. Fixit chops. Struggli and Bom confer and head offsite, Clint orders us to put the tarps back on Enterprise and stay onboard.

Merzifon neglected to send his top cooks along with his top techs. The Zilch crew carries our personal belongings to the tanker's dining hall where we pass time by drinking bad coffee and eating stale rolls.

I finally get some face time with Manuel by grabbing a seat at his table; unfortunately Clint has latched onto him like a new-found best friend. Darthy and Hel are safely out of earshot across the long room.

I pick a safe topic. "Your friend Merzifon sure came through for Zilch. Did you hear about the tanker and *Potent Bull* decoys?"

Chin's eyes light up, "I have heard only the barest outline of your saga but I gather that Odysseus would have fled shrieking from the dangers you faced down. Would that I had been there. My good friend Merzifon Karabuk showed commendable allegiance."

Clint listens, but I doubt that he understands half of what Manuel spouts.

I say, "Good thing Merz is such a huge Trekkie. Enterprise means a lot to him."

Chin looks puzzled. "After you left Istanbul, friend Karabuk contacted me rather urgently trying to invest in Channel Zilch. He talked about a movie. It seems that he is not concerned about financial return, which concerns me a great deal. Did my daughter have anything to do with this?"

I check over my shoulder to see that Heloise is well out of earshot before I say, "Hel did a number on Merz, all right. She told him he'd be wiping his ass with Benjamins when he kicked the bucket, but if he invests in Zilch we'll all live forever. She was on quite a jag that night. Whatever the hell she was yammering about didn't sound like Channel Zilch to me."

Chin noses in. "So it wasn't an affectional bonding she engineered in Karabuk that motivated this?"

I roll my eyes. "Cupid the Affectional Bonding Engineer. Nobody can top you for a euphemism, Manuel. You know I don't read your daughter real well. Did she play the lust card with Merzifon? Don't think so, probably, who knows?"

"And how has your relationship with Heloise progressed?"

I sigh another in a long series of sigh. "Same. Noble and unrequited love on my side. On her side, well, I'm the same old cat toy that she bats at every now and then when she's bored. Other than that she ignores me, except for business."

"Poor Mick. Did my warning help?"

I blush, recalling dropping the bomb secret. "Yeah, thanks, changed my life." Can't make myself tell him, so I change the subject. "So did you cut Merz in for some Channel Zilch action?"

Chin shakes his head and looks at me proudly. "We need no partners. Our costs are manageable and our investment is undiluted. Channel Zilch remains a wholly owned subsidiary of Chin, Ltd."

Chin stands. "You must excuse me. Right back." He heads off toward the can. Clint is up getting a refill of something. Time to buttonhole Manuel.

I catch up with Chin in the men's room. I'll spare you plumbing details.

I say what I need to say first, "Manuel, I don't like dealing with these hoods. That one bullet reward thing is heavy shit. I know that your friend Merzifon doesn't do business in this part of the world but couldn't you find a legitimate freight service?"

Chin says dismissively, "Listen to yourself. What legitimate freight service would touch our stolen Enterprise? Capitalism is still raw in this part of the world—every deal is clandestine to some degree."

"Russian Mafiya is no joke. These guys…"

Chin brushes me off, "At the end of the day these guys want to earn a profit, and I am paying them well. If I had not contracted with Delp I would need to find someone just like him. Now let us return to our atrocious coffee."

I persist, "But how do we know they aren't going to turn us in for Ishwald's million?"

"Mr. Delp, the Mafiya boss, agreed to a fee of six hundred thousand dollars to facilitate our trip. He says that his word continues to be good and that he would never cooperate with NASA Security in any case. A matter of honor among thieves. And did our friends not produce the fuel you need for your tests?"

"That was impressive. I'm not so impressed with their crane handling so far."

Chin shrugs. "Clint promises a fix within hours. He sounds extremely confident."

I get to the tough point. "We need to talk about Head."

Chin looks a bit peeved. "Still going on about Richard? You never accepted his hiring."

I say, "I tried, Manuel. But did you hear how he acted when we came through Gibraltar? The guy is going—"

The bathroom door slams open and Clint strides in, relaxing when he spots Chin. "Manuel, is good see."

I'm blunt. "Clint, I need a moment alone with Manuel. Business, you understand."

Clint says, "Is business then talk. I am partner."

I consider—Richard really has nothing to do with these guys, so I dive in. "We've got to fire Richard. The guy is a danger to himself and to those around him. Richard has to go."

Chin narrows his eyes and holds up one hand. "I will not discuss Richard without Darthy and my daughter at hand."

"Richard Head is bad news," I persist. "He's got a drug problem and he nearly killed Ishwald with a flare gun. I want you to fire—"

Out of nowhere Clint butts in, "Stop talking bad of Reeshard Head. My boss has seen wideo of Reeshard Head and is beeg fan."

I react angrily, "I don't care—"

Clint grabs my collar, twists it tight on my neck, and yells, "SHUT UP OF REESHARD HEAD!"

I go rigid and lock eyes with him. Chin bellows at top volume, "UNHAND HIM!"

Clint jerks away from me, evidently hearing The Voice for the first time. The bathroom rings with echoes.

Clint goes from shock to anger in an instant. I'm pissed but I'm not going to escalate this battle. I don't know the rules.

Chin is furious and his voice swells to rattle the loose plumbing, "I will talk to Mr. Delp about your treatment of our astronaut."

Clint smiles without a crumb of sincerity and brushes off my collar with the back of his hand. "Is mistake. No problem. We friends, yes?" He gestures toward the restroom door. "All peoples outside. We are lifting Enterprise."

I dig in. "But Richard."

Clint's eyes narrow and Chin shakes his head. "Mr. Delp is indeed a huge fan of Richard Head. When explaining Channel Zilch to Delp I showed him a video of Richard's oatmeal box audition and it mesmerized the man though he knows no English. Delp was starstruck by Richard, insisted I fly him out with me to Baikonur."

I knew I'd have a battle to ditch Richard, but I never foresaw a gangster fan club.

Clint points toward the door. "We now are lifting Enterprise. Outside please."

"Cheer up, Mick," says Chin. "Let us go assist with the transfer of Enterprise."

When I get out on deck the sight takes my mind off personnel issues. A monstrous grey crane hoists Enterprise like a balsawood glider. Our resourceful chums borrowed the crane from a local nuclear reactor site.

Clint shadows Manuel and makes it impossible for me to say another word about Richard. I'm helping tie down Enterprise to an enormous military truck when I see Manuel get in a car with Darthy and Head. I may have to learn to live with Richard Head. I just hope he self-destructs in front of Manuel's eyes.

And then I feel bad for hoping that. Maybe, just maybe, Head will pull himself together under Darthy's care.

Sure thing.

A little jaunt from the Black Sea to the Caspian. Our itinerary is by massive military truck from Poti to Oni, across the Georgian/ Russian border to Niz Zaramag, then Ardon, and on to Terek. Then by train to Prochladniyj where we hang a hard right to Mozdok and points east to the port city of Makhachkala on the Caspian Sea. This is maybe 500 miles. Except for the fact that we're travelling at 7 mph rather than 70, it's just like traveling from Minneapolis to Chicago—a middling day's drive through Wisconsin.

Except Wisconsin isn't split into a dozen regions, each of which hates the entrails of every other region. This is the Caucasus mountains, home to some of humanity's ugliest ethnic and religious hatreds. Everyone worships different gods or the same god in different ways, so of course it makes perfect sense to beat the crap out of one another. Mix in some Russian military forces trying to keep a lid on the strife by playing favorites with one ethnic group after having been whupped soundly by other tribes, stir in Iran to the south giving support to some of the Islamic groups, the terrorist training grounds set up by America's historically screwed-up foreign policy in the region, and you get one of the most lethal slices of real estate in the Solar System.

When this region came out of the Commie deep-freeze, it thawed and sent up an unholy reek of rancid history.

Struggli is a Chechen, and Chechnya is the center of the region's Mafiya. The Chechen Mafiya thrived during the past year of the brutal Third Chechen War, running guns and carrying out mercenary hits for both sides. Our Chechen gang have ties with the Ossetians and a few of the gangs on the Georgian West coast. The crazy quilt map of these alliances dictates our route.

The first day of our trip is through Georgian territory controlled by gangs warring with our guys' gang. So we deck the big transport truck out in Georgian military markings, swaddle the shuttle in grey canvas, and convoy with jeeps fore and aft.

Hel, Gritch, and I stay inside the shuttle. She's determined to fire off some of that new tet to track down those thruster anomalies.

The three of us spend the first day of our trek under the covers together, the covers being mildewed grey canvas tarps wrapping the shuttle. Hel has installed a PC joystick for me to fly with, a top-of-the-line force feedback model used by gamers to slaughter monsters in dungeons. While I go through a rigidly-ordered sequence of flight maneuvers, she monitors the response of the thruster fuel valves in an endless series of dry runs—tests where we don't actually feed the thrusters any gas. Gritch traces wires in the wall panels looking for an intermittent short.

Clint checks in occasionally via walkie-talkie from the trailing jeep. Bom drives the mega-truck Enterprise rides. Struggli leads the way in the second jeep.

I'm an utter drooling idiot from lack of sleep but Hel the Inexhaustible is on task, hunched over in the CDR's chair beside me, her custom amber spex flickering from within their cheesy pink plastic frames, typing in air, pissed when I blow a simulated maneuver or when she has to nudge me awake.

It becomes one of those timeless stretches that could measure days, weeks, eons. Seems like I've always been here sitting in the pilot seat of a shuttle, canvas shrouding the cockpit windows, rumbling along a potholed Georgian back road, listening to Heloise drone orders at me, "...translate full starboard 5 seconds, rotate z-axis 15 degrees, center stick, initiate x-axis negative..."

Clint on the radio, voice tight, "We haf problem." The transport stops hard with a dry rasp of brakes.

Hel queries, "'Sup?"

"Road is block. Eight men with weapon. No uniform. Tree on road. Struggli in front jeep they argue. They walk along truck. One walk toward me. Two go look under tarp."

Heloise yells to Gritch, "Go live! I need hydrazine and tet NOW!"

"The hell you say?" Gritch's reply is muffled. Gritch's feet twitch in agitation, sticking out of an access panel.

Hel yells louder, "Give me juice, NOW!"

Gritch's feet jerk once, and then again. "You got it. This better be good."

Heloise radios Clint, "On my three we give them a scare and step on it."

Clint hisses, "Struggli is pulling gun. Is wery, wery bad."

Heloise turns to me. "Fuck three. Jam it, Mick."

I slam the joystick full forward and a gout of flame rips the canvas from the windshield and blows it blazing into the air. I rock the stick side to side and blue snarling torches lance out the sides of the nose.

Our thruster blasts illuminate the night scene around us. Men run or lie flat on the snow. Struggli busts his jeep through the roadblock, scattering the log barrier. Bom starts the transport lumbering forward while I play deranged dragon with the thrusters. A big hunk of burning, sparking canvas spins crazily down to drape over a running man who dances with it for a second and leaps into a snow bank.

I release my tension with a roaring "YeeeeHaaa!" I've got a rhythm going with the thrusters which starts to rock the whole transport side to side as we pick up speed.

Heloise belly laughs like I've never heard her. She whips off her glasses to wipe her eyes. "Cut, Mick. Funfunfun."

She goes all business, data-seeking, "Did you get a visual on the flame length from number one x-axis port nose thruster?"

What a gal!

At Prochladniyj we ditch the transport and take a train skirting well north of newly-ruined Groznyj, the epicenter of the Chechen/Russian dirty war. Struggli's gang retook this piece of turf the hard way—they own the place. We make no attempts to act covert except for the usual gift wrapping on the shuttle.

We get a sleeper car all our own. Much vodka gets drunk in the lounge by our three helpers. I choose catching up on my beauty sleep over bonding with gangsters.

Clint and Struggli are no fun to be around, every interaction is a power struggle—exhausting. I can't wait to get to Baikonur and be done with our Mafiya guides.

I can't wait to get to Baikonur and be done with Earth.

Hel is lost in her laptop, writing code for our live thruster tests. Whenever I doubt this crazy Zilch scheme, I only have to look at Heloise Chin—totally focused without a doubt in her mind.

I stare out the window at beautiful country, mountainous and wild. Villages are war zones. Walls tumbled by shells and clawed by bullets. No children. Women walking in small groups, heads down, carrying water in yoked buckets. Men with hard faces and worn guns. Good times on the borderlands of the Jahweh/Allah fan club turf wars.

Ishwald can't touch us here.

CHAPTER TWENTY-NINE: A ROMANTIC CRUISE ON THE FABLED CASPIAN SEA

WE RIDE THE MILITARY FLATBED to Makhachkala, port city of marshes and mosquitoes. The lands of the old USSR never really got into the new-fangled ecology craze. In the U.S. we try to potty train our industries and cities, but in this neck of the woods, if you've got garbage or industrial waste you dump it out of sight.

Makhachkala is one of the biggest cities on the Caspian. The Makhachkalese employ a small fleet of garbage barges to carry their trash out to sea and drown it. A garbage barge can be rented for peanuts, just buy the fuel and give the captain a couple hundred American bills and you can call one your own for a pleasure cruise anywhere on the Caspian Sea. Don't bathe in or drink the water.

Garbage scows stink. They rock with every wave. Enough said. A two-day crossing to Aktua on the Kazakhstan coast. I ate maybe three crackers and they didn't stay ate long.

Clint's been hitting hard on Heloise ever since Chin left us. Crude stuff along the lines of "Hiya, baby. You like go with real man sometime?"

Struggli eggs him on and adds his own rude harassment, makes kissing noises and rubs his pinky on his wrist, a gesture which must be chockfull of sexual innuendo in his culture.

Bom stays out of it. He grins and reddens whenever Heloise glances his way.

The second day on the boat the constant, crude lechery wears on my nauseated nerves. I'm not fool enough to fantasize that Heloise needs my help. She's studying these guys under her psychroscope, brushing them off in a bristly, firm manner that leaves them unbalanced and upset.

Gritch shakes his head slowly. "Them boys better watch it. Little lady's liable to take em up on their offer and then we'd have a couple dead Mafiya stinking up the ship or some freaked up crazy gangsters runnin round with guns. Gonna happen. Betcha she calls em on it."

So she did.

We're all in the Enterprise's cargo bay. Clint is sitting on top of Captain America's Harley making motorcycle noises while Gritch and Heloise do some technical stuff with a bay door motor. I slump against a carton of Monkees albums staring listlessly at the group, all puked out and no use to anyone. Struggli and Bom play cards on a wooden carton.

As Hel strolls past Clint he pinches her bottom. Snake-strike quick her hand lashes out and snags his wrist. He laughs and tries to shake her grip off, but she holds firm, locking eyes with him, her mind chewing away behind those green slits.

She lets go and chucks him under the chin with her thumb. "You sure know how to turn on an American girl."

Clint looks startled. "I am radical love engine. Hot ladies fall over me at all times."

I can see it coming. Gritch tinkers intently with the bay door motor.

Heloise purrs, "I'm ready to fall."

She grabs a lapel of Clint's leather jacket and yanks him off the Harley. "Follow, stud-pig."

Clint flashes me a triumphant look as she leads him toward the airlock. I wink at him and give him thumbs up. Gritch stifles a chuckle that turns into a cough.

Struggli and Bom watch the exchange quizzically. Clint Russians at them and their eyes bug out. As Hel drags Clint past them her other hand snakes out and snags Struggli's collar.

"Tell Struggli to join us."

Clint looks dubious. Hel hectors him, "There's plenty of Hel to go around. I'm no piteous male with finite fluid reserves. Go on, ask him."

Gritch breaks into a fresh fit of coughing.

Clint translates and Struggli gives a big nod and shrug. Bom blushes infrared and looks concerned.

"Tell Bom not to worry, Clint."

Clint rolls his eyes to the ceiling and grins.

"You tell Bom I'm okay or I'll fuck Struggli dry and leave you sucking wind."

Clint hastens to translate Hel's message to Bom. Heloise dishes him one of her snake-charmer smiles. He nods and gives a little wave as they head toward the airlock. Heloise has set up her boudoir inside the middeck, and that's where she takes them.

Gritch looks over at me. "How long you give em boys?"

I smile a crooked smile and shake my head.

Gritch cackles and glances at his watch. "I give em less than twenty minutes. Care to put ten bucks against me?"

"You're the expert there, Gritch. I got no data to extrapolate from."

The airlock door slams shut.

I have no right to feel jealous but it surprises me that I don't even feel a twinge. Whatever Heloise is about to do to those two, it's got nothing to do with love, sex, or lust. Can't feel jealous of dudes I pity.

We hear the first muffled howl and Gritch checks his watch. "Seven minutes, forty-seven seconds."

The airlock door swings open and Clint scrambles out, wearing a pair of baby blue underpants, one cowboy boot, and a look of dazed revulsion on his face. He stands in front of the airlock goggling at us, takes a deep breath and gives his head a quick shake as if to clear it. He forces a smile and gives us thumbs up and a nod, when he gets hit from below and his knees crumple. He collapses on Struggli who is crawling desperately out of the airlock, away from Hel's "orgy," mumbling a long, low babble of Russian.

When they untangle, Struggli stands. He's got red tights on his legs. His arm is wound round with duct tape and trails a dozen feet of what looks like black vacuum cleaner hose.

The two give each other a long look, and an entertaining sequence of emotions wriggles across their mugs: relief, horror, embarrassment, anger, confusion.

Gritch cuts in on their special little moment. "You boys sure were quick. Forget yer rubbers?"

Clint barks a phony laugh and fumbles in his shirt pocket until he extracts a pack of Kools.

Gritch leans close to Clint. "Jess give us the highlights. How many times y'all do it?"

Clint slowly brings a cigarette toward his lips and drops it just short of its goal. He doesn't bend to pick it up but slowly puts the pack back in his pocket.

Gritch cackles. "Know watcha mean. I tapped that ass. Words can't get aholt of the real thing. But give it a try."

Struggli starts to mumble, fast and low. He looks up at me beseechingly and his voice gets louder.

Clint still won't look in our direction, but he speaks. "I tell you words from Struggli. He says the crazy woman tell us she need work math problem. Sex math she call it. Then she put on her computer glasses and take shirt off. Better, I think, she joking about math, but no. Writing on wall many numbers, she ignore us, stands looking at numbers. I come to touch her a little bit and she turn around, so beautiful tiny tits, but she say wait and I will set things up. She go in closet, Struggli and me start take clothes off, expect her come out maybe naked, but no—she have on suit with lights on belly. The lights are making numbers. She carries box, takes out tape, hose, red pants, tells Struggli put on, then tapes hose to arm. Struggli getting nervous. Don't feel sexy, how can I, she so crazy? Then from the box takes metal crab with long pink willy like donkey and is moving like alive. She give me look in eyes and walks to me, crab starts wave legs and make noise like kitten. I am gone from there. Is no way, man. Up fucked she is in head."

Amen, brother, you read that one right.

Struggli stops talking and Clint goes silent. Bom takes in the scene with a frown on his face and a crease of concern on his brow.

Gritch snorts. "You guys never had sex with an American woman?"

Later that night, I bump into Hel and ask, "Clint said something about a metal crab with a big pink willy. One of your pets?"

"One. Willy, huh? I like that. He's Mr. Willy from now on. I made it for a friend but it creeped her so I kept it, since it's an amazing little beastie. I power it up for special occasions."

"Clint thought it was real special."

"Made that boy a sweet n sexy horror story to scare his grand-kids."

We dock in Aktua, Kazakhstan, in the wee hours of the night. It's a railhead port often used to transship huge sections of rockets floated down the Volga and bound for Baikonur.

Our final mode of transport is an old diesel locomotive pulling Enterprise on an oversized flatcar. There is one other car in the train—it carries two big orange shipping containers. The long sides of each container are boldly labeled "ChoirWorks".

Hel squeals, "They delivered the server farms. The Choir comes through again."

"What are server farms?" I ask.

"Server farms are lots of hard drives and processors."

"Why do we need two server farms?"

"To save all our video. Video takes lots of disk space. Lots. Oodles and oodles of gigas and teras."

I like it when she confides in me. Treats me as a peer. "They going to fit in the shuttle bay?"

"All calced into load distribution. They're half-length, twenty by eight by seven. Plop em in side-by-side."

We keep up our numbing workpace on the trip. I get back to pulling my weight now that the sea and stink are behind us and food stays in my belly. Clint and Struggli give Heloise a wide, nervous berth. It's good to see the boys knocked down a notch. Can't wait to see the last of them when we get to Baikonur.

We stop the train at night in the open desert near Bejneu and run a series of live thruster tests. As I work her controls I feel Enterprise come alive. The RCS thrusters boom and kick precisely to my stick inputs. No trace of the previous anomalies—OMS and RCS thrusters are ready for operation. Sitting on a train in the midst of a vast desert plain, it's hard to accept that the next time Enterprise fires her thrusters we'll be a hundred miles high.

CHAPTER THIRTY: MAFIYA ZAP

NEXT AFTERNOON I'm sitting mesmerized by the flat landscape— I swear I saw some camels in the distance—when the train's brakes shriek. A humongous green Russian army chopper stands beside the tracks and as we roll past, brakes squealing, I see Chin standing beside it. The train screeeeches to a long, slow stop a mile down the track. The chopper lifts off and lands near our locomotive, stirring up a pink cloud of dust.

I watch Struggli and Clint saunter to meet Manuel. Something about the cocky way they walk gives me the willies. Chin looks glum as they escort him to the shuttle's flatcar. GritchHel and I go to meet him.

He doesn't quite look me in the eye as he shakes my hand. A cursory greeting to his daughter and Gritch. He launches right into a briefing.

"Delp was unable to extend our launch window at Baikonur. You will arrive late tonight and we have eight full days to prepare for launch. As per plan, our good friend Mr. Kropotkin has arranged for the bulk of Russian supervisors and workers and international satellite personnel to be transferred away from

Baikonur on an extended planning and training assignment to the new Russian Vostochny launch site. All untrusted personnel will be absent from Baikonur for nine days. They departed this morning.

"A small contingent of trusted Kazakh Energia specialists was left behind. They will do the bulk of the work to ready and launch the Energia. It is our job to mount Enterprise on Energia and launch before the Russian personnel return. We have eight days to mount and fire the shuttle."

Gritch rolls his eye at me.

"Any questions?"

Gritch pipes up, "Eight days from tomorrow. You mean that, dontcha? I ain't even got a look at that Energia and you want a shuttle mating and launch in eight days."

Chin nods emphatically. "You approved the Energia-Enterprise interface plans. The Kazakh engineers are excellent and the booster is prepared for flight."

Gritch nods, "I don't deny you got me to give thumbs up to the plans and timetable. And I know the Russians got damn good techs and booster hardware. But we got no margin for fuckups, bad weather, bad software—"

Heloise cuts in, "My software will run. You don't trust your hardware?"

Gritch faces her, "Your software came through trackin down them thruster glitches but listen, little lady..." He pauses and looks uncomfortable. "Sorry, Heloise. Look, I'm not gonna bullshit you—I'm as crazy as all y'all but I need to know I have authority to scrub the launch if I can't give it a thumbs up. I want to hear you all say it."

Heloise: "This sucks razors. You do your work and we'll decide if we take the risk. Pop, tell him."

Manuel shakes his head.

Gritch looks hard at each of us, his gum-chewing slow and heart-felt. "Sure, you're taking the risk. But if the shuttle dies you die. It's over for you and I'm on the ground watching my friends die. I did that already with Challenger and Columbia. You don't think that tears a man's guts out?"

I feel the tearing in my own gut, the sorrow, rage, helplessness on seeing that white puff of death at the pinnacle of Challenger's pillar of smoke.

Gritch continues in a low shaky voice, "Listen, we had this talk before but I gotta hear it again. I'm not holding us to NASA standards, but I gotta feel you got a real chance or I pull the plug."

Chin nods, "You make the final call, Gritch."

I pat Gritch on the shoulder. "You give the GO/NO GO, Gritch. I'm not driving this bird until I see your scrawny thumb sticking way up."

Heloise squints and nods. "One, Gritch. That's the way it is. You're hardware; I'm software."

Our approach to Baikonur riles Struggli and Clint—they get even more edgy and rude. Baikonur Cosmodrome was the Soviet Union's doorway into the cosmos. All cosmonauts from Gagarin on blasted off from its parched clay soil.

When the CCCP went FFFT, Baikonur happened to wind up deep inside the newly independent Kazakhstan, and the Kazakhs played their advantage to the hilt. One of the first post-Soviet cosmonauts was a Kazakh. Russia gets to lease the Cosmodrome from K-stan for a hefty penny, but it has to treat it as a jointly run facility and hire locals and train them in space operations until it gets its new Cosmodrome at Vostochny online. This creates an unwieldy bureaucratic beastie that gives us a loophole big enough to fly a shuttle through.

The shuttle train is dark, creeping over the rail spur that runs around the perimeter of Turyatam. Struggli and Clint and a couple of their heavily armed buddies ride shotgun, scanning for Russian military. Seems that they've tangled with the Russian military before and won some, lost some.

The gangsters have Chin cooped up with them somewhere on the train. Heloise's temper is operating in the red.

Gritch, Hel, and I are buttoned up snug in the shuttle, all sprawled out on sleeping bags on the middeck floor. Gritch and Hel discuss a wiring diagram and I'm trying to pick up a decent rock station on the radio. Nothing but staticy Arabic wailing and American preachers trying to ring up a few more ex-commie souls.

A rapping on the side hatch. Gritch gets up and swings it open. Chin steps in and Gritch slams the hatch behind him.

"What the hell you up to?" says Gritch. "Them heavies after you?"

Chin slowly rolls his eyes upward and sighs.

"Spill it, quick," Says Hel.

Chin looks down and says quietly, "Our gangster acquaintances have become quite avaricious."

I strike my forehead and act stunned. "Say it isn't so! Clint and Struggli? I thought this escort service was like a Boy Scout good deed type of deal. Did they have the gall to ask for money?"

Chin grimaces. "I wish that were all. You won't often hear Manuel Chin doubt himself, but I feel like an idiot thinking I could best the Mafiya. Big American businessman pulling a fast one on a bunch of yokel crooks."

"Don't be so hard on yourself," says Gritch.

Hel: "You screwed up, didn't you, Pop? Slap yourself one for me."

I interrupt this heartwarming family exchange, "We're still launching, aren't we?"

Chin nods and smiles a weary flicker. "The launch goes on. But we now have a partner."

Loud knocking on the side hatch. Chin freezes.

Gritch says, "Locked. They can't get in."

Chin lowers his voice, "The gangster boss, Mr. Delp, wants a cut of Zilch. And we have to take his son along on Enterprise."

Heloise growls, "Zero."

Rap, rap. A muffled yell from outside.

Chin flinches. "Best let our rude friends enter."

Heloise tilts her head and her eyes go tight, slits of green lava. "Sure thing, Pop." She takes two purposeful strides and yanks the hatch open. Clint stumbles into the room. Heloise throws her arms around his neck, jumps up and hugs his waist with her legs. He struggles to catch his balance but topples and falls forward onto a sleeping bag right on top of her. A pistol clatters out of his hand onto the deck floor near my feet. Great, a gun.

"Crazy woman!" Clint shouts and strains to push himself up but Hel has all four limbs wrapped tight around him and his arms tangle in the sleeping bags. Gritch slams the hatch shut.

"I KILL YOU!" Clint screams.

Chin walks towards me, eager eyes on the pistol at my feet. I quickly pick it up.

Clint frees one arm and pulls it back to wallop Heloise in the face. I see it coming, step forward and raise the gun to womp the side of his head, but Hel presses her face to Clint's ear and blocks my shot. As I shift to get a crack at the back of his skull, she blows a hard lungful straight into his ear hole and Clint shrieks, stiffens, jerks, and slumps slowly like a lousy actor milking a death scene.

His body shudders as Heloise jerks herself out from under him. "Give me a hand, spaceman."

I roll Clint off her. "How bad did you hurt him?"

"Deaf in that ear. Had it coming. He was annoying Pop. Right, old man?"

Chin nods. "And now we have gravely annoyed Boss Delp." His brow wrinkles sadly.

Hel snorts. "The night is but a blastocyst. How many gangsters?"

"Moonchild, things have gone quite far enough. Zilch isn't in danger; the launch will go on, albeit with an unwelcome partner."

Hel says fiercely, "We conned NASA, we escaped the U.S. Navy, we whipped Ishwald. Maximally suboptimal to cave to these guys, especially after the way they jacked you around."

Chin purses his lips and nods. "They have been rather rude to me."

Hel smiles, pats him on the elbow. "How many gangsters are out there?"

"Five. Bom and one other in the engine. Clint was holding me in the last car with Struggli and one other very unpleasant young man."

Heloise takes a deep, satisfied breath. "We gone have funs, peoples."

She runs to her locker while Gritch ties up the unconscious Clint. Chin gives me a quizzical look. I roll my eyes and shake my head; he smiles and nods. He did his best to warn me but I'm still lost in the girl.

When she returns, she wears her pink rhinestone computer sunglasses and carries a nasty-looking toy—one of her robot pets—a scorpion of matte black plastic and grey metal about the size of a cat.

She sets it down. Her hands do the air-typing thing and the wicked little critter whirs and scuttles toward the door. I open it, and the evil-looking metal bug climbs the wall, swings sideways through the door, and skitters out into the night.

Our train creeps through Kazakh darkness. Intermittent metal squeaks remind us that we are on a train within ten miles of the Cosmodrome, our last stop on Earth til launch and/or death.

"That's my taserbot, Zsa Zsa Gabot." Heloise's hands dance in a regular rhythm, like she's massaging a porcupine.

Gritch hmms. "Gonna make them Mafiya monkeys twitch, huh?"

"Zsa Zsa's got eight taser stinger darts and only needs twenty-two seconds to recharge between jolts. A lightning-tailed scorpionbot is ultradiscouraging to its victims."

You ever watch someone play a computer game when you can't see the screen? They look like lunatics, and that's Heloise for the next half-hour. Only her voice clues us into how she's scoring at Mafiya Zap.

"I'm going for Struggli and gangster number one in the back."

Gesture, gesture. "See their train car. Good thing Zsa Zsa's got a superb gecko-inspired traction system cause I'm going up that wall. Now peek in the window from the top. Thoughtful boys got it open a crack. There's the Strug, looking at his watch, getting worried about Clint, poor baby. We'll take care of that."

Her hands go into a slow, weavy snaking pattern, aiming.

"VOICECAP ZAP! Bingo. That boy crumpled like a stunned ostrich. Backing the bot away from the window to let gangster one think about it while I recharge."

She hums a low string of monotone notes and nods her head in rhythm. I look over at Gritch—he stares intently at her from the side. He sees me watching and makes big eyes, sticks the tips of his fingers into his mouth and chatters his teeth up and down on them. I nod. Heloise Chin is indeed the scariest thing I've ever ogled.

Her hands flex. "Contestant Number Two, what special gift does Zsa Zsa have for you? Oh, sentimental boy, he's leaning over Struggli, can't zap a guy in the back can I? VOICECAP ZAP! Sure I can. Visual confirmation—gangster Noname twitches and he's one... two... three... out."

She lifts the pink glasses. "Gritch, go back and tie those two up while they're weak. I'll send Zsa Zsa forward to stun the rest."

Gritch: "Better leave Bom awake to drive this train."

Hel smiles. "Bom's a sweetie. I'll knock out the heavy. Bom will do whatever I ask him."

She proceeds to do exactly that. When Gritch, Hel, and I go up to the locomotive to tie up the zapped Mafiyoso, Bom looks worried for about two minutes until Hel calms him down. She mimes that she wants him to keep driving the train. He nods and turns to the throttle.

Our master plan is to choo-choo up to the gate at Baikonur and face down head gangster Delp, using his men as hostages. Chin says Delp only keeps half a dozen men with him at Baikonur, since there are only about thirty Kazakh techs manning the base. Chin seems to think our captive gangsters give us some sort of leverage over the Big Boss, so after Delp caves and slinks off we'll turn once again to the sacred business of getting our asses into space. Right. I've seen enough gangster movies to have my doubts about Chin's plan.

Manuel doesn't seem real gung-ho about his own plan, but it's the best any of us can come up with on short order. Heloise is our insurance in case Delp isn't sympathetic to the plight of our hostages. She recharges Zsa Zsa and hides out on the flatcar behind Enterprise.

I'm with Gritch and Chin in the locomotive. Bom drives. I've got one of the thugs' pistols pointed in the general direction of the cluster of tied-up Mafiya goons. Clint is groggy. We bandaged his ear and the bandage shows a few leak-spots of blood. The other three keep their hard eyes on me, waiting for me to do something stupid. No matter how I scowl they can tell I'm not the kind of guy to plug them. No fear in their eyes. Hard to feel lousy about not being respected by thugs.

Bom spots signs of Baikonur Cosmodrome and waves us to look out the window. Far out on the horizon, stark yellow light bathes a tower that's got to be our launch site being prepped. He slows our train with a banshee squeal of brakes and crash, crash, crash as cars slam against couplings.

Baikonur station creeps up on us—a dimly lit gaggle of low buildings and looming train cars. Bom inches along, throttling back the engine so it's hardly more deafening than the old *Potent Bull*.

Under a faded streetlight stand a big car and a man waving both arms. Bom hits the brakes, and metal screams like tortured robots until we grind to a halt. I look from the engineer's compartment down at a black Cadillac old enough to have futuristic fins. Waving guy opens the car door and out steps a short, puggish man in a grey double-breasted suit straight out of prohibition Chicago. And—get this—he's got a Thompson machine gun cradled in his arms. Not pointing at anyone, but very much a fact.

My tied-up bundle of goons see Delp and his Tommy gun through the open doorway. The bound thugs somehow scooch, wriggle, and roll en masse to a spot shielded from Delp by the locomotive wall. I sidle out of the open doorway myself.

A car door opens and I hear Darthy's voice, "Hey, guys, things have changed."

Darthy! We knew she was at Baikonur but hoped she wouldn't show up to greet us. That complicates things. Darthy is out there with a gangster holding a machine gun. Our leverage is problematic.

I'm the voice of Channel Zilch tonight because Manuel said that Delp didn't fear him. So I pitch my voice as low and mean as I can muster. "Tell Delp that we are ready to bargain with him. We want him out of Channel Zilch."

Darthy speaks slowly, as if to a child, "You want me to lean on Delp? He's not a nice man and he's standing next to me holding a machine gun."

I reassure her, "Delp wouldn't kill a woman. There's a Mafiya code about that."

Darthy translates this. Delp and his flunky laugh. Not a pretty sound.

I continue, loud and low, "Tell Delp that we have five of his men. If he leaves Baikonur we won't hurt the hostages. Once we get confirmation that Delp and his men are far from Baikonur we will let these guys free."

"You sure you want me to tell him that?" Her voice is shaky.

"Be forceful, Darthy. Don't show him any fear."

She translates.

A blast of machine gun fire. I yell, "NO!" and charge the door to avenge Darthy. But she's fine, standing beside Delp watching him fire his racketing gun down the side of the train.

I yell, "NO!" But he's not shooting Enterprise; he's peppering some twitching piece of junk in the gravel beside the tracks.

A Helish scream of "Shitfire!" and I realize that Zsa Zsa is scrap, no longer our secret weapon. Whoa, Hel has failed!

Delp stops shooting and barks a few lines of Russian. Darthy translates. "Delp says go ahead and shoot the hostages, or better yet let him shoot them. They—and these are his words—fucked up, and Delp hates fuckups."

Chin says, "Time to fold our hand, Mick. You were most valiant."

I wince. Delp wins.

We have a new partner in Channel Zilch.

Delp climbs into the locomotive and gives each of his terrified minions a kick in the face before having them untied.

Struggli and Clint aren't our buddies any more.

CHAPTER THIRTY-ONE: THE GANGSTERNAUT

I SLEEP THROUGH most of the first night at Baikonur alone on a metal cot in a drafty room sloppily painted a greasy yellow that made my skin crawl. My blanket scratches and leaks cold air and doesn't cover my feet but I'm beat, depressed, just generally not fired up with my usual piss and vinegar. I thought that when we got to Baikonur we'd be free of the Mafiya, but instead their heel is squarely on our neck.

I sleep, eat the hunk of cheese and half loaf of bread left by my bed, and sleep again. I worry—How are the others? Is the launch still on? What should I be doing to help? Will I ever see Heloise again?—but not enough to keep my eyes and brain from drifting shut.

I wake at dawn, tired and grumpy, and press my nose against the single pane that's not smeared with snot-colored paint. There's the gantry a couple miles away, lit by spotlights and strings of walkway bulbs. Working on our launch.

Okay, so where does that leave me? Unless they've hired another shuttle jockey I need to be knee-deep in launch prep. I feel the old pre-flight jitters rise, adrenaline molecules percolating in the blood, attention sharp, muscles cocked and ready.

The door swings open behind me and I jump. Darthy enters and I relax. A big, lumpy guy in a purple jogging suit follows her and I tense. He's sporting a holster filled with a mean hunk of lethal silver metal. The guy's dome features an enormous pompadour stiff with product.

Despite Darthy's companion it's great to see her. "Got yourself a bodyguard! Autograph hounds pestering ya?"

Darthy smiles ruefully while purple dude gives me the once over. He grumbles a mouthful of Russki and Dar speaks, "This is Blegnor Delp, the head gangster's spoiled brat of a bastard son. He welcomes you to Baikonur and offers to shine your shoes with his nose hairs."

I hold out my hand to Blegnor and ask Dar, "I take it his English is rusty."

Blegnor snorts at my offered handshake and looks away as he sweeps his hand up to his forehead to smooth his pompadour. His eyelids do this creepy pucker like his eyes bit into something nasty. Darthy smiles and winks at me and translates something at the guy who rolls his eyes and sniffs. He does a bored look around the room while speaking in a monotone for a full minute.

Dar tries to mimic his monotone, "Mr. Bigshot Delp here says that he is attracted to female chickens but they won't give him the time of day because he has a male member the size of a maggot."

I snort, choking the laugh off. Delp narrows his eyes at me. "Dar, cut it out."

She continues in the same monotone, "Can't a girl have fun? Okay, here's the story. Delp here wants you to teach him to be an astronaut in the next week."

I cringe inside but keep a neutral expression. "So it's true. We have to take this guy into orbit with us?"

Dar turns to Delp and jabbers and he spits out a single, "Da."

She turns to me and I nod. "Got it."

"That's what you think, smarty-pants. I asked him who's the ugliest guy at Baikonur and he said it's his Da." I bite my lip and Delp makes a curt cutoff signal and spews a couple paragraphs of stuff.

Darthy, "He says that he will be driving the shuttle, you will be his copilot. He's flown as passenger on many planes so he figures a week will be plenty for training."

I whine, "This can't be happening, Darthy. Look, can't he help you with the life support systems? You could train him to change carbon air scrubbers, vacuum the can?"

Darthy says angrily, "What a delightful inspiration. I'll ask him."

And she does, because he looks pissed and cuts her off. "Nyet..." and a whole string of nasty stuff aimed in my direction. He strokes his pompadour in agitation.

"He says he appreciates the career counseling but he's got the I.Q. of a clam and can't begin to understand life support systems so he's afraid he'll just have to lower his sights and drive the rocketship."

I nod and say in an enthusiastic tone, "Could you tell him to go fuck himself?"

I cringe as she "translates", but he cracks a smile at me and gives thumbs up.

I have a Mafiya babysitter wherever I go. After my introduction to Blegnor, a tiny, bald gangster walks into my room and jerks his thumb toward the door. When I hesitate he narrows his eyes and points emphatically at the door. I have a strong inclination to sit on my ass but I take the hint. If I fight every little pissing match with these guys I'll wear myself to a nub.

It's a raw day outside with a steady cold wind. My minder leads me down a gravel road among a few disused warehouses to a newer building made of white brick. I get a name out of him—Fodor.

Fodor leads me into the building and takes me to an office where I meet an English-speaking Kazakh[10]. Fred is one of the trainers at the cosmonaut training facility. He's already met baby Delp so Fred shares my insensitive attitude toward him. Fred leads me and Fodor on a tour of the training facility and makes sure to highlight their state-of-the-art centrifuge.

It's a brutal-looking contraption, especially if you've ever spent chunks of time whirling around in one. Russians build strong; they tend to over-engineer things.

Shuttle crews never did centrifuge training because the most we hit is 3 g's. I saw pictures of the scrapped NASA centrifuge—it didn't look too different from a carnival ride painted drab green—the gondola where the victim was strapped hung at the end of a fifty foot metal boom balanced with a VW bug-sized counterweight. The whole whirligig was mounted on a vertical metal axle about the thickness of a telephone pole. The thing could spin up to generate a 14-g force—enough squash to put someone in a coma.

As a trainee pilot I did a few pukey spins in a lot wimpier

---

10   I'll call him Fred. I'm not naming any of the Kazaks who helped the Zilch launch. I don't know what line of b.s. Kropotkin sold them to persuade them to help us, but I have a hunch they got nothing for their trouble but more troubles.

centrifuge. I never took over nine g's. Nine g's is a brutal crushing that leaves you aching for a week.

Baikonur's centrifuge is a centrifuge on steroids. Bigger radius, massive girder in the swinging arm, Humvee-sized counterweight, all painted the same snotty yellow as my barrack room. Fred smilingly assures me it can generate 19 g's. A 200 pound dude will mass almost two tons—cracked ribs, punctured lungs, cerebral hemorrhage, rupture—party on, dude! Blegnor must weigh in at 240.

I open the door from the centrifuge control room and walk into the huge cylindrical centrifuge chamber. Fred leads me to the passenger gondola and pops open the hatch. The familiar reek of vomit and sweat and plastic spills out of the tiny chamber. My Mafiya minder gags and backs away. Fred hops up into the gondola and gestures for me to follow. I look at Fodor and he looks away which I take as permission to step up into the stinky little shell. Fred is seated in the padded victim's seat and I stand on the tiny shelf of floor. Fred motions at the door so I swing it shut.

Fred reaches into his pocket and holds up a pen. "From Kropotkin. This for talking. Listen is here." He pulls off the pen cap and unrolls a length of thin wire. He puts the cap in an ear. "Say here." He holds the end of the pen towards his mouth.

He hands me the pen and instructs, "Talk only night. Plan launch with no gangster."

I place the cap in my ear and hear a faint hiss.

I ask, "How did you guys...?"

A jerk and then a knock at the gondola door. Fodor doesn't approve of our little tête à tête.

Fred says, "Take." I pocket it.

I swing the door open and beckon for Fodor to join us but he is content to stand and listen.

I confirm the evil educational plan with Fred, "I agree with you. The core of an accelerated cosmonaut training program has got to be frequent and prolonged sessions in the centrifuge."

Fred nods seriously and somehow keeps a straight face.

I climb into bed that night clutching Fred's magic pen. Fodor has been replaced by bland Azonov who sits outside my locked door. I put the pillow over my head to muffle the sound before I uncap the radiopen. I feel like an idiot when I put the pen cap in my ear, but there's that hiss. I speak into the pen: "Test. Test."

Nothing. The hiss is steady. I try again, "Test."

I lay there, head under the pillow, sporadically talking to the pen for a good ten minutes before the pen answers. Unfortunately the pen answers in non-American. Another voice speaks in the same language. I tentatively say, "Test" and they stop speaking.

I listen to the hiss and yawn a big yawn.

"Ping!" Even through the lo-fi earpiece, the flutish voice is clearly Hel's.

I "Ping" back at her.

"Mick! Welcome to Kazakhcomm." Heloise Chin sounds thrilled to hear me!

"Heloise!"

"Anyone else?"

I say, "I heard a couple people talking earlier, not English or Russian."

Hel says, "Kazakh. Kazakh workers use this covert comm system to go behind their Russian bosses. I call it Kazakhcomm."

I ask, "So what do we do? Can you think of a way to get the gangsters off our neck?"

A male voice, "Allo. Can you hear?" A Russian-accented tenor.

I ask, "Who is this?"

"Is Kropotkin—Wasili Kropotkin."

Hel says happily, "Dad's Russian space bureaucrat buddy. The Monkees freak."

Kropotkin laughs heartily. "Soon rich Monkees freak."

I say hopefully, "I assume you got these talking pens to us so we could pull one over on the Mafiya."

Hel, "Can you get a trick pen to Pop?"

Kropotkin says quietly, "Is not adwisable. Big Delp keep Manuel close. Pen would be danger for him. We three only are needed for planning."

I ask the big question, "So how do we arrange to leave baby Delp on the ground? No way will I share a shuttle with that..." I don't say it.

Kropotkin asks, "Why you say share?"

"I thought you'd know. I'm training baby Delp to be an astronaut so he can come along on Enterprise."

Kropotkin says quietly, "Is you who not know. Boss Delp son replace you, not be passenger."

I start to yell, but stifle my voice. "I'm training my *replacement?*"

Hel sounds like she feels this: "Oh, Mick."

"I'm going to max that centrifuge until that gangster whelp is pulped to lumpy gravy."

Hel laughs. "Sick, O-man. Vasili, how we gonna screw Delp? Any thoughts?"

Kropotkin has some well-thought-out, concrete thoughts. We make a standing date to talk every night an hour after the gangsters lock us in our rooms.

Baikonur is where The Dream was born. Gagarin launched here, the first human in space, a personal hero. I want to wander around the place like the awestruck schoolboy I was and still am. Boss Delp has other plans for me—I'm to spend this week training his son to be the astronaut who takes my place on Enterprise.

Baikonur Cosmodrome is the size of Vermont, but I'm confined to two buildings—an isolated barracks of which my Mafiya buddy and I are the only occupants, and the cosmonaut training complex.

We all have full-time Mafiya babysitters who tag along everywhere, even to the can. Delp keeps Clint and Struggli off babysitter rotation because they are emphatically empty of empathy for Zilch employees.

The gangsters have us each sleeping in different and (Kropotkin informs us) widely separated buildings. We don't see Richard or Manuel. but Kropotkin assures us that they are being well cared for.

I still haven't seen Enterprise or the promised Energia booster, but I get to play with my new best friend: Delp Jr., first name Blegnor. Now that I know he plans to take my place I have no qualms about the hell I put him through. I've got him convinced that riding multiple centrifuge runs day after day is the royal road to cosmonauthood. I admit I get a kick out of the fact that every time I see him, Blegnor looks a little worse for wear.

My third day at Baikonur I get an English-speaking Mafiya minder who wants me to call him Pete. Pete gives me great news, "We see rocket now."

The word 'rocket' perks me right up.

Pete drives us toward a massive building that I know from a distance is the Buran program's Site 112. The top of the high white wall is jagged where the roof collapsed in 2002. When you work around rockets you get used to BIG. I crane my neck upward to appreciate the scale of the walls as Pete drives around the building.

As we reach the end of the long wall we see tiny workers and then a locomotive; and beyond that—big goofy grin—is Enterprise, still on her flatcar and lookin good. Gritch's team did a great job touching up her black paint.

Something odd on her flank. As our car pulls closer I see the unmistakable purple and yellow CZ logo of Channel Zilch. Gotta admit that looks sort of sweet.

All the parts of this unlikely mission are here. We beat Ishwald and we're going to beat these thugs.

I get out of the car and look back at Site 112. The hangar doors are open, and two locomotives wait silently to pull the Energia/Buran transporter out of the cavernous space.

Above the transporter, the Energia hangs suspended under a grey frame of girders, its business end pointing our way. I've studied this Energia's configuration and seen pictures, but staring into the throats of twenty clustered rocket nozzles is a kick.

Energia is second only to NASA's historic Saturn V in boosting power—100 tons to Low Earth Orbit. Rather than developing huge rocket engines like Saturn's F-1s, Russia built their heavy-lift Energia by strapping four four-thruster Zenit boosters around a central four-big-thruster core. All twenty nozzles ignite at liftoff, and eight minutes into the flight, when the boosters run out of fuel, they drop off and the four big nozzles in the central block keep roaring all the way to orbit.

The sight of all those magnificent engines hardens my resolve to hoodwink these gangsters. I *will* ride those beauties straight up out of here.

Gritch hustles over to us, trailed by his Mafiya minder. He's grinning wide. "At Energia is some damn fine rocket. Twenty freaking engines—WHooEEE!" We shake hands and he keeps going, "Ese Kazakhs stored at Energia in tiptop shape. It should fire just as good as the last one."

The last Energia launched the single successful Buran mission! I clap Gritch on the shoulder. "You mean that?"

Gritch looks me in the eye and levels with me, "Feels like a launch comin on. Course the ony reason I'm givin thumbs up is our Enterprise/Energia matin tech is dead simple. Enterprise is just dead weight to ol Energia. We run into no ugly surprises the next few days I'm spectin to launch you folk. We got a few more touch-ups for Enterprise, but ese here Kazakhs know how to work. Enterprise is right on schedule."

I take a deep breath and look back at Enterprise. If that pretty bird is gonna fly, Mick Oolfson flies her.

A locomotive fires up its engine, and in the din I lean close to Gritch and clue him in, "Kropotkin is going to make sure the control room is clear of gangsters for our practice launch. Only it's not going to be a practice launch. We're gonna launch a day early."

Gritch recoils in real horror. "You cuttin a day off my schedule!"

Pete asks, "What you say?"

I wink at Gritch who coughs into his hand then says, "I said don't dare cut off your moustache. It's a beaut."

Pete looks at my bare lip and considers.

That night on Kazakhcomm I deliver the good news about Gritch's assessment of our chances. Kropotkin shares the good news that he's got his hands on a second Orlan spacesuit—twin to Blegnor's. Because Darthy is our Channel Zilch spacesuit specialist,

Kropotkin agrees that she should be given the dangerous gift of a talking pen.

The next few days we get to talk among ourselves under the eyes of thugs. We have to talk to get our job done, but we don't always talk business—not many of Delp's minions know American.

Hel and Gritch prep the bird for mating with the Energia and work with the Kazakh launch crew. Darthy works with life support techs—she's got her pen now, so she's inside our early launch plan. Kropotkin hustles to round up the last few parts we need. I spin baby Delp and occasionally get to visit the rocket and shuttle.

Darthy's Russki lingo pays off big-time. Kropotkin bribed one of Russia's top life-support system experts to spend time with her, dumping know-how on nutrition, exercise, and psychology for long-duration space flights. The two hit it off, and Dar manages to liberate some Russian "surplus" supplies and tech for the Zilch cause.

On my second visit to Site 112, Gritch puts his hands on his scrawny little hips and gives me some great news. "Energia got some spare horsepower, so Darthy got Enterprise a couple sweet upgrades." He points toward some large metal canisters shrouded under canvas. "You crazy folk talkin about nine months in orbit. Thought you better have a big margin of breathables. Gonna put that big thermos in Enterprise bay and top it off with LOX before y'all launch—a shitload of oxygen. That smaller jug is extra water."

Enterprise is provisioned for an unprecedented extra-terrestrial excursion. I *will* fly her.

The next day I get my morning off to a swell start by personally pressing the button on the centrifuge control panel to kick off Blegnor's first spin of the day. Fred promises to keep a good eye on him and to keep the g-force sublethal.

Pete drives me out to 112 to be a gopher for Gritch. I'm itching to lend a hand with the bird.

Gritch doesn't bother with pleasantries—I don't think he got eight hours of sleep the whole week. He leads me to the rump of the Enterprise and points up. "Lookee what Heloise just had me mount on the ass of Enterprise—that weird-fuckin-shaped titanium plate. Heloise had it shipped here aheada time. Told me I need to mount it back ere where Enterprise used to have em fake main engines."

The metal plate has a concavity with the damnedest pattern to it, like it's designed for a pinecone about the size of a truck to be installed in its hollow.

I ask, "So what are you installing there? A pinecone about the size of a truck?"

Gritch is irritated. "Not a goddam thing. She tells me it ain't none of my beeswax and that nothing goes in there before launch."

"So what do you think it is?"

Gritch says irritably, "I ain't got the slightest. I know they worked damn hard gettin that shape just the way that freaky lady wanted. Ats where most of the cost of this doohickey went, carvin that hollow shape. And here's a fact'll shrivel your sack—there's about a half inch of lead bonded to the titanium in that hollow."

That knocks my head back. "A half inch of lead. Heavy as hell."

"That lead must be real, real important to haul it up into orbit."

"You're not thinking…"

He shrugs and makes a mouth. "What else is lead juju for?"

"Channel Zilch is not doing a damn thing that requires us to mess with radioactive material."

"Just wanted you to know about it. You're the pilot of this flight. It's your ship."

"Thanks, Gritch."

That night on Kazakhcomm I ask Hel about the lead-lined titanium pinecone cozy. She laughs and says it's a surprise.

Gritch and I decide to check progress on the shuttle radiator system. He's been overseeing a group of Kazakh techs installing a heat dumper, and it's supposed to make deadline in the next few hours.

We climb up the rusty yellow scaffolding to look down into the shuttle bay. Heloise is inside working with four techs to tie down a huge wad of purple plastic, securing it tight in a web of red nylon cord.

I feel Gritch go tense. He's tired and cranky. "Scuse me for asking a dumb question, but is that thing listed on the payload manifest?"

Heloise looks up and smiles one of her arc-light dazzlers. "It's a gift from Pops. Bow-koo surprise."

Gritch looks at me and squints, leans over, and whispers, "I ain't askin her what it is. Probly some kinda sex thingy."

I do the asking, "What the heck is that thing?"

Heloise tilts her head and shakes a finger. "A surprise, I told you. I calced it into launch mass and weight distribution, so don't worry your pretty little buzzcut thinker. A girl gets to have her secrets." She turns back to her techs and they get back to snugging up the cord binding the purple plastic wad.

Gritch rolls his eyes and starts down the creaking scaffolding.

I'm right behind. We'll deal with the radiator later.

I get only one glimpse of Head during our week at Baikonur. Late at night I'm walking back to my dorm with one of my Mafiya shadows when Delp's big old high-finned black Cadillac pulls up beside us.

Down rolls a window and Richard Head looks up at me with a broadcast-ready smile beaming from his face. He asks, his voice making it clear that he is doing me an immense favor by caring about my humdrum life, "Oolfson, how goes preparation for Channel Zilch's launch?"

I lean down and peer into the car. Boss Delp sits beside Head in the back seat, studiously looking out the other window. I lean in and say, "Tell Mr. Delp I don't think Delp Junior will be ready for launch."

Someone translates from the front seat and Delp turns toward me with blood in his eyes. Head shrinks back into the seat.

Boss Delp barks something which is translated as, "Make Blegnor ready or Boss shoot you in balls watch you die slow."

The black Caddy motors off before I can catch up further with Dick.

That night Darthy is pissed. She signs into Kazakhcomm, "Vader here. Let's screw those bastards."

Hel is amused. "Yay, Darthy!"

Kropotkin says, "Is our plan, screwing uff Mafiya bastards. Good talking second time today, Ms. Darthy Wader."

"Great to hear your voice, Dar," I chime in,

Darthy asks, "Anyone heard from Richard?"

"I saw him today," I say.

"How was he?"

"We didn't talk. Boss Delp seems to be treating him well."

That's all she wants to know. Darthy switches from pathetic into competent mode. "Vasili told me about his second Orlan spacesuit. We've got to make the switch when I'm suiting up young Blegnor before the practice launch. Here's how we'll do it. I'm going to set up the Orlan-fitting station in the cosmonaut training building."

"The place where Blegnor loves to ride his little centrifuge," I say.

"Exactly."

We do a last-minute mod to the exterior of Enterprise to raise the probability we'll survive the ascent. Enterprise never got the expensive, ceramic foam heat-tile treatment that its sisters got, but it's covered with a layer of tough polyurethane foam tiles, plenty good for the free-flight drops it made but way too flimsy for the aerodynamic forces of rocket-powered ascent.

Turns out that the cheapo tiles are fine for Enterprise's sides but we have to reinforce the surfaces that bite through the air—leading edge of wings and tail and the nose. Kropotkin finds just the thing: some rugged thermal blankets. The crew fits and bonds them over the stress-points.

I just wish they had had another color thermal blanket in stock. The pink swatches make Enterprise look like Barbie's Space Shuttle Bordello.

Enterprise is used to indignity. She'll forget her years of ignominy when she is in her glory high above this silly world.

I spend quality time watching Blegnor spin in the centrifuge. One of those I-shouldn't-enjoy-this-but-it's-just-so-damned-satisfying kind of things. He pukes almost every ride, but he's determined to get his training done to make his pop proud. The centrifuge doesn't require him to strain his brain—just his belly.

I hang with a few Kazakhs in the centrifuge control room and am feeling right at home with the training and launch personnel.

One of the Kazakhs, Shokan, has perfect English. Guy grew up in Missouri through third grade before his homesick Dad dragged the family back to the wind-swept plains of Kazakhstan. He's the language funnel between me and the rest of the ground crew.

Shokan buttonholes me with three of his buds one night after we've spent a long day working on finishing touches to various life-support systems. We're all a little giddy from long hours of meticulous tedium.

"Mick. Tell the story. We want to hear about the shuttle roll."

I jerk back in surprise. "Wait a minute! Nobody knows about that. Not one frigging word got into the American press about that."

Shokan translates and his buds whoop, like I've told a good one.

"You mean you guys in Russia—excuse me, you guys in Kazakhstan—all heard about the little screw-up that got me canned from NASA?"

Shokan nods. "We know NASA, Mick. We're fans."

"So what do you need to know? Why don't *you* tell *me* about the shuttle roll?"

"It's your story, Mick. You tell the boys."

Pilots love to tell stories. In case you haven't noticed. So...

"Here goes. It was my second ride in space—a picture-perfect mission doing secret naughty work for the military... But you guys probably know all about it. Do ya?"

Shokan translates for his buddies. One of them nods and speaks and Shokan Englishes, "The SDI package. Mother Duck and her Ducklings. Code named Boo…"

I interrupt, impressed, "Boojum, you guys know the code name. Well I'll be double-dipped. We do a black mission and you guys even know the nickname—Ducklings—we used for the payload. Can you tell me what the damn thing was good for? They never told me."

Shokan translates and everyone smiles quietly.

"Okay, forget I asked. The flight was about as routine as a shuttle flight could be from my point of view as pilot. That is to say, it was absolutely wonderful—loved every minute of it. Went as smooth as silk, almost no malfs, uh, major malfunctions, nits, glitches, or even anomalies—nominal all the way! Parked our package in orbit, did some science stuff. Although less of it because it was a black mission.

"Looked like another notch in my career. I was sitting pilot seat even though I'd already piloted a mission because my first flight commander asked for me and she was one of the best. I could still learn a lot from her.

"It was on landing that I made my boner. I still can't believe I was that dumb. But pilots have got a long history of doing dumbshit, hotshot stunts to impress their buddies.

"I had a bet riding with a few of the other astronauts. We'd done some calculations and modeled some envelope-pushing shuttle behavior in computer simulators and arrived at the conclusion that a lightly-laden shuttle could do a few maneuvers it wasn't strictly rated for. We each[11] put in twenty-five bucks and bought a very good bottle of Dalmore single malt whiskey for the winner of the bet. Lucky stupid me—I won the bet and shit-canned my career.

"Since it was one of the quietest military missions to date, we broke protocol and didn't announce landing place or time to the public. We pulled a dawn touchdown at the lakebed at Edwards so I figured—no news cameras, minimum civilian exposure."

---

11   Four of us, though I never let on to the panel of inquiry that this bet existed, and you'll never get the names of the other three out of me.

I give Shokan the time he needs to translate. I can tell he's trying to get it right, speaking slowly and pausing to think. His audience of Kazakh techs listens raptly. They'll pass this story on and I'll be on my way to mythhood.

Shokan finishes and turns to listen to me blather on about my exploit.

"During re-entry, just under Mach .4 on the final dogleg approach, I did a beautiful 4-point barrel roll, banked in and landed right on the money with no damage to the craft, crew, or payload. I became a hero to a bunch of shuttle jockeys but was drummed out of the corps by outraged apparatchiks." Apparatchiks... And, it hurts to say it, a few astronauts who I thought were buddies.

Shokan finishes translating and his buddies all smile. One of them gives me a good thump on the shoulder and thumbs up. These guys get it.

This chapter deserves its own book for all the hard, smart work we did, but only space tech hypergeeks would enjoy that book.

Boy, did we work. Tuck every last little thing into the shuttle. Spin Blegnor. Mate Enterprise and Energia—what an amazing, unnatural, magnificent sight!

We work. Check off checklists. Spin Blegnor. Wheel the whole whangdoodle out to the launch pad. Spin Blegnor some more.

The days tick by fast, but by crazy-hard work we keep on schedule. These Kazakhs know how to put big things into orbit.

Under my pillow with Kazakhcomm:

Darthy: "On the morning of the launch you're going to have to put on that Orlan spacesuit all by yourself, Mick. We need to meet tomorrow night so I can train you."

Cool! "Where?"

Kropotkin: "Darthy will go to cosmonaut building. Three in morning. Kazakh will drive her. You must walk. Tomorrow Kazakh will unscrew bars of your window and leave worker's clothes. Is not many Mafiya and never out late night. Walk quickly. Door will be open at building."

Heloise hums the opening bars to the James Bond theme.

Two days before show time Gritch seeks me out. He's got a serious expression on his mug which I don't know how to read.

"You're spam in a can on ascent. We got no abort options. You got that? Once Kropotkin hits that ignition button it's orbit or fry. We'll feed you some data on the way up, but it's only to keep you guys from going buggy. If you start to go anomalous we may just feed you some bullhooie to keep you calm before she blows. Got that?"

I grimace and nod. "Gotcha, Gritch. We don't have the usual umpteen abort options. I don't like it, but I'm a passenger till we hit orbit. My only job is to enjoy the ride and not shit my space diapers." I look him in the eye. "Is this your warm and fuzzy way of telling me we're on schedule?"

Gritch shakes his head and looks befuddled, like he can't believe he's about to say these words. "These Kazakhs know how to prep rocketships. Unless they's a major fuckup we gonna punch you outta Baikonur right on schedule." He gives me a big, big wink to make sure I know he's talking about our unscheduled premature launch.

It's Saturday. The Delps are expecting a Tuesday morning launch but we're punching out of here Monday. Late tonight I've got to learn how to put on a spacesuit.

Gritch is happy. Hel is happy. Dar is smug.

This Channel Zilch freak show is gonna fly.

I set my watch alarm to vibrate at two thirty but I never fall asleep. Tomorrow is my last day on Earth if we can pull off the old astronaut-switcheroo. I roll over my ideas for grounding Richard Head and look at my watch every three minutes until it's time to roll.

The window bars are indeed unscrewed. It opens, but it's a tight slide, so I take my time, inching it slowly. Don't want a squeak to wake up my Mafiya minder in the hallway. The promised worker's clothes are in a bag outside the window—a stiff brown jumpsuit and an orange plastic hard hat.

I walk quickly toward the cosmonaut building, a walk I take every morning to start Delp on his morning spin. Streetlights are dim and far between, and the quarter moon does a lousy job of filling in the gaps. I startle something small and fast—a lizard or rat.

A jeeplike vehicle is parked in front of the cosmonaut building: Darthy's ride. The door to the building is wide open and a light shining from a trophy case illuminates the entry hall.

Darthy's spacesuit-fitting emporium is behind the first door to the left. The door is shut, but a slit of light spills from below it. Darthy awaits to conduct a seminar on donning an Orlan.

I don't bother knocking—the door is unlocked and opens at my push.

I stare down the muzzle of a revolver aimed at my forehead by a very attractive nurse.

CHAPTER THIRTY-TWO: UNDEAD SOULS

MY FOREHEAD STARTS to itch right where the nurse's gun points. Her eyes tell me she wouldn't be sympathetic if I explained my allergy to high-speed metal.

A New Jersey-tinged voice from behind me, "Isn't she adorable, standing there with her gun? Nurse Motorcade, dear, you are truly adorable."

The pistol-packing nurse sneers over my shoulder at the reedy voice. Her head starts to jerk rhythmically side to side. She's wearing earbuds, rocking out.

A voice I recognize, our old Mafiya buddy Clint, commands from close behind me, "Hand behind, wrist together. Be good boy."

The Jersey twang urges, "That's a good boy." The nurse flourishes her gun to encourage me to be a good boy. Her bobbing face looks bored and distant. Her shoulders sway with a beat, blank eyes saying that she doesn't give a shit whether or not she pulls the trigger. I put my hands behind me, wrists together, a good boy.

The reedy voice continues, as Clint binds my wrists tight, "Let me introduce you to my personal assistant, Nurse Motorcade. My darling Motorcade takes good care of her Gogol, isn't that right, dear?"

She yawns and ignores him. Probably doesn't hear him. Her upper body dances, but she keeps her gun leveled at my brain. Clint clucks, and she holsters her revolver in time with her beat.

As Clint tightens my wrist restraint, I take in the sight of Nurse Motorcade—or rather "Nurse" Motorcade, since her skimpy white uniform is clearly a fetishist's checklist: a stiff white hat perches cockeyed on a geometric helmet of bleached silver hair; big pale blue heavily-eyelashed-and-mascaraed eyes peer unblinking from behind geeky black glasses under ruler-straight bangs; pale pink glossy lipstick coats bee-stung lips; a copious bosom cantilevers the blouse of an erotic parody of a nurse's uniform; a wide black belt droops on one hip with the weight of a holster from which peeks the pearl handle of the silver revolver I just got to meet; garter belts play peek-a-boo from under the short tight skirt as her hips buck; white fishnet stockings grace muscular swaying legs shod in sensible white nurse's shoes—sensible but for the stiletto heels tapping the tiles as she dances. Nurse Motorcade is in her prime, an ageless beauty thirty-forty-fiftysomething into music, guns, and gangsters.

Channel Zilch has dragged me to some weird places, emotionally, technologically, geographically, and ethically, but this scene outweirds them all.

Clint jerks the wrist restraint tight—feels like one of those plastic zip-strip wrist-ties cutting into my wrists.

The voice commands, "Turn around, Mr. Oolfson."

I hesitate. Clint yanks my arms up and spins me.

"Call me Gogol."

Gogol is a bland-looking, thin, well-tanned man recumbent in a high-tech wheelchair. Grey silk tie, light grey shirt, dark grey jacket cut well from shiny fabric, grey pocket square, grey hair, mild blue eyes. His wheelchair is an ultramodern angular contraption—a sling of black webbing strung on a skeleton of metal struts riding thin black wheels.

I smile a sour smile. "Gogol as in the writer."

Gogol lauds me, "Ah, you are literate. Gogol—isn't that a clever alias? Adds cred to my rep, as they say. Motorcade, dear, come close. Gogy may need you." She's looking right at him but keeps on bopping.

I glance sideways and there is old buddy Clint, making big eyes at Gogol like he's Elvis.

Gogol says pleasantly, "Please forgive me your restraints, Mr. Oolfson. I am a simple accountant, but Mr. Delp values my services and insists on my absolute security. When my people discovered Kazakhcomm, your friend Clint eagerly volunteered to chaperone you here tonight."

Kazakhcomm is busted. I'm stunned.

Clint leans into me and asks, "Who laughing now, astronaut?" Don't think I'll inquire if he's deaf in the ear Hel blew into.

Gogol waves around me to get his assistant's attention. "Motorcade sweety, Gogy needs his tea."

Clint jerks my wrists high behind me and I bow involuntarily. "Go." He pushes me toward a metal scaffolding from which cords dangle—Darthy's suit-fitting frame. Clint pushes me under the frame and hisses, "Put knees on floor." He's got the leverage, so I sink to my knees. "Stay."

I'm not going anywhere. This guy Gogol knows it all. Looks like I'll be training my replacement after all. If I walk out of here.

Clint spins me by my arms to face Gogol. He hauls painfully upward on my hands and I bow forward with the leverage. He threads one of the dangling cords between my wrists, tightens it with an upward yank, and knots it. Zero percentage in trying to be a hero when everybody in the room but me has a gun.

I am immobilized on my knees, bowing toward Gogol with

my wrists tied high behind and above my head. I have to tilt my head up to look at Gogol. My shoulders complain.

Motorcade boogies to Gogol's side and unstraps a thermos from a dock on the futuristic wheelchair. Her head starts to sway hard as she pours a smoking stream of dark liquid into the cup lid and shoves it toward Gogol, spilling a little on his jacket as an urgent beat makes her twitch.

Gogol's voice is full of gratitude, "Thank you, dear. A tiny stain. Think nothing of it."

Gogol's upper lip rises like a rabbit's when he leans forward to sip—teeth brown as flint. He takes a long, noisy sip and sighs. "I do love my boiled tea. Such a comfort it was in the old Gulag."

Nurse Motorcade grabs his cup and screws it back onto the thermos, spilling a dollop as she starts to dance.

Gogol says in all sincerity, "Thank you, dear. You are too kind to your Gogy."

Noises from the hallway. The door swings open and Darthy walks in, her hands bound behind her. She takes in the scene. I don't say a word, don't know what to say. Her minder, Fodor, enters the room right behind her.

Gogol greets her, "Ms. Vader, welcome."

Darthy asks weakly, "What's going on here?"

Gogol says mock-sadly, "Please excuse my poor hospitality, Ms. Vader."

Clint says, "Tie here, Fodor."

Fodor leads Darthy under the frame and kneels her down beside me. I give her a sad smile as the two thugs tie her wrists to a cord. Darthy gives a groan as Clint pulls her wrists up to tie them.

"Go easy on Darthy!" I say.

Clint hisses, "SHUT!"

Gogol chides, "Temper, Clint." Then mock-sadly, "My hands are tied, so to speak, by Boss Delp's security policies. He flatters me with these strict precautions. It is not in my nature to question my boss's wisdom."

Darthy totters on her knees, trying to find a comfortable position.

I whisper to her, "They nailed us."

Clint snaps, "Shut up!"

Gogol tuts, "Manners! We must pass the time until our party is complete. While we wait for the stragglers, let us get to know one another. Would anyone like to share an amusing anecdote?"

I look over at Darthy and make a disgusted face. She shakes her head and looks a little woeful. What sort of fallout will this mean for her? She's still a major part of the Channel Zilch show, so they have to launch her. Me, not so much.

Gogol says, "Very well. I will play my role as host and make small talk. Did you know that there are acts of violence which even gangsters find beyond the pale? Blegnor told me a particularly gruesome story today. Would you like to hear it? A child of two, daughter of a captured rival of Mr. Delp, was taken to visit her tied-up father, given a knife, and ordered to..."

I beg him, "Please, please, no."

"No?" Gogol sounds disappointed. "Perhaps you are right. My small talk has been coarsened by conversing with the violent element—a sad commentary on the nature of my profession."

A car pulls up outside.

Gogol says, "Our last guests have arrived." Who? He calls plaintively, "Gogy wants more tea, Motorcade, dear, before he has to talk boring old business."

Nurse Motorcade happens to be dancing in Gogol's direction but doesn't hear. He gets her attention with a wave and mimes drinking from a tea cup and saucer. Motorcade stops dancing and looks at Gogol like he's a four-year-old pestering her for candy. Darthy's eyes get big as she watches Nurse Motorcade go through her pissed-off tea-maiden routine. Pure surrealism.

Hel enters, followed by Gritch, arms trussed behind them, trailed closely by two familiar Mafiyoyos.

Gritch bellows, "What the hell you got Darthy tied up like at for?"

Clint sneers at him, "She is present for boss."

Gritch puts his head down and charges straight at Clint, screeching like a banshee with a stubbed toe. He bounces off Clint and all four thugs close on Gritch and subdue him while he yells, "Pissant hog suckin freaks, LEMME GO, ya butt chompin…"

BOOM! Nurse Motorcade's gun flashes and shards of plaster drop from the ceiling. Hel steps away from the door and says cheerfully, "OK. I'll stay, Nursey. Nice try, Gritch. Sweet diversion."

Gritch stops struggling and says proudly through gasps, "All right, you goons got me. Did my bit for the freaky lady."

They truss Gritch in the kneeling bow position and then all four of them cluster around Hel and kneel her down beside me and haul her hands high behind her. I whisper to her, "I'm screwed."

Hel scowls as the Mafiya tug her arms high. "Hell of a thing," is all she says.

Gogol hands Motorcade his empty cup and asks her quietly, "Please wheel me closer to our guests, sweet." She snatches the cup from his hand and without missing a beat shoves him angrily toward us. He stops himself with a handbrake before he collides with Darthy.

Gogol simpers over his shoulder, "Thank you, nurse." He wheels himself back a step and faces the four little helpless Zilchers kneeling in a row. His voice becomes flat and business-like, "I am Gogol. Let me tell you why I have called you here, why I spoiled your absurd plotting.

"I see in the assets of Channel Zilch a golden opportunity for Boss Delp. I am an expert at transferring money from here to there, from you to me. I run what has recently become the most profitable division of Delp's empire, an elite stable of what some might call black-hat hackers, spammers, phishers of logons, masters of Dark Design Patterns, online scammers. I prefer to call my people Financial Misdirection Engineers."

Gritch snorts. "You found you some evil—"

"LISTEN GOGOL!" shouts Clint.

Gritch snorts, but holds his tongue.

"You seem like fine people," Gogol continues, "with admirable ambition. But I am in a tough line of work with little room for sentiment. To be blunt, I must make drastic changes to your mission in order to optimize profit for Boss Delp.

"I have analyzed the Channel Zilch business model and find it ludicrous. I see no revenue stream for a Channel Zilch reality show beyond a paltry few tens of thousands in t-shirt sales. No foreseeable web-ad revenue, because I smell flop." Gogol looks at Heloise severely. "And frankly, I am surprised at you, young lady, for talking your father into investing in this dud.

"I am interested only in your server farm. I...that is, the Delps...order you to transport your server farm to geosynchronous orbit and to keep it there for as long as you can stay. You have no other objectives on your mission.

"As a consequence of this change I have decided to strike Delp Jr. from the crew roster and reinstate Mr. Oolfson. Mr. Oolfson's inclusion in the crew will improve the odds of a successful insertion of the payload into geosynchronous orbit."

Completely sideswiped, I blurt, "What? I'm back on Enterprise?"

Gogol gives me a bland smile and nod and continues, while I chew on the news, "My techs are at this instant reconfiguring the server farm and loading it with intellectual property. My assistants are packing your racks of empty hard drives with all the most popular movies and games and software and songs and porn."

"We need those servers for video!" Heloise protests.

"I am not here to argue. Pay attention. I have cancelled your reality show, so you have no need for massive video storage. In fact, that storage capacity was several orders of magnitude more than a video station could reasonably need."

Hel says, "Redundancy."

Gogol sighs and rubs his head. "Your lies are giving me a headache. Does Nurse have something for a headache?" Motorcade isn't facing anywhere near him. She's doing what looks like the authentic Twist with an expression on her face like her pet scorpion just died.

Me: "Can I ask a question?"

Gogol nods.

"I don't quite know how to put this, but... You're grounding Delp Junior. Won't both Delps be a little miffed?"

Gogol snaps, "Not your affair."

I try to process this. *What's going on?* Gogol spilled the plan for ditching Junior in front of Clint and Fodor. Don't know if the other Mafiya here speak English. Gogol is going behind Delp's back and it looks like he's got some of Delp's gang on his side. Can I make any hay out of this?

Motorcade has Twisted around toward Gogol who waves frantically toward her and begs, "A little temple rub, Motorcade, love?" She rolls her eyes and Twists away from him.

Gritch says, "Anybody else feel like they hopped up on a hippie drug trip?"

Gogol resumes his businesslike tone, "Where was I? Ah, yes. We are severing Enterprise's internal control and monitoring of the server farm. We will handle all that from the ground. My organization has installed a high level interface called MAGOOG to supervise the server."

Hel: "May I ask a question too?"

Gogol shrugs and nods. "Since you asked politely."

"What the hell do you want with the server farm really? Haven't you heard of Bittorrent? There's no business model for an orbiting digital pirate hoard—bandwidth and latency Earth/Enterprise will be shit."

Gogol smiles wide. "Ah, what you ask about is the future of Delp Enterprises. Boss Delp himself has said that Gogol is the future. Most of Delp's revenues now come from the Internet scams Gogol's boys run. How does Gogol see the future? I could tell you that my next source of income is massive twitch farming, a term that means nothing to you. I could tell you about our Zombie Meatnet, but I'll wait to brag until it's up and running.

"My ultimate goal is to build an evil captive Singularity. You look surprised, Heloise. I know about your hobby and am a fan. I employ a horde of brilliant Financial Misdirection Engineers working tirelessly on new methods of relieving the credulous of their cash. I watch closely the efforts of your friends in the Singularity field. When your open-source brain becomes useful, my coders will copy it and patch over its ethical restraints."

Darthy looks at Hel quizzically. Hel doesn't react to Gogol's bombshell.

"Heloise Chin, as a software engineer this should amuse you. You are aware of Google's policy of allowing its engineers to work one day a week on a blue-sky project?"

Hel says, without inflection, "I asked about the server farm."

Gogol responds testily, "I am getting to that. I, too, insist my engineers spend one day a week working on their own wild and crazy and, yes, thoroughly evil projects. Once you have delivered it to high orbit, we plan to use Enterprise's server farm as a test bed for some of the more advanced of my engineers' experiments.

"I have a great advantage over Google. As a practicing libertarian—some would say outlaw—I have access to motivational incentives that Google lacks. Twice a year I run a competition among my researchers to encourage bold new advances in technologies of graft. We run my hackers' blue-sky software projects live online for a week and the researcher whose autonomous-thievery app reaps the most cash is allowed to keep one percent of its ill-gotten gains from that day forward." Gogol smiles and leans down to Heloise, "The loser, the one whose program swindles the least cash—and this is the Darwinian freedom to motivate that Google lacks—is tortured in a most grisly manner in full sight of all my researchers. To encourage the others, as they say.

"Are you aware that living skin and muscle can be dissolved, and nerve endings teased out of the living pulp and laid out on a grid of electrodes? The screams of the victim can be played like a pipe organ. Oh, how my minions are inspired by that twice-yearly culling."

Gogol looks down at Heloise and she stares at him, not reacting. Finally he says, "Heloise Chin—it would pay you to treat me with respect. I want a long-term relationship with Channel Zilch, a goal not fostered if I turn you over to Clint and company for an evening of amusement."

Heloise doesn't react. Her green eyes say it all.

Gogol breaks eye contact with Heloise and wheels himself back from her. "It is getting late and we must sleep. Before we break up our little party, let me repeat so there is no misunder-standing: the ludicrous reality show is cancelled. It is your job to fly the Delp organization's server farm to geosynchronous orbit. I will assist you in your endeavor to launch a day early, sorely disappointing the heir apparent. I will be the only member of the Delp gang in attendance in the control room. Any questions?"

Gogol looks at each of us, but even Gritch is quiet.

Gogol continues indulgently, "I am quite aware that you may well pursue your plans to broadcast. That is no concern of mine. I hope it amuses you to sell t-shirts. And if you should think about reneging on our pact once in orbit, let me remind you, Ms. Chin, that we know where your father lives." Gogol gives Gritch a thin smile. "And we know where *you* live. If the server farm does not make it into geosynchronous orbit, Clint and Blegnor will fly to America and..." Gogol cocks a finger at Gritch. "Boom. Manuel Chin... Boom."

After that sentimental message, Gogol adjourns the meet-ing, "Your minders will untie you one by one and escort you to the door. Oolfson and Ms. Vader, I will see you in this very room tomorrow morning at four sharp. We will switch Mick with young Delp. Good night. Motorcade, dear." He waves to get her attention.

As the Mafiya minders lead Hel and then Gritch out of the room, I try to make sense of what just happened. I'm back on-board. Gogol is going to help switch me with Delp Junior.

I nod to Darthy as Fodor escorts her to the door.

"And, not least, release our Mr. Oolfson. He should get what sleep he can."

As Clint starts to fumble with my knot I say, "Stop. Don't untie me. I need to talk to you, Gogol. I need to talk to you alone without Clint in the room, so keep me trussed."

Clint keeps working on the knot. "Are crazy? Is no way you—"

"It's about Blegnor Delp. Believe me, he wouldn't want you to hear this little bit of gossip."

Clint starts to protest, but Gogol is intrigued. "Go. Leave Mr. Oolfson safely secured. Stand well away from the door and do not listen."

Clint gives me a nasty glare. As he walks toward the door, I say, "Motorcade should also—"

Gogol cuts me off, "You push your luck, Oolfson. Nurse Motorcade is always in attendance." The door closes behind Clint. Gogol prods, "Out with the tidbit about the son and heir."

I look up at him. "I got nothing. Needed to talk to you private."

Gogol's face goes grim.

I say quickly, "It's about business—increasing the probability of success of the mission. You want your server farm in orbit, right?"

He looks at me placidly, "Go on. Motorcade, dear, Gogy wants some tea. Yes? Go on."

"It's about Richard Head. I don't want him on the shuttle—he's a nutcase. If we leave him on the ground…"

"Mmmm, not possible. Big Delp dotes on Richard Head and keeps him—"

I cut in, "You pulled the plug on the Channel Zilch reality show, so Richard doesn't have a thing to do up there but suck down air and supplies that Hel and Dar and I could use. Head's got a drug problem and he nearly killed some people with a flare gun. All you gotta do is make him miss the practice launch. Tell him to sleep in tomorrow. Tell him we don't need him at the practice launch since he's just a passenger."

Gogol looks at me, thinks, and smiles. "A certain beauty to your suggestion in that Channel Zilch's launch will assist Gogol with a personnel issue as well. Isn't that right, Motorcade?"

Motorcade's music must have been between tracks because Gogol says something to her in Russian and she laughs—an ugly laugh, but she laughs. Gogol claps his hands and says loudly, "Clint, you may come back in and untie Mr. Oolfson."

My shoulders are killing me, but when Clint unties me roughly I don't give him the satisfaction of a groan.

As I walk back to my room through the thin light of dawn I realize that Darthy never did teach me how to get myself into that Orlan spacesuit.

CHAPTER THIRTY-THREE: PARTY CRASHER

THE LAST FEW TASKS fall into place. Gritch is grouchy in a way that lets me know he's pleased. At the end of the day he gives me a big thumbs up. Everything is ready for our "practice" launch tomorrow.

If Gogol keeps his word, Richard Head is going to sleep in and miss the boat. The boat will NOT miss Richard Head.

I'm not optimistic about getting anywhere near eight hours shuteye tonight. Kropotkin has been making noises about a vodka-swilling party and then I have the 4 am switcheroo. My Mafiya keeper of the day, Tazkan, is all for partying. After a long day we are just leaving my room, heading toward his car to drive to Kropotkin's apartment.

It is a quiet, quiet night. I make a whooshing noise, shake my head, and point to the sky. Tazkan gives me a wide-eyed gander and then he realizes I'm commenting on the lack of wind.

A popping sound far in the distance. Tazkan tenses. Another pop. Probably bored Mafiya potting coyotes. They got coyotes in Kazakhstan?

Tazkan motions me to stop and unbuckles a massive walkie-talkie from his hip. Looks like it's got vacuum tubes in it. There's a cellphone coverage hole around Baikonur "for security reasons," so old tech is back in style (iGlasses don't work without 6j coverage). I wait while he does the language. His tone is all business.

He shakes his head in disgust as he sheaths the antenna and holsters his toy. He points back to the car and starts to trot. A jeepish vehicle, two Mafiya on board, squeals by us and heads out toward the perimeter noises.

We hustle into the car, and as Tazkan drives he listens on his overweight gizmo to the Mafiya voice traffic, occasionally chiming in. I can't make out a thing. I keep my eyes on the buildings and empty spaces passing by, trying to get my bearings.

I get Tazkan's attention and make a motion like drinking a cup of vodka. He shakes his head. Something damned important to postpone a vodka party.

The night is riled up, motors revving, tires crunching over the gravel streets of the deserted spaceport. Tazkan follows another car into a cluster of buildings I don't recognize until I see the green tile residence the Delps have been using as their HQ. Lots of Mafiya around tonight. Tazkan brakes to a noisy stop and we double-time past a couple of guards into the building.

Struggli waits with two others inside. He scowls when he sees me and turns his back. An unforgiving nature.

A car squeals to a stop outside and everyone orients toward the doorway. The door flies open and Delp Jr. strides in. Behind him, two Mafiya musclemen manhandle a hefty guy with a coat thrown over his head. He's in for it.

Baby Delp stops in front of me and looks at me squint-eyed. What gives? He's never stopped to exchange pleasantries before. He beckons me to follow and gives Tazkan a signal to stay put.

I follow the grim little party into a small room. The two bullyboys fling their captive down into a metal chair. His wrists are tied in front of him. None of these Mafiya do American, so I lean against the wall to wait.

Someone comes in with a cup of tea for the boss's son. They talk, gesturing toward the captive. He sits there quite still, head shrouded in the jacket, taking it all in. Cool customer.

This could get ugly. I'm not sure what my moral duty is here. If this guy tried to rob a Mafiyoso or steal something from the launch site while the Mafiya are feeling proprietary, he's liable to wind up inanimate. Seeing as how I'm a prisoner here myself, there's not much I can do to save him from whatever they dish out. So why the hell am I here? They want to throw a scare into me? Make me watch them torture the guy to show me how deep their evil runs?

The tea dude heads toward the door and as he passes, the captive shoots out his foot and trips him, twisting out of his chair and flipping the jacket away from his face. He knows right where the door is and I inwardly cheer as he makes his break. One of the big boys saunters after him. No hurry, the escapee fumbles at the doorknob with his tied hands. A piledriver wallop knocks the poor guy crashing to the floor, spinning so that when he lands sitting against the wall I see his face.

Ishwald!

His eyes bug out. "Oolfson! I knew it!" A chill wind blows through me.

The door bursts open and Delp senior strides in, scowling, Darthy Vader at his heels. Darthy takes in Ishwald and her whole body gives a little jerk. "Shit."

Ishwald snarls up at her, "That's right, lady. You're in a heap of shit."

I blurt, "You got us surrounded, Captain Ishwald."

"You guessed it." He narrows his eyes and lies. "I've got a battalion of SEALs just outside the Baikonur base perimeter set to sweep in and take your sorry operation down."

I shake my head. "In Kazakhstan? I don't think so. My guess is you're solo." I can tell by his look that I nailed it. "You still working for NASA?"

Ishwald's eyes narrow and his mouth trembles with the effort of keeping quiet.

I read it on his face. "So NASA finally fired you?"

Ishwald looks away.

Big Delp takes in this little scene and adds it up. He snaps at Dar and she translates some version of what got said. He looks at me and Dar translates his question, "Who is this?"

I think it over. Best let him think Toby is still a NASA bigwig. "Captain Tobias Ishwald. Head of NASA security. He wants the keys to Enterprise so it doesn't miss the shuttle reunion."

Delp's mug clenches as Dar translates. He stands for a full minute glowering down at Ishwald. Ishwald glares back with equal rancor, not cowed an iota.

Daddy Delp beckons his son over and they confer. Darthy strains to overhear while keeping an innocent gaze fixed on Ishwald.

Ishwald hisses at me, "You're not getting away with this, Oolfson. Give it up."

"How'd you find us?"

"Come on, after Istanbul where else could you be heading with a space shuttle? Fucking Kazakhs wouldn't cooperate with NASA. I had to enter as a tourist."

The Delps are still jawing it over. They ignore our little chat. They've got all the cards. Nothing we do matters.

Ishwald's tone gets confidential. "I talked on the phone to a Russian here at Baikonur, Vasili Kropotkin. You must have that guy in your pocket. He tried to put me off the scent."

"Kropotko? Never heard of him."

"You're a lousy liar, Oolfson."

Dar nods at that.

Delp senior is done with this scene. He barks at his troops, and the two strong-arms hoist Ishwald to his feet.

"Watch out for his teeth." I can't help saying it.

Dar snickers. Ishwald shoots me a glare that would set fire to a glass of milk.

Delp leads his son out the door, muttering in a low, bored monotone. The two hard guys drag Ishwald between them. Dar and I take up the rear.

"Where they taking him?" I'm getting worried.

"No idea. Couldn't make out what those two were saying."

"They're not going to kill him—are they?"

"I think they'd have done that by now."

"Can you convince them it would be stupid to kill NASA royalty? This whole thing would escalate into a blood feud with the US government."

"I'll give it a shot." She rolls her eyes, takes a deep breath, and goes into passing gear around Ishwald's honor guard. I feel a little twinge of guilt—Darthy doesn't know that her dear Richard is going to sleep in and miss our launch tomorrow.

She pulls even with the Delps as we hit the front door. She's in full Russian as we beeline to a black Cadillac idling in the center of the dirt road. They let her get into the car—good sign—but the doors slam in our faces.

Ishwald and his pals march toward a covered army truck. Tazkan and I tag along. When one of the toughs clambers up into the truck Ishwald makes his move, sweeping the guy's feet out from under him with his tied hands. As the guy topples off the truck, Ishwald shoulders his startled partner under his falling weight which takes both down in a heap. Ishwald turns and eyes Tazkan and me. He makes his break toward my side.

I hesitate an eternal half-second. Ishwald free on the base the night before launch? Gotta do it. As Ishwald starts his sprint past me I stick out my foot and trip him sprawling on his belly. Cue the sound of grit scraping fabric and skin and a shrill, loathing-drenched, *"OOOOOOOLFSON!"*

The truck crunches to a halt in front of the base clinic. Ishwald's taken a few licks from the goons but he's toughing it out, giving them no groans for satisfaction. He sits straight on the wood bench across from me in the covered truck bed. His keepers sit snug by his sides.

I find myself reassuring him, "Hang in there. We're at the base clinic. Looks like they're going to patch you up."

Ishwald snarls, "And then shoot me?" He gets an elbow in his ribs from a goon.

I wish I could reassure him on that point.

Inside the clinic, Dar paces. The Delps are doing their bored gangster act. Dar falls in with me as the parade clomps down a long, tiled hall.

"Any clue what's up?"

"They won't say. Mini-Delp giggled a few times in a nasty way. I think I got through to them about not killing Ishwald, but they're being real bastards about telling me what future they have planned for the Captain."

I act astonished, "Delp and Delp? Bastards? They just have self-esteem issues."

Darthy says with fervor, "I can fix that. Engrave 'I'm OKAY' on a hundred bullets and pump them one by one into their malignant bloated bellies."

"Whoa, Dar." I give her a look. Her mouth twitches with malice.

The gangster marching club tromps through a pair of swinging doors. As they swing back at us Dar puts her hand up to stop the one with a short Cyrillic label.

"Shit, Mick."

"What?"

"This says, 'Morgue'."

o   o   o

I'm inside the room inches from big Delp's face. "No."

A meaty hand yanks me back. The scene registers. One whole wall is a cadaver filing cabinet. One of the drawers is pulled out, empty. This is a big base and accidents happen around rockets. Is there one of these rooms at the Cape?

Delp barks at Dar and she sidles toward me. "It's okay, Mick. He says they're not going to kill Ishwald. Just store him in one of the body drawers until after the launch."

Ishwald's eyes go wide and he starts to struggle.

I remind her, "He's got claustrophobia bad, Dar. They can't."

"Claustrophobia?" She squints and I see her ransacking her Russian vocabulary for the word. She launches into a description of the problem.

Delp Senior laughs deeply and whelp and gangsters chime in. Seems Ishwald has made himself quite a fan club here. Brutal laughs. One of the bad guys is part hyena from the sound he makes.

Boss Delp stops, and the chorus stifles in mid-guffaw. He jerks his head toward the drawer. Ishwald's keepers drag him by the arms.

Ishwald's mouth pipes a high, quavering mewl. His face goes dead and his body limp. The thugs drag him, feet scraping. Delp Junior has an avid grin on his mug, still learning from the big boys how to be a big bad gangster.

I take a step to get between the gangsters and the long, grey drawer. Their eyes go small. Ishwald tilts his face and registers me. His body spasms, feet catch the ground, and he lunges at me. The gangsters yank him hard. Ishwald's teeth snap shut inches short of my...lower belly. I shuffle back and watch, numb, as they heave poor Ishwald, squealing, cursing, convulsing, into the drawer bed. His squalling grows distant and hollow as they roll the drawer shut. Delp steps forward, turns the key, pockets it.

Ishwald's shrieks rattle the wall of metal drawers. The gangsters are all smiles. Ishwald screams even louder.

Got to get out of here. Nothing I can do for Tobias.

I need to find my way back to Tazkan. I'm thinking *no* on that vodka party. I need to hit the hay. Gotta wake up at four again, sneak over to the cosmonaut training center, and switch my ass for Blegnor's. I've got a rocket to drive tomorrow.

I ask Darthy, "Are we dismissed?"

The morgue door swings inward and Gogol wheels into the room pushed by Nurse Motorcade. He points at me and snarls in Russian. The Delps' faces get angrier with every word he speaks.

Darthy translates: "The astronaut is planning to take your son's position—uh, *job*—on Enterprise through a...a trick. I suggest that you—Oh, Mick!—I suggest that you lock him in one of these drawers."

Delp Senior barks an order and a thug pins my arms behind me. Delp Junior pulls open a long drawer, leans close to my face, and smiles.

The gangsters find my struggles hilarious.

CHAPTER THIRTY-FOUR: SHOWTIME

MORGUE DRAWERS aren't made for napping—evidently cadavers don't bitch about resting their asses on cold metal. Not that I could sleep even if the drawer was a feather bed—Ishwald's shrieks would wake the corpse of a deaf man.

They didn't stick me into the drawer right next to Ishwald's, so his screams are mercifully muffled. Shame we can't talk over old times. I make soothing noises to calm him but his claustrophobia is overwhelming.

I spend a good hour feeling around inside the drawer for a release. They stuck me in the drawer feet first, so I fondle all the mechanisms on the inside of the drawer front. I can wiggle a few thin metal rods but they don't budge.

As the night wears on, Tobias stops screaming but emits frequent trills of falsetto sobs, which gives me the creeps.

I can't fathom why Gogol has turned on us. I'm grounded and the early launch is dead. The good news is that I don't have to spend months trying to get along with Richard Head.

I need to switch the positions of my head and feet, so I spend a good chunk of time folding myself in half and wriggling. My healing arm-bite makes itself known. When I get reoriented I brace my feet against the front of the drawer and take a minute to breathe. Ishwald's high-pitched sobs sound like a tantrumming three-year-old. Freaky.

I pull up my knees, gather my strength, and slam my feet hard against the front of the drawer. The pounding triggers a squeal from Tobias but doesn't budge the drawer. I give a few more fruitless kicks.

Time to deal with the looming issue. They may keep me in here until the scheduled launch, which is over twenty-four hours away. Pilots are well-versed in the eternal struggle between bladder and small enclosed structure. I can't ignore it any more—as we astronauts say: time to vent waste liquids. I refuse to wet my pants. If I roll on my side and unzip, the piss will puddle in this drawer soaking my clothes anyway. Only thing I can think of is to take off my t-shirt and use it as a sponge. I start to struggle with my shirt in the cramped space.

A sound: door. Another: footsteps. Mafiya checking on us? I freeze and listen. Ishwald screams shrilly at the disturbance. I hear a click and then a rumble as my drawer lurches open. I blink at the light and suck in a welcome lungful of cool air.

Nurse Motorcade looks at me without expression, turns and walks toward the exit. I sit and call after her, "Wait. What?"

She turns and casually beckons me to follow her. I hop out of the drawer in a clumsy flurry—shit!—scraping my palm on a metal edge. I stop to examine the scratch, and Motorcade says something hard in Russian. I hold up my hand to show her my owee, admittedly well short of lethal, but it stings! She rolls her eyes and turns to leave. Great nurse.

"Wait!" I point toward Ishwald's drawer and raise my eyebrows expressively. I mime opening the drawer.

She shakes her head angrily and says, "Gogol."

I say loudly toward his drawer, "Toby, old pal, I tried to get you out, but I gotta leave. I'll make sure they free you. Hang in there." Tobias answers with a shriek like a scalded cat. I doubt he caught a word of my little pep talk.

I hurry out of the morgue to catch up to Motorcade. Ishwald's pitiful squalling dies to dim echoes. The building is empty. I follow the sound of her footsteps out an exit. She walks straight to the only parked car, a standard black gangster Mercedes.

Let her shoot me in the back—but when you've got to go... I beeline to the nearest bush and let fly. Motorcade waits in the car, jerking her head and keeping her empty blue eyes on me. Guess it's okay for her to watch me whiz—a nurse, right?

I get into the Mercedes and Motorcade hits the gas. She's a hard driver who knows how to cover ground in a big car. Whatever is playing in her ears is fast and heavy because her head whips front to back in a headbanger's thrash. She sings in low, harsh perfect English. "...a snake in a closet, holding sway in the boulevard..."

The dimly moonlit Baikonur landscape screams by, punctuated by clumps of dark buildings. Motorcade sings loud, "...into the null and void he shoots..." I have no idea what the hell she's singing and what the hell is up. Am I going to be hauled in front of Delp and dismembered? What's Gogol up to? If he wants to launch tomorrow he would have left me in the drawer. Optimism and dread do a sweet and sour tango in my gut.

When I recognize the familiar road leading to the cosmonaut training center I relax and let my hopes out of their box. Blegnor Delp should be here right about now, getting fitted into his spacesuit for today's "practice" launch. Definitely looking possible for me to take a little rocket ride today! Gogol, do it for Mick!

Nurse Motorcade slams us to a stop with a sliding crunch. She gets out of the car without a word and I follow her white uniform into the building, hoping, hoping. She beelines to Darthy's spacesuit prep room and I let out an internal YEEHAA!

Darthy is bent over a huge body lying on a table—Blegnor is out cold! She turns, and when she sees it's yours truly, runs at me full-tilt. She wraps me in a hug and beams up into my face. "It's on, spaceman! Let me get you into your spacesuit."

Gogol the Grey, in his futuristic wheelchair, waves at me and gives a big meaningless smile. "Did you despair in your little drawer, Mr. Oolfson?"

I give him a trainwreck of a facial expression trying to cram anger and elation and relief and disbelief into my face muscles all at once. I add sarcastically, "I never doubted you."

Gogol laughs loudly—a cold sound. "I very much doubt that."

I'm disoriented on every axis. "Clue me. The original plan was for me to climb into the backup spacesuit and then do some sort of switcheroo at the launch site to fool Delp Senior."

Darthy gives me a squeeze and looks up at me happily, "Change of plans. I told little Bleggy that I needed to put a saline drip in a vein before I put his spacesuit on. Gave him a knockout hit of valium."

Blegnor does indeed look like he's relaxing hard.

Gogol explains complacently, "I was able to place some of my men around Blegnor so there was no need to fool anyone but Delp's poor mentally challenged heir."

"Your men?" Looks like Gogol is building himself a gang within the gang.

Gogol ignores my question and simpers at Nurse M, "Gogy missed his Motorcade. Did Motorcade…?"

Motorcade sighs in disgust and turns her back on Gogol. She sways to a sultry tune. Gogol looks hurt. He wheels to Motorcade's side and taps her wrist. When she turns, he mimes drinking from a tea cup and saucer. While Nursie does her bored-waitress act, Gogol addresses me: "You have a rocket to catch. Get into your spacesuit now."

I suddenly feel a familiar sensation. Suiting up before a mission always goads the tummy-caterpillars out of their cocoons. Up until now I've had no time to worry about launch. Never had that dubious luxury before—a first just like so many other things about this consistently singular Channel Zilch operation.

Darthy hugs me and heads back toward the tabled Delp. "Let me get the little shit ready for his nap. Get started suiting up, Mick. Orlans are a cinch. I'll help you with the tricky parts at the end."

The Orlan spacesuit is hanging from the very frame all of us were tied under yesterday. I give Gogol and Motorcade a wide berth as I walk toward the suit. It hits me: did Gogol get Head to take some extra beauty sleep this morning? Can't ask in front of Dar.

Darthy says with satisfaction, "There. Delp Junior should sleep safe and sound for four to six hours. Let me help you, Mick."

Gogol commands, "Wheel the little shit to the centrifuge

room, Ms. Vader. Fred will meet you there to start Blegnor on his daily spin."

Fred's here?

Darthy beams. "With pleasure. We'll give little Blegnor a nice, long ride. If we set it to spin creepy-crawly slow it shouldn't wake him up."

I say, "Why the hell are we spinning Blegnor when he's out of it? Can't we just lock him in a room somewhere?"

"I can't have young Delp suspect my involvement in this subterfuge," Gogol explains. "He associates the centrifuge with Mick Oolfson. And, truth be told, I, too, maliciously welcome any opportunity to strengthen the young heir's character through torment. Off with you, Ms. Vader. Oolfson will don his spacesuit while you do your good work."

Darthy wheels the sleeping gangster from the room. I face Gogol. "Head?"

He smiles a bland smile. "Richard will accompany you on your launch today. In fact I have offered him the use of the backup Orlan spacesuit. Darthy fitted him before Blegnor arrived. He awaits transportation to the launch site in a quiet room in this building."

I knew it! "You lying sack of..."

Gogol flashes into rage. "SILENCE!" And then calmer, "I am a man of my word. Richard Head was determined to 'practice' with you today, so Nurse Motorcade and I quickly devised a work-around. I convinced Richard that it was much safer to launch in a spacesuit. The rest is up to you." He taps his mascot on the hip. "Motorcade, sweetie, give the nice man his device." When she looks down at him he mimes holding something small and pressing it repeatedly with his thumb.

Nurse Motorcade gives me a smile as dazzling as it is frightening. She stops dancing and looks me in the eye as she reaches into one of her bosom pockets and holds a small cylinder out toward me.

It looks like a pen. "What the...?"

Gogol says proudly, "We were inspired by your friend's clever Kazakhcomm pen sets. Richard Head's head is in your hands with this transmitter. Simply press the button during launch and Richard's spacesuit air supply will tragically malfunction. So sad that such a promising lad should suffocate due to a wiring fault in a secondhand spacesuit. Give him a suitable space burial to premiere your silly reality show."

I take the pen from Motorcade, who still looks me square in the eye, smiling hugely. "I can't..."

Motorcade says something and Gogol barks a laugh. "Naughty Motorcade. I assure you that Mr. Oolfson is almost certainly equipped with male genitalia." She resumes spasming rhythmically.

I take the damn thing. No way will I use it but I won't leave it in their hands. I gingerly slide it into a shirt pocket.

As promised by Darthy, Orlans are a cinch to put on. First I slip on the cooling layer woven with flexible tubes of coolant. The back of the suit opens up like a clam shell and I climb in and wiggle into the arms and legs. The fishbowl helmet glass is smudged and scratched.

The suit is Blegnor-sized. The little shit is five inches taller and sixty pounds heavier than I am. Let's just say it's roomy.

I get a feel for how the arms move—different from NASA's suits, stiff, but a slightly larger range of motion side to side. The gloves are miles too big but it sure feels sweet to be back in a spacesuit. Makes up for a hell of a lot of Mafiya soap opera.

Darthy returns from spinning Blegnor. She leans into the Orlan and pats my back. "We're going to do this, Mick. We're going to blast into space."

She leans close and whispers, "Richard will be ok, Mick. Really. Give him a chance."

I remember the death pen in my pocket. Yeah, Richard will be ok.

Darthy slams shut the back of the suit and buttons it up. Things go quiet. Takes her only a couple minutes before she flips the switch to turn on the pumps. Compared to suiting up in a NASA rig, the Orlan is a cinch. As *not* mentioned by Darthy, Orlans are hell to walk around in. That convenient clamshell backpack is a serious hunk of hardware that makes me lean far forward to counterbalance.

Darthy walks to my front and taps on my fishbowl. She flips down the sunshade on my helmet, a gold reflective visor that will keep my identity mum. She points to a rocker switch on my chest control box and flicks it—a hiss in my ears.

"Speaker comm, Mick. How do you like the Orlan?"

I give thumbs up. "Slick but damned awkward. Are we ready to rock?"

Gogol wheels himself in front of me, whining back over his shoulder, "Could you please help Gogy, please, nurse?" He looks up at me and says, as if lecturing a two-year-old, "You will be driven with Richard to an assembly point with the others. Richard expects you to be Blegnor Delp. Not every member of the Delp gang knows of this subterfuge."

Oh, shit. I've got to make Head and the gangsters believe I'm Blegnor in this spacesuit. I should have stuffed a few pillows inside and worn high heels. I'll have to act like that obnoxious thug somehow. After a lousy night of no sleep in a morgue drawer I get to give my premiere improv theater performance. Nice to know the audience will throw lead instead of tomatoes if I bomb—it's really, really swell to have other matters take my mind off the little worry of being blown to bits launching our "experimental" spaceship.

"Forward, Nurse Motorcade!" Gogol is propelled out of the room by his medically-themed henchbeing.

I take my first step—damned awkward. The next step is nearly my last as I stumble when the oversized boot twists and catches its heel. Darthy grabs me before I fall.

"Steady, Mick. I mean Blegnor."

She keeps two hands on my arm as I walk through the door.

I'm not ready to see another spacesuit walking toward me: Richard "Richard" Head, I presume.

The spaceman raises his arm and hails me in a media-ready voice, "Blegnor. How do you feel about today's launch of Channel Zilch?"

Improv time. I draw a blank. Line?

Darthy saves the day. She looks up into my helmet and speaks Russian at me.

I gulp. She winks and nods a tiny encouraging nod.

I never took theater class. I hope the comm speaker is cheap and nasty because I don't do impressions. Somehow I manage to spew five seconds of pathetically lame low-pitched fake Russian nonsense, rolling random vowels and gurgling at least one consonant unknown to earthbound linguists. Darthy nods and tells Head cheerfully, "Delp Junior is ready to rock."

Then I get an inspiration. I picture Blegnor's characteristic gesture and sweep my hand up to stroke the crown of my helmet as if smoothing my pompadour. Darthy loses it. She doubles over snort-cough-laugh-braying for quite a spell. She's got a great laugh, but it's out of control.

Quick! What would Blegnor do if a woman laughed at him? I put my hands on my bulky hips and stand tall, cocking my head back in wounded pride. Head is frightened. "Watch yourself, woman. That is Mr. Delp's son you're laughing at."

Good thing my face is invisible behind my golden helmet because I'm sure my eyes bugged out at Head's groveling. The guy is a willing tool of the Mafiya! Papa Delp must have treated Dick right. I will savor watching Head's face when Mick Oolfson jack-in-the-boxes out of this spacesuit inside Enterprise.

Darthy's laughter must have cut through Motorcade's earbud din because I see that the unholy pair have stopped and turned around to watch. They didn't see my Oscar-caliber pompadour sweep so they haven't got a clue. Gogol looks dourly at Darthy and Motorcade looks over my head, head bopping to her soundtrack.

Darthy pulls herself together and stands straight. I point angrily toward the exit. Motorcade spins Gogol around with a jerk and we proceed.

A van is waiting for us outside. Playing my part to the hilt, I push Richard aside to climb in first. He is forced to sit in the front, beside our chauffeur, Fodor. I don't have to talk to the Mafiya-loving tool.

Darthy gets in beside me and pats my leg. She looks up at me and smiles a wide-eyed, joy-filled, bakery-fresh smile. Darthy Vader is thinking about Blasting Off Into Outer Space, and I should, too.

Outside the window, Gogol smiles blandly and waves. Nurse Motorcade Frugs with abandon. I don't bother to wave. I'm glad I've seen the last of that sick pair. Once we're in orbit we'll deal with Gogol's server farm. Heloise Chin will nail that sucker in no time.

Darthy talks to me in Russian but holds her finger to her lips: I guess I shouldn't spew my Russki gobbledygook in front of Fodor. She repeats to Richard, "Gogol said this van would take us to a bus. Heloise will be there."

Wonder who else? We drive in silence for the stretch of a few minutes. I realize that I haven't worried about the launch enough, so I worry about it hard until Fodor swings us to a halt beside an old bus. A few gangsters I don't recognize stand guard.

Darthy helps me out of the van, and as I straighten up I see Gritch sprinting full tilt at me. He whoops and raises his hand, and I high-five him instinctively. A gangster saunters over, looking puzzled.

I do a slow, exaggerated pompadour sweep. Darthy snorts and Gritch grins up at me. "Sorry, Blegnor yer highness. Thought ya was some other damn asternaut."

The Mafiya dude stops and squints at us dourly. As I stride toward the bus, Gritch sidles up beside me and pokes my ribs with his elbow.

As we reach the door, no gangster around, Gritch grabs my arm and leans in close. A young boy's eyes shine at me out of his wrinkled face. He whispers, "It's gonna fly. We did our damnest and everthing feels right."

I whisper, "You did good, you old rocket tinker. We're big boys and girls, now it's up to us."

Gritch says soberly, "Up to you and a few hundred thousand bolts, switches, valves, and pumps that have to work together damn near perfect the first time ever in this bastard Energia/Enterprise launch configuration." Gritch is rightly nervous. I feel a good healthy jolt of the old launch jitters myself.

I ask, "Did our supplemental LOX tank get topped up?"

"To the brim. Frost all over the sucker."

"Have you talked to any of your buddies at SpaceX and Orbital Sci about buying a ticket down?"

"Gimme a break. Ain't sayin a word to no one til you fools up there beggin to come down."

A Mafiya guy leans down from inside the bus and we step apart, still eye-to-eye through the golden visor. We'd never have got this far without ol Gritch.

Time to go. I stand tall and trundle up the stairs into the bus.

Hel sits way in the back, dressed in grey sweats. I give her a little wave. She beams for real and my heart goes gooey and warm. Soon, Heloise Chin will see Mick Oolfson in his element.

I lower my bulk into a sideways-facing seat near the front and Darthy sits beside me. She leans against me and puts her hand on my arm.

The others board—gangsters and techs. A short fireplug of a guy stops and faces us. The guy is jittery, nervous. He speaks in Russian and I know who he is instantly—the distinctive voice of Kazakhcomm: Wasili Kropotkin.

I stay silent, wary—am I supposed to react? Finally he smiles, satisfied, and walks to the back of the bus.

As Richard boards, Darthy leans close and whispers, "That was Vasili Kropotkin."

I roll my eyes to let her know that I recognize our Mr. K, then realize that Darthy can't see through my golden helm.

No sign of Manuel Chin.

The bus we ride to the launch pad is splotched with sandblasted rust peeking through ancient layers of grey and blue paint. It rattles like a sack of cheap aluminum pans over the red dirt road. The wind is back to the same constant whooooOOOOoosh as every day at Baikonur. I hear all this through my tinny earphones on top of the whirs and hums of my Orlan spacesuit.

Darthy leans against me, quiet. I look down and see her face beatified by a rapture of solemn joy. She's not thinking about gangsters. She's thinking about Outer Space.

I crane my neck to see Heloise. Hel can't quite keep the smirk off her face, but then her face is usually like that unless she's up to something.

Across the aisle a Mafiya dude picks his teeth. I scooch my torso sideways to look out the front of the bus. The Energia/ Enterprise starts small on the horizon and grows until it looms against the pale dawn sky. It still looks wrong to see the shuttle strapped to the gargantuan Russian booster and not to its natural belly tank and twin solid fuel boosters.

Details emerge as the bus gets closer. Those pink thermal blankets on all the leading edges set my teeth on edge. I almost half-hope someone's forgotten to take a pictures of Enterprise tricked out like this but the sight will stay lodged in my mind, and I know I won't be able to keep from wincing every time I conjure up the image. The pink trim screams girl's toy.

The bus grinds to a halt. Looking up at Enterprise, I feel like a doll playing inside a Barbie the Astronaut Shuttle Set. Which I guess makes me Ken. I lurch to my feet, swivel, and walk unsteadily up the aisle while pondering the horror of being Ken.

I reach the front of the bus and take my time going down the steps. As I take a few steps from the bus, Kropotkin grabs my arm and talks to me in Russian. This is awkward. He knows I can't speak Russian. He points toward the back of the bus. Ok. Kropotkin is on the good guy's side, so I pretend to understand. He starts to walk and I lumber along beside him.

When we reach the back of the bus, I turn to see a gangster on our heels. I sweep my hand through my non-existent pompadour and angrily wave the gangster away. He stops, unsure. I make a fist and shake it at him and he backs away, smiling abjectly.

I turn and follow Vasili to the far side of the bus. He leans close to me and says clearly in English, "I need piss, Mick."

I flip up my gold visor to look at him through the scratched fishbowl. Kropotkin looks quite serious and whispers urgently, "Always cosmonauts piss on bus tire before launch. Is habit... not right word. Better than habit but always happen. Is hard explain with not right word."

I suggest, "Custom?"

"Custom is word I was looking. But why, you wonder. Here is the why: Yuri Gagarin piss on bus tire very first launch. Every cosmonaut piss on tire after."

That makes me smile. "Gagarin? A hero. Say no more. If Yuri Gagarin pissed on the bus tire, no one better try to stop Mick Oolfson from pissing on the bus tire. It's an honor. It's also a crying shame that my..." I gesture toward my crotch, "...is locked up in this spacesuit."

Kropotkin whispers cheerfully, "I piss for both."

I watch solemnly as he pisses, washing red dust off the tire in a bright black streak, feeling like I should salute a custom that flows straight from Gagarin. An ancient, cracked, and bald-to-the-lining tire. Bet Gagarin pissed on this very same one.

Not going to belittle Vasili by cracking that joke. These people don't need every passing Westerner busting a gut over how their country squandered seventy perfectly good years in a hideous nightmare. Poor bastards, even the rich ones.

I lean toward him. "Shouldn't I call the women cosmonauts over?"

Kropotkin looks serious. "No time for Heloise and Darthy. Women cosmonaut piss in bottle before launch and bring here to pour."

Whoa—they take their customs seriously in old Kazakhstan.

After he zips he reaches out to shake my hand, and I feel something small and slim and stiff through my glove. I hold it up in front of my helmet. A sprig of some grey-green plant.

Kropotkin tells me quickly, "Take. Another custom, wormwood take with you into orbit."

I shake my head. "You Russkis sure have your customs. I hope you had the customary vodka binge last night."

I stuff the wormwood into a belt pouch. Kropotkin helps me snap it shut. "Wery old Russian custom. But not need launch for wodka."

My turn. I take a step back from the bus to make sure we've still got our privacy. All the hoods and techs and Zilchers are heading away from us toward the Enterprise/Energia launch pad, so I say, "Speaking of custom, you could do me a huge favor by cooking up a NASA launch custom."

Kropotkin's eyes get big. "NASA haf customs?"

"Sure thing. Open a can of beans or a dozen if you got em and start them heating up on a stove. Keep em heating during the countdown, throw in some ham, onions, whatever. When we make orbit I want everyone in the launch center to eat the beans. We call em launch beans."

He nods, serious. "We will eat launch beans for you, Mick. Is good custom. Is short countdown so we use microwafes oven."

I slap him on the shoulder with my empty glove. "Thanks for

everything, Kropotkin. You got a hell of a team and I wish you luck for your retirement."

Vasili nods. "I will take luck when you are finished with using it. All luck is for you this morning."

I smile. "We'll try not to use it all up. Gritch and Manuel are gonna need Lady Luck's strongest juju to get out of Gogol's reach."

"Escape plan is go. When Energia launch early, mafiya run to Delp for instructions. Kazakh pilot fly Manuel and Gritch far to safety. I will be on plane and also Kazakh Enterprise team. All is good."

"Thanks, Vasili. Thanks."

He sticks out his hand and says seriously, "Droog."

"Droog?" I hesitate. Sounds sinister.

"Russian word is mean friend." He looks a little sad. Hadn't thought about Vasili being upset if we blew on launch.

"Droog," I say warmly, as I shake his hand through my Orlan's clumsy glove.

The gang's all here and we've got a spaceship to launch.

Time to walk up the flight of old metal stairs someone scrounged from the airstrip. Propped on top of that is a long metal ladder leaning against Enterprise. There isn't a gantry in all of Baikonur that fits the Energia/Enterprise stack, so we make do with what works.

One of the Kazakh ground crew holds the ladder as first Darthy, then Head in his Orlan spacesuit, then Hel, then I climb. Kropotkin follows me to button up Enterprise's hatch. I hang onto the ladder as we wait for Head to struggle through the tiny door. I take one last look back at Baikonur. Won't miss it—nope. Then I see tiny Gritch waving up at me like a maniac. I wave back hard.

As I get to the top of the ladder and look through the hatch, Hel is already strapped into the commander's seat. Enterprise's nose is pointed toward space, so she lies on her back facing upward.

I hear Head's and Dar's muffled voices arguing from middeck. Their "chairs" are foam cushions attached to middeck's back bulkhead. Darthy's first task is to strap Head in. I think of the pen in my pocket. Damn Gogol! He knew I'd never use that thing.

I lean into the hatch and grab the webbing strung to help us get into our seats. I roll onto my back and pull myself in and then let my legs swing down. They drop heavily against the back bulkhead. I stand and consider. Wait for Darthy. Can't talk. Head has to think I'm Blegnor until we're out of here.

Kropotkin sticks his head through the hatch. I hold my upraised forefinger to my helmet to shush him and he nods. He knows the score.

Darthy says to Head, "I've got you all strapped in, Richard. How does that feel? Cozy?"

I can't make out his reply, but it doesn't sound happy.

"I have to help Blegnor now, Richard. I'll adjust that in a minute."

Darthy's next task is shucking me from this damn spacesuit. No way do I want to be in this thing when we launch. It's an EVA suit, not an ascent suit. We only talked Blegnor into wearing one for launch to help us make the switch.

Darthy pokes her head through the middeck hatch and worms her way through with amazing grace. I turn my back toward her and she immediately starts unlatching the clamshell. Kropotkin watches her with great interest.

The spacesuit's back springs open and fresh air rushes in. I tilt forward and Darthy helps me lower the bulky carapace to the deck beside me. I bend toward Dar and give her a big hug, my legs still deeply enmeshed in spacesuit.

Head cries plaintively from middeck through his cheap suit speaker, "Darthy! My leg is cramping in this awkward position. When you are quite finished with Mr. Delp, please assist me."

As I let go of Darthy something in my pocket snags on her shirt and flips to the floor. Head's death pen!

"SHIT!" I see it lying on the bulkhead and lunge for it. The spacesuit trips me up and I fall heavily forward. The suit crumples so noisily I'm not sure if I hear a crunch.

My mind is spinning as I fumble with both hands to find the pen. What will I tell Darthy? Damn awkward stuff.

Darthy asks sharply, "What are you doing, Mick?"

Head calls from middeck. "What is going on in there?"

Hel yells to Kropotkin, "Seal it."

I roll onto my back, tangled in spacesuit. I yell, "Seal it!"

Darthy yells, "Seal it!"

Kropotkin heaves a worried sigh, shakes his head, slams shut the hatch, and torques the bolts.

It gets real quiet inside Enterprise without the constant whoosh of that old Kazakh wind.

CHAPTER THIRTY-FIVE: PRODUCT LAUNCH

"IS THIS WHAT you're looking for?" Darthy bends down and examines something in her hand. "It's crushed. The clicker is missing. Oh, there it is." She bends and grabs it.

I'm still sprawled on the bulkhead in a heap of spacesuit and fear. Did crushing that pen sentence Head to death? Darthy sounds justifiably confused, "It's just a pen, Mick. Was it a gift?"

She bends and hands the pieces to me. I peer hard into the wreckage of the splintered pen searching for wires. I pry apart the pieces of the flimsy barrel. Sure enough, it's just a pen. Bastard Gogol gave me a bogus Head-snuffer. Guess you can't trust a crook—who'd a thunk it? I remember Motorcade yucking it up over their little con. I briefly consider telling Darthy that Gogol wanted me to kill Head with that pen just to watch her face. File it for later. Much later.

Flashback of Ishwald mock-stabbing me with the butter knife. Wonder how he's doing in that drawer?

Richard calls, "Darthy, what's going on in there? Is young Delp injured?"

Head is still oblivious. Darthy looks at me, relieved. I hold a finger to my lips and smile ruefully.

"He's fine, Richard," she calls back. He got his spacesuit caught on a thingy and tripped."

Richard, peevishly: "My leg is cramping. Help me with these damnable straps."

Darthy looks at me and smiles a sad little smile. "Be right with you, Richard." She bends and says, "I'll turn off Richards' speaker comm. Tell him he'll wear down his batteries."

I nod and hold out my hand for help. Darthy gives me a boost to vertical and I shuck off the suit legs while she makes her way back through the middeck hatch. As I start to climb up the web ladder to my pilot seat, Darthy calls out, "Richard's comm is dead, Mickster. Jabber away!"

With any luck I'll be able to talk freely to the control room during launch. Gogol promised us he'd be the only gangster in the control room. I climb into my pilot seat and strap myself in. Up through the windshield the Kazakh sky is mottled grey.

Up is where I want to be.

First we've got to sit a spell here in old Enterprise. Hel and I talk tech until the control center checks in. I don't remember what we said. I do remember that her smile looked real. I basked in it.

While we sit, I indulge in a few launch jitters. We're in an American space shuttle strapped to an Energia. Foolish. But here we are. Gritch didn't scrub the launch.

Darthy calls from middeck, "Richard has conked out, poor baby. I'll let him sleep."

I say, "Let blastoff wake him."

Darthy scolds, "Wake up inside a launching rocketship? That would be cruel, Mick."

"Exactly," I explain.

An unfamiliar voice from control starts our abbreviated countdown at T minus sixty minutes. Enterprise is just dead weight hung on Energia so I don't have much to do but listen and occasionally confirm some minor point. Minutes tick by like heartbeats and my heart beats faster and faster.

"Sixtin, fiftin, fourtin, threetin, we have hold at threetin second..."

Exhale. A bead of sweat trickles into my left eye. "What's the glitch, control?"

"Wasili wants speak you…"

I expect the worst. "Must be a glitch. We scrubbing the launch?" I glance over at Heloise in the commander's seat. She glowers at me.

"Is not so much glitch, Mick. Haf a bit patience. We will do countdown in moment." Kropotkin's unmistakable growl in my headset. There's a jerky cadence to his voice like he's reading the words off cue cards.

"No glitch? What are you recycled pinkos up to then?"

Vasili speaks slowly and carefully, "Is no hurry. We have talk first and then we gif you wery, wery good PRACTICE launch. Do read me, Enterprise"

Shit. I look at Hel and whisper disgustedly, "Gangster in control room."

She rolls her eyes and I see her brain engage.

I hear an angry voice, not Vas's, bark something in Russki or Kazakh.

Kropotkin says carefully, "Shall countdown after few minutes. No problem just little wait. We are all happy in control room. Warm happy like Beatles say is happiness, you know, Enterprise."

It registers: Kropotkin is a 60's rock and roll fanatic. He's not raving; he's alluding to the Beatles' tune, *Happiness is a Warm Gun*. Delp's got wind of our plan to cut out of here a day early and some Mafiyoso is holding a gun to Kropotkin's head and has ordered him to kill time chatting with me.

I beat my helmet back against the restraints of my acceleration couch. "No! No! No!" I slam shut that emotion. Do or fry time again.

I look at Hel and snap, "Delp's onto us and Vasili's got a gun to his head."

Heloise closes her eyes and nods slowly.

I say, "Vasili, I read you, man. If Mr. Happy can hear me, say a sentence with the word red in it."

"I know it is blue sky out, Enterprise. Is not a weather problem. Be bit patient."

"Good, good Vasili. Here's my take on the jam—you have a gun to your head. You gotta be careful what you speak, but he can't hear me. If it's Delp Jr. say something about sports."

"Okay, Mick. We talk about hockey while problem is being fixed." There is no quaver in his voice now. "You think Bulls beating Raiders in World Series this year?"

Blegnor Delp! I picture his bullish, looming frame—taut with fury and oozing rancid sweat—pointing one of his daddy's precious Tommy guns at Vasili. Nothing uglier in body or spirit than that spoiled whelp of a Kazakh gangster.

"But Darthy conked him out and strapped him into the centrifuge for a good long spin while we launched. Someone ratted on us. Ran to Daddy and told him we were gonna launch without his son on board. Damn his pimple-plated butt."

"That is right, Mick. Good thing we practice today. Is might be jam in LOX coupling."

I remind him, "You know we mounted a backup decoupler for the LOX hoses onboard Enterprise, Vas. That's the last thing tying us to the ground. Wait, you want me to cut them?"

I look at Hel and she gives me a vigorous nod.

"Then you can launch me with one button press so the little shit doesn't get any warning! If that's it give me a sentence with the word persimmon in it."

A very long pause. Persimmon? What the hell made that jump out of my mouth?

Heloise cuts in from her commander seat, "Cheese."

I relay it to Vas, "Use the word cheese."

"You want we bring you nice snack while you wait? Bagels with cream cheese and lox?"

"Got you, Groucho. Initiating LOX coupling jettison."

I signal to Heloise and she releases the emergency LOX jettison toggle switch from its safety lock and thumbs it hard. A muffled *kachunk!* signals the cutting of our final tie to the launch pad.

"It's in your hands, Kropotkin. Don't do anything stupid like get your head blowed off."

"ENTERPRISE IS LAUNCH!" Kropotkin's panicked squawk rattles my helmet.

What the...? We've got thirteen seconds of countdown to go.

"GO! ENTERPRISE IS GO!"

I can't light the damn thrusters—my ass is strapped to this

metal skyscraper. Kropotkin is Launch Control—he's got the red button.

Clatter as chips fly from the shuttle's nose and ping off the windshield. A ragged row of bullet scars in the nose tiles.

"BULLETS!" I scream.

Kropotkin, shrilly: "Is Boss Delp shooting machine gun!"

"PUNCH IT!"

A burst of lead claws the tiles on the cockpit roof. A slug rips a screeching groove in the thick windshield.

"PUNCH IT!"

BOOMGROWL! Energia's engines roar to life. Twenty howling thrusters jam the seat hard into my spine.

"Whee doggies!!" I whoop. Back into the wild black yonder!

Space shuttle Enterprise scrams on treadmarks of smoke up, up, up into the grey Kazakh sky.

continued in

HEL'S BET
coming from Panverse in Summer 2014

Author's Note & Acknowledgments

Channel Zilch started as a story-telling screensaver project in 1992. It morphed into a novel and was written between bouts of employment, game coding, disabling epilepsy, cognitive problems, and Central Pain Syndrome. I finished the first draft of Channel Zilch during the 2007 Clarion West Write-a-thon and rewrote it three times over the next three years.

Thanks to all who read the manuscript, wrote orbital mechanics programs (which I ignored), inspired me, backed me with generous patronage, and kept me alive and (relatively) sane: Margaret Sharp, Almira Sharp, Jack Sharp, Joan Sharp, John Sharp, Diane Sharp, Ray Romano, Rob Erickson, Chris Hecker, Casey Muratori, Jeff Roberts, Brook Waalen, Stephanie Lundeen, Gisela Scherer, Mika & Travis (my horrible dogs), Daisy dog, Larry Heyl, Earl Johnson, Eileen Kinney, Paul Pfalz, Mandy Dumins, Alia Eleu Thera, Becky Brandt, Louise Mowder, my colleagues at the Central Pain Syndrome Foundation, Stuart Rubio, Eric George, Michael Antonio, Kevin Goldsmith, Jon Blossom, Sam Ross, Martin Skoro, Tony Santucci, Tom McGrail, William Hsu, Neil Morrison, Mark A. Horowitz, Dan Moynihan, Jason Kavanagh, Elizabeth Veldon, Blunt Jackson, Dan Sheehan, Mary Ann Sheehan, Lucas Sheehan, Michael Johnston, Emma Johnston, Harry Chesley, Laura Mixon, William G. M. Leslie, Lyn Aspey, Kristine Rudin, Aurelia Shaw (thanks for the great cover art!), Grant Orndorff, Steven Drucker, Marc Smith, Stephen Coy, Kirk Goddard, Myrna Mae Berg, Jim Preen, Bonnie Randall, Kurt Shusterich, Trevor Nolte, Scott Swink, Nicholas Wilt, Mike Perren, Amanda Rutter, Tony Manson, Linda Whitaker, Don Mitchell, John W. S. Marvin, James Mahoney, Dr. Vernon Neppe, Gary Saaris, Robert Brown, Stan Kelly-Bootle, Russell Wallace, Keith Amarak, Jessica Geiger, Stuart Driver, Inga Velde, Bruce Warner, Debi White, Kate Mylecraine, Maggie Bucka Bauer, the inmates, teachers, and staff of Clarion West 2002, Café Wren in Luck, WI, and the brilliant writers of my crit group, *Written in Blood*: Janice Hardy, Juliette Wade, Aliette de Bodard, Keyan Bowes, Traci Morganfield, Genevieve Williams, and the Pharaoh.

I apologize to all those CZ backers whom I have forgotten

to include. Twenty years of work on Channel Zilch and a faulty memory adds up to an imprecise list. Please contact me so I can add your name.

Heloise wishes to thank: Diana Rigg as Emma Peel, Kat Bjelland and Babes in Toyland, L7, The Blue Up?, P.J. Harvey, Patti Smith, Greta Christina, Oneida, Lightning Bolt, Joan Jett, Chrissy Hinde, Kathy Acker, Tribe 8, Aeon Flux, Mecca Normal, God is my Co-Pilot, Coughs, Free Kitten and the riot grrrl bands.

I apologize to the people who work at Baikonur. A handful of gangsters taking over the busiest spaceport in the world is one of the biggest and most libelous stretches in Channel Zilch, and that's saying something.

Doug Sharp does not officially advocate stealing shuttle Enterprise and launching it on a stolen Energia.

The blame for any infelicities of fact or style should be laid squarely upon the person responsible: Dario Ciriello.

Northfield, MN, 1992—The Pad, Comstock, WI, 2012

ABOUT PANVERSE PUBLISHING

Panverse Publishing is an independent press dedicated to publishing original work, both fiction and nonfiction, by new writers and established professionals. Our titles are readily available in both print and digital formats from Amazon, Barnes & Noble, and other online retailers, and in print from your local bookseller. You can read about current and upcoming titles at our website at http://www.panversepublishing.com

Reader support and word-of-mouth is vital for independent publishers and their authors. If you enjoyed this book, please help spread the word by telling friends, mentioning it on social media, or posting a review online. Thank you so much.

Panverse Publishing. Story. Wonder. They're back.

15% of royalties and 10% of Panverse Publishing's profits from Channel Zilch will be donated to the Central Pain Syndrome Foundation for brain research. You can visit the CPSF website at http://centralpainsyndromefoundation.com